THE DEAN OI

DEGREES OF
PUNISHMENT

By

Dee Vee Curzon

CONTENTS

PROLOGUE

Taken from St James' College Instructions to Students.

Clause 25.6

I, the undersigned, agree to the rules of the College as presented. I have read and understood them and hereby promise to conduct myself in a quiet and orderly manner.

I undertake to at all times observe the orders and regulations of the College and pledge obedience and loyalty to the institution.

It is my wish that the option of corporal punishment be applied if my indiscretions deem it necessary and appropriate.

I undertake to accept disciplinary punishment in any form and as proposed by the College's Dean of Discipline and would welcome the opportunity to be educated and improved by such punishment as deemed fit.

I request that the College accepts my signature as evidence of my commitment and I hereby authorise the said powers to carry out any requisite action to ensure compliance and obedience for the good and benefit of myself and the College.

Please accept my signature as my promise and commitment: To the aims and ambitions of the College; to my welfare, my education and my improvement through learning, mentoring and discipline.

Student's signature confirming acceptance of clause.

....

(Print name..)

Parent(s) or Guardian(s) signature of affirmation to the above clause.

....

(Print name..)

....

(Print name..)

Signature of the College's Dean of Discipline witnessing.

....

(Print name..)

CHAPTER 1

IN WHICH EMILY AND GEORGINA

VISIT THE PROFESSOR

Professor Stones looked hard down his long nose at the two miscreants standing before him; he thoroughly enjoyed their discomfort as they shuffled about under his penetrating stare. The report did not make comfortable reading for the two pretty young blondes standing before him.

"We are so very sorry, sir, it won't happen again," said the taller girl, Emily Govan, daughter of Sir Alec Govan, a senior figure in the Civil Service. "If you could just give us a chance to make things right please."

"If I remember, girl, you were very sorry the last time you stood in front of me and STAND STILL, girl," Professor Stones boomed in response before turning his gaze upon her companion. "Exactly how proud do you think your parents would be to hear about your recent actions, Georgina Fawcett-Jones? You bring disgrace to your family name, you may well be shame-faced, young lady."

The professor's face betrayed no sense of the growing pleasure he felt as he watched the two females squirm before him. Well aware of his reputation for firmness and severity in his position of the famous college's Dean of Discipline for the last 40 years, the professor was well versed in gradually turning the screw tighter and tighter as he led the badly behaved students to the inevitable conclusion.

"I am sooooo sorry, sir." Georgina found her voice.

Stones could see the concern cross her face as she realised how shaky her voice sounded. He could see there was a desperate air about her as she tried to hold it together but from her demeanour he thought that it was more likely that she would collapse on her knees at his feet and beg for mercy.

"I really don't know how it all happened, I have never behaved like that before and I promise that I will never do so again."

Stones knew Georgina's father well, another prominent figure in his field, being an eminent archaeologist who was often called on by the media for his thoughts on current events in his speciality subject of early Roman construction and design.

"What on earth would your father say?" he taunted her, enjoying the look of panic as her face contorted and she spluttered incomprehensibly.

The professor sighed, and looked off into the corner of his room and pretended to contemplate the fate of these two, a practised move which he often employed in a sadistic manner to heighten fear and expectation.

"You, girl," pointing at Georgina. "You are a major disappointment. I see no record of any misbehaviour during your first two terms here, so maybe you need to have a rethink about your choice of friends."

He peered dismissively at Emily causing her to blush deeply.

"This one has lived on the edge of a cliff called Trouble and has finally toppled over and fallen into a valley below called Serious Punishment." The professor ranted on in the manner he was renowned for throughout the college.

"Sadly she's taken you over the edge with her, hasn't she, girl?" Georgina trembled from head to toe.

Stones watched as she displayed signs of willing herself to retain some element of dignity but only succeeded in coming across as the naughty little schoolgirl she was being treated as.

"I really am sorry, sir," she whispered. "It won't happen again, I will do anything to put things right. Please sir, my father doesn't need to be told, I have learnt my lesson, I am really sorry..."

She spluttered to a painful halt as the professor's face reddened and his lips twisted into a sneer as he moved menacingly towards her.

"I will decide who gets told and who doesn't and all the snivelling in the world from a spoilt and ridiculous child who needs firmly taking in hand, will not deter me from fulfilling my obligations to the college and your parents to put you on a straight path. A straight path that will have an end result in moulding you into a young lady that both this college and your parents can be proud of!

"Do not say another word, girl, I don't wish to hear your pathetic, grovelling little squeaks. You will go back to your room and have two days to deliver a one-page record of what occurred last night, exactly how you came to be drunk and singing half-naked around the Founder's statue and how you feel about it now. You will also write a letter of apology to the night porters who had to deal with you, and then, you will suggest what you think is an appropriate punishment. If, and it is a big if, I am satisfied with what you have to say, a punishment will be set and your future behaviour will be monitored. Now get out, wretch!"

He flicked the girl's mobile phone across the desk towards her; although Stones had invested much of his substantial wealth in security and electronic gadgets galore, he nonetheless always insisted that any of the reprobates sent before him had to deposit their devices to ensure any temptation to secretly film or record was removed entirely. Many students had incorrectly assumed that being played Tchaikovsky or Wagner during punishment sessions was to drown out any sounds of the process from prying outside ears, the truth was that the cleverly designed habitat with its large central room surrounded by a ring of external rooms was not only fully soundproofed but extremely well-constructed. No, the classical music was yet another safety aid in blocking potential recordings that any of the punishment candidates might attempt. There were plenty of recordings made in the room but they were all at Stones' instigation from the array of secret cameras carefully positioned to cover every conceivable angle and cleverly placed in the specific areas of the room to pick up the sound of punishment and discipline being dished out. Everything recorded, audible and visual, was for the professor's pleasure, amusement, protection and reference!

Needing no further bidding, Georgina grabbed her device and, giving her friend the quickest glance of sympathy and support, left the room, still voicing pointless apologies that would have little effect on the hardened heart of St. James' College's Dean of Discipline.

"Emily Govan," snapped the professor quickly, alerting Emily to put on her most apologetic and respectful expression.

"I think we have to move to a different level with you, don't we? Please don't even think about interrupting me." The professor raised his voice as Emily opened her mouth to start with more pleas for forgiveness and mercy.

"In fact, go and stand facing the corner of the room with your hands on your head and spend some time thinking about your behaviour and how it should be dealt with. I am seriously considering whether or not the college needs to put up with your presence for much longer. You've been here barely six months and I am not sure whether we need you here any longer, young lady! MOVE!"

Emily obeyed and walked over to the corner of the room facing the bookshelves that filled every single piece of wall space in Professor Stones' main Study and Tutorial room, which also served as his living room.

Professor Stones went to sit back at his desk. This one looked like he might at last be able to turn to his unlikely accomplice, Jamie Adams, an evening porter at one of the minor colleges across the city. The two of them had formed an unusual alliance and friendship, of a kind at least, based on their shared interest in a certain practice, and this episode looked like it was going to bring a plan to fruition. He smiled at the back of the silly young woman with her nose to his books and contemplated an interesting few days ahead. His glance drifted lower as he appreciated the nice rounded form of her buttocks under the tight jeans, recalling the firmness of them when he had spanked her previously, certainly well suited to what the professor had in mind as regards punishment. He decided to let the girl stand and suffer for a while and then see what she could be encouraged to offer up in way of punishment. It had been a little while since he had been able to indulge in his 'little foible' as he liked to think of it, but since a chance meeting with Jamie off-site, he was confident that things were looking nicely encouraging. He hadn't yet been able to call on Jamie to get their joint venture up and running properly, as the cases he dealt with just lately had been of the less serious misdemeanours, not the fully fledged floggings he had enlisted Jamie's assistance for.

Emily was a young lady who had clearly not taken on the lessons she should have learnt from earlier encounters with the Dean. He was aware that she possessed the intelligence and perception to have realised that there was little action or words to be said that would appease him and suspected that her brain had started to tick over rather frantically for a plan and line of defence to ensure that her parents did not come to hear of her disgrace. Being cognizant of Emily's background he supposed that when you had a trust fund of a million pounds coming to you when you reached the age of twenty, which was likely to be subject to her eminent father's strict rules on upholding the family name and honour, it tended to help you bring certain things into focus. Obviously scrubbing toilets and a few days doing the worst jobs set by his colleagues in the Domestic Household Department had not struck home, nor the embarrassment of a sound spanking of her bare backside that had taken place shortly after. He remembered the tears and remorse that had followed and was a trifle disappointed that Miss Govan had failed to heed the warning of what she could expect if a spanking failed to correct her behaviour.

However, on the plus side she had now earned herself a rather unpleasant Friday afternoon ahead; serious beatings always being designated for a Friday, or Saturday on a particular busy weekend, principally to allow recovery time and not interfere with their academic timetables, with the secondary bonus of possibly ruining their social plans for that very weekend! Certainly the professor had always imagined that quite a lot of plans would have had to have been changed due to a sore and painful backside.

The professor had no doubt that Georgina Fawcett-Jones, Emily's partner in crime, would have been easily led by her wilful friend, and it intrigued him to hear what she proposed as her punishment. He generally liked to be lenient with a first-time offender, his preference being to instil the fear of God plus the threat of much more serious punishment coming their way if they didn't keep to college rules. Sometimes, however, that just wasn't appropriate and menial tasks and a bit of sweat and grime plus a fierce dressing down and threats of much worse were just not enough to hammer a message home.

Georgina, he felt, might well benefit from a few minutes with her knickers down over his knee but, he contemplated, he would keep an open mind and not pre-judge. He didn't believe that a spanking for a spanking's sake was a fair course of action however much he enjoyed the experience; he had always deemed it important that punishment beatings were appropriate, justified and in the best interests of both the college and the student in the long run. Obviously for a man with tastes such as his, a seemingly never-ending supply of misbehaving young ladies' bottoms that he had the power and good reason to have draped over his knees or furniture, was not much of a chore at all!

Some of his colleagues wondered why Stones had gone on after reaching retirement age, he reflected, particularly as it was well known that he was a spectacularly wealthy man. Were they serious? He loved his work and he especially loved his role as Dean of Discipline and all that involved. Of course he wasn't considering retirement!

CHAPTER 2

JAMIE'S PAST

As Jamie Adams had been busy doing one of his least favourite tasks of filing his paperwork from his productive small business venture, his mind drifted. There had been some dark, difficult and miserable days for Jamie since the death of his wife, Angie, from a long illness five years ago. After a real struggle to conquer his grief and desolation at the end of a relationship spanning over 20 years and the loss of his soulmate, Jamie had faced his demons. Gradually he had been able to move onto a place wherein he felt that he was painfully aware of what he had lost but had accepted the situation and started to rebuild his life without Angie. Nowadays treasuring her memory and concentrating on the good times rather than the illness and eventual demise of his beloved sweetheart and partner.

Left financially sound, Jamie had left his senior civil service position and set up his own small business trading in ceramics and pottery. Working principally from home, Jamie travelled around the south of the country attending auctions, trade fairs, markets and large car boot sales. With dedication and hard work, he had soon turned an interest into a thriving little business. Wanting a bit of stable income and not wanting to spend too much time alone in his 3-bedroomed house on the outskirts of the city, the perfect house when you had planned a two-child family, he had looked for a part-time position locally to keep himself occupied. Jamie had successfully found employment as an evening porter, working four days a week, 5pm until 9pm, at one of the newest and least known of the famous city's university colleges. This suited Jamie perfectly, he carried out his own business when it suited him on odd weekdays and occasional weekends, whilst covering his desk duties at Parkinson College late afternoon.

Whilst Jamie had enjoyed an occasional one-night stand since Angie's passing, he recognised that these had been entirely driven by normal sexual appetite rather than any search of desire for emotional attachment. He would have struggled to put names to all of his couplings and none had he entertained the idea of seeing on a regular basis. However he did miss some of the activities he and Angie had enjoyed and had wondered more and more frequently about how he could satisfy the urges and frustrations that had built up inside of him. Jamie and Angie had discovered their shared love of spanking and bondage by accident after a silly argument and a bit of tipsy teasing from Angie that had pushed Jamie's buttons enough to react. A quick struggle had ensued and suddenly Jamie had Angie positioned so that she found herself staring at the carpet from an undignified position over his knees. The jeans she was wearing had given her scant protection from the avalanche of smacks he had landed but he had been surprised when it became apparent that there was a lack of fight or resistance, her lowered head and submissive body language just serving to egg him on. As Jamie had paused with slight disbelief at what he was doing, he became aware that his wife had ceased her writhing and twisting but was to the contrary lying supine in the punishment position and breathing quite rapidly. Jamie remembered the conversation that followed word-for-word.

"Have you learnt your lesson, young lady?" There had been no response. "Answer me and answer me at once, young lady, or I may feel the need to apply a few more sharp slaps to teach you some manners."

Jamie had paused as yet again Angie failed to answer, realised that this was a now or never moment and had grasped the nettle (so to speak!).

"Right, young lady," he had barked. "I am clearly not getting through to you yet. So you better stand up and put your hands on your head. These jeans are coming down and you'll get fifty more smacks on your bare bottom to teach you a damn good lesson in how to behave!"

Again to his astonishment there had been no resistance from Angie as Jamie had unfastened the jeans' button and tugged her trousers and panties down in one swift movement. He pulled her back into position over his knees and stared at her glorious naked pert bottom with total lust.

"Take a breath, young lady, the next few minutes are going to be very painful," Jamie had said in his sternest voice, before he started to spank the cheeks of Angie's rounded bottom.

Although she wriggled and moaned, there was no effort to avoid his hand or attempt to stem the flow, encouraging Jamie to believe that she had fully engaged in the role-play fantasy. Emboldened by this Jamie spanked harder and harder so that the sound of the slaps was resounding throughout the room and her backside was turning a deep shade of crimson under the relentless assault. The hardness of his throbbing cock must have been apparent to Angie as she changed position and spread her legs apart, presenting Jamie with a view of her exposed pussy lips, already clearly glistening with her wetness. The added sight of her enticing arsehole clenching and relaxing between smacks excited Jamie even further.

He delivered way more than the fifty promised and he only stopped as his arm tired with Angie's bottom having turned a vibrant bright red and Jamie could feel the heat that radiated from it. Angie had sniffled and snuffled for a few seconds, as Jamie waited to see where this was going to lead and had been slightly apprehensive as to whether or not he had gone a step or two too far. He needn't have worried as the next words from Angie's lips were music to his ears.

"I am so sorry for behaving like a spoilt brat, Master, thank you for punishing me. What would sir like to do now?"

Never one to look a gift horse in the mouth, Jamie quickly adjusted to this sudden change to their normal sexual routine.

"Upstairs to bed, young lady, while I consider whether or not you have learnt the error of your naughty ways. It might be just as well for you to have a taster of what will happen if there is any repeat of your disgraceful behaviour. I'll have you on your knees, head down on your arms, legs apart and that very naughty bottom up in the air to greet me as I come in. Off you run, pretty lively now, MOVE!" he instructed Angie with a hard slap on her much admonished rear end as she scurried from the room, scrabbling to pull her trousers up and leave with some sense of dignity.

Jamie went into the kitchen and casting his eye around selected a large wooden serving spoon as the perfect implement to take things one step further. Jamie decided to allow Angie time to contemplate what had happened and, more importantly, to imagine what might be going to happen next, before he made his way up the stairs. Part of him was apprehensive that Angie may well have changed her mind and be regretting what she had allowed to take place. He needn't have worried, Angie was as she had been instructed, and Jamie felt his stomach flip as he entered the room to the stunning sight of his wife's bottom displayed in all its splendid glory, her long legs wide apart, head down resting on her crossed arms. It was a view that Jamie would never tire of over the years as they played out different versions of this scenario although none so overwhelmingly sexy for Jamie as in that moment as he took in the glory and splendour of his wife's outstanding body being presented to him for his pleasure. Spurred on by Angie's newly discovered submissive nature, Jamie slipped his belt from his trousers, aware that there was no guarantee that his young wife would offer herself up so readily in the future.

"Right young lady, let's make sure you understand the way things are going to be from now on. I am going to give you six hard strikes with the wooden spoon." He patted Angie's bottom gently with the implement as he spoke. "Then another, and hopefully for you a final, six which will be lashes from my belt." His eyes widened and a smile pulled at the corners of his mouth as although Angie tensed all over at his words, she didn't speak or move from her position.

Jamie's hand slipped between her legs and fleetingly played with the very wet pussy lips that were so available and almost irresistibly displayed for him. He licked his fingers, enjoying the taste and put them towards Angie, who opened her mouth, flicking a knowing glance at her husband, and sucked them clean of her own juices.

"Brace yourself!" As Angie tensed her buttocks rather over-dramatically in readiness, Jamie brought the wooden spoon down in a sweeping motion to land on her left cheek with a resounding splat. Angie's muted yelp gave him what little encouragement he needed to apply the second stroke to her right cheek. He deliberately went lower with the third stroke on her left and quickly followed with a fourth in line on her right cheek. Angie had begun to sob quietly by now but made no move to avoid the swinging wooden spoon, which encouraged Jamie to apply two more firm strokes to the centre of her naked bottom across her crack. Already still displaying a red hue from the spanking, her bottom was now decorated with six bright red round spots where the back of the spoon had struck home. Jamie laid his hands on the beaten buttocks and stroked her silky spheres with tenderness and love.

"Well done, that's the way to take your punishment. I think you might be getting the message at last, young lady. Right, let's see how you cope if I take things to a different level. Prepare yourself. Are you ready?"

There was no response from the naked form, her head down and long hair covering her features.

"I said, are you ready, girl? How dare you ignore me? That's three extra lashes coming your way!"

A spluttered, "B-b-b but," was the unwise response that escaped from Angie's lips. "That's so not fair, I didn't realise..."

Jamie cut her off. "Right, three more, I am not having this backchat. Be quiet. Now!" he barked.

Angie came to her senses, strangled off her further protests and dropped her head back down.

"And you can damn well count these out loud and thank me for each stroke, young lady. I will not tolerate dissent, backchat, cheek or any other form of disobedience. DO YOU UNDERSTAND?" Jamie roared at his quivering lover.

"Yes sir, sorry sir. I promise I'll try to stop being such a naughty girl and will do my best to improve my disgraceful behaviour," Angie simpered in response, clearly taking the course of least resistance.

"So how many strokes with the belt would you like to receive then?" Jamie cruelly asked.

"Hmm, I think I need twelve, sir, please?" was the hesitant response.

"Exactly, sounds like we are making progress now, bottom up high and prepare for the first lash."

A meek Angie obeyed and tensed her taut cheeks tight and still in

15

readiness but then found herself sprawled in an undignified manner as the belt struck home with force.

"Yaaanaaanaaaaaa!" she screeched as the pain spread across her already tender rear end. "Oh please, oh no, it hurts, oh stop please, oh my god."

Jamie watched as the thick bright line developed across the crack of her buttocks.

"I'm waiting," was all the response Angie got.

There was a pause and then she reluctantly struggled slowly up into position taking a deep breath.

"Yes sir, I am very sorry, sir. One, sir, thank you, sir. I am ready for the rest of my punishment now, Master," whispered his now fully subservient wife.

Oh yes indeed, thought Jamie. *Life has taken an enjoyable turn.* The rest of the belt thrashing passed in a blur for Jamie, although perhaps not so for Angie as she struggled to maintain both her position and her dignity as the next eleven strokes burned into her sore bottom.

At last she was able to say, "Twelve, sir. Thank you, sir," before meekly adding, "I am sorry I have been so naughty, sir. I will try to behave better in future, sir. Thank you so much for punishing me like the disobedient and shameless little girl I am, sir."

Jamie looked lustily at Angie's fully exposed pussy, bright red bottom and the puckered rose of her arsehole displayed in all its beauty. He wondered briefly what had happened to the rather shy young wife that had rarely allowed herself knowingly to be so open to his view in this manner, always just a little embarrassed to show her lower orifices openly for him to feast upon… and feasting upon them is exactly what he had in mind now.

"Stay exactly where you are, young lady. I haven't finished with you yet. There's a dripping wet cunt and tight little arsehole that need some attention." Jamie being deliberately crude to see if there was a reaction from his more usually inhibited partner.

"Oh yes, sir, Master sir, please sir. I am yours to command, sir," was the startling response that was all the encouragement Jamie needed. Quickly stripping naked himself he knelt down on the bed behind his now truly submissive wife and bent to gently kiss her scarlet cheeks. Angie let out a sigh and Jamie knew that this was going to be a memorable occasion as he dipped his head and positioned his mouth in front of his wife's fully exposed arsehole. He snaked his arms around her kneeling body, taking a rock hard little nipple between one set of fingers whilst the other hand slipped down to fondle her soaking wet pussy. For the very first time Jamie was able to plant a lingering kiss on what he had always thought of as Angie's forbidden entrance without her jerking away from the contact and manoeuvring her bottom from his reach. As he pinched her nipple and slid an investigative finger deep into her sex, he tentatively pushed at her anal opening with a wet tongue, gently forcing himself into her, savouring the taste of his wife's most inner sanctum.

Jamie lapped up the erotic musky scent of the treasure hole that he had previously only dreamed and fantasised about. Probing in and out, deeper and deeper he feasted between her cheeks with his tongue while his fingers moved faster and faster inside her pussy. Angie started to thrust herself back into his face and Jamie sensed that she was close to orgasm, he twisted her nipple roughly and rubbed one knuckle really hard against her clitoris. Angie screeched in ecstasy as she came, her head tossing from side to side, thighs gripping Jamie's hand tight. A brief respite then she clenched again, Jamie released her breast and swapped hands, bringing his juice-drenched fingers around to her arse crack and replacing his tongue with a forefinger as he breached her virgin anal hole properly for the very first time. Again Angie came and then again as Jamie used his fingers alternatively thrusting in and out at speed in her welcoming open entrances.

"I love you," Angie whispered as her body slumped onto the bed exhausted and fulfilled.

"Oh no, don't think your work here is done," jested Jamie as he stretched out on the bed and deftly pulled Angie's body on top of him in the classic sixty-nine position with Angie's dripping pussy and twitching arsehole above his face whilst his throbbing cock leapt up in anticipation of his wife's wet mouth coming down to greet him.

Another first, thought Jamie, as Angie had previously only let this activity develop if she was the bottom and Jamie the top. As his tongue started to gently lap at the wet folds above him, he almost swooned when Angie's lips and tongue first gently licked and then sucked at his straining cock. He moved his tongue to the hard little nub of her clitoris and took the opportunity to dip his nose into her pussy, covering it with liberally with her sexual juices. He paused for a moment, wondering whether this would be a step too far even for the suddenly newly liberated and decidedly less sexually restrained Angie, before he apprehensively slipped his nose from her pussy, and positioned it between her bottom cheeks, carefully easing it into her arsehole. He wasn't to be disappointed as Angie bucked her legs backwards pushed her bottom hard into his face and forced his nose deep into the secret dark cleft while his tongue worked hungrily on her pussy. Jamie felt like he had suddenly been offered paradise as his cock throbbed and pulsed in Angie's mouth. She must have sensed his approaching orgasm as she started to move her torso, releasing his cock from the heaven of her warm mouth.

Grabbing her thighs Jamie instructed her, "No, don't turn over, slide down and take me into you in the 'Reverse Cowgirl' position. I want to watch as I fuck you."

Coyly looking over her shoulder Angie did as she was told. "Yes Master," she simpered. "You'll then be able spank my naughty bottom some more, won't you?"

Jamie was now beyond being amazed at the sudden release of this highly erotic and sexually charged side of his long-term lover. Soon he sighed in ecstasy as she rubbed the tip of his erection against her glistening wet pussy lips before squatting down quickly to take him completely in as she fully displayed the split peach of the still-pink globes of her bottom. Torn between wanting to just hold her cheeks and watch his cock sliding in and out of her pussy or pushing a wet finger up her gaping and almost beckoning rear pleasure hole, Jamie had his decision made for him.

"Please spank me, darling, spank me hard and make me come again."

Jamie immediately brought his hand down hard on her cheek as she thrust it backwards at him. Expecting a scream or at least a yelp of agony, Jamie was astounded to hear his wife pant and moan and then clearly offer up her backside for further punishment. *OK,* thought Jamie, *if that's what you want, let's see what you can take.* Jamie began to spank Angie's bottom rhythmically, left then right, again and again, harder and harder as she offered no resistance. While her marked cheeks again began to almost glow bright red, Jamie knew that his own climax was not to be denied for too much longer. Sensing this, Angie quickly slipped him out, shuffled backwards to cover his face with her pulsating pussy and spread cheeks and dipped her head to suck greedily on his twitching cock.

"Aaaaarrghhh!" screamed Jamie spluttering into the folds of her sex as he exploded into her willing mouth. His orgasm was intense and he spurted copiously into the warm wetness as Angie sucked harder and harder to drain him of his cum. Expecting her to reach for a tissue, Angie had never minded bringing him off in her mouth but had always drawn the line at swallowing his ejaculation, Jamie was amazed and excited to see her grinning over her shoulder at him. She licked her lips provocatively, allowing his spunk to bubble on her lips before making a show of swallowing hard and then opening her mouth wide to prove that she had swallowed his offering for the first time. Jamie doubted that he had ever been happier, more sexually fulfilled and more deeply in love than he had at that moment. Angie then lay down fully on Jamie, moving to allow his tongue to enter her again. She rubbed her mound hard against his face as she drove herself again to orgasm.

"I'm fucking your face, my love, I'm fucking your face," Angie breathlessly cried out as her body spasmed once more and Jamie was treated to the tip of his tongue being sprinkled with her cum, his face becoming covered with her love juices. She spun round and slipped into his arms and they kissed and stroked each other for several minutes while their breathing returned to normal and they enjoyed together the coming down period after making love as only two people truly committed and in tune with each other can, as they lay looking lovingly into each other's eyes.

It would probably be fair to say that in the days, weeks and months that followed, their sex life became more vigorous and more intense than it had ever been, the introduction of many accessories and love toys of all types certainly widened their scope and there were many visits to 'Knickers Plus', the local outlet for what was basically an underwear and lingerie shop with an additional room full of sex toys and all manner of sexual aids displayed imaginatively and creatively so as not to appear crude or perverted in any way. Eventually after a lot of persuasion Angie would join Jamie in his visits and with the expansion of online shopping covering every taste and aspect of sexual adventure under way, their boundaries widened and they became more and more adventurous. Jamie snapped out of his reverie as the sharp ping of his mobile phone alerted him to an incoming message and he reached hopefully for the instrument. His face lit up as he realised that the sender was Professor Edward Stones, a man Jamie looked upon, and up to, as his mentor albeit the professor would always refer to him as his colleague.

"We have a little situation to deal with, please indicate your availability to assist by return. Regards, Stones."

A smile spread across Jamie's face as he knew that this was a message telling him that the professor had just condemned a student to corporal punishment and that Jamie was required to carry out the act, or part of it. He quickly responded giving the professor the agreed standard days and times that he was available knowing that the professor would already have seen from Jamie's shared online calendar, when he was free. Jamie fired off his reply then he sat back and waited for the professor to determine with his 'victim' the most suitable time for the punishment to take place. After much planning, the reality of the weeks of discussions and plans, with some interesting active sessions to be going on with thanks to their shared membership of a very particular and specialist club, were finally going to come to fruition. Jamie could feel his erection growing as he contemplated the chance to give one of the female students from the prestigious St. James' College a damn good thrashing on her bare backside very shortly.

The professor had intimated that if things worked out there would be many more opportunities for Jamie to indulge in his passion for beating the bottoms of recalcitrant young ladies and he could hardly wait to get started!

CHAPTER 3

DEALING WITH EMILY

The professor let Emily Govan stand and contemplate her doom for almost an hour as he got on with college business.

"Right, young lady, you've had long enough. Go and sit down at the corner desk, there's pens and paper aplenty, and you can do a spot of old-fashioned comprehension using your fingers and a writing instrument... a pen, a pen, for goodness' sake..." he said, exasperated, as Emily looked rather mystified at his words.

"Write me an essay, reasonably concisely if you will, which will convince me that I can apply a suitable punishment that will allow you to remain in college to complete your degree. It was six months ago that I tanned your sweet derriere for drunken behaviour, at your own request I may add, and you assured me then that there would be no repeat. Well here we are again, young lady. I hope you have been sensible enough to use the last hour to have come up with an option that I will find acceptable. You have thirty minutes to decide your future so best sit down and start writing."

Emily moved quickly across to the desk, saying, "Yes sir, I certainly will do so. I am very sorry and hope that I can truly show that I can mend my ways, sir."

Stones watched as she picked up the pen, steadied herself and began writing, the expression on her face suggesting to him that her mind was frantically working overtime. Set discreetly amongst the bookcase-covered walls of the Dean of Discipline's spacious and rather distinguished-looking central room, which worked as both his office and his main living room, were a series of cupboards and shelving units at various heights. A keen observer would have noticed that some of the cupboards had number dial locks secreted amongst the shelves and may have wondered what lay hidden inside. The professor languidly got up and walked across to one of the larger cupboards now, pausing to select a book from the shelves as he passed. Casually with one hand holding the well-worn tome, he flicked at the key pad of the nearest cabinet with the other. The door sprung lightly open revealing the contents, however rather than remove any item the professor turned away, book in hand, and returned to his desk leaving the door very much open. He then wandered over to where Emily was staring into space, having written down very few words.

"Ten minutes gone and very little down, it seems," mused the professor. "One hopes that you are just formulating your thoughts before finishing your rather simplistic task, eh?"

The look that Emily gave him indicated a certain degree of panic; he could see that she knew what she had done wrong and was sure that she pretty much accepted that any chastisement was likely to very much involve a sore backside. The quandary that he knowingly had set her, having previously laid her across his knees and subjected her to a long, painful bare bottom spanking, was for her to propose an expansion on this theme and he could see that she was a little unsure on exactly what she would be expected to suggest.

Stones loved these mind games with his young students; their reluctance to offer themselves up for punishment was natural but they were usually bright enough to realise that there was no escape clause available. He had hoped that Emily had fully understood the direction that the conversation had taken and that she would realise that the end result for her was bound to be something more severe than a straightforward spanking. Eventually she put into words her thought process.

"Yes sir, just thinking hard to make sure that I can put into words how sorry I am and how I need to be effectively punished, sir... it's just that I am not sure what form exactly you would find acceptable for my punishment to take," was what she ventured.

"Oh for pity's sake, girl!" Stones barked. "Have you not learnt anything, yet? I suggest you start thinking a bit faster and come up with the answer very shortly or I will have to think about who to contact to help clarify your thinking!"

Emily blanched, and he could see that this was clearly not an avenue she wanted explored, but as she went to respond, Stones exasperatedly slammed the book in his hand down on the table next to her and walked back to his desk. "Eighteen minutes left," he snapped.

He could see that he had now got Emily's full attention as she stared in horror at the book beside her: *Thrashing and flogging to cure disobedience: A Victorian Governess' answer.*

At this point, as Emily's eyes spun round to face where the professor was sitting she espied the open cupboard door.

"Oh My God, what the fuck!" she said, the words tumbling from her mouth before the wisdom of doing so kicked in.

As the professor's head slowly turned towards her, she tried to retract the unwise exclamation.

"Sorry sir, I just saw, I just, I didn't... I'm so very sorry, sir."

Her eyes were pulled back to the contents of the cupboard, where, hanging neatly in rows on gleaming steel hooks, was an array of some of the most terrifying implements Emily had ever laid eyes on. There were canes of differing thicknesses and lengths, paddles – wooden and leather, a riding crop, a small whip, leather straps and pronged belts, a cat-of-nine-tails and several odd-shaped handled wooden accessories.

"I, you can't, just, just, just… Professor no, please no, you can't, you can't, I won't, I will not….Oh my god!" Emily blustered, her face clearly displaying a rising agitation and approaching panic.

"Child, you are digging yourself in a deeper and deeper hole. You have just a few minutes left to illustrate that you possess some English composition skills in that tiny, poorly used brain somewhere before I may sadly have to consider the action to start your removal from college. For a start you will not speak foul language to me ever again, without serious repercussions. I am already pondering on what additional punishment I can give you to get that message into your head. You are clearly not learning how to correct your behaviour and you seem to have a flagrant disregard and disrespect for authority," thundered the professor.

"I'm sorry, I'm sorry, I'm sorry sir. I just was not expecting… I didn't dream…"

Taking a deep breath, Emily turned back to the desk, picked up the pen, concentrated on steadying her hand, and started to write. She sighed deeply but Stones noticed the clear look of acceptance settle on her face and she moved the pen towards the sheet of paper with her body language indicating that she seemed resigned to her fate. Stones watched as her eyes strayed towards the array of implements of punishment displayed and with a quick shake of her head turned back to the desk and she began to write.

The professor went over to his beloved selection of, what he liked to refer as his "improvers", each one had a tale to tell, and a tail to tame, and he chuckled to himself as he ran his hand lovingly along the row. He smiled further as Emily flinched at the sound, this was one young lady who would thoroughly deserve her fate, Stones mused as he strolled over behind her, glancing at his watch as he did so.

"Two more minutes, Emily, so finish off please. I think you'll find you need to add the word 'bare' into that sentence." Emily jumped at the professor's words but quickly amended her text, her earlier resistance seemingly confined to dust. Finishing off as fast as she could, Emily signed and printed her name at the bottom of the page, Stones suspected that she well remembered how her reluctance had resulted in her falling foul of the professor's wrath previously, earning extra swats on her backside for not following instructions and "failing to comply". As she handed over her work, Stones was delighted to see how nervous he had made her.

"Just like handing over those so important essays to your tutors, eh girl? Do you always hand those in late as well?"

"So sorry sir, yes sir, no sir. Oh God, no I've never been this nervous handing in work, sir. I am sorry I am late." Emily rather whined as she stood anxiously before him.

"Well thank you, at last, just three minutes late, but who honestly would have expected anything more from a wilful, disobedient, cheeky and rude girl? Whilst I read through this, you will return to the desk and write a further essay apologising for your failure to comply with the time limit set and, most importantly, what you now feel about your foul-mouthed outburst given that you have had time to consider your actions. Of course, you will also suggest a punishment appropriate to this that you would like to undergo. Then we can get on with sorting out the details of how and when the punishment will be delivered…"

The professor looked in astonishment as Emily's face clouded over and she literally stamped her feet.

"This is so unfair," she unwisely blurted out.

Professor Stones fixed her with his most steely gaze and watched as she seemed to shrivel under the stare.

"Oh God, I am so sorry Professor Stones," was as far she got before Stones interrupted her with a voice of like a clap of thunder.

"Emily Govan, I absolutely despair. You are now entering Last Chance Terminal, my girl. Right, take off your clothes. I am not putting up with your nonsense for very much longer, you need to learn a small part of your lesson now. You clearly haven't been taking our conversations seriously. Do not speak," he snapped as Emily began a protest.

"Strip naked now or by Christ girl I will have you frog-marched from this college, file your expulsion papers and contact your parents. Now, I said!"

It only took a split second for Emily to realise that she had no option but to comply as she quickly stripped her top and jeans off, down to her brassiere and knickers. She paused and risked a sneaky glance at the professor, who met her eyes as he stared unblinking and unmoving at her. He allowed himself a smile inside as Emily was wise enough to read the unspoken words in his eyes, unhooking her bra and letting her voluptuous breasts swing free. She took another breath then, presenting her behind to the professor, bent and pulled her knickers down, exposing her bare bottom to his gaze, adding them neatly to the rest of her clothes – another lesson she had learned from her previous visit.

"Now, young lady, I seem to finally have your full attention. Put your hands on your head and face me when I am talking to you." Emily complied, closing her eyes as she turned to show her full-frontal nudity to him.

"Where were we? Yes, you were going to go and write me another little report, weren't you? Now move the chair away, you can write standing up, or, more appropriately, bending over," smiled Stones, "and whilst you are at it, you had better read this little excerpt from the college's Disciplinary Code, Rules and Conditions of Entry. As you can see, I've also attached the end page of the contract, showing your signature alongside your parents'. As we discussed previously you have been made aware of the contents and I remind you again that this shows that your parents have kindly signed the page I have given you laying out the application of the corporal punishment process and their acceptance of the college's full authority and permission to execute any deemed chastisement thought fit by the Dean of Discipline. You will note that the options to exclude certain elements of the agreement have not been taken and that your parents have signed sanctioning the Dean of Discipline full powers 'in loco parentis' to inflict whatever necessary punishment is required to ensure that all possible attention is given to developing a fully-rounded, well educated, erudite and discerning adult who will bring pride and honour to her family and the college. As you will also note it further states that all punishment will be delivered to the student in the state of undress as determined at the time by the said Dean of Discipline. As I say I am aware that you have been presented with this before but it is part of my duty of care to both you and your parents to ensure that you understand that punishment at St. James' is never a malicious act, nor an act of anger, nor an act of vengeance. We seek purely to improve by reparation and correction. This may well be painful, you may be hurt, you may suffer, you may be humiliated, you should feel disgraced and ashamed, but ultimately you will be improved and therefore we will have achieved progress. You will learn many things here at college, but one of the most important will simply be learning how to behave for the greater good.

Do I make myself clear, do you understand?"

Emily gulped and blanched under his ferocious gaze; Stones was well aware that like most students she had barely glanced at what she had been advised to read, both when becoming a college member and when disciplined previously. He knew that like others before her she had assumed that none of this would apply to her, never dreaming that she would face the shame of being treated in such a manner, bent over the professor's knees with her bare bottom in the air, utterly humiliated and humbled. Stones knew that her parents had signed this off possibly thinking that their sweet and perfect little daughter would never transgress and so be unlikely to need be concerned with any of this side of college life. Or, as in the case of many of the mothers sending their daughters to their alma maters, having a fair idea of what their little dears could expect and being perfectly at ease with the possibility that sore bottoms would be heading in that direction! Like most students in trouble, Emily was unlikely to want to appeal to her parents and Stones was confident that her mother would have been horrified to hear of her daughter's predicament and would, in all probability, be encouraging his actions. For once Emily had got on with the job in hand, quickly having written down a short statement signing with a flourish and turning to hand the sheet over. Another long sigh escaped her lips as she waited while Stones finished reading through her earlier piece.

Stones let her stand by his side before acknowledging her presence.

"Hands," was all he said and Emily obediently placed her hands on her head, apologising immediately.

He stared at the naked, very attractive young woman standing before him and then read through the short essay she had just delivered. Placing it alongside her earlier work, he made sure that she was well aware that he was scrutinizing her uncovered body in detail, sensing that she was becoming a tad too comfortable considering her circumstances. He looked into her eyes with his sternest expression, pleased to see the earlier anxiety evident there, before speaking slowly and dispassionately.

"This will suffice, Emily, thank you. Let's just go through the formalities of the details. I accept that you have apologised fully for your disgusting behaviour and that you have requested that you should be thoroughly flogged in way of a suitable punishment for your disgraceful conduct. I also take note that you have also apologised in full for your misdemeanours and foul language today. You will report here next Friday evening at 5pm, freshly bathed and wearing lightweight easily removable clothing. Your underwear will be clean and fresh on, please note."

Emily gritted her teeth but refused to rise as he continued.

"You require a note from the college nurse, counter-signed by the tutor responsible for your pastoral care, to justify any reason why the punishment would need to be postponed. You are required to advise me by midday of your appointment of the reasons you are requesting a delay and due consideration will be given and usually a new date set."

The professor went through the mantra laid out to every student due to be subjected to corporal punishment, ensuring that a record was preserved of the student's compliance and agreement to be so punished.

He continued, "I hope you do not need to be informed of what would happen if it was to be discovered that deceit is involved in any such request and that you must display full contrition to atone for your sins. Over a period of about an hour or so, you will undergo a complete and intense thrashing and be sent back to your room when

I decide that the process is complete and that you have sufficiently paid your dues. If it is necessary, due to any failure on your part to accept the punishment in a correct and dignified manner, you will be requested to return and the punishment will then be repeated. Note I say repeated, not continued, it is important that you understand that stipulation. Otherwise I would expect everything to be resolved by the time you leave on Friday evening, hopefully as a chastened but improved young lady. Is that all clear?"

Emily nodded her assent and Stones enjoyed the moment when the dreaded words "complete and intense thrashing" seemed to penetrate her consciousness. Stones watched as she processed his words, he wanted her thinking about the fact that she was now facing the additional punishment that he had promised because she couldn't just keep her thoughts to herself.

As Emily waited patiently, standing still, silent and proud, Stones adopted a more conciliatory and forgiving expression hoping to encourage slight hope growing that maybe he had just been taunting her with the threat of separate punishment for her slowness in writing her essay. Stones smiled at the rather desperate-looking student whose eyes seemed to sparkle with desire to please. Stones prepared himself as he got ready to crush her hopes of forgiveness; as if he would ever forgive such an outburst and such insolence. The time had come to enlighten her, he thought, time for Emily to discover that the Dean of Discipline did not waste words and energy on idle threats.

"Now young lady, just in case you might be thinking I was in some bizarre way going to forget or relent concerning your earlier behaviour," the stern words of the professor causing Emily to blanch and stiffen, the hope of any mercy being shown draining visibly from her face. Stones, noting her reaction, continued with a smile, adding to Emily's nervousness.

"I note that you agree that a spanking would be the most suitable and appropriate punishment for now. I would now like you to go over to the cabinet that concerned you so much earlier on and bring me the dark brown round leather paddle please."

Emily gulped and, under the unblinking gaze of Stones, she slowly made her way over to the open door of the cabinet. Stones noted her cast a brief glance at the contents displayed before she duly selected the described paddle; her reluctance to look at the canes, straps, crops and wooden paraphernalia and implements, which suggested much harsher experiences, very evident.

"Come, girl, come. Bring it to me quickly or would you rather select an alternative?" barked the professor as Emily paused with the paddle in her hand. She handed the paddle over suddenly looking very aware of her nakedness and vulnerability in front of him.

His next action left her clearly stunned as Stones rose and leaned towards her sniffing at her upper half, before suddenly he bent down and took a deep breath in. Emily's face was one of pure abject horror as Stones first sniffed at her fanny and then his large hands grasped her hips before propelling her round and making a performance of taking large sniffs around her backside.

"When did you last wash, girl?" he snapped but before Emily could answer, he continued, "Don't bother as you smell a bit rank and since I don't wallop smelly girls, you need to take a shower. Go on, in you go, everything is in there." Stones pointed to the automatically opening door as his fingers manipulated his laptop keyboard and a door opened within the book-cased lining of the walls, revealing a luxurious bathroom.

Stones enjoyed Emily's look of amazement to see the beautiful décor of the large en-suite room containing two sinks, a large freestanding bath, a toilet, a bidet and a top-of-the-range shower encased in glass. Towels, flannels and mats were everywhere and the walls were heavily mirrored from floor to ceiling.

"In the shower you pop and get yourself properly clean." Emily's face once more was bright red as Stones yet again chose his taunting words to reduce her to feeling like a naughty little six-year-old. The fight seemed to drain from her though, as she padded obediently across to the bathroom attempting to pull the door behind her. She almost lost her footing as the door stayed absolutely firm against her pressure.

"Ah, it stays open," said the professor, clearly controlling the workings from his computer. "I am not having you locked in there wasting time, hoping, rather pointlessly I might add, that your punishment somehow won't happen if you prevaricate."

Although he realised that it had to be perfectly clear to Emily that he was toying with her and teasing her to see if she would react he suspected that this was a strong-willed young woman and his battle to break her will was not yet over.

"Realisation dawning, is it at last?" he sneered. "Yes, it is degrading, yes it is humiliating and yes I am making you feel so very small... There are two threads to effective discipline, Emily, one is the pain caused and the other is the humiliation of the experience. The idea is that to teach you a lesson that you won't forget, the two combine to ensure that it is a memorable experience that you won't want repeated. Effective and efficient improvement of miscreants is the aim, young lady. Hopefully you are now beginning to understand my methods."

He could see that she clearly wished to speak and watched with amusement as she hesitated as if she didn't dare ask whatever was concerning her, presumably fearing the answer.

"Come on girl, spit it out. Something is obviously bothering you, out with it," he probed.

"Oh God… um… but, but, um you see sir, I need to go to the toilet, please," she asked plaintively, but then gulped in horror at the response she received.

"Of course, you may relieve yourself my dear, it's never good to be beaten with a full bladder. I am sure you will find the facilities up to standard though. Please carry on."

Emily just stood frozen to the spot, her hand still applying pressure to the unmovable door.

Stones encouraged her. "Come on, come on, please relieve yourself and get into that shower so we can get on with the main business of the day." His tone then hardening as she remained in position.

"Come along, girl, come along. I haven't got all day but I can certainly make time for additional swats on that cute derriere of yours if that's what it needs to encourage you to do what you are told. You have clearly realised that the door is staying open so just get on with your business."

Emily let loose a long sigh but the need to pee evidently overruled any reservations concerning the shame and embarrassment of using the toilet in front of her smirking tormentor. In truth Stones got no sexual thrill at all in this blatant act of voyeurism but was totally aware of the degradation that he was adding to Emily's experience and saw it as just another stage to fully mastering the errant student. He watched dispassionately as she perched on the toilet bowl, squeezing her eyes tightly as she obviously attempted to disconnect from the situation enough to relax her bladder to be able to pee. As her flow finally gushed out she let out a long breath of relief but on opening her eyes was shocked to find the professor standing beside her.

"Done?" he queried, reaching down beside her and tearing off a few squares of toilet paper. "Well, wipe the drips off and let's get you into that shower."

Emily's face was a picture and Stones suspected that she would not be able to think of a time when she had felt made to feel quite as small and insignificant as she did at that moment, notwithstanding that he was a man who had already spanked her and seen her most intimate body parts up close. Hers was a look of pure despair as she once again coloured scarlet in embarrassment and humiliation. Flushing the toilet quickly she nipped into the shower, with a look of relief that suggested that she was grateful that she at least had had one door that she could close behind her, even if it was hardly opaque!

Stones watched her as she turned her back to him and switched the water flow on; he was thoroughly enjoying causing Emily such discomfort and was pretty sure that he was getting through to her. For all the unforgiving thoughts the students often considered concerning his behaviour, most would accept that generally his punishments were designed to discourage repeat offending and found it hard to argue that it was not effective. Although Emily was a disappointment in that she was a returning offender, the professor's method tended to be very effective in quashing bad behavioural patterns amongst the ladies of St. James. Stones beliefs in his methods were supported wholeheartedly by the college council committee and most importantly by the Mistress, the President, the Senior Bursar and the Senior Tutor, who along with Stones himself made up the powerful quintet that basically set the tone and direction of the college. St. James' record of success academically meant that little resistance to their thoroughly un-politically correct disciplinary procedures was encountered and with so many of the students being offspring or close relatives of alumni and college members, that was unlikely to change. Graduating from St. James' was virtually a passport to success both career-wise and relationship-wise, as the circles opened to former members of college were very wide and very influential. Stones sat back in one his many purposely and carefully positioned chairs observing Emily Govan as, now out of the shower, she towelled herself dry.

"A little tip, dear. Towel that bottom nice and dry as rest assured that a wet or damp backside will accentuate your upcoming painful improvement process even more so."

Emily snarled under her breath but quickly obeyed. "Yes sir, thank you sir," she ventured, having correctly surmised that now was most certainly was not the time to annoy this man who basically, and rather literally, had her fate in the palm of his hand! Stones move over to the seat that he considered his spanking chair, positioning it so that the hidden cameras would be recording his favoured angle to view at a later date.

"Right, Emily, time to spank and paddle your bottom now, if that is what you wish?"

Going by her expression, what Emily wished and thought didn't necessarily tally with the professor's words but a wiser student now deemed it more politic to concur.

"Yes sir, I wish to be punished for my earlier rude and tardy behaviour and agree that a spanking and a paddling would serve me well as a reminder to behave in an improved manner in the future."

Stones could see that she had steeled herself to submit to a spanking and was well aware that it was under duress and that he was a long way from producing a compliant nature in this rather strong-willed and headstrong young individual.

"Right young lady, I can see that you have decided that you might as well grit your teeth and get this over with. After all, it's only a spanking eh?"

Stones' words were rewarded in the startled expression that crossed Emily's face and he knew that he had hit the nail on the head. She wasn't the first person to have been shocked by the professor's apparent ability to read their thoughts and double-guess every action.

Breathing slowly and steadily, Emily placed herself beside the professor and waited for the inevitable instruction to position herself for the spanking. Stones was pleased to see some trepidation in her eyes as she espied the paddle sitting within reach and was no doubt hoping that it would prove to be a softer option than it appeared. He noticed her gaze drift to the cabinet of punishment implements on the wall and she perceptively trembled all over as, no doubt, her thoughts flashed to what was promised to come.

"Bend over, Miss Govan, and present yourself in the accustomed manner, hands on the floor and spread your legs, if you wouldn't mind please," he instructed. Emily displaying an expression that suggested that she might not totally appreciate that it sounded very much like she might have a choice in the matter, nevertheless complied exactly as instructed.

"Excellent. Now as you should know, I have no wish to engage in conversation during your punishment so please keep any thoughts and observations to yourself. You may answer any direct questions, you may thank me, and you may of course sob your heart out. Please however refrain from screaming. It is a spanking, it will sting, but it is perfectly bearable without any histrionics so I would be grateful if you would accept it with a degree of decorum. I will now begin. You will receive a spanking of a mere twenty-five slaps followed by a thorough paddling of a further dozen. If you kick or fail to keep your legs open for the duration I will have to use the leg-spread restraints, this, of course, will also earn you further punishment strokes and the paddling would be doubled. Do you understand and are you ready?" Stones asked, one hand firmly on her lower back whilst the other was gently stroking Emily's raised bottom cheeks, his fingers fluttering over her opened crevice, in a manner which he knew from experience would be quite disconcerting for his subject.

A last deep breath was heard from Emily, who, Stones was interested to see, showed no reaction to his intimate touch.

"Yes sir, thank you, sir. I am ready for my punishment to begin, sir."

As she tensed to await the first stroke as his hand moved from her bottom, Stones decided to test her stoicism and shake her calm demeanour. He paused before speaking the words that would produce a visible response as though a chill had run through her.

"Oh dear, not carried out a very effective drying process then," his hand had returned to her cheek swiftly joined by the other. Suddenly he parted her buttock mounds completely and let out a sigh that clearly signalled a deep disappointment.

"There's a veritable pool of droplets in your crease, young lady, how hard is it to dry a bottom now?" he muttered.

He reached across her body to his desk and opening a drawer, produced medical gloves which he proceeded to put on as Emily attempted to peer through her legs, wanting to see what fresh horrors might be about to befall her.

"Eyes down, retain the position while I sort out your failure to carry out a simple everyday task," he barked.

He then slid cupped fingers between her bottom cheeks, running them up from her pussy lips and firmly over her arsehole, scooping out the drops of shower water and flicking them over her bottom. A sob escaped from Emily's lips and her legs began trembling as he repeated this manoeuvre several times with one large hand holding her cheeks prised wide apart. Stones then proceeded to gently smooth the water over her cheeks.

"This will serve you right and teach you to prepare yourself better in the future. I do not expect to have to wipe the backsides of my students before dispensing punishments!" he snarled.

His reward was several deep shuddering breaths as Emily obviously struggled to retain her composure, much to the professor's merriment.

"You are now going to learn that the stinging sensation is heightened when applied to wet flesh."

Stones waited to see if this last taunt prompted Emily to react but it appeared that she was now beyond a response; he hoped that she no longer harboured hope of there being any possibility of coming out of this episode with any shred of pride or dignity left. Not only had she endured a senior member of the college having just touched her pussy, he'd basically just wiped down her bottom crack with his fingers. Stones was well aware that like every student treated thus before her, nothing would have quite prepared Emily for the shock of the first slap landing forcibly on her left buttock. The muscular but fleshy surface undulating and reshaping before the initial white impact mark began to be replaced by a keen hand-shaped reddening. Despite her best efforts, Emily shrieked with the shock, albeit a shriek that was cut off in its prime as the right cheek received the second stroke.

"Decorum, Emily, decorum," reminded the professor, probably rather too cheerily to Emily's mind!

She certainly would not be able to dispute his promise about the effect of having wet flesh as she mewed at the effect of the stinging pain.

"Legs apart, girl," she was reminded and her lower body tensed and she automatically closed her legs.

"Keep in mind that you should be presenting and pointing your anus at me at all times. That should help you keep those cheeks apart!" He goaded her, knowing full well that she would detest the instruction.

He paused and Emily took her cue, spread her legs fully apart and raised her cheeks, fully exposing her arsehole and most of her pussy. Stones sensed her resolve to retain some sort of dignity and suspected that she was keen for her castigator to appreciate her compliance less retribution be earned.

"Yes sir, sorry, sir," she obediently complied, appearing to concentrate on preparing to absorb the blows as silently as possible as the spanking continued apace.

"See how you are learning already," he smirked as he added a bit of additional swing to his arm.

The slapping sounds were all that was heard for the next few seconds as he completed her spanking, Emily's body taut as she struggled to keep her cheeks unclenched.

"Well done, good girl, that's your little hand-spanking completed," said the professor. "I'll pause to allow you a moment's grace before I commence the paddling. You may rub your bottom if you wish."

Emily hesitated and Stones knew full well her quandary: much as she wanted to rub and squeeze her stinging cheek she would know full well that the downside would mean exposing her private parts even more than they had already been. Added to this the weight shift without her hands firmly on the floor would result in her rubbing her lower torso into his lap which she might not realise until she committed herself. However, as often happened, the students in her position found the overriding need to play for time to allow them an opportunity to somewhat recover from one thrashing before the other one began.

"Thank you sir," was her response as she manoeuvred to rub her bottom. Stones felt her tense as she now became aware of the hard ridge of his erection. There was a moment's pause and he could almost feel the working of her mind before she continued with the kneading of her rosy buttocks, making no indication that was in the least bit aware of his state. Although generally most cautious in ensuring that his reprobates were not aware of how erotic and sexually charged he actually found the act of thrashing young and naked female bottoms, Stones found himself strangely unbothered and, if he was truthful, far more aroused than he would normally be. There was definitely something about Emily that appealed to his most base senses; however he was experienced enough in these circumstances to be able to display complete nonchalance concerning his state. He smiled to himself; he was far too long in the tooth and well-practised in his art not to realise what had just occurred and although he deliberately wore tight thick underwear designed to contain his swollen length he knew that the over-the-knee experience by its nature left him a little exposed with the bodily contact being so unavoidable. Her demeanour gave him pause to think that here was a young lady that normal rules might not apply to. Whilst she appeared well aware of her nakedness and vulnerability, he suspected that she was a pragmatic woman who well appreciated the lack of options open to her.

"Shall we get on, girl?" he queried. "What would you like to happen now?"

Emily, to his approval, said the words she would have known that he was expecting, she reached for the paddle, offered it over to the professor and dropped her hands to the floor once more.

"Sir, I would please like to receive the severe paddling to my bottom that we have agreed that I thoroughly deserve and which I am sure will teach me a proper lesson."

Stones was impressed once more, the carefully chosen subservient words and tone of delivery were evidence of a quick learner, albeit with a speedy temper to match, as without a further word the paddle was taken quickly from her hand and whipped through the air to land on her left cheek before Emily had had time to prepare in any way whatsoever.

"Yaaaaaaah!" she screamed and then again as the second stroke arrived. By the sixth stroke she had lost control, her legs were kicking, her body twisting as she tried to evade the stinging leather.

"Last warning, Emily, if you don't keep in position, still and with your legs wide apart, then the punishment will be doubled and I will have to put you in the leg restraint."

Emily whimpered but settled back into place. "Sorry sir, please carry on and I will do my best to receive my punishment in the correct manner."

The submissive words and cringeworthy manner indicated that she was now at the stage that she was beyond caring about anything other than getting to the end of this session without incurring any additional punishment. Stones surmised that at this point she was desperately trying to put to the back of her mind what exactly she would have to ensure next Friday and hoped that she was beginning to realise that she may just need to change her attitude to authority if she to actually get through three years at the college.

Any such thoughts that Emily was having were interrupted as the paddle descended onto its exposed intended target for the seventh time, and then an eighth. An ear-piercing scream came next as two strokes landed in quick succession on the softest skin of her lower cheeks and top of her legs, Emily's body bucked, her arms and legs flaying, almost propelling herself off the professor's lap in the process. Scrambling to retain the correct position her head twisted back to show a face with wide appealing eyes that told Stones that she knew what was coming and was begging for him not to say the words she dreaded.

Emily burst into tears finally as he began to speak.

"Those puppy dog eyes count for nothing with me, missy. That's three additional strokes for non-compliance of basic instructions, Emily, now will you please hold firm now and show some decorum. Try and retain some sense of any dignity you still have and present your bottom in the correct manner. Any repeat and I will not only apply the leg restraints as I have warned you but I will also restart your paddling from the beginning."

Emily was now sobbing disconsolately, the fight all gone. "Yes sir, sorry sir." She raised her bottom and surrendered herself to her fate as the final two strokes became five and were applied in quick succession to the sobbing student, her cheeks on fire, her shame fully formed, her dignity lost in the room at the hands of her irresistible tormentor. As Stones let the paddle drop back onto the desk she lay supine across his lap, beaten and cowed, tears falling onto the carpet; she seemed to barely register the fact that Stones was now gently stroking and kneading her stinging posterior.

"Shush, shush, my girl, it's all over for the time being, shhh, shhh, shhh," he murmured as his soothing hands worked on relieving the stinging.

Emily was beyond any objection, and Stones felt that sense of triumph in knowing that yet again he had mastered his prey completely.

"Stand up, young lady, tissues are here, wipe your eyes, blow your nose and make an effort to pull yourself together. Now hands on head, up against the wall, time for reflection."

Emily obeyed, any thoughts of resistance appeared to have been wiped from her mind entirely, as she did as he instructed, and positioned herself against the book-lined wall.

"Thank you, sir," she said meekly. Her dropped shoulders and lowered head signalled her defeat.

The professor paused in his work to stare at the source of that afternoon's activity. *Yes,* he thought. *Progress is being made with this one.* He partly admired her spirit and feistiness and knew that to a degree it was probably an essential part of her make-up and character albeit over-emphasised and poorly controlled. However, this was why he truly believed in the discipline he dealt out for the college, as he was confident that this young lady would surely benefit from his "improvement" process in the long term. He was not entirely convinced that the flogging to come would be the last time he would need to give this impetuous young lady help along the way, but it was a good start on the road! He wandered over to her pile of clothes and picked up her underwear.

"You may reunite yourself with your clothing," he said, handing over her bra and panties. "I suppose you will have to put those knickers back on, rather grubby though they are," he added, knowing full well that this could provoke a response. Emily reared and reacted to type.

"How dare you, you fucking old—" was as far as she got with her unwise words and her quick temper as suddenly a vice-like hand gripped her neck and bent her forwards. Emily would have barely had time to register what was happening as she was marched a few steps, vaguely hearing the sound of something being unhooked and briefly registering the rapid air movement behind her before an unbelievable pain exploded across her already sore buttocks. Her scream was one of pure shock and agony, all air being expelled from her body, her eyes bulging wide and her legs going akimbo as she struggled to maintain her footing. Released by Stones she fell to the floor, her underwear falling beside her, her hands scrabbling to grasp her cheeks as her body rocked and shook.

"When you have quite finished with all your histrionics, you will pick up your grubby underwear and hold them in your hands on your head. This little beauty will remain beside me until I believe that I no longer require to dispense further correction to you today," he said as he placed his favourite thick leather strap on the desk.

"You, my girl, still have a lot to learn, it seems. Hopefully some more progress with your improvement can be made next week."

A few minutes later, as Stones allowed Emily the time to contemplate yet again the trouble her quick mouth had landed her in, there came the sound of a gentle buzz. The professor turned to his PC, looked at a monitor and tapped a few times. Emily turned, a look of sheer horror and panic on her face as a door at the rear of the room began to automatically open and the clear sound of someone entering the building became apparent. She spun around, her mouth falling open in wordless astonishment, her eyes casting around as though an escape route was about to reveal itself to her.

"Face the wall, girl, do not move!" was the response that that action brought her as Dr Celia Ford, the Senior Tutor, appeared in the room via the back entrance that Emily, like most people, had hitherto been completely unaware of.

"Oh my, Emily Govan, I see. Clearly still here and evidently still being dealt with," were the Senior Tutor's opening words. "Thought she was just in for her little chat, today, Dean?" she queried, seemingly not the slightest bit taken aback to see a naked student, hands on head with a blazing red stripe across her bottom, standing against the wall in Stones' room.

"Yes, so did I, Senior Tutor, so did I. But Emily has a little problem controlling what comes out of her mouth, it seems, so she has been having some immediate lessons in improving her behaviour, but sadly without making much progress so far. We do have time, however, we do have time. That and another appointment next Friday when, I am pleased to report, Emily has decided that she would like to return here for a thorough thrashing as punishment for her lewdness," responded Stones.

"Oh, excellent to hear, Emily, is this correct?"

Emily's body had tensed at both their words but was evidently still struggling to get her head around the fact that she was fully exposed in front of this senior member of the college staff, someone that all of St James' students generally held in such high regard. Her lack of response, however, did not go unnoticed by the professor.

"You have just been asked a question by the Senior Tutor, where the devil are your manners young lady, have you really learned so little today?"

Stones moved swiftly across and before Emily had regained her composure enough to formulate an answer his words were followed by two sharp stinging slaps with the flat of his hand on the back of her legs. Emily yelped in pain as once again tears filled her eyes.

"Yes sir, sorry sir, sorry miss... I am so sorry, yes, of course I deserve to be beaten properly. God I'm sorry, please no more, I am so sore, sir," she cringed imploringly.

Turning away from her, Stones addressed Celia. "We have plenty of time before the restaurant booking, would you like to see this afternoon's goings on?"

The Senior Tutor smiled. "You know me so well, Dean. Shall we have Emily watch it with us? Such fun that would be."

Ten minutes later, a distressed and shamed Emily was standing, hands on head and still naked, between the two seated academics in front of a large screen that had appeared from its previously concealed position in the ceiling. Compelled to watch a replay from the moment Emily and Georgina had entered the rooms with every word and action being played out before their eyes. Emily's face was bright red but transfixed as the scenes of the afternoon unfolded before her eyes. Whilst Celia was engrossed in the activity being screened, Stones watched Emily's reactions. He could see the clenched teeth as she was angered by her own outbursts and lack of control, the wide eyes and appalled expression as she relived the moment the professor sniffed at her nether regions and screwed his face up in distaste; relief and temporary relaxation took over when it became apparent that there were no cameras filming inside the bathroom with only her knees and feet on show, while she was seated on the toilet. He smiled as Emily's face contorted, her cheeks turning bright red, as on the screen Stones strolled into shot and handed her sheets of toilet tissue, followed by that returning spirit and anger as she heard the Senior Tutor chuckling out loud, a slight look of disgust appearing, her disapproval of the lack of empathy shown on her face. No footage as Emily showered, and Stones fast-forwarded through until Emily re-entered the room and placed herself over the professor's knees, readying herself to receive her punishment after listening once more to his padded-out description of what was to come whilst she lay fully exposed. Stones smirked in anticipation as those moments of sheer absolute horror and disgrace were replayed as he spotted the shower water droplets between her open cheeks and then removed them. Emily did not disappoint, her cheeks aflame and her eyes lowered in shame as his fingers flicked down the crack of her divided buttocks.

"Oh, masterful, Dean, absolutely masterful. But did the young minx leave herself wet on purpose I do wonder, eh, Miss Govan?" said the Senior Tutor, leaning to gently pat Emily's cheeks as she stood between them.

Emily started in surprise and opened her mouth but was unable to form a response before the Stones' booming voice brought her up short.

"You are not required to answer that, Emily. Mouth firmly shut, eyes back to the front please."

Emily meekly complied, her body language once more taking on the appearance of a defeated and deflated opponent. He knew that he had been quite severe in his quest to belittle and conquer her but hoped that it had served to teach her that she had taken on a battle that was never to be won. Interestingly she seemed more connected with the film as the punishment took on the more formal aspects of her actual thrashing: her expression becoming much more engaged and attentive as she watched her own humiliation as the professor spanked and then paddled her. Stones had to admit that he found this young lady quite enigmatic, her face clearly showing shame and horror as she viewed her own disgrace but there was undoubtedly a contrary message from her eyes that betrayed a sense of excitement and perhaps longing. Her beaten cheeks were probably no more than just a little warmed now, the pain of the spanking would undoubtedly be diminishing by the minute. He couldn't resist a smile as Emily's face cringed and her mouth fell open as the film rolled onto the episode when she reacted most unwisely to his words concerning her underwear and he could sense her shrivelling inside as she saw the strap swing through the air before exploding onto her taut cheeks as his hand forced her body down, bending her over to be perfectly placed for the stinging and forceful strike.

"Ooooh, ouch," muttered the Senior Tutor, seemingly in sympathy and again reaching forward to very softly stroke Emily's bottom.

"You are really quite an extraordinarily silly thing, aren't you, my dear? Luckily the Dean has you in hand now, so hopefully you can be sorted out and put on the road to redemption."

That prompted a wry smile from Emily and Stones noted her relaxed stance completely accepting the calming hands of Celia as she continued to lightly massage the girl's red cheeks. Stones decided to bring this session to an end, wanting to ensure that Celia's touches remained supposedly sympathetically maternal rather than moving on to anything more sensual, instances from the past reminding him that she could easily give into temptation!

"You may dress yourself and leave my quarters now, Emily. We look forward to seeing you next week to continue your education. Thank you for attending, now cover yourself up and be off with you," were his dismissive final words that evening, as he flicked her phone towards her.

The relief on Emily's face was replaced by a more puzzled expression at the last words spoken by the Senior Tutor. "Yes, off you go, dear. I look forward to seeing you again shortly."

This was followed by the aside to Stones, "She's currently down to be Porter's first victim then I assume?"

The questioning features of Emily were now highlighted and Stones realised that the student had heard and was perplexed by the remark. Not that he thought it would do her any harm to be left wondering and maybe a little bit tormented by what had been said.

CHAPTER 4

YISHEN TELLS HER STORY

A new week, a new problem, thought the professor as the clearly terrified young Chinese beauty stood blubbering and shaking before him in response to his summoning email. The professor allowed her the moments she needed to recover; he was not affected in any way by female tears, he had seen and heard an awful lot of distressed young women over the years, and, of course, had been the cause of many of those tears.

"When you are ready, young lady, have recovered some decorum and pulled yourself together, we will discuss the matter in hand," he said in a seemingly disinterested manner.

"Y-Y-Yes sir, Professor, sir, sorry s-s-sir," was the stammered response.

She took a deep breath and exhaled slowly. Stones was happy to wait and allow the errant girl time to get used to her presence in his set (or his parlour as he liked to think of it). He had read the report from the porters as well as the student's tutor and was looking forward to what was likely to be quite an opportunity for him to deliver his favourite form of punishment. After a bit of a barren spell when pickings had been slim with just a few minor miscreants to deal with resulting in menial task punishments handed out, this incident, following on from his Friday session with the rather impetuous Emily Govan, was just the sort of episode and opportunity he loved to fall into his lap!

Admittedly the Gardens Department of the college were always quite pleased to see students out on the expansive and well-kept greens, picking litter or pulling weeds, the Kitchens were always happy to welcome pot scrubbers and the Housekeeping Department over the moon to receive candidates sent for toilet cleaning. Nonetheless, to Stones, these minor, annoying crimes warranting trivial but soul-cleansing and chastening activities were hardly an opportunity to enjoy his more favoured form of punishment. They were satisfying punishments in their own way, but Stones knew that far worse crimes were occurring in the college that would earn the reprobates more severe and entirely appropriate, in his mind at least, castigation. His challenge was to bring these abusers of college rules, these ruffians and pests to justice, and to ensure that they faced up to their responsibilities as they properly entered adulthood and prepared for, hopefully, a successful career and future.

Stones fervently and sincerely wished for the students who left his college to be ready to take on the world, to make their parents proud and to enhance the college's reputation for producing world-class leaders, thinkers and movers & shakers. He held in his hands the weekend's reports including the apology he had requested from Georgina Fawcett-Jones, wherein he noted that she had taken the easy option amongst her grovelling words of apology, by stating that she would be prepared to face up to whatever punishment the professor saw fit to impose.

He quickly tapped out an email informing her that she was to report to him just after lunch on Friday and to be prepared to face immediate punishment due to her failure to comply with simple instructions concerning the content of her report, combined with what, as she herself had noted, was 'appalling, drunken and lewd behaviour unbefitting a member of such an illustrious college.'

Stones then warned her that unless she now specifically requested the appropriate punishment he would have to consult with her parents to determine the best course of action, knowing full well that this would add to her terror. *Serves her right,* he thought, as he had been toying with taking things easy with Georgina but her evasive and timewasting tactics were not endearing her to him. He sighed, dismissing the silly girl from his mind and returned to Yishen's document.

The reports cited 19-year-old Yishen Yiam as not only being drunk and disorderly in the famous courtyards of the college, she had also not only thrown up when carried into the Porters' Lodge overnight sick bay but then, to the disgust and anger of all concerned, she had proceeded to wet herself and soak the fold-up camping bed she had been lain upon. Unfortunately for Yishen there wasn't much that earned the wrath of the night porters more than dealing with bodily fluid expulsions of any sort from the students. Three days had passed since the incident on the Friday evening, when from all accounts, Yishen had taken to alcohol for seemingly the first time at a student gathering to celebrate one of her college friend's birthdays. Up until then she had been an exemplary student with stunning 1st year examination results and unbeknown to her, a student that the ruling counsel of the college were counting on to perform strongly and be a worthy addition to the list of high-achieving Chinese ladies. Overseas money via the lucrative Asian market was paying dividends indeed for St. James as it was for many of the country's top universities. Not only from the high fees that they could charge for educating the up-and-coming elite youth of a part of the world most keen to add a prestigious University education to the backgrounds and CVs of their future experts in many fields, but also from the lucrative investment and sponsorship their parents, potential employers and leading institutions were so keen to splash around. Let alone the kudos gained for the college from whichever political party was in power at the time.

The professor knew only too well that at least one or two drunken escapades were the norm for most students and whilst the college would routinely turn a blind eye to situations that usually resolved themselves peacefully and without any real involvement from the watchful eye of the porters, there was a point at which disciplinary action was called into play. At least in a female-only college they were often spared the extreme excesses of some of more easily-led, machismo outbreaks and testosterone-driven antics of some of the male members of the City's colleges. The young ladies also tended to be more self-recriminating and shame-faced when facing up to what they had done after the event. Which suited the professor perfectly as he had discovered to his absolute delight that this made them far more pliant and accepting that they deserved the punishment that he was only too keen to hand out.

"So Ms Yiam, not only disgustingly drunk to the point of vomiting all over college property you also then disgraced yourself by flooding the Porters' Lodge with your urine. What sort of state do you think you were in to be voiding your bladder in the presence of the college porters? Which they then had to clear up, as you were blatantly too inebriated to even known you had performed so disgracefully. Would you like to attempt to explain yourself at all?"

Yishen had turned a bright shade of scarlet as the professor recounted the circumstances of a night that she would so like to just wipe from not only her memory but also those of everyone who now seemed aware of the dreadful occurrence. "S-s-sir, I am so sorry, Professor, sir. I don't know why I did these terrible things, I did not realise that this alcohol would affect me this way. It is a terrible lesson for me sir, I will never ever drink again sir, I am so sorry sir, Professor Stones, sir."

"Oh stop babbling, girl," snapped the professor. "It's not me you need to apologise to, is it? So, firstly you will need to go to the Head Porter and the Senior Night Porter and apologise to them and then you need to personally apologise to any other porters involved. Of course, we then have to punish you severely for your behaviour. What on earth will your father and mother say when we report to them?"

Yishen dropped dramatically to her knees with a look of pure horror on her face.

"Oh sir, I beseech you, please do not report this to my parents. It would break my mother's heart. Please sir, please. I will do anything, accept any punishment if you don't inform my parents."

With his back to her, apparently in deep thought, the professor allowed himself a self-satisfied smirk. This was going exactly in the direction he had hoped.

"Well," he said, "I don't know about that, what punishment could be given to you that would be appropriate and would clearly match the obvious distress that the thought of informing your parents has caused you? Your behaviour has been outrageous as well as truly disgusting, I am very much tempted to ask your father what punishment he thinks would be fitting."

Yishen sobbed loudly. "Oh please sir, please do not ring my father. I will accept any punishment you decide on. I am already so ashamed, I could not bear to anger my father and disappoint my mother through my actions, I beg of you Professor, sir, please, please, please."

The professor fixed the clearly suffering errant student with a steely gaze, making her squirm.

"How exactly do you think you should be punished then, young lady? Albeit I should hesitate to refer to you as a lady when you have urinated publicly in college, if this had happened at home what on earth would your parents have done?" he barked at the shaking student.

Perceptively he had clearly picked the right words as Yishen flinched abruptly and the colour began to drain out of her face. Stones slammed his hand down on the desk beside him.

"I asked you a question, gal, now speak!"

Yishen was startled into speech. "My mother would, my mother would… oh no sir, I could not possibly say." As she stumbled with her words, the professor pushed home his advantage.

"Yes, yes, yes you can and you will, girl. What would your mother do? Come on, child. For goodness sake, spit it out!"

She could clearly see no alternative and out came the words that he had been anticipating and hoping for.

"Oh no, sir. Oh, I don't want to say this. She would spank me, sir, she would spank me most comprehensively." Yishen blurted out the words with a look of sheer horror on her face.

The professor changed tone and encouraged her to go on. "Yes child, she would spank you, at the very least I should hope, for your disgraceful behaviour. But details, girl, details. We may have a solution in view that would not involve the college in officially notifying your parents, and indeed making public your shameful behaviour."

Yishen, of course, grasped at the lifeline that the professor appeared to be kindly offering her. "Oh sir, my mother would thoroughly spank my bottom sir, until her hand stung too much to continue, and sir, I would offer to fetch her a wooden spoon from the kitchen to continue my beating, it would be my duty as a good daughter to save her poor hand, sir. Then, sir, my beating would be continued until she was satisfied that all the naughtiness had been beaten out of me, sir."

Sensing there was more Stones egged her on with a tilt of his head; Yishen breathed in deeply and continued.

"I would be sent to bed then, sir, and would be expected to lie face down on the bed with my bottom on show and the door open, signally my disgrace, to await my father's return from his workplace."

Yishen took another deep breath and, in vain, gave the professor a pleading look.

"Now what exactly would your father do? I hope that you don't imagine a mere spanked bottom is a fitting punishment for what we have suffered from you," he said. "Pray do continue, I hope this tale has an appropriate ending or I can see I will have to make that telephone call after all."

"No sir, no sir, please sir. Let me tell you what would happen sir, because it has happened sir, only once have I misbehaved so badly before, sir, so I truly know what my father would do sir. Where I come from, sir, the mother administers punishment to the daughter and the father punishes the sons. However if the mother feels that the daughter has not been sufficiently punished by her beating, then she will tell her husband that she has beaten the daughter and that it has upset her very much to do so. She will say tell him that because the daughter had been so badly behaved that she has shamed the mother and has made her feel as though she has failed her husband in not bringing up her daughter better." Yishen hesitated.

"Carry on, child," prompted the professor.

"As the mother has deemed to have failed her husband by not raising a better behaved daughter, then the mother would tell her husband that she should be beaten to punish her for her poor skills in raising her daughter. The father would then come upstairs to fetch the family bamboo cane which is kept for the most severe beatings. This cane hangs at the top of the stairs in most houses to remind the family that the father expects a well-behaved household. At this point, sir, it would be expected of the daughter to defend her mother and ask the father for his forgiveness on behalf of both herself and her mother. She would also then ask if she could take the mother's punishment instead as she has brought shame and disgrace to the house, sir." Yishen hesitated again, her face ablaze, a picture of shame and self-pity.

"So at this point the daughter would then be thrashed instead of the mother?" encouraged Stones.

"Yes sir, exactly sir. It would be very shameful and dishonourable for the daughter not to ask to take the punishment. Any daughter would not disrespect her mother by not asking, sir, especially as the whole village would........" Yishen stumbled to a halt, her face flushing an even deeper red.

The child was very unfortunate to have such an expressive face, mused the professor, and he appreciated that she clearly was not used to being in such an unfortunate position as the one she had landed herself in.

"Well? The whole village would what exactly? I should not need to remind you that if I believe that for just one moment you are misleading me or telling me lies any way, then I will revert to my original course of action and contact your father. Is that understood?" Stones raised his voice knowing that the girl was very fearful of his authority and had become completely compliant.

"Oh sir, no sir, sorry sir, please forgive me, sir. I am your servant, sir."

There could be no doubting that Yishen had indeed lost all

resistance or self-respect in the face of the stern demeanour and authoritative voice of the professor. She clearly was in awe of his position and what she saw as his undoubted jurisdiction and command over her future aspirations and ambitions. Yishen's upbringing meant that she had little intransigence or defiance to oppose someone in a prominent position, and in particular an elderly man, in her nature. Yishen gulped and took a deep breath to steady herself and at a sharp nod from Stones rushed to give him the information he requested.

"Sir, when the head of the household has to deliver a thrashing due to dishonour and shame being brought on his family, then every door and window is opened in the house and the curtains are pulled completely back. This announces to anyone close by that a family member is to be given what we call a 'bamboo beating', sir. These are only given when the head of the house has deemed that the offence committed by the sinful member of the family is so bad that the family's long bamboo cane will be used. This will occur one hour before the time that the father has allotted for the thrashing, sir, and this gives the whole village time to be made aware by the neighbours that a serious misdemeanour has occurred and that a thrashing is imminent. The shame and dishonour of the family is considered to be eliminated if the village has been invited to attend to hear the thrashing.

Once the beating is completed the father will display the miscreant's thrashed body at the bedroom window and the gathering will applaud them both to show that the village approves the punishment and forgives the behaviour of the beaten reprobate."

Once again Yishen took a deep breath, causing Stones to admire the spirit she was showing whilst attempting to still the obvious panic and fear building within her.

"Sir, I have to tell you that the beaten, wicked rascal will then have to stand shamefully naked against the wall in the front room of the house, which is then open for any relatives or village elders to come in to inspect and approve the beaten areas at close quarters, sir. At bedtime the punishment is considered over and it is not polite for it ever to be mentioned again, apart from by the father. That is everything that happens, sir, I promise you."

The professor stared at the totally embarrassed and stricken young lady.

"So, my gal, I think that I understand from this, is that what you are saying is that at home you would be most severely beaten for the disgraceful actions that you have made this proud and illustrious college a party to. I would like you to put your hands on your head and go and stand in the corner of the room and consider exactly what action you think I need to take to ensure that you receive the appropriate punishment for what you have done; especially for the distress, shame and clear dishonour your poor parents would feel if they were to be informed of this. Go on, gal, move yourself."

The professor pulled her by an earlobe to guide her to the corner and then gave her backside a quick swat with his flat hand to set the tone for her contemplation. The professor mentally rubbed his hands together at the thought of what was to follow. He very much doubted that he would get anything but compliance and acquiescence from the cowed and traumatised student who was gently sobbing in the corner. He decided to leave her there to stew for a few minutes as he checked the girl's study roster, comparing it to his own diary and the shared calendar that he and Jamie Adams used to keep each other up to date with their availability for the "little arrangement" as he always referred to it.

Minutes later a date and time had been agreed between Stones and

Jamie. Still sitting at his desk, Stones snapped the trembling girl back into the present.

"Right, young lady. Come here and stand in front of me. Hands on your head until I say different. Firstly you will go straight back to your room and write me a one thousand word essay describing what you have done wrong, why you need to be punished severely, what you think a suitable punishment would be and why you think that this punishment should be carried out within the college. You will deliver that through my letterbox by eight tomorrow morning before you toddle off to your lecture, which I can see is an hour later. At 11am on Saturday morning you will return here ready for your punishment and dressed appropriately, assuming that I am happy with your essay, that is. If, of course, I am not happy with your scribblings, then obviously things will have to go from my control and will be passed over to your parents to deal with."

Yishen started to babble. "Oh sir, I will surely please you with my report, sir, you will surely need to punish me yourself, sir, please we do not need to inform my parents. Sir, it would be an honour to be punished by you, Professor, sir."

The professor looked sternly at the young Chinese girl still shaking before him with pleading eyes, but inside he was so enjoying her discomfort and subservient manner.

"You most certainly will be punished, young lady, and certainly under my instruction, now shoo!" said the professor, dismissing the student, and she gratefully scuttled from his room.

The nuance of his carefully chosen parting words appeared to cause her slight confusion, as he had intended. He felt satisfied that he had left her mind awhirl with the likely dreadful repercussions to come for her evening of madness.

CHAPTER 5

JULIE WANTS TO BE DEALT WITH

QUICKLY

The letter from Yishen Yiam came through the professor's letterbox at a few minutes before eight o'clock the following morning and gave Stones a boost for the day as he relished the words of sorrow and repentance. She had spared herself nothing, admitting to her appalling behaviour, regretting the trouble and inconvenience she had caused, apologising for severely letting herself and her family down and begging Stones' forgiveness for any distress "her woeful tale" had inflicted upon himself and the college. He could only wish that all of his miscreants could accept responsibility and their forthcoming fate in the manner that Yishen had been doing so far. He did wonder whether this apparent stoicism would be continued when it actually came down to baring her bottom for the considerable thrashing that she had, for time being at least, rather willingly put herself up for.

The professor somehow doubted that such exemplary conduct in her acceptance of the misery that she had to come would be continued once her punishment got under way; but for now at least she was being granted pride of place in his mind as an example of how to accept your shortcomings and put your hands up for the ordeal to come. He had seen copies of her written apologies to the appropriate staff in the college and had been impressed to find out that she had faced the porters who had dealt with her on the fateful night and verbally apologised as well as putting a heartfelt apology in writing. Stones contemplated what was to come later that week, and mentally rubbed his hands in gleeful anticipation. With Georgina Fawcett-Jones set to visit on Friday afternoon followed by Emily Govan to deal with later on that evening, both he and Jamie were, he was sure, likely to have an enjoyable and entertaining Saturday morning with Yishen to follow. *Roll on the weekend,* he thought. He wandered across to his "improvers" cupboard and pausing to consider the implements hanging there, touching an occasional item. "You, my three beauties, and you I think," he spoke out loud as he stroked his leather paddle, a wooden long-handled spoon, one of the more formidable-looking canes and the black, thick leather strap.

Meanwhile he had some more disciplinary notice reports to look into…

The first one looked straightforward enough:

NATURE OF INCIDENT: Noise complaint

DETAILS OF INCIDENT: At 01.15am Miss Claire Pritchard, third year student approaching examinations, of Courtyard 3 Block A Room 6 telephoned the lodge in a distressed state to say that her neighbour was keeping her awake with a gathering of raucous people in a drunken state.

Ben and I attended and spoke to Miss Pritchard who was very upset and insisted that her neighbour was making her life a misery with her continuous noise. Refused to keep things down or agree any kind of time limit imposed on noise levels and continually said unpleasant things to her to wind her up and upset her.

ACTION TAKEN: We went and spoke to Miss Vanessa Bertrand, second year student, of Room 7 adjacent to Miss Pritchard who indeed had a few guests in her living room that were making a fair amount of noise.

After explaining the situation and the complaints made by Miss Pritchard, Miss Bertrand referred to her neighbour "the stuck-up geeky bitch" and retorted that she was making her life at college difficult and not as enjoyable as it should be due to her constant sniping, complaining and banging on the wall. She then broke down sobbing for a few minutes. After these tears, Miss Bertrand calmed down. By this point all the guests had made their exit apart from one young lady, a Miss Julie Rolfe, second year student, most guests had left once they realised what was going on with porters attending. Miss Rolfe was quite rude to the porters, making offensive remarks and not helping the situation. Eventually Miss Rolfe required escorting back to her own room, Courtyard 4 Block B Room 2, and continued the abuse until deposited safely in her own room.

REQUIREMENT OF ANY FURTHER ACTION:

HEAD PORTER'S COMMENTS: The Head Porter and Senior Tutor confirm that there have been previous complaints and some history between the students' neighbours which has involved porters and both tutors. It is a cause for concern as both students are getting very distressed over these incidents. A previous minor incident had caused them both to have been sent to the Dean of Discipline and led to cleaning duties in the kitchen being set as a punishment. This can be taken to have failed as a deterrent and further action is now requested.

The College Pastoral Care Tutor has spoken to Claire Pritchard and Vanessa Bertrand together and found that their animosity and intolerance towards each other very concerning which led to her being required to actually hold them apart as the atmosphere had turned disturbingly hostile and both had resorted to threats of physical violence. After discussions with the Head Porter, and a precise briefing with the Mistress, the Senior Tutor passes on the issue to the Dean of Discipline as both feel that they have exhausted their remits in dealing with the two of them, and that this has well passed the bickering stage.

The Dean of Discipline is thereby requested to talk seriously to the two *students as to their future within the college and is requested to impose and carry out just punishments.*

The third party, Julie Rolfe, has been spoken to by the Head Porter, the Senior Tutor and the Pastoral Care Tutor and has apologised for her behaviour to all concerned. The recommendation is however that she deserves a punishment on file and the request is made that the Dean of Discipline submits her to a formal disciplinary interview to agree a punishment that would be mutually beneficial to the college and Miss Rolfe, to improve her behaviour, point out the error of her ways and to warn her of the repercussions of any further poor discipline.

Stones quickly sent off an email to Julie Rolfe, thinking to get the less complicated issue out of the way before he attempted to unravel, resolve and correct the major problem between the main two warring students. Pondering for a while Stones decided that he would speak to Claire, the supposed victim of the conflict first and then invite Vanessa to join them. He suspected that this relationship would need a firm hand to settle, but he had handled far worse and always enjoyed the challenge of these sorts of conflicts. In his position he knew where the real power lay and by the time he had finished with these two, he was fairly confident that they might grasp that too. Composing invitations to attend a disciplinary hearing notice was a pleasure as he well knew the apprehension that the formal wording usually created when they pinged to announce their receipt in the students' inboxes.

What Stones wasn't expecting though was an instant reply from Julie Rolfe asking if she could report for her disciplinary meeting without delay and requesting that consideration would be given to her undertaking any punishment with immediate effect. Having a spare hour or so, Stones decided to grant her request and ordered her to attend in one hour's time, appropriately prepared and dressed with a one-page essay confessing to her misdemeanours and suggesting a punishment most apt. *This should be interesting,* he mused. Within the hour the buzzer went signalling the girl's arrival. Stones studied her on screen and duly noted that she looked quite confident and self-assured under the circumstances. Something he felt confident that would be subject to alteration over the next hour. He allowed her to enter and signalled to the pretty young student to stand before him. He held his hand out for the folded up sheet of paper she was holding.

"Let's see what you have to say, my dear," adding, "if that is a mobile phone you need to put it on my desk now, students are not allowed to bring their devices in here."

Some of the student's confidence immediately dissolved. "Oh sir, sorry sir, of course sir." Julie handed her mobile over cursing herself quietly, obviously angry for making this stupid mistake and putting herself on the back foot straight away. For the first time since she had emailed him, Stones suspected that doubt was entering her mind concerning her decision as to whether or not this had been such a great plan! Stones was satisfied that the sudden realisation that she had been totally fooling herself into believing that she was going to control this situation had now hit home.

"So to cut a long story short," Stones began as he finished her written offering. "You behaved like a nasty little bully, you were drunk, abusive and failed to cooperate with the porters who came to deal with the rather childish and quite ridiculous situation that you unwisely got yourself involved in the other evening. You wish to now reiterate your apology to the porters who dealt with you and the Pastoral Care Tutor and you have formally requested that you be allowed to undertake immediate disciplinary action in the form of a spanking and any other corporal punishment that is considered necessary to draw a line under this episode. Is this correct?"

Julie smiled and seemed to have recovered her poise.

"Indeed sir, I am asking to submit to whatever punishment is deemed fit, sir. I am totally aware of my breach and accept that my behaviour was appalling and that the pain and humiliation involved in a thrashing is the least I deserve, sir. I fully appreciate that you are willing to allow me the favour of taking my just desserts immediately rather than go through any protracted period deciding my fate and having to wait to be punished. I am ready to be punished, accept that a bare bottom thrashing is appropriate considering my behaviour and am happy for that to commence, sir."

The professor fixed her with a piercing stare. "Your sister was Gina, if I remember?"

"Ah, yes sir, you remember her then sir?"

"Certainly do, I enjoyed her company, did she tell you?"

"Er, yes sir, she did tell me about her time in this room with you, sir."

"Expand, girl, what exactly did she tell you?"

"Sir, it was Gina who told me that the waiting was the worst bit. She told me that you spanked her, sir, and that it seemed to last forever. She told me about the pony training ritual you made her go through to learn obedience, sir. You put her in reins, sir, and made her trot round the room on the end of a rope while you smacked her bottom with a bat, sir."

"Hmmmm seems like she did, indeed. It was a paddle actually, but granted it is in the shape of a small cricket bat. So, Julie, is that what you want then? To experience what Gina went through?" The professor's tone grew sharper and he watched the girl struggle internally, but she was resolute.

"Yes sir, I probably deserve worse, sir. Gina was always the well behaved one, I was always the one who got into trouble."

"Not playing a game here are we, Julie? It's not a contest, it's a chastisement. I am considering postponing and reviewing your situation in lieu of this, I think you need to realise that I am the person who decides who gets punished, when they get punished and how they get punished. Is that clear, young lady?" he barked at the now slightly less composed student before him.

"Y-y-yes sir, sorry sir, please sir, I didn't mean to annoy you, sir," she rather spluttered.

"Right, get your clothes off and stand in the corner over there." Stones opted for a harsher tone as he decided that the time had come to disabuse the student of the idea that she had any kind of control of their meeting.

"Oh, um, all of my clothes sir?"

"It doesn't require an exchange of views or further questioning. It was a clear instruction."

"Yes sir, sorry sir." She quickly removed the simple dress and underwear she had on and moved naked to the corner as instructed; instinct told her to place her hands on top of her head. She stood straight, feeling his eyes on her backside and she tensed the cheeks in anticipation of what was to come.

"In time, my dear, in time." His words were as unsettling as he had intended. He could tell that Julie was now disconcerted and had lost her earlier confidence so never being a man who had failed to take an advantage of a situation, he decided to take things up a notch.

"Turn around for me for a moment please." The polite words did nothing to disguise the sense of total control that he had now imposed.

Julie turned slowly, keeping her hands clenched together on her head, and there was no surprise showing when she heard his next words as Stones was clearly staring directly at her pubic area as she turned to face him full frontal.

"Well, well. Is that a French Wax, my dear?" said the professor, coming to squat down at her midriff.

"Yes sir, it's called a Landing Strip, sir." Julie still managed to maintain the voice control of someone confident in herself and Stones was impressed with her seeming lack of self-consciousness with his face now inches from her vagina. Once naked most of the more resilient students were unable to keep up any pretence of nonchalance when he began his practised process of gradually dismantling their composure and self-assurance with his blunt and rather personal remarks about their nakedness and body make-up. Although the young lady's continual swallowing and pink blushing cheeks were evidence of her vulnerability and fear, he did feel that she was reasonably relaxed considering the circumstances. He decided to give her time to let her mind run loose and unhinge her a few degrees more.

"Very pretty," he said, gently spinning her back round to face the corner and returning to his seat.

A few minutes later Julie was horrified to hear a buzzer go and the professor clearly allow entry to someone.

"Stay exactly where you are and do not move, look round or speak. Do you understand?" Stones snapped.

"Yes sir, but sir…"

"Quiet," he warned ominously as gentle steps heralded the arrival of a female guest to both of them and Stones saw Julie's shoulders relax somewhat, presumably, relieved that the visitor was to be a woman.

"Good afternoon, Professor," said the new arrival. Stones saw the tension immediately return to the student's upper body as she undoubtedly recognised the voice of the Pastoral Care Tutor, Sonya

Coombs. Sonya's integration into the college's traditions and processes hadn't been totally smooth so far, her connection with other staff with their entrenched views concerning St. James' values having been somewhat lacking. On the grapevine, something that the professor paid constant heed to, the word was that a number of the students were taking advantage of her apparent discomfort with the strict disciplinarian policies. However, it often took a while for new colleagues to bed into their set ways and Stones was prepared to give her time and the benefit of any doubt for the time being. He'd chosen now as a good a time as any to see for himself the way she would react to being thoroughly involved in a punishment scenario.

"Reporting for duty, Professor Stones. My honour to be here to witness a scoundrel get her just dessert!"

A good start, thought the professor, although he only nodded perfunctorily in greeting.

"Yes well it's time you were included in a more participatory role rather than just as an audience member for these unavoidable little sessions. Only your third time in attendance I do believe. I presume you remember the protocol?"

"Oh yes, Professor, no worries on that score I can assure you," was the confidently spoken response.

Stones was referring to the basic code of conduct of the chosen few in the college who had been given rights to view, and in some cases participate quite actively in, formal and documented discipline and punishment sessions. Sonya would be well aware that, as a junior member of the selected union, she was there to carry out any wishes of the Dean of Discipline rather than to act in any way of her own accord. He had ensured that she had been well tutored in what occurred in the room albeit the only chastisements she had witnessed had been simple cases, quick bare-bottomed spankings and a tongue-lashing, rather than any higher level of more severe corporal punishment. She had witnessed the professor's methods, his use of barbed threats, psychological mind games, humiliation and shaming techniques including the rather physical manhandling and sexual exposure route that this often took. As perceptive as always, Stones had been well aware that she was not entirely comfortable, possibly from a feminist viewpoint, but had previously spent time explaining to her that every student that had suffered a thrashing in college, damn well deserved it and that the alternatives and options open to the miscreants were less palatable. Sonya would have been so conscious that her position in the prestigious college would only be tenable if she gave her total support to the rules and regulations that she had gladly signed up to, but Stones suspected that she would be far more comfortable if she could turn a blind eye to this part of college life. As Dean of Discipline he felt that it was high time he started to test her resolve. The college allowed no dissenters or non-believers amongst their ranks and part of Stones' job was to ensure that any weak links were discarded early on in their time on the payroll. The positions at St. James' were much in demand and extremely well-paid, there was no need to carry passengers and Stones relished the task in applying the pressure.

"Let's get started then, Julie, come to me, over my knees now, girl. Let's see if I can get home our message about disreputable behaviour in college."

Julie immediately moved to comply and settled herself over his lap. He noted that the flicker of excitement he had seen in her eyes when discussing this earlier had long disappeared as the reality of the situation she found herself in was likely not matching the fantasy. Her buttock cheeks tightly clenched, awaiting and anticipating the feel of his hand slapping down on her bare skin.

She flinched rather dramatically as she felt Stones' hand just rest across her cheeks.

"First you can spread your legs wide apart and let's have a good look at the target area before we begin and second, you might like to note that we will start with unclenched buttocks please."

Julie audibly gulped but after just a second's pause she duly obliged. Stones always enjoyed the moment when he felt his victim accepting that any sense of control whatsoever had finally slipped away. The professor's next actions and words would now set the tone for the rest of the session. He placed both hands on her bottom cheeks and eased them much further apart than they already were, before he delivered his verbal coup de grace.

"Oh look, we have a shaved crack, Miss Coombs, to go with the nicely trimmed pubic hair. It's a long time since I've seen such a bald anus, although you have missed two stray hairs, my dear."

He motioned to Sonya. "Hold these cheeks apart for me for a moment and I'll do Julie here a favour and pull out those two little strays from right by her anus."

The mewing coming from the student's mouth was music to Stones' ears. Julie's head lowered dejectedly even closer to the floor, her total submission plain to see. Her buttocks were being held spread apart by a female tutor whilst an elderly male professor was attempting to pluck hairs from her anus. Stones hoped that she had never felt more humiliated, humbled and mortified in her life. Unfortunately for her, he was just warming up!

"Got it! That's one, just stay still my dear and stop opening and closing your anus for a moment. There, got the other little blighter. Thanks Miss Coombs, you may return to your seat now. Hmmmm I have to say young lady, you do have a very nicely perfumed bottom crack and anus. I presume that you had a jolly good wash and shave before you came across? Your crack is definitely lovely and smooth."

As he spoke he ran a forefinger right down between her bottom cheeks. "That was a question, you may answer, child."

"Ooooh my! Yes sir, I shaved my bottom in the shower when you granted me the request to meet," she answered meekly, her voice subdued and shaky.

"Yes I suppose then it was quite easy and convenient to slip a soapy finger up your back passage, eh?"

A swallow and a long sigh followed before Julie quietly responded.

"Er, no sir, not exactly, I, um, use a long-handled lady razor to shave myself and... Oh my god, why I am telling you this? Oh God! Right, I am just going to say it. Sir, I soap up the handle and slide it up my bum, sir, and then, just well, you know, sort of flush myself after, using the shower nozzle, sir."

"Interesting," said the professor, "and how do you see to shave yourself in such an intimate area?"

"I, um, oh God, I have a suction-headed mirror, sir, that fixes onto the shower wall. So I sort of spread my cheeks with one hand, sir, squat a bit, look over my shoulder and shave with the other hand." It was obvious that Julie could hardly believe that this conversation was happening and undoubtedly was grateful that her face was hidden from view just inches from the professor's patterned carpet. Stones was actually quite impressed that she was holding herself together under this most intimate of questioning; he relished breaking the spirit of his delinquent culprits and was convinced some of them would prefer to take harsher physical punishment than face the intimate probing that he had become so practised at.

"Well I very much approve of your ablution regime, Julie, very successful and admirable too. Now let's see if you can take a bare-bottomed hand spanking like you obviously think you can."

With that and without Julie having a second to prepare herself, Stones' large flat hand landed with a resounding slap across the centre of the rounded buttocks facing him.

"Yaaaaar!" was the response before the hand flashed down again, which was repeated rapidly as the professor initially opted for a fully-fledged fast attack.

Julie's cheeks quickly turned pink under the onslaught, which continued for thirty slaps before he took a breather. Julie's cries had turned into sharp yips of shock and pain in reaction as each strike had landed with tears flowing freely down her face and her body wriggling and squirming under Stones' muscular arm.

"Not quite so composed now, eh girl?" Stones chided her. "It's amazing how a glowing bottom soon knocks the cockiness out of these youngsters. Sonya? Come and keep an eye on the crying end for me. I think Julie may be starting to feel a little bit sorry for herself now," Stones said, indicating for Sonya to come and sit at Julie's head.

"Take her face in your hands please Sonya, I doubt she'll appreciate someone watching the way her face will be distorting and showing her discomfort but she's not here to enjoy herself. Always good for our young scallywags to know that someone has watched them in their moments of private distress," chuckled the professor as he turned the screw on Julie's sense of shame and humiliation.

"Actually I am fine, thank you sir," responded Julie, showing spirit that was perhaps admirable but more certainly unwise as the next occurrence was the swinging hand of Stones resuming its onslaught on her tender behind.

Seventy further slaps of equal force and no recuperating break followed and by halfway through Julie had been reduced to blubbering and howling like the thrashed child she was. All fight gone now, just a tossing and turning wreck looking for the nonexistent escape route from the torrent of blows. As the professor completed this stage of her punishment with a final wallop, he laid his sore hand on her blazing cheeks.

"Any sign left of that smart alec with the lip?" he queried with Sonya. "What's happened to the cocky young imp? Describe her demeanour now for me please."

"As expected I think you'll find, Professor Stones," she answered with a small smirk of satisfaction. "We have a pitifully sobbing naughty young girl, with a dribbling mouth and a rather disgusting runny nose!"

Sonya couldn't have sounded more triumphant if she had delivered the cause of the girl's misery herself. She had recognised Julie as one of the many students in the college that seemed to treat her rather disdainfully and was really enjoying watching the girl's misery and pain etched in her flushed face. Julie, meanwhile, couldn't have hated the Pastoral Care Tutor any more than she did at that moment.

"Here's the tissues, clean yourself up a bit and try and gain some sense of dignity back. Rather pathetic now, aren't you girl?" snapped Stones.

"Yes sir, sorry. It hurt far more than I expected, sir but..." Julie hesitated, realising that it might be imprudent and possibly impertinent to say too much more.

"No Julie, please continue. I am always interested in a recipient's viewpoint and it's good to get feedback. You can speak freely and honestly without fear of repercussions now," prompted the professor.

"Well, as I think you suspected, sir, I was quite looking forward to being spanked, a sort of new adventure so to speak. But sir, it hurts like hell when it's happening, sir, so much more painful than I'd thought. However now it's over, sir I, um, quite, um, like the feeling now, sir. So the anticipation, you know the thought of having to get naked and bend over your lap, sir, was actually really exciting and the after feeling is quite, sort of, um, sensual, sir. The trouble is that the spanking itself was far longer than I thought and the stinging was quite awful, sir. Is it OK to say that, sir?" Julie tailed off looking quite apprehensive particularly as Miss Coombs was looking haughtily down her nose at her.

"That's absolutely fine, Julie, thank you for your honesty. Now let's have a good look at my handiwork. Turn around and bend over, legs wide apart and point that rather sweet-smelling lovely little anus at me now."

Just as Julie was regaining some composure he again threw a curve ball at her and with a face colouring to match her backside, she did as she asked, fully displaying herself.

"Yes, pretty good distribution, if I do say so myself. Nice deep red all over, lovely white crack dividing the orbs of crimson and oh, what have we here Miss Coombs?" Sonya looked at the girl's sexual folds and saw immediately what had caught the professor's eye.

"Looks like the disgusting slut is thinking improper thoughts, Professor, she's clearly sexually excited and in need of a cold shower. I am not sure that this punishment is achieving what it's intended to!"

Sonya couldn't help but allow her dislike of the student to show and the professor was fully aware that she would like to see Julie suffer far more.

"Fair point, well made, Miss Coombs. Right Julie, a sopping wet aroused vagina is not what's aimed at so we really do need to put paid to whatever disgusting sexual fantasies you have been having otherwise it's not that much of a punishment, is it? Right, let's see if you find being harnessed and beaten as much fun as your sister did."

Throwing the equipment at Sonya, he continued, "Strap her up, Miss Coombs, and we will put her through a training session. I'll get the paddle to encourage her with and you can get her walking in a circle at the end of the reins to start with."

Clearly enjoying the opportunity to humble and demean Julie more, Sonya strapped the girl into the reins, rattled them and ordered, "Walk on, walk on."

With which Stones slammed the paddle across her cheeks to good effect.

"Naaaaaaaoooooowwww," screamed Julie, faltering badly and turning in an attempt to remove her bottom from the line of fire.

Sonya quickly yanked the reins forcing Julie to keep the line of her designated circle. The professor gave the exposed cheeks two quick hard slaps, causing desperate howling and stumbling from Julie and a wide grin from Sonya.

"Trot now, you little tart, knees up, straight back, arms in front of you in trotting fashion. Let's hear you 'neigh' as well. Come on, come on." Sonya's relish was absolute.

The professor obliged with encouraging strikes across her flanks. Stumbling as she tried to retain the speed of the trot, the severe sting of the paddle caused Julie to trip over her own feet attempting to avoid further blows and she sank to her knees. Sonya now totally lost in her role dragged the girl to her feet.

"Canter, bitch, canter. Hit her, Professor, hit her good and hard!" Sonya seemed unaware that she had rather lost control but it certainly wasn't escaping the professor's attention.

Julie tried valiantly to increase her pace around the circle as Sonya manipulated the harness and reins to control her; the professor now waited on the outside of her circle cracking her writhing buttocks each time she passed producing a shriek of pain as the paddle slapped hard against her extremely sore bottom, her faster pace now allowing her next to no recovery time at all. Finally it became too much and she keeled over and lay prone on the carpet despite Sonya's attempts to drag her to her feet.

"Get up you slovenly bitch, take what you have coming to you."

"That will suffice," boomed the professor, asserting his control. "Stand down, Miss Coombs, stand down."

Sonya tugged hard on the reins, causing Julie to clamber painfully to her feet.

Julie turned angrily on her. "You fucking bitch, no wonder students call you the Past-Caring Tutor, by the time you get round to finding anything out, everyone is past fucking caring, you useless evil fucking cow!"

The slap that landed on Julie's right cheek spun her head completely round as it resounded throughout the room and Julie crashed into a chair in an effort to stay on her feet. Her hand went to her face, her ears ringing and tears once more poured from her eyes. There were several seconds of silence before the Pastoral Care Tutor took a deep breath and turned to the professor and spoke in a halting whisper.

"I am so sorry, I don't know what came over me, Professor. Julie I, er, I…"

Stones moved her away, saying, "You may leave now but I will email you shortly as we need will discuss this further."

Sonya grimaced and, continuing to apologise, hurriedly left the professor's quarters as Julie struggled to her feet and looked imploringly at the professor, seemingly oblivious to the severity of what had just happened.

"Oh my god, I am so sorry, sir. Shit, sir, I'm really sorry, she just pushed my buttons. Oh God, I lost it didn't I? I am soooo sorry. Oh shit, what's going to happen to me, sir?"

"To start with, young lady, and I hesitate with the word 'lady', I strongly suggest that you please shut your mouth now. You may well have a lovely clean and pretty little anus, Julie, but it rather contrasts with your foul potty mouth that needs a bar of soap rubbed firmly into it. The point of a good hiding is to right wrongs and improve your outlook and behaviour. Well, it seems to have failed with you. Firstly we have seen your desires awakened with your sexual lust bring displayed so blatantly with your love juices virtually dribbling down your legs, then we have this appalling offensive rant using disgusting language. This has resulted in the Pastoral Care Tutor being pushed to her limits to such a point that she has been reduced to losing control and striking you."

He paused; the situation was tricky and bearing in mind everything was being recorded, Stones was picking his words and actions carefully and accordingly. However the blessing was that Julie was far more concerned over what she perceived as her violations and the additional trouble she could now be in.

"Sir, I am really sorry. God, if she makes a complaint, sir, will I be expelled, sir. Oh sir, oh God I am such an idiot, sir. Can I go and see her and apologise, sir? Please sir, will I be expelled?"

Stones fixed her with his most fierce gaze.

"Julie, listen to me. We don't expel, we send down. 'Sent down in disgrace' is the actual terminology." Julie started to tremble and Stones made a decision. "Pull yourself together, child, you can choose to volunteer for a severe flogging, and I mean severe, young lady, we're not talking about a few pats on this backside." He gave her bottom a couple of hard slaps, bringing her alert. "No, now I am afraid that you require a proper, damn good thrashing. It will be very painful, very brutal with a lash, a cane and a strap. This will require you to be tied and buckled down to be able to withstand it. It will be long-lasting on the day, long-lasting in recovery and a long-lasting memory. I can assure you, girl, that if you opt for this route it will not be the easy option."

Julie's eyes were lighting up with relief and respite, she saw salvation like a beaming light and she was certainly going to walk towards it.

"Sir, please sir, yes sir, can I volunteer to be flogged, sir? I am so sorry, sir."

The professor nodded solemnly. "You will return shortly to your room and you will write the required words similar to before. What you have done wrong, a full apology to Miss Coombs and myself and a description of how you feel you should be punished. I will ask Miss Coombs to write independently to you to apologise for striking you, that should not have happened and she will face repercussions for that. I assume you are happy for us to deal with that internally?"

Julie was clearly only too keen to go along with anything suggested by the professor. "Oh of course, Professor. I don't want her to get into any trouble, it was all my own fault."

"Full marks for that, Julie. I do believe we can make something of you, you do have certain charming attributes and appear to have generally good standards and an acceptance of wrongdoing. A thorough flogging might end up being the best thing to ever happen to you."

If the girl had any idea how she was being skilfully manipulated by him she showed no appreciation of the fact, and Stones felt that a bit of a crisis had been nicely averted.

"I think we do need to just finish off your paddling and then you can pop off."

Julie's face dropped but then the twinkle returned to her eyes.

"Yes sir, of course, sir. Shall I take the harness off, sir?"

"Yes please, and then bend over my special desk here, bottom up high, legs apart. Think of that fascinating and cute little bald anus as the bullseye and point it at my face please." Julie jumped to obey and took position as instructed, settling herself over the mound that raised and parted her cheeks.

"We won't have the cuffs on for this as long as you can stay in the correct pose."

"Yes sir, thank you sir."

The professor slammed the paddle down hard on her right cheek, causing a long intake of breath and a low moan, followed by a stifled yelp as the left cheek received the second stroke. Pausing, the professor watched in wonderment, and a touch of admiration, as he could see that she was pushing herself against the rubber mound between her legs. He slammed the paddle across the tender stretched skin at the very top of her buttocks where there was no protection from any layer of fat to provide padding. Julie screeched and writhed but remained totally in position and within seconds resumed her gentle squirming. Stones took a closer look and could see that she was coating the leather-covered mound with secretions from her vagina and was clearly very aroused.

"To help you concentrate and make sure you fully understand that this is a punishment, I will not start counting the final three strokes until you have had the orgasm that you are striving for. So the sooner you climax the sooner the punishment will be over, until then, these are all extra strokes."

With that the professor started to paddle her cheeks without pausing to allow any recovery time between blows. A frantic Julie started grinding furiously against the desk in a desperate attempt to bring herself to orgasm as quickly as possible, but the constant barrage made it hard to concentrate on the pleasure aspect especially as she was now reduced to crying out with one seemingly never ending scream. Feeling no need to be surreptitious or discreet, Julie slid a hand down between her legs and frantically began to openly masturbate her clitoris. The professor had slapped the paddle against her ruby red buttocks a good thirty times before the screams of anguish turned into a grunting roar of orgasm as the girl's body went into a prolonged spasm before she collapsed limp onto the desk, sated albeit with a blazing bottom.

"Please lick your fingers clean, dear, and then kindly resume the position." Julie struggled with the effort to present herself correctly, apparently exhausted from her experience, but obediently arranged herself into position after quickly sucking the slickness from her fingers.

"You might find these last three a little bit more effective as chastisement now your mind is a bit more focused. Trust me, young lady, now you've had your little distraction sorted and your mind clear, you will now just have the pain and discomfort to deal with. "

CRACK, the first blow sounded across the centre of her buttocks.

"Yaaaaaaaaar," screamed Julie as suddenly she understood the reality of the professor's words. CRACK, the second blow struck the fleshy lower buttocks.

"Naaaaaaaaaaa," the response from Julie.

Stones paused, he knew exactly where he next was aiming for, taking a moment to look over the bright red and mottled dark blood-red patches of her thoroughly beaten and somewhat battered bottom, the hairless arsehole twitching madly between her splayed cheeks. He waited until she settled down and then slammed the paddle down with all of his might to strike her one last time across the top of her cheeks.

THWACK. There was a moment's silence as the echo of the blow died and then Julie screamed in shocked anguish before sliding back and collapsing at his feet grasping her bottom.

"Oh, oh, yaaar! Fuck, fuck, fuck."

Stones sighed in exasperation, leaned down, grabbing a handful of Julie's hair and threw her back across the desk. He slapped her bottom hard three times with his flat hand, and then as she tried to protect her sensitive throbbing cheeks, he went lower and stung the backs of her legs.

"Enough with the foul language, young lady. You will learn," he berated her. "A proper apology and a thank you is what is required at the end of your chastisement, not foul language."

"Sorry sir, I am so sorry sir, I apologise truly sir, and thank you sir. Thank you so much for my beating, sir." Julie babbled desperately.

"Well pull yourself together please. You'll find cleaning equipment under my sink in the bathroom. You can ensure that my desk is cleansed of any sign or scent of your masturbatory activity and then you'd better shower. Then you can write me a short piece apologising for your misdemeanours and thanking me for taking it upon myself to apply corrective treatment. If you are quick and everything is to my satisfaction, I may have time to rub some rather luxurious, cold soothing cream into your sore bottom before you leave."

Her tasks completed a few minutes later, Julie now felt like she was in heaven, as sprawled across the professor's lap on his sofa, she was in a blissful state as he gently and sensually rubbed the cooling cream expertly into her cheeks. As he fingers slid into the hair-free divide of her cheeks she automatically opened her legs and pushed her bottom up towards him, allowing his creamed fingers to slide over her arsehole and down towards the lips of her sex. She sighed audibly and attempted to raise her body to allow his fingers to travel further down, her sore bottom undoubtedly adding to her aroused state.

"That is quite enough of that, young lady, I think you've been allowed one sexual episode too far as it is," scolded the professor, deftly moving his hand away from the danger zone and easily flicking Julie up beside him on the sofa. It was the professor's rule to avoid blatant sexual contact with the students so as to keep an objective viewpoint as far as chastising them went and also to avoid leaving himself open to any charges of abuse.

"Yes sir, sorry sir. Oh dear, that was a bit shameful, wasn't it?" Julie responded in her openly refreshing manner that, in truth, Stones found very endearing.

"Well now, I am sure you have someone more appropriate who can help you out later," the professor teased.

"Oh I don't have a regular boyfriend, sir, just a good friend who sort of acts as an occasional lover, sir. Trying to avoid getting emotionally tied down while at University, sir."

"Fair enough, however I am not here to encourage your sexual promiscuity so you do need to show some self-restraint. I am well aware that we may have inadvertently let free a sexual need in you that will possibly lead you into having a sexually adventurous and interesting private life and I wish you luck with that, it's nothing to be ashamed of, we all have our foibles, but tread carefully, Julie. Choose your partners with care and don't give your body and your trust too easily. Right, lecture over, bottom nicely creamed and relatively recovered, a flogging for us both to look forward to soon, but in the meantime you need to get dressed and leave me."

He rather lovingly patted her bottom one last time and directed her to her pile of clothes, returning her mobile.

"I'll be in touch regarding your return to these rooms once you have written to me as requested. I would suggest that we look at about a fortnight's time early on the Friday evening. Let's hope that a thorough flogging will sort you out, you certainly seem destined to suffer." These were the professor's parting words as Julie left after her extraordinary afternoon.

Well, well, that was interesting, pondered the professor, however he knew he couldn't put off what needed to happen. Taking a deep sigh, he reached for his phone.

"Afternoon, Mistress, we need to have a chat about a little problem. Sonya Coombs."

After a long and detailed conversation with Professor Winslow-Bellingham, the Mistress, Stones pondered over their decision concerning the Pastoral Care Tutor's future. The Mistress had watched the relevant short clip from Stones' recording of the slapping incident and was clearly angered at the loss of control by one of her trusted staff. Sonya had had little expectation that she would receive much in the way of mercy for what was a straightforward assault on a student and even in this unusual college with its specialist and old-fashioned approach to disciplinary issues, there was little sympathy towards anyone crossing that particular line. It had been no surprise therefore that she had tendered her resignation in writing immediately in the hope that she could leave quietly and discreetly with no mention of the incident and with no stain on her character or recorded disciplinary action. Stones wondered whether or not she would be amenable to the obvious alternative and had contacted Sonya to request that she attended his study to discuss her resignation. As Senior Tutor, and her immediate superior, Celia's opinion had been sought and although Sonya had transgressed badly and indeed had found her role very challenging since joining the college, hence the difficulties experienced with Julie, the feeling was that she would progress into a valuable member of staff. Moreover the college prided itself on employing top-quality individuals and retaining staff long-term, certainly once they had embraced the college's peculiarities and points of difference, therefore was reluctant to lose people they valued. Sonya would have appreciated that the college paid over the odds, rewarded staff loyalty, was supportive and inclusive and importantly had a reputation for turning out some of the most successful women operating in many spheres worldwide. In addition it was in a beautiful part of the country, assisted with the finest living and working conditions and was the envy of its peers both nationally and internationally. The job may have had its challenges and hurdles to overcome, some of the most intelligent and promising young female minds had also long proven to be some of the most headstrong and ill-disciplined individuals but the college had developed its own philosophy, rite of passage and strict protocol to deal with this. The proof was in the pudding, as Stones liked to say, and it rarely happened that an old girl failed to live up to the promise shown. However the staff were not excluded from the expectations in the same way that they benefitted from the college's success, as such they were required to keep to the highest standards of operation and service in all things and woe betide them if they failed to deliver.

CHAPTER 6

WHERE THINGS GET WORSE FOR

GEORGINA AND EMILY

Friday came around far too quickly for Emily Govan's liking and after attending her morning lecture she was back in her room, a three-student apartment, separate bedrooms with en-suite facilities and a shared kitchen and lounge. A simple snack for lunch hoping to settle her uneasy stomach as she tried so hard not to contemplate the thought of the beating to come and then she had thoroughly showered. Naked in her room, she checked her bottom in the mirror; like so many times before since the horror of the previous Friday and she was pleased to see that, at last, the bruise from the lash of the strap had cleared and her bottom was free of blemishes once more. *Not for long,* she thought rather ruefully, gently parting her cheeks and bending forward. She looked over her shoulder at the mirror image as she opened her legs and pulled her cheeks further apart. She studied her crack and open arsehole and bent further to expose her pussy lips – *So this is the view I am giving* – and was quite shocked to feel a frisson of excitement pass through her as she imagined presenting herself for the professor's cane. Her mind started to race as she imagined the moment when she would presumably be instructed to bend over and touch her toes, in her mind and with no experience to fall back on other than received wisdom, which was the only way a caning would be carried out. She supposed that the minimum number of strokes would be six but suspected that her punishment would be far more severe. As she imagined the cane falling and cracking against her she slipped her hand down to her already moist sex and gently teased her lips and clitoris.

Soon her pussy was slick with her juices; she picked up her floor mirror and placed it at the bottom of her bed and knelt on the duvet. Dropping her shoulders to the bed she returned her fingers to her glistening pussy. Looking back at the mirror she widened her legs, slipping a finger inside of herself. She envisaged the professor's arm swinging down repeatedly as the cane cracked down on her undefended and totally exposed bottom. She laid face down on the bed in her favoured masturbating position with the heel of her hand hard against her mound, her middle finger embedded deep inside her pussy whilst the others worked against her wet lips. Emily raised her left hand and brought it down on her bottom cheeks, slapping from side to side as she lost herself in the build-up to the coming orgasm. Totally engaged in her lustful and passionate fantasy, Emily failed to hear the door of the adjoining room open, the muted conversation that was quickly hushed and then fell silent. Harder and harder she spanked herself as her right hand began to piston at rapid speed between her legs. Suddenly she tensed and then convulsed, letting out a moaning scream which she muffled by plunging her face into her pillows as the climax overcame her. With her hand now resting on the crack of her reddening bottom, she gently caressed her own bottom hole for the first time in her life, as with one final thrust of her other drenched hand she yielded to a second orgasm.

"Maaaaawwwwwww," she incoherently moaned as her shuddering body subsided and she relaxed sprawled on the bed.

Sated and content she returned to the bathroom to quickly wash down and refresh herself, a brief glance at her bottom to reassure herself that there would probably be no evidence of her self-spanking by the time she reported to the Dean. She was pleased to see a healthy pink glow that should soon disappear. *Jeez,* she thought, *what has become of me?* Masturbation she had no qualms about; Emily had enjoyed satisfying herself even when she had had a boyfriend, not that she was overly experienced but she had slept with three of her last boyfriends, one of whom she had been in a ten-month relationship with. She reflected on the thoughts that had led her to become so wanton; her ex had barely laid a hand on her bottom, let along spanked her or fingered her bottom hole. *How did I end up here?* she wondered. Turned on by the thought of being thrashed, slapping her own cheeks, her fingers often deeply encased in her vagina, she shuddered to remember the picture she'd had in her mind at the moment of her climax, that of the Senior Tutor stroking her sore cheeks!

Oh Em, aren't you a mixed up, silly girl? She wondered if this indicated lesbian tendencies, she shook herself to dismiss the thoughts. It was just her way of dealing with the fear of the thrashing to come, she firmly decided. At that moment came a gentle knock at her door.

"Hi Em, we're back, come and have coffee," called Josie McPherson, one of her two flatmates, Georgina Fawcett-Jones being the other.

"OK," responded Emily, thinking that it was a good job that they hadn't returned a bit earlier and she smiled at that thought as she went through to the shared lounge. That smile froze on her face as she entered the room to see that her flatmates Josie and Georgie were indeed present, but was rather surprised to see a second-year student seated in the room with them. Not any second year either, thought Emily, but one of the rather ominous ladies of the much-feared circle of second-year students known as the Seven Sisters, renowned for being the coolest girls within college and certainly not a clique to be messed with.

"Zoe Taylor, isn't it?" volunteered Emily.

"Yes," she replied, "and you are Emily Govan, of a recently spanked bottom and a further thrashing to come later on today, I do believe." Emily's mouth dropped open and she looked accusingly at Georgina, who had clearly recently been in tears by the state of her eyes.

"Oh don't be cross with her, the poor dear is in such a state worrying about her own visit, aren't you, darling? Under an hour to go mind, so it will soon be over," added Zoe as Georgina looked forlornly in apology at Emily. Never one to hold a grudge, Emily went over to Georgina and gave her a hug.

"Go and shower now, Georgie, and dress yourself in simple virginal-looking clothes, look like an angel and you may be treated a bit more like one. Remember what I said, it only smarts for a while and once it's over it soon dies down."

Georgina scuttled from the room, saying, "I am really sorry, Em, none of this was my idea," closing the door behind her before Emily had a chance to question her in response.

"Sit down and drink your coffee, Emily, we need to have a little chat," said Zoe and by the way that Josie shuffled around on the chair avoiding meeting Emily's eyes, she could see that trouble was on the horizon. Emily sipped her drink as Emily produced her mobile.

"Let's all have a little listen to this recording I made earlier," said Zoe mysteriously.

Still intrigued and a little bit suspicious even though Zoe's nature appeared to be friendly and open, Emily was soon to be disabused of any notion that friendliness was in Zoe's mind. The grainy recording was not perfect but was clear enough for there to be no doubt as what was happening as Josie bowed her head in embarrassment as the evidence of her compliance and betrayal became clear to Emily. The sound of Emily's hand cracking and slapping down on her own bare bottom echoed around the room, followed, to Emily's great chagrin, by the clear sound of her muffled scream in orgasmic ecstasy.

There was an eerie silence in the room as the recoding came to its conclusion and Zoe switched it off. "Well that was both interesting and entertaining," chuckled Zoe as Josie continued to stare at the floor in deep embarrassment and shame. Emily waited her out. She knew that this was not going to be a simple case of begging, Zoe's demeanour suggested that there was a proposal of sorts coming.

"So, I was wondering what someone might be prepared to do to stop this being circulated on social media platforms. If I was that way inclined, of course."

Emily held her gaze and her nerve before responding.

"Firstly, Zoe, how despicable and how low can you go? Secondly, I would just deny it as faked, there's no video and my voice isn't that recognisable on it and thirdly what would be the point? What do you want from me?"

"Oh, you want to play hard ball, do you? Well firstly, fuck you, bitch, I'm not the one having a wank while spanking my own arse, so don't try the little Miss High and Mighty act on me. Secondly, people will believe it because they will believe me and let's face it, little Jodie here is probably not going to be a very good liar on your behalf." Josie tried to correct her error over her name but was promptly dismissed by Zoe.

"Shush dear, don't interrupt your elders and betters. Thirdly, what I want is not that big a deal and won't take too much effort on your part."

Emily waited her out again.

"So I'll take that as a maybe for now. All you need to do is to secrete your mobile somewhere so that when you return to see the Dean of Perversion for your super thrashing this evening, apart from giving you more memories to wank over, you will set your phone on record and give it to me to download afterwards. How simple will that be, dearie?" Emily paused to consider, this didn't seem too onerous or anywhere near as bad as she'd expected.

"So, I give you a recording of the Dean thrashing me and this is somehow better for me than the recording you already have?" she queried.

"You're overthinking this. We are not actually interested in you, your thrashing or what you choose to get your rocks off over. What we want, and the 'we' isn't open for discussion but I suspect you know who we are." Emily nodded. "What we want is to sort the old letch out once and for all. You are just the means to an end, sweetie. You are providing ammunition; you, yourself are actually irrelevant. So you'll do as I ask then?"

Emily thought quickly. "I will, but on one condition and that's that you delete that recording now."

Zoe stared thoughtfully at her and came to a decision. "Clever girl, I approve. You are showing promise, have you thought about joining the Little Sisters? I rather like you, Emily," she finished condescendingly.

Emily knew about the Seven Sisters, the influential group of second years who prided themselves on being the college's ultra-cool alpha females amongst the undergraduates, and their first-year sycophantic followers known as the Little Sisters. Emily thought they were a bunch of wannabe middle-class gangsta bitches but felt it best to keep that thought to herself. Certainly at least while this arrogant, smart arse bitch thought she had one over on her.

"OK," said Zoe. "Let's roll, Emily." Holding her phone in front of Emily she deleted the file and handing the mobile over, she invited Emily to check. Emily quickly scanned her phone in case this was a double bluff but it appeared that the file was permanently deleted.

"Thank you Zoe, I will hide my phone in the room this evening while I have my punishment session and you can have it tomorrow."

"No, my sweet, I'll collect it tonight. You can tell us what it was like then, and you can show us your bottom, can't you?" said Zoe, emphasising her superior standing in the relationship. Emily nodded her assent and checked the time, 90 minutes to go before she was going to go through possibly the most painful experience of her life and here she was negotiating with this blackmailing bitch.

"Enjoy tonight, sweet cheeks, I'll see you and those sweet cheeks later, don't go masturbating in front of the pervert, will you?" Her parting shot sending another wave of embarrassment through Emily.

"Fuck off, you shit-faced little bitch," swore Emily under her breath.

Minutes later Georgina was standing shaking and tearful in front of the Dean and Sara Morgan, the Chief Administrative Officer for the Senior Tutor's department.

"Sara is here at my request to help you cope with this disciplinary action but can be sent away if you choose." Sara moved towards Georgina and took her hand.

"It's your choice, Georgina, but I am here to help you, give you strength and support and help you cope with the process." Sara smiled and squeezed her hand and Georgina almost collapsed into her arms.

"Oh yes, please stay, thank you, thank you." Georgina was ridiculously grateful and Sara's libido stirred and her stomach churned as always when a fresh face turned to her in gratitude, trust and hope. However, any sense that things might turn out better than anticipated for Georgina were extinguished with Professor Stones' opening words.

"As you know, young lady, you are undoubtedly guilty of disgracing yourself and behaving injudiciously and offensively in public view on college grounds. You have admitted this and your rewritten document of contrition accepts full responsibility for your actions with appropriate apologies to all affected by the evening's events. Sadly I have to say that on further viewing of the CCTV recording I have been shocked to see that your behaviour was a bit worse than I had previously been aware of."

Georgina's mouth dropped open. "W-w-w-w-what?"

"Don't interrupt me again, please, young lady, when I want a response from you I will ask you a direct question." Professor Stones' voice turned to take on the sharp edge that instilled fear in most of those that had stood before him. Georgina was certainly not an exception to that rule.

"Oh, sorry sir," was her timid apology.

From her expression, Stones could see that Georgina's mind was now whirling; he doubted that she had much of a memory of that night. He was aware that she had allowed herself to become thoroughly intoxicated along with Emily and a couple of others, and from experience he doubted that during the episode it would have crossed her mind that she might ever face any consequences of her drunken shenanigans. Georgina's face contorted rather comically and he surmised that although her memories were clearly hazy, the sense of sheer panic showing in her eyes now suggested that she was gradually piecing things together.

"Tempted as I am to leave you with your feeble mind struggling with its faulty memory bank, I have a little aide-memoire for you now, my pretty little one." Stones was enjoying taunting her and had always been an advocate of allowing his miscreants time to dwell, time to dread, time to imagine – punishing bottoms was a joy but he did so enjoy the anguish that his mind games delivered to the little horrors that found themselves before him.

Georgina wasn't to wait long to find out full details as Stones flicked a switch and a screen dropped down from the ceiling, seconds later a fairly sharp pictured recording, albeit from some distance, appeared on the screen. The next few minutes were easily some of the worst of Georgina's short life; watching herself dancing around drunk and acting very silly was bad enough but then the horror show started. Suddenly the picture zoomed in as Georgina pulled down her top, popped a breast out of her bra and placed it in the marble hand of the reaching arm of the college founder's figure, you could also see that she was making provocative motions with her mouth, licking her lips and then forming a sucking motion. Rather than watching the footage – he had viewed it many times – the professor concentrated on the student's reactions. Georgina started to tremble, as realisation now hit home; what before had seemed a nightmare scenario was now surely a little bit of a bad dream in comparison to the trouble that he hoped she appreciated that she was in now. Unfortunately for the wretched girl, it was not yet over as the film moved on and Georgina and Emily could be seen to squat down at the statue's feet and, having pulled their knickers aside, appeared to be miming relieving their bladders. The film rolled on, as both girls displayed their bared buttocks to the statue, to the point where one of the night porters appeared in the distance and the group had been in charge enough of their senses to run off. The screen went black and rose into its casement in the ceiling. There was a deathly hush in the room. Georgina looked at Sara for support but could see from her shocked and slightly disgusted face that she hadn't been previously aware of the contents of the film.

Stones broke the silence. "Well Georgina, I am also not forgetting that your original report did not specify what form of punishment you felt your actions deserved regardless of the fact that you knew full well exactly what was required of you. Oh, you think that a look of petulance directed at me is warranted, do you?" He paused as Georgina seemed to shrink before him, with a look that illustrated regret that she had allowed her annoyance to show. "Yes, you would be well advised to keep that face wiped of sulky little looks!

"So not a very auspicious start to your first few minutes in this room, is it now? You have been exposed as behaving highly offensively to college property, and the founder's statue at that. You were clearly inebriated and out of control and you have decided to shirk your responsibilities when it comes down to accepting consequences and proposing appropriate punishment. Oh dear, young lady, oh dear. Your crimes are mounting up, are they not? Could well be that we will need to replicate the punishment being handed out to your partner in crime, Emily Govan, who will be joining us later this evening for the higher level chastisement process. It is very difficult to see why Emily deserves a much more serious punishment that you now that we have seen in detail that you were not quite so much of a hanger-on, as first thought, during this disgraceful episode. No indeed, seems a bit unfair for Emily to be taking the brunt of the punishment on her own, don't you think?"

"Oh sir, no sir, I am so sorry sir, it was Emily's fault I was drunk sir, I don't normally drink much but she had these bottles of wine, sir, and I didn't realise... ouch oh." Georgina dried up as Sara squeezed her hand really tightly, digging her nails in to shut the silly girl up.

"Well Sara, not a very bright girl is she?" Stones stared at the miscreant. "I presume that you did rewrite your report and that you have brought it to me today?"

"Yes sir, I did, sir," she hastened to reply, desperate to please her tormentor in any way possible.

"Fetch it from your folder then, I presume that is the reason you have brought possessions to my room for a disciplinary process. You do know, I am sure, that nothing unauthorised in advance is allowed to be brought into this room on punishment days?" Stones as usual emphasising his oft-made point concerning any temptation to film or record the disciplinary process in any way.

Georgina almost ran over to her folder, pulling her report out and rushing it over to the professor.

"Go and stand in the corner please, Georgina, face the wall, hands on head. For the time being at least you may keep your clothes on." Georgina scuttled across to the indicated book-lined wall, and adopted the pose as instructed.

"Hmmmm, has the penny dropped? Has this silly girl finally realised that her future is hanging in the balance, has she put forward a suitable punishment?" queried Stones as he began to read Georgina's report. "Oh scrub that, apparently not. I asked you to be specific but you have again not accepted the invitation, and basically fudged the issue. Right Georgina, back here in front of me, hands on head. Would you like to take this opportunity for a final chance to offer up a proposal for your punishment before I ask the Mistress to attend to formally put into place your removal from this college? You are a very silly young lady, and I will not be offering you any more chances to cleanse your conscience and wipe your slate clean. Naughty girls I can take but liars, sneaks and cheats do tend to bring out my harsher side." The professor was becoming a tad fed-up of

Georgina's fecklessness and apparent lack of moral fibre and had decided that she needed a few harsh words to shock her into total acquiescence and obedience.

"Oh my god, no sir. Sir, please sir, please don't, sir. I'll do whatever you say, sir. Please sir don't call the Mistress, sir. Oh sir, don't send me down, sir, I'm so sorry sir. Oh my god, sir, please sir I am not a bad girl, sir. I didn't mean to be untruthful, sir, I am just so scared, sir."

"For crying out loud, do shut up and let me hear an articulate pleading as to an alternate punishment to being sent down. Get a grip, girl, focus on the task in hand and, for pity's sake, save us from all these dramatics and histrionics."

"Oh sir, please sir, just punish me, anything sir, I'll do anything," said Georgina, to Stones' frustration still not quite grasping that she now needed to be very specific.

"You are really a very ridiculous young lady. Do I have to spell it out? Listen very carefully to my next few words. What do you think I should do to make you appreciate that you have a very special place here, that you have behaved appallingly and that you wish to take your just desserts? This is your very last opportunity. I am fast losing patience with you and am not entirely sure that I believe that you are this dim. Sara, you may talk to her for a moment and give her some much-needed advice."

The professor moved over to his cabinet and perused his implements of correction and improvement, as Sara moved beside the clearly stricken Georgina and took her hands in her own.

"Sweetheart, why are you making him so cross? You must know what you need to go through to save your place here, don't you?"

"I don't want to be spanked, Sara, please don't let him hurt me."

"Now you damn well listen to me, young lady, a spanking is the very least of your worries. What you have done deserves a real thrashing, and only when you accept that can you count on still being here at the end of term. Otherwise Georgina there is going to be an excruciating interview with the Mistress followed by your parents being summoned to listen to you being expelled in disgrace, with the reasons being spelled out. Now buck up, do the decent and correct thing, and for pity's sake ask the professor if he will please be so kind as to allow you to submit to a thorough thrashing to make amends for your filthy and insulting behaviour. Quickly now before he loses patience." Sara berated her forcibly, to Stones' approval.

Georgina began to tremble all over but took a long breath as she gathered herself. Stones knew full well that thoughts and images of distraught, angry or ashamed parents were often the key element in a student accepting their fate and finally facing up to the punishment they were to receive.

"Sir, please sir." She turned to the professor. "I am so sorry, sir, and I need to be punished, sir." She stole a quick glance at Sara's face that Stones could see was imploring her to get the dreaded words out.

"I need to be thrashed, sir, please sir," she almost shouted at the professor.

"Sounds like you may be coming to your senses at last. Please continue, expand and elucidate."

"What? Oh sorry, um, er."

"Professor Stones would like you to put your request for punishment in plain and simple words," interjected Sara, her whispered words in the reticent girl's ear being intentionally loud enough for the professor to appreciate. "For Christ sakes, Georgina, ask him to wallop your bare arse until you can hardly walk, ask him to beat you within an inch of your life, ask him to batter the blazes out of your backside; because otherwise the only walking you will be doing will be out of the door for good!"

"Oh sorry, sir. Please sir, I would like you to give me a thorough thrashing on my bare bottom." She looked at Sara, who nodded to encourage her. Suddenly the words started to spill out of her mouth. "Sir, I want you to beat me sir, please sir, can I be given a walloping, sir? Please sir, please. I need to be thrashed to within an inch of my life, sir. I am a very bad person, sir, who has behaved disgracefully and need to beaten, sir. Will you please allow me to take the walloping of my life, sir? Shall I bare my bottom immediately, sir?"

Sharing an amused grin with Sara, the professor beckoned the girl over to the cabinet. "Fair enough, and which of these articles do you think would best help you to amend your disgusting habits and follow a more improved route to academic success?"

Georgina and Sara went over to the cabinet. On seeing the contents the younger girl burst into tears. "Oh no, no, no," she cried. Stones ignored her entreaties.

"With Sara's help you are now to choose the three implements that you believe should be used to thrash your naked buttocks, after you have been put over my knee and spanked of course. You have two minutes to bring three items to me." With those words he walked off and picked up Georgina's report. "If I agree with your choice you can then rewrite this, specifying exactly, exactly mind, let's have no ambiguity on this, how you wish to be punished to atone for your sins. Then young lady, we will see about starting the first part of your punishment now while we still have to time before that reprobate friend of yours Miss Govan arrives for her thrashing."

Georgina suddenly perked up. "Sir, can I tell you something please sir?"

Stones nodded his assent.

"Sir, Emily is going to be asked to record her thrashing for someone else, sir, she called Zoe sir, she's a second year, sir. She's taped Emily doing something disgusting, sir, and she's going to blackmail her, sir."

Within minutes Stones had heard the story from Georgina to the point that she had left the room, not knowing what the outcome was but sure that Emily would probably do what she was going to be asked. Georgina was undoubtedly a little bit taken aback that the professor seemed well aware of the Seven Sisters, but from her expectant expression he could see that she hoped her that ruse was about to get her some leniency of treatment.

"Well, thank you for that, Georgina. I do not condone tell-tales, so you will not be rewarded other than that we will not disclose where we obtained this information. Now that I am aware of the fact that you are such a proficient snitch, young lady, I may call upon you in the future for information or favour. Now bring me three implements quickly and rewrite that report now."

Georgina blanched and froze; Stones could see that this had not gone according to plan. Of course, he was relishing her discomfort; not only was she clearly terrified of him, not only was he was making her write and ask him to give her a good hiding, she was also expected to select the form of punishment, and then strip naked in front of him. Sara nudged her and indicated for her to unhook the leather paddle, the riding crop and the thin cane with Georgina cringing with each touch.

"Give them to the professor and get writing," she urged.

Georgina handed the three to the professor, rather timidly asking, "Will these three do, sir?" barely receiving much more than a grunt of apparent disinterest in return as Sara guided her to the desk to start her rewrite of her punishment request. Within a matter of seconds, Stones could see and hear that Sara was getting exasperated at

Georgina's unwillingness to be straightforward and succinct and eventually dictated the wording while Georgina sniffled with self-pity.

With the report finally in his hand, Stones questioned her to reiterate and clarify her division.

"So to try and make amends for your disgusting performance the other night, and for your continuing inability to follow simple rules of procedure and instruction, you are requesting a thorough spanking and paddling. Which is to be carried out shortly, to be followed by a further thrashing with crop and cane, which will be carried out either today or I may decide to hold that over for a later date dependent on how time goes. All punishment to be applied to your bare buttocks. Is this correct, Georgina, can you confirm your wishes please?"

Georgina hesitated and received a sharp dig in the ribs from Sara.

"Yes sir, please sir, that's right, sir. I do, sir."

Sara sighed. "Georgina will you please specifically ask the professor for the punishment that you are requesting or it's going to get worse for you." Her patience clearly becoming exhausted with the reticent madam.

Georgina took a breath. "Sir, sorry, sir. Yes sir, I would like you to spank my bare bottom now, sir, and then use a p-p-paddle, a crop and a, oh no, a cane please." This further hesitation resulted in an exasperated sigh from Sara.

"Well, well. At last, young lady, we seem to be making progress, looks like the penny has finally dropped. I have considered your request and am pleased that you have volunteered to take the appropriate corporal punishment for your misdeeds. I think it is time to get those garments off and get your naked naughty backside over by my chair and we will finally get on with it."

Georgina locked eyes with Sara, who nodded to encourage her, and began to disrobe. Hesitating once she was down to her undies,

Sara stepped forward and unclipped her bra releasing a pair of small perky breasts, then bent forward and pulled her knickers down and off a compact little bottom. Finally naked, Georgina stood now compliant but clearly terrified. She moved over to stand before Stones, her hands trying to cover her breasts and her pubic area.

"Hands on head," sighed the professor and hesitantly Georgina obeyed.

Smoothing his hands over his lap, he indicated for her to position herself in the expected manner. One last deep breath and she laid herself over him, her hands reaching for the carpet, her bottom fully exposed. Sara knelt down in front of her.

"Open your legs wide, keep them still and raise your bottom to offer it properly for your spanking. That's it, nice and wide, open both those cracks up, always like to see the anus of my rascals. Oh, and what a cute tight little anal hole we have here too." One hand resting on a cheek and flattening the skin to open up Georgina's bottom crack fully.

Georgina gasped in shock at his words, but obeyed although the professor could sense her stifling the urge to burst into tears. At that point a buzzer sounded loudly in the room. Stones reached over and pressed a button, his other hand gently resting on Georgina's buttocks, a finger resting in the top of the open cleft of her bottom. Georgina's body froze and stiffened across his lap as a door opened; her view being somewhat restricted, her head down and peering through the gaps between Stones' legs. It would have been obvious that the first person through the door was a man, followed closely by a clearly feminine pair of legs behind.

"Welcome, Porter. Welcome, Senior Tutor. I am afraid we are running late but I am sure that Sara and Georgina won't mind if you wish to witness Georgina's spanking."

Sara held on tightly to Georgina's hands as the girl tried to struggle up. "Shush, stay still, there's no way out of this, just steel yourself and try and behave so that this is over as quickly as possible. Tell the professor that you are happy for people to see that you get what you deserve for being such a naughty girl."

Stones could feel the resistance ebbing as Georgina lowered her head and slumped in surrender. Sara meanwhile was glad of the restraining task in-hand to distract her from Jamie's presence, but Stones had noted the exchange of looks and Sara's blushing cheeks and guessed accurately their shared experience the evening before may well have created the start of something. The possibility caused him no heed, he liked to feel he was a romantic at heart and was happy to see how this would play out. Georgina's answer interrupted any pursuance of those thoughts.

"Sir, thank you sir, I am happy to be p-p-punished by you in front of your guests, sir, as I have been such a n-n-naughty girl, sir."

The professor smiled. "Good girl, well done and thank you Sara for guiding Georgina so well. I am heartened you are performing so ably under the circumstances."

Sara beamed up at him, her blush growing ever pinker as she looked into his all-knowing eyes.

Stones smiled; he was well aware of his attraction to women of a certain type. A type that did not shy away from the obvious sexual element in the disciplinary quirks that he excelled in. He accepted that his powerful position, deep voice, physical size and domineering personality were the key factors and that he allowed very few to really get to know the man beneath the outward features and performances. He had learnt over the years to apply himself to the role that allowed him to make such good use of his position to be able to pursue his favoured activities. Even in the presence of Jamie, who Stones could see she was clearly attracted to, he still felt that, at least for the time being, he was her master.

"Right, back in position please, my dear. Let's get on with business."

With that remark the professor brought his hand to Georgina's bottom with an almighty crack. This was followed by an equally almighty scream from Georgina who immediately started to struggle against Sara, as a second blow landed and her scream doubled in volume.

"If you don't stay in position with your legs apart and bottom up then you'll go into leg restraints and, more importantly, young lady, I will start your punishment again."

The third slap was just as hard and had the same reaction as Georgina fought to get free and crossed her legs as she fought Sara's attempts to hold her in place. Stones flipped her off his lap onto the floor, grabbed her by an arm and marched her over to his punishment desk. With Jamie's help he quickly fastened her into ankle and wrist clamps despite Georgina's writhing and crying uncontrollably throughout.

"Let me go, I don't want to do it, I don't want it, what's that, what's that?" Georgina yelped in outrage as her groin met the raised rubber mound on the table edge that forced her legs apart to display her intimate areas openly.

"This is a way to keep disobedient rascals, who won't take their punishment properly, presented for a good hiding with their bottoms raised and their legs spread wide apart. You are now going to get your spanking doubled and I fully intend that you will learn how exactly to take a thrashing before you leave this room."

Stones then proceeded to start walloping her buttocks methodically and with much force with his large hands, meanwhile

Sara held her head and mopped up her tears as Celia and Jamie watched with dispassionate expressions. It was quite a ferocious assault and the others were suitably impressed at the professor's stamina and resilience as well as his consistent timing as the slaps landed virtually every two seconds apart and with unerring accuracy. After one hundred slaps, Georgina had wilted and submitted, the fight had gone and the yelling had been re-tuned into a series of low throaty grunts of pain accompanied by copious tears.

The professor continued, however, Georgina's buttocks bright red and completely covered, only stopping after his hand had slapped her sore cheeks two hundred times. The professor paused to admire the results of his efforts. Georgina's bottom and the tops of her legs looked as though they had been painted scarlet.

"Right, shall we give you a moment to recover and then I think we will keep you positioned like this for a paddling followed by a good flogging with the crop and the cane to reinforce the message and hopefully bring you to a state of redemption. I think you should receive the full punishment in one go to truly teach you a lesson. I really wouldn't relish the thought of having to go through your ridiculous wittering and complaining a second time. Obviously this will intensify the pain somewhat but I cannot see that you don't deserve a higher level of suffering, eh? Have you anything to say yet, Georgina?"

With Sara aiding her like a theatre prompt, Georgina managed to gasp out.

"Oh yes sir, thank you sir for spanking me. But I have learnt my lesson already, sir. I am so sorry for everything I've done wrong, sir." And before Sara could stop her, "I think that is enough, sir, I've learned my lesson. Please can you release me now, sir?"

The tutting of the professor was only the precursor for a follow-up response that Georgina obviously had not considered.

"Oh dear, oh dear, oh dear. Sadly not a success so far then. Even with your help, Sara, she hasn't really grasped the seriousness of her crimes and how the punishment needs to be appropriately applied to ensure full understanding and contrition. So Porter, if you would pass the wooden paddle bat we can step things up, and based on Georgina's latest contribution I think we will have twenty rather than the planned ten strokes."

This final comment reawakened Georgina's rebellious side and she immediately tried to struggle before realising that her head was basically the only part of her body with any real freedom of movement.

"No, that is not fair, I've had enough. LET ME UP!" She demanded loudly, completely ignorant of how dangerous and injudicious this was.

"Fair enough. We will make that twenty-five then. Now listen carefully, young lady, you are coming close to earning yourself a strapping which I can assure you will make your spanking seem like a tickle. For a flogging with the strap, I have a special contraption which in your position I can't really show you but let me tell you that you would be restrained in cuffs on your back with your legs pulled up, spread apart, towards your head. Now please picture that for a moment, this little beauty," the professor deliberately paused for effect, then tapped a fingertip against her anus, "would be forced wide open as will this special work of art beneath," and he moved his finger to flick her lower pussy lips that rested on the leather mound.

"Then, my sweet, this…" He had picked up the thick strap from cabinet and now waved it in the absolutely flabbergasted and terrified young woman's face. "This will be brought down ten times, with real venom on your already spanked, paddled, cropped and caned little bottom cheeks. If you are lucky, your anus and vagina will manage to avoid the lashes but regardless it will hurt like you'd never believe, the pain lasts for quite a while and will leave you very bruised. Now do you have anything to say, young Georgina?"

Sara did not need to prime her this time.

"Sir, sir, I am sorry. I do not want the strap, sir, please. Oh God, sir, please sir, I am so sorry, sir. I will be good now, sir, but please sir, not too hard, sir. I am not used to this sir, please sir, please. Please don't hurt me too much."

The professor sighed and picked up the paddle bat.

"Nice try but no prize," he said, bringing the paddle down in a sweeping stroke across her cheeks. The resulting scream was loud, high-pitched and long-lasting, Sara held Georgina's face tightly in her hands trying to quell the noise. Once more the tears sprang forth and Sara had to wipe her nose.

"Don't worry about the screaming, Sara. She won't have the breath soon to keep it up, but hold her very firmly, and yes, get ready with the tissues to mop up the snot and tears as we go. Disgusting child! The next few are going to be fast and furious." Stones never liked to miss a trick in adding to his victim's humiliation as he leaned over to raise Georgina's head by her hair to make it easier for Saar to administer to her.

He was correct on all counts. The paddle landed in a blur repeatedly slamming into her lower cheeks, the redness deepening. Georgina's scream turned into a panting wheeze then, as the professor paused, into a more desperate sobbing.

"Fifteen to go," he taunted her before raising the wood and this time aiming for the sensitive tighter skin across the top of her bottom.

"Yaaaaaaaaaaaaaaaaaaaaaa!" was the new cry from Georgina, as showing no mercy Stones repeated the blow precisely nine more times. A few seconds' pause and then he laid on the final five dead centre, her bottom now evenly covered in a bright, angry-looking coating of crimson. He put down the paddle and joined the others in contemplating the sight of Georgina's well thrashed throbbing behind.

"When you are ready, Georgina, you may thank me."

Stones knew that the response now should illustrate whether or not he had bested the young student and the voice, when it came, quivered, but was undoubtedly defeated.

"Oh sir. Oh, oh, oh thank you sir. Oh my word, sir, it stings so much. I'm sorry sir, please sir, thank you sir."

The professor smiled. "Yes that's much better. In a few moments you will receive your cropping and then finally a damn good caning, then your ordeal will be over. While she's in position, I think I'll just give her a cropping quickly then perhaps you would like to step in, Porter, a bit earlier than planned but now is as good as time as any for you to show the ladies how you handle the cane. As she seems to be coming to her senses at last, I think just ten strong and true strokes with the thin whippy cane on top of the crop strokes will suffice. It tends to mark well and the narrow stripes on the smaller derriere always seem a good fit."

He went over to the cabinet, replacing the paddle and picked up the crop and the thin cane which he flexed and swished in the air deliberately to further disconcert a trembling, quietly weeping Georgina. Stones enjoyed using the crop and cane in tandem, as although similar looking, the two implements produced differing effects. The crop was made of fibreglass and had a thin leather covering, thickening at one end to form a handle and tapering down to a fine tip, covered in a leather tongue to reduce greatly any chance of breaking the skin. The cane, and Stones had many of different thicknesses and lengths, was one of his thin rattan ones, more whippy than the longer bamboo sticks. The strokes of the crop tended to produce an immediate stinging sensation that would pass quicker than the cut of a cane that was more likely to bruise and have a longer throbbing discomfort.

Jamie took the cane and began gently patting Georgina's clearly throbbing cheeks, causing her to flinch and clench rather dramatically. "I can't wait to get started on this bottom, sir. I'll be seeing to you in a minute, young lady," said Jamie, moving quickly aside as Stones approached with the crop flexing in his hands.

Stones didn't waste any time and the crop suddenly flashed through the air, his arm swung backwards and forwards at great speed as twenty strokes of the crop, landed in perfect grouping from the very top of her cheeks to the top of her legs. Georgina began howling as the first crop stroke hit home and this turned into one long continuous banshee shriek as the strokes landed with no pause or hesitation, her bottom now aflame with pain.

"Give her two minutes to stop her nonsense then give her a damn good caning please, Porter. Let's leave her in this position, I don't think we can trust her to bend over and take the cane unbuckled." The professor returned the crop to the cabinet as Sarah desperately tried to calm the hysterically sobbing, shaking girl down.

Jamie leant in closely looking at the expert grouping and consistency of the older man's work, raised welts forming in perfect symmetry earning Jamie's admiration and respect. He prepared himself slowly for his first performance in the professor's room. He was determined to ensure that he carried out his task to his new mentor's satisfaction. He so wanted to please this man and earn his respect and admiration. He addressed the now gently weeping and quietly moaning girl.

"Right, young lady, ten strokes hard and true, but first you will kiss along the length of the cane to honour it."

Georgina noisily gulped and uttered incomprehensible sounds as an answer, causing Sara to tug her hair sharply before whispering into her ear. There was a moment when the cane hovered in front of the sobbing Georgina when it seemed that she was not going to comply with the instruction before she took in one long breath and moved her mouth to the base of the cane. Jamie and the professor exchanged a knowing smile of victory as Georgina began to kiss along the cane's length as Jamie slid it slowly along her lips.

"Good girl, you may now address the cane." Jamie was testing her compliance further but made contact with Sara's eyes and winked to encourage her to manipulate Georgina to comply. Sara again murmured into her ear.

"I would like to ask the cane to punish me for my disgraceful crimes against the college and to make me a good g-g-g-girl," Georgina tentatively volunteered, much to the professor's delight.

"Excellent, Porter, well done young lady, that's the ticket, much better, much, much better."

Jamie could see the relaxation seep through Georgina's body, her head hung lower as Sara cradled it in her arms, and her bottom cheeks lost their tension, her crack widening as they did so.

"Lovely," purred an appreciative Senior Tutor.

"Down girl, down," mumbled a chuckling Dean of Discipline.

"Right young lady, let's make a start then," said Jamie, swinging the cane down in a vicious arc.

The relaxed cheeks became a thing of the past as Georgina's body gyrated phenomenally considering she was fastened at hand and foot. She was panting frantically, gasping with the pain and shock of the cane's biting contact on her already very sore buttocks. Sara held onto Georgina's face as though willing the girl to lock her eyes to her own as they widened to perfect circles and her mouth seemed to freeze in a strangled groan of pain as the cane fell again and the fire in her bottom intensified. Thwack! Thwack! Thwack! Thwack! After the first five Jamie took a moment to silently critique his own work, causing both the Professor and the Senior Tutor to join him in perusing the girl's flinching backside.

"Nicely spread and a lovely welt coming up for each one, don't you think, Professor?" sighed the Senior Tutor, running her finger along the fast rising bright red stripe of the first laid strike.

The professor leaned forward and put both of his huge hands to cover the entirety of the girl's small bottom, causing her to desperately attempt to close her cheeks. Even in her agony, Georgina was clearly aghast as she became aware that she could feel the professor's breath on her arsehole but had no choice to submit as, seeing and feeling her tense, he dug in his fingers and roughly held the cheeks wide apart. He sensed that this was one student who would learn her lesson and doubted that he would see her in his room again for punishment, but as always was keen to ensure that her disgrace and humiliation was complete. It was his intention that, like many others before her, she would never be able to see any of the people who were witness to her punishment and degradation, without her face reddening and shame spreading throughout her body.

"Uh-uh," he warned. "You should have learned by now, Georgina, you have submitted your body over for punishment. You are allowed no dignity, no pride, and no sign of any arrogance. You are just a shamed, disgraced little hussy getting her just desserts. Any further show of disobedience or resistance then I will instruct Porter here to start your caning again but this time with a thicker cane. Do you need to feel the thicker cane to help you decide on the best direction to take now? Or there is always the strap, remember what I said, I would be perfectly happy to strap you on top of your caning if that's what your behaviour deserves."

"Oh God, no sir, no sir, no sir, thank you sir. I am so sorry, sir. Please do whatever you want, sir, but I don't need the thicker cane, sir, or the strap sir, please sir," sobbed Georgina.

"Seems like she is ready for her final five, lay them on thick and hard, Porter," instructed the professor.

Jamie pulled back the cane, then swiped and whipped it past Georgina's ears causing the girl to flinch in terror. He raised the cane high and waited, and waited and waited. Georgina's bottom seemingly developed a life of its own and began twitching in anticipation; a dribble of sweat ran down her open crack settling in her anal entrance. Jamie relented and whipped the cane across the centre of the trembling bottom inducing a strangled gasp from the suffering culprit. He went high and low in quick succession with the next two, Sara holding her head fast in her hands as the thrashed girl howled in anguish. Jamie took careful aim and swept the final strokes down across the centre of her bottom, landing one on top of the other, raising an immediate thick angry welt and provoking an ear-piercing shriek from Georgina. He returned the cane to the cabinet and resumed his seat with a nod to the professor and Senior Tutor.

"Awesome," was the only word that the professor said, to Jamie's relief and satisfaction. Stones indicated to Sara to release the sobbing and distraught girl from her restraints and led her round to face the professor, Jamie and Celia.

"Turn her around until she stops the blubbing," said Stones in a dismissive tone. "I'd rather look at her thrashed disfigured backside than that miserable facial mess."

The three of them were joined by Sara who came to stand beside them all looking studiously at the ravaged cheeks before them. Raised welts from the bottom of her buttocks to the top decorated the wretched specimen before them.

"Well young lady, landed yourself in a far bigger pickle than you thought, didn't you? Turn round now, have you anything to say?"

Georgina turned to face her audience, her sobs having subsided to gentle sniffles.

"I would just like to apologise to everyone concerned, sir. I am sorry and thank you both for punishing me as I deserved, sir."

The professor nodded his approval.

"Good girl, well said and well taken. I admire a young lady that can take what she deserves and take it with some honour. Sara, please take Georgina into the bathroom and give her a couple of minutes with her poor red bottom in the ice in the bidet. It'll take the sting out a bit and help the bruising come out early so your lovely little bottie isn't too disfigured for long." He patted Georgina's stinging cheeks as she scurried past with Sara.

The professor turned to his companions, opening a bottle of claret and filling four glasses.

"A little tipple well deserved I think. Good show, Porter, a good start and we have still got the delightful Emily to deal with this evening and then back again tomorrow. Celia, if you wish to join us again before 11am tomorrow, I think you will appreciate my intentions towards young Yishen Yiam."

"Ah yes, Little Miss Pissy Pants, isn't it? Why thank you Professor, I most certainly will."

Sara came through and joined them, accepting the glass of wine from the professor albeit slightly reluctantly. She wasn't a great wine drinker but knew from experience that the professor liked his little rituals and his wines tended to be of such fine quality that they slipped smoothly down.

A few minutes later, a very chastened Georgina was led back into the room, head bowed and suddenly very conscious again of her naked state. Sara placed her before the professor, nudging her to indicate that she needed to stand straight facing him with her hands interlocked on her head.

"Right, young lady. You may now dress that pretty little body, complete and sign off this document signifying that you have received, and were happy with the designated disciplinary action and then you may take your leave of us."

Georgina hurried to obey, and without hesitation quickly annotated the form to say that she agreed that she had fully deserved the beating that she had requested and that it had been conducted to her satisfaction. Stones quickly perused it and nodded at her to leave and Georgina scurried from the room.

He looked at his watch. "Just about time for a cup of tea before young Emily is due to join us. Ding ding, round two," he chortled.

With that, the three of them finished their wine and contemplated a job well done!

CHAPTER 7

EMILY'S TURN (AGAIN!)

Georgina crashed into the room. "I got fucking caned! I got fucking well caned! He's got a recording of us pretending to pee on the fucking statue, you fucking moron, Emily, it's all your fault, it was all your idea. 'Be a rebel for once in your life,' she says, and I end up fucking arse naked bent over, displayed in front of a fucking audience. I get felt up by an old man and fucking spanked then fucking paddled then fucking beaten with a bloody horse crop and then I fucking well get caned! My arse is on fucking fire and it's all your fucking fault, you fucking bitch!"

"I take it things didn't go well?" sighed Emily. "Look, I am sorry Georgie. Let me see, come on, darling."

"Fuck off, Emily, I hope he beats the skin off your arse." Georgina was not to be placated.

Emily followed her into her room where her friend threw herself face down on the bed sobbing disconsolately.

"Shush, sweetheart, shhhh, now." Emily lifted her dress and stroked Georgina's bottom, feeling the heat radiating through her knickers.

"Right, stay where you are and let me look after you for ten minutes." Emily left the room, returning a few seconds later with a bottle of massage oil and a glass of cold white wine.

"Sit up for a minute, slip your dress off and drink this." Emily wrapped her arms around the shoulders of her tear-stained chum. "Emily's going to make you feel better and then Emily's going to go and get her arse crucified!"

Georgina managed a smile. "I suppose that it's over, at least for me, but I had no idea it could hurt so much, Em. He's such a bastard, I have never been made to feel such a silly little girl in my life. Oh God, he's seen more of me than I have!"

Emily turned her friend over and laid her down. "Lift up, lie still and trust me, darling," said Emily as she slipped her friend's knickers off her legs and sprinkled oil all over her bruised and beaten bottom cheeks.

Gently Emily worked her fingers over the swollen globes, soothing expertly as she worked the expensive luxurious oil into the swollen striped buttocks, glad to have something to do to take her mind off of what was coming to her own bottom shortly. Georgina soon found herself dozing as the pain subsided and her friend's sensual and calming massage alleviated her distress and spread calm throughout her body.

"Time for me to get myself ready now, darling. Maybe you could give me a massage later when that bitch Zoe has been and gone." She kissed the slumbering Georgina and crept out of the room.

By the time Georgina snapped awake, thinking of how she should have warned Emily that she had spilt the beans on the plan to record her session for Zoe, it was too late as Emily was on the professor's doorstep waiting to be allowed entry.

"Step inside, young lady, although I suspect that you've spoken with Georgina so you can understand why we may be reluctant to use the word 'lady'." Professor Stones decided to go in hard and get straight to the point.

"Yes sir, I have talked to Georgie and I am aware of what we were seen doing that evening…" Emily paused.

"Don't stop now and be specific, I am not interested in anything ambivalent and vague, Emily. I would appreciate your honesty now, I cannot offer you a way out of your predicament but you can certainly stop it becoming more severe than is already planned. Let's face it, Emily, you managed to talk yourself into a heap of trouble when you were here the other day. So no repeat, continue with your little resume of the other night please," Stoned encouraged Emily.

"Yes sir. I would like to apologise for my dreadful behaviour, showing disrespect to the college founder, the college itself and the staff and academics therein. Sir, I was drunk and out of control and apart from exposing myself and using foul language, I also simulated urinating and encouraged my friend Georgina to do the same."

Stones turned to Celia, Sara and Jamie. "Emily, we are joined this evening by the Senior Tutor and the Chief Academic Administrator who will be the observers of your punishment and Porter here, who will be carrying out the punishment."

This news jolted Emily, as Stones had expected; she had been trying not to think about the man's presence since she had entered the room but hadn't anticipated that this stranger would be the one wielding the cane. *So,* she thought, *on the plus side, this Porter,* and she didn't recognise him as one of the college's team, *is fairly good-looking and about thirty years younger than the professor. Maybe,* she contemplated, *this could be the silver lining on a very dark cloud,* although there was a definite part of her that she had to admit was disappointed that the professor wasn't going to be the one giving her the thrashing.

"So Emily, after some discussion, I have decided that you will be given twelve strokes with the tawse, which, for your education, is a leather strap with a forked tail end. You will then have twelve strokes of the heavy cane and then six lashes of the thick strap to finish off your ordeal. A total of thirty strokes in all, but I should warn you, young lady, that I seriously contemplated giving you twenty-five cane strokes as I very much feel that you have pushed the boundaries. However I did sense a deal of shame, a willingness to commit to improvement and a commendable attitude to accepting responsibility for your actions. So twelve with the cane it is, I do hope that you won't cause me to reassess my thoughts on this?"

Emily blanched, and Stones could see her mind ticking over and wondered if she was going to come clean about the proposed secret recording she had apparently committed to. He'd secretly rather hoped that she might make a clean breast of things and confide in him. He suspected that she was bright enough to doubt that she could place an awful lot of faith in Zoe's loyalty and that she would be reluctant to betray him as planned. He recognised that he undoubtedly had developed a soft spot for the young woman and was mildly disappointed that she looked as though she was prepared to betray him. Any sense of loyalty and obedience that she had developed towards the man who seemed to derive great pleasure and satisfaction in inflicting severe pain on her was probably placing her in great conflict he surmised. He decided to give her one final opportunity to tell all.

"No mobile on you, I presume?" He sensed that she was wavering and there was a long pause before she drew in a deep breath and replied.

"No sir. I am ready to present myself if the professor is ready for me to start paying my dues."

He supposed that Emily understandingly wanted to get this done and dusted, and then get out of the room with her recording and hand it over to Zoe as fast as possible. She slipped her jacket off, her mobile already recording, and turned to hang it on the coat rack behind completely unaware that it had been positioned between two speakers in preparation. Wagner was just being introduced to the room as Emily stood before them, blissfully unaware that her duplicity was going to do her no good whatsoever.

"Fair enough, don't say you weren't given the opportunity. Rest of your clothes off, girl, don't be shy. Let Porter get a look at what he's got to work with."

His words caused Emily's visible confusion but she duly stripped down unashamedly in seconds, her audience did not intimidate her and she was fairly proud of her body and secretly quite turned on to be naked in front of the professor and her new acquaintance, Porter.

"Porter, lead her over to the hanging cuffs. We are going to see how Emily copes with our freestanding crucifixion pose while she takes the tawse." The cuffs had dropped from the ceiling, controlled electronically by the professor with his fully automated and interactive setup. He had already removed the two floor tiles that exposed the foot restraints for Emily to place her feet into. A little moment of electrically inspired whirring and clicking and Emily found herself with legs wide apart and arms spread and splayed above her.

Now Emily's facial expressions changed, the confidence and composure previously displayed drained from her face, her eyes widened and for the first time the onlookers could see fear. She was barely able to move and spread-eagled upright with the full knowledge that very shortly her backside was going to be extremely painful. She may have enjoyed her fantasies of being naked and having her bottom thrashed but as Professor Stones well knew, in your fantasies it certainly didn't hurt like hell as it did in reality. Stones stood directly before her and looked deep into her eyes; he was certain that she would rather not have someone watching her break down and cry her heart out and he was pleased to see the terror in her eyes.

"All ready then, my friends. Sara, it might be useful if Emily was to have a chance to appreciate the role you play with some of the scoundrels in this room. So can you take the tissues and assist this young lady with her facial ablutions while Porter tries out the tawse on her. Ready when you are, Porter. Happy for you to take up the position and let us proceed discussed please."

Emily flinched, her buttock cheeks clenching at the air rush as Jamie tried a few practice strokes with the implement. A tad less thick than the thick leather strap, slightly shorter and a fair bit wider, but the devil's horn cut divide at the tip was what gave it its own particular sensation on landing. Emily discovered this as the first stroke lashed down unexpectedly across the backs of her calves.

"Hiiieeee. Fuck! Aaaaahh," was Emily's greeting back to the tawse at their first meeting, followed by, "Niiiiiaaaooo! Shit. Fuck. Shit," as the second stroke landed on the backs of her knees!

"Sara, have a word," warned the professor.

"Shhh, shh. Hush with the swearing, sweetheart, you'll only end up receiving punishment strokes. Try and count them and if see if you can concentrate on thanking the professor for correcting you so kindly rather than this use of foul language." Emily's look implied that she had no idea what Sara's role was and that she was perhaps not the most willing recipient of her advice! Stones suspected that her impulse was to tell Sara exactly what she could do with her sage words but he was impressed that she managed to stay tight-lipped and just grimace as the pain message from her throbbing legs seeped through into her brain. The next stroke was full-blooded and at the top of her legs, almost causing Stones to wince himself as Emily screeched, her body bucking wildly within the limits of the restraints. He doubted that she was thinking too much about taking issue with Sara now.

Crack! Crack! Crack! As prearranged with the professor Jamie laid the next three strokes across the top of Emily's back, then two in the middle of her back avoiding the lower back and the vulnerable kidneys as instructed. Emily was panting and seemed beyond screaming now, her mouth open making deep guttural noises and her eyes wide and staring with Sara dabbing at her cheeks and whispering soothing words to help her bear the pain.

"That's eight, sir, thank you sir," Emily gasped out, remembering what Sara had said and desperate to do anything to ensure that the punishment did not get prolonged.

"Continue, Porter," were the only words she heard back.

Splat! Splat! Two vicious strokes were laid at speed across the centre of her buttocks and Emily writhed and swung in her bindings.

"Yaaaaaazaaarrrr! No, fuck no. That bloody well hurts. Aaaaargh, you fucker!"

"Extra one on top of those two, please Porter." Stones' voice was sharp, loud and clear.

Sara tapped her face and pointed a finger at her, "Don't!" as Jamie swung the tawse and cracked her again on the bright red ridge that was now glowing across her flanks.

"Yoooooo! Oh my god. Thank you, sir, thank you."

"You do take a while to get the message, don't you my dear?" laughed the professor.

"She certainly has got some spirit, I do have to say," chuckled the Senior Tutor alongside him.

Jamie went low on her cheeks for the next and then completed the thirteen strokes with a hard and accurate stroke across the remaining white unblemished stripe of skin at the tops of her cheeks.

"Oooooooh! Ooooh! Ooooh!" Emily's suffering was clear to all present as her sobs filled the room and her body continued to jerk spasmodically as though further strokes were falling.

Stones stroked her ravaged mounds gently. "Feels like we applied red hot pokers to your derriere, does it, my precious one?" His words spoken quietly into Emily's ear instantly calmed her. The tears continued to flow down her face as Sara cradled her nodding head.

"Well done, darling. Thank them both now, come on, you can do it, come on," urged Sara.

Taking a deep ragged breath, Emily forced the words out. "Thank you for punishing me so well, Porter, thank you for my punishment, Professor. I am so sorry for my disgraceful behaviour, sir. I am so very sorry."

"Excellent. OK, shall we grant her two minutes' grace and then release her, Porter? Emily, you will then present yourself for the cane. Back to us, bend over and put your hands on your ankles. Legs well apart, bottom cheeks nice and relaxed, that lovely anus open and pointing the way like a beacon lighting up the target area," chuckled the professor, continuing with his taunting and provocative words to see if Emily would carry on biting.

"Yes sir, of course, sir," was the delivered response with Emily attempting to gain some composure.

Jamie fetched the thick, heavy cane from the cabinet and gave it a few practice swipes through the air, causing Emily to shiver and shake with trepidation.

"A fine job indeed," murmured Stones as he inspected Emily's bottom. "I almost feel some sympathy thinking on the damage that the mighty cane and then the thick strap will do on top of the bomb site she's presenting at the moment. Oh well. C'est la vie. Live by the sword, die by the sword… or should I say the tawse. Ha ha!"

Moving round to face Emily again, he chuckled into her face. "What fun, eh? I think it's time we unbuckled you and got you ready for round two. Sara, Celia, please unfasten her."

The two women moved quickly to free Emily, who almost stumbled into Celia's arms as she was released.

"There, there, my sweet," said Celia as she wrapped her arms around the naked, still trembling blonde. A finger gently moving her golden tresses back into position before wiping final tears from Emily's flushed cheeks.

Jamie moved to take her from Celia, spinning her around to face him.

"Open your mouth and hold the cane for me please, Emily," he said, playing along with the professor's teasing of the girl.

Emily obeyed, gripping the cane between her teeth as Jamie bent behind her, giving himself a few seconds to assess the state of her bottom from the wicked tawse. Stones noticed the ridge at the front of Jamie's trousers so suspected that his inspection was not just professional interest, so to speak. Emily certainly had some deep red stripes, and the professor was sure that further admonishment to those sore cheeks with the cane were going to test her to her limits. Sara came and stood beside Jamie and Stones caught the drop of her head and widening of her eyes as she stared at Jamie's groin. Stones allowed himself a smile as he thought of the moment when he had first seen a naked Jamie, rather impressive. The fleeting thought crossed his mind that maybe Sara would perhaps appreciate that honour. Sara glanced across at him as him, her gaze meeting his before quickly looking away.

"If you could focus on the task in hand, Sara, and bring Emily over before me please."

Sara blushed and he knew that his suspicions concerning her probable improper thoughts were being confirmed.

"Yes sir, sorry sir," she responded and rather tugged Emily towards him.

"I am ready for you to cane me now, sir, if you wish," announced Emily, although Stones rather doubted that she was as nonchalant about what was coming as she was intending to convey.

Stones positioned two chairs side by side in front of Emily, before motioning to Sara to sit beside him.

"Sit in front of her, bend her over and hold her hands on her ankles please, Sara. Porter, give her a few taps for both of you to get the feel of the cane, then strike her slowly and hard. I suspect we may have to consider a change of position. To be fair to you, Emily, stretched buttocks thrashed with a thick cane can be a savage and bruising encounter, and your fortitude is admirable but may not be enough to get you through this. Let's see how it goes with you counting these strokes loudly and clearly please."

Emily remained tight-lipped and silent but her trembling cheeks and twitching arsehole rather gave away her trepidation. Jamie swished the cane as Sara settled in front of Emily, stroking her hair before covering her hands and locking eyes with the clearly terrified young woman. The cane began lightly tapping her bottom as Jamie took careful aim before raising it high. He held it up in the air for over twenty seconds and then brought it swinging down to crack against Emily's lower cheeks. There was a silent pause before Emily grunted in pain, her knees buckling and her bottom swaying. She sucked in a deep breath, straightened her legs and spoke clearly.

"One, thank you, sirs."

Jamie swung the cane again, landing fractionally above the first stroke, producing a stifled yelp from the recipient, who held her stance albeit helped by Sara's tight grip and whispered encouragement.

"Good girl, good girl, you're doing superbly."

Emily took another breath. "Two, sirs, thank you, sirs." The third stroke whistled through the air before landing perfectly again just above the first two, creating tramlines across the suffering girl's buttocks.

"Oh my, oh my, oh my, ooooooooer," gasped Emily before adding, "three sirs, thank you, sirs. Oh my. Oh my. Jeez. Jeez, it bleeding stings."

Again, with Sara strong grip assisting her, she stayed in position, although her legs had now started to tremble and Stones was aware that her knees would likely crumple soon. With tight stretched buttocks bent over adding to the tautness, there was little in the way of a fat layer to absorb the force and lessen the impact. The heavier, thicker cane was indeed a much harsher mistress and her watching audience stayed respectively silent knowing the girl was taking a pitiless and earnest beating. The fourth stroke slammed down, Emily noisily expelled the deep breath she had just taken in and Sara struggled to hold her still as her legs again wobbled.

"Oh no, oh sir, oh God it hurts so much, sir. Please stop, please stop."

Jamie paused to give her ample time to continue her count, but the professor was quick to interject.

"You are doing well, my dear, so don't spoil it now. You will be able to change position shortly but I want two more delivered in this position to ensure that you appreciate the finer points of a severe thrashing and your bottom gets bruised evenly all over. So, we are waiting for your count or do I need to instruct Porter to add punishment strokes for further disobedience?"

Emily let out a long rather woeful sigh.

"No sir, sorry sir. Thank you, sirs, that was four, thank you. I am ready for my next stroke, sirs," she finished mournfully.

Stones nodded to Jamie, who already had the cane raised, and he slashed down into the centre of her cheeks.

"Aaaaaaaaarrgghh! Ow! Ow! Nooooooooooooo! Fucking arseholes! Shit! Bugger! Fuck!" was the response that fifth strike garnered as Emily started to sob in clear distress.

Sara released one hand to stroke her face. "Come on, sweetheart, you must stop the swearing. You are doing really well, just focus on the counting and getting this over with."

Once more Emily took a deep breath as the initial pain receded.

"Oh my, oh my. Five, sirs, thank you, sirs. I am sorry for my foul language, sirs."

Jamie took careful aim at the strip of skin still unmarked by the wood at the top of her crack and swung the cane with great accuracy to land on the taut vulnerable surface. To the surprise of no one this sent Emily over the edge and there was nothing Sara could do to hold her as she fought to release her hands, grasping her bottom cheeks her legs akimbo as she fell to the floor. She screamed in anguish, tears streaming down her face, distraught and distressed.

"No, no, no, no, no," she wailed.

The professor waited, holding his hand aloft to indicate to the others that he was prepared to allow her recovery time.

"Oh shit, oh fuck, oh shit, arseholes, arseholes, arseholes!" Emily unwisely bleated away with profanities before belatedly remembering the previous repercussions of her foul language.

"Oh no, I am sorry about my language, sir, I am trying not to swear so much, sir, but it hurts so much. Oh. Oh. Oh my, that's six, sirs, thank you both, sirs, thank you, thank you." She wittered and was clearly struggling so for once, so the professor decided to be merciful.

"I think maybe an essay on the use of bad language, its place in society, when it may be appropriate and in what company. Yes, that could be entertaining. Let's have one thousand words by first thing Monday morning delivered to me personally at, shall we say, 8am my dear!"

Emily's relief was obvious, although Stones noted that the fire was still in her eyes and suspected that the rebellious part of this headstrong young lady wanted to tell him where he could put his thoughts on her use of swear words.

However she confined herself to, "Yes sir, of course sir, 8 o'clock Monday morning with a thousand-word essay, sir. Thank you, sir. I know I have a potty mouth, sir, and I really ought to have learnt to control it by now, shouldn't I?"

This earned her a smile from Stones in acknowledgement, before he asked Sara and Jamie to secure her over the main punishment desk for the second half of her caning.

"Well stretched over, make sure her thighs are forced apart by the mound, legs well apart to open her buttocks properly. Make sure she pouts those vaginal lips up at you and gives you a nice view of her anus. We always want our ladies to give us a nice floral display of their blossoms to look at whilst we perform our mundane but necessary tasks. Ha, ha, ha! Celia, just check those luscious lips to ensure that there is no seepage. I would like to make sure that we are not causing her any excitement or entertainment before we proceed."

As sheer horror formed on Emily's face, her mouth dropping open and a lovely pinkish hue spreading all round her neck, she gripped the desk legs tightly as she suffered the indignation of Celia's hands parting her thigh completely. Stones watched in amusement as

Emily fought her instincts to give Celia a piece of her mind, whilst he noted the discreet licking of her lips as Celia ran her fingers along the length of Emily's vaginal slit. He enjoyed tempting Celia like this, he knew full well from his sexual adventures with her over the years, that she had inclinations towards bisexuality and that Emily's looks, gorgeous body and spirit would appeal to her base instincts. However, she followed his instructions and stood away from the tense student.

"All good, Professor Stones. No dribbling from her pussy, I think maybe the severity and seriousness of the punishment has actually hit home."

"Excellent, Porter, now don't spare her feelings, repeat the six exactly as before. Let's see a nice second layer on top of the first and lay them on quickly this time, no respite. Let's hear this scoundrel roar, Porter!"

Sara took position in front of Emily, grabbing her distraught and defeated face. "Concentrate on breathing through the pain and counting the strokes," she implored her, turning to the professor. "No need for her to count out loud presumably, sir?"

"Oh no, she won't have time or probably the ability," he laughed heartily, nodding to Jamie.

Jamie gently tapped the cane against Emily's quivering buttocks, prolonging the torturous anticipation for her, tapping harder and harder as she tensed then he suddenly raised the cane high and brought it down with real pace and force. Thwack! Thwack! Thwack! Thwack! Thwack! Thwack! For five seconds, Emily's world seemed to freeze as she experienced torment and agony like never before, just before the final slash of the cane she began a full-throttled scream that filled the room.

Sara grasped the girl's frantically shaking head hard. "It's over, it's done, sweetheart. Take a deep breath in and hold it, now slowly release it, breathe through the pain, Emily. Better thank them for your caning as soon as you can speak without swearing," she finished, pinching the girl's cheek to keep her attention.

"Naaaaarrrrrr, f-f-f-f-flippety flippety flip," was Emily's response, as tears flooded down her face, she did her best to heed Sara's advice. "Yah! Yah! Yowsie! Oh God. Thank you both for my c-c-caning, sirs, oh. Ow! Ow! Ooooeeer!"

The professor and Celia moved in to inspect.

"Wow, impressive targeting, Porter, lovely straight lines and these welts are getting more raised by the second." Celia ran her fingers up and down Emily's bruising and almost lacerated cheeks.

Emily could hardly not be aware of the fingers gently probing her buttocks but this imposition was evidently nothing to what she was experiencing. A feeling of total loss of control and dignity became second nature in this room of dread and punishment for the college's errant students.

"Up you stand for us, girl. Now I am sure that all you really want to do is to plunge your roaring bottom into a bucketful of ice but you have been promised the thick strap to finish off. I hope you recall the sting and after-burn just from the one lash that I applied previously, my dear?" Stones' words seemed to snap Emily back into full consciousness and her sobbing ceased immediately.

From her expression as she turned to face him he could see that she did, apprehension and despair written all over her face as her mouth opened and closed as she failed to form any coherent form of response.

"I'll have a bit of pity though. Unbuckle her, Porter, good job, and sit her in the bidet please Sara, the ice should have melted enough to accommodate this naughty bottom by now." His hand stroked her throbbing cheeks tenderly as Jamie unhooked her and Sara led her into the bathroom.

While Emily was enjoying some relief out of sight, Stones went across to her jacket and found her mobile still recording. He switched it off and slipped it into his pocket.

"I'm a little disappointed that she didn't come clean about this, she's a clear submissive albeit with an attitude and I would have thought her willingness to please me and earn my favour would have broken through her fear of young Zoe and her cohorts. Pity, but I suspect it takes something to make her give anyone up, sadly for her, young Georgina isn't made of the same stern stuff that she is. Let's have the table down and strap her up in the most demeaning position on her back. We will use the pulley process to have her spread legs up above her shoulders, bottom in the air and see if she wants to tell us the story of her mobile. Then, I may give her a hint that all is not well. She's a bright young thing, let's see if she figures it out."

Jamie went to the cupboard indicated and got out the professor's pride and joy, the specially adapted massage table with its attachments and strap system ready for Emily's return. Meanwhile the professor was listening to the beginning of Emily's recording and looking very self-satisfied.

Celia was keeping an eye out in the bathroom, where Emily was sitting with her backside planted firmly in the bidet bowl just savouring the ice water calming her inflamed cheeks, all thoughts of retaining any element of self-respect long gone. A couple of minutes later Sara wrapped a bath towel around her shoulders and wiped her face gently with a flannel.

"You're almost there, sweetie, just be obedient, polite and honest from now on and you will be out of here in no time and this will become just a memory," Sara said dispassionately. Stones had placed

Celia in earshot of the bathroom both to keep Emily unaware of his activity back in the main room but also to ensure that Sara did not succumb to temptation and take pity and warn Emily that that her secret task had been blow wide open. Stones felt he had chosen well in recruiting Sara into the punishment process but was always aware that others found it harder to distance themselves from the pain and despair he inflicted on his victims. All members of staff were employed on the clear understanding that they approved and supported the principles of corporal punishment, whilst the implication of repercussions if they did not, generally required no further comment or reminders.

"Right, Sara, get the young rascal back in here. I've got a thick heavy strap that has an appointment with a very naughty girl's bottom," the professor's voice boomed out, intending to send a chill through Emily to match the ice-frozen sensation of her cooled derriere.

Sara towelled Emily dry before leading her back into the room, her bottom still smarting and the welts raised and sore but much relieved by the freezing water. Emily's eyes widening in horror as she saw the contraption awaiting her. Her terrified look rather warmed his heart.

"Oh no, what is this?"

"This, my dear child, is a device that keeps you still and perfectly positioned for a very harsh punishment whilst also making you present yourself in the most demeaning and humiliating fashion. What fun, eh?" he chortled.

To his delight Emily started trembling in fright as Sara and Celia walked her across to the padded table with its ominous hanging belts, buckles, cuffs and chains.

"Oh my god, it's the massage table from hell," said Emily as her gallows sense of humour again came to the fore. Her eyes widened as she took in the thick strap in Jamie's hand and she visibly shuddered. As Stones had intimated, that memory of the one stroke fully revealed on the look she directed at the potent implement. He imagined that she was remembering the long-lasting burning sensation that the strap was renowned for producing that followed the fearsome initial impact slap. Her defeat was apparent and she acquiesced in silence as Jamie came forward to help bind her into position. Emily allowed Jamie to lay her down on her back flat on the table, flinching and closing her eyes firmly as Sara and Celia took a leg apiece at opposite sides of the table, spreading her totally and pulling her bottom off the support into the air, as they harnessed her ankles stretched above her shoulders. Emily grimaced as she opened her eyes to stare straight into the professor's as he stood between her wide-open legs. Celia then raised her head to give it cushioned support so that Emily's forward view was of her own pussy displayed wide open directly at eye level, her bottom presented in its full glory.

With Stones directly staring deep into her eyes, Emily was obviously prompted into a moment of revelation and blurted out, "Sir, Professor, sir, I've done something bad and I need to tell you about it! Oh God, I'm sorry but I don't know what to do, I've got myself in a bit of a pickle, sir."

"Not sure if you might be a tad too late with your news, young lady," said the professor enigmatically. "Might you be referring to this?"

Emily looked up in horror as the professor pulled her phone out of his pocket.

"Oh no, you knew, how... Oh Georgie, Georgie, Georgie. I should has have known."

Stones kept his hypnotic gaze fixed to her eyes. "You are clearly in even more trouble now, Miss Govan, so let's hear it from the horse's mouth from start to finish. As you now realise, a tad too late sadly, we have a certain amount of knowledge so I'd suggest that you keep to the truth. Honesty now will be a small saving grace for you."

Emily let out a heavy sigh. Stones had enjoyed his mind games with Emily and with the look of her misery and defeat written all over her face he hoped that she would realise that she should not persist in any further attempts to outwit him. He had second guessed her continually, had seemed able to read her thoughts, had always been one step ahead of her, had humiliated her, had demeaned her and had completely mastered her. Yet he could still sense a certain amount of adoration from her, either regardless or perhaps because of that.

A miserable and downcast Emily told her story, she left nothing out even as she stumbled red-faced over the words to describe how she spanked herself as she masturbated. Her audience listened respectively in quiet admiration as she opened up completely and honestly, they would know full well that he would have to take action against her regardless of how regretful and ashamed she plainly was. Stones hoped she appreciated, as she came to the end of her tale, how ridiculous the situation was, addressing senior staff of the College whilst spread-eagled naked, tied up and peering through her legs over her pussy!

She finished her tale mournfully, her misery complete.

"I am so sorry, sir, I really didn't want to have to do this but taking on the Seven Sisters as a first year just didn't seem to be sensible policy."

"Oh Emily, you have such little faith. I will break them apart, piece by piece, I promise you that every one of those little hussies will be in this room eventually, buck naked, backsides afire, crying their little hearts out, begging for forgiveness with their dignity on the floor and their self-respect in tatters."

Emily smiled, her faith in him apparently restored by those words. He was quick to wipe that moment of pleasure off her face.

"Nice to see that lovely grin on your face, Emily, in a minute Porter will make it a distant memory by way of the strap. So you like to spank your own bottom whilst imagining someone else doing so then? Self-gratification is all very well, young lady, I have no actual issue with you bringing yourself off in private or using fingers, artificial penises, vibrators or whatever comes to hand on or in your vagina, I am sure that you are an inventive debaucher, but masturbating prior to attending for a thrashing puts you in an interesting category, do you not think?"

The grin had long gone from Emily's face as the professor yet again ensured that he stripped her bare of any sense of worth. Intended to shame her beyond what she would have thought possible, as the occupants of the room all rather smirked or sniggered in enjoyment at his description of her bedroom antics.

"Oh God, yes sir, I can't really explain it, sir. I think it was just a release for the apprehension and fear as I waited for the time to tick around."

The professor just smiled at her.

"Nice try Emily but I think we all know exactly what was going on. Being naked and defenceless, humiliated and spanked over my knee turned you on to such a degree that you couldn't keep your eager little fingers out of your pants or your hands off your bottom. I am correct, aren't I dear? You are required to answer."

Emily took a breath. "Yes sir, you are correct, sir. I am such a slut. I am sorry to have been such a disappointment to you, sir."

At Stones' nod, Jamie stepped forward.

"Right, Porter, time to make young Emily's bottom sing once more. She may enjoy masturbating and playing with herself while fantasising about having her bottom spanked but I very much doubt she'll be pleasuring herself thinking back on her strapping. Give her the promised six for now, I need to think exactly what punishment would be appropriate for someone who has disappointed me so much, tried to breach the rules of the Code of Discipline and was quite prepared to betray her mentor and protector. Very disappointing, Emily, and I know you will wish for me to punish you appropriately for your deception and treachery."

He nodded towards Jamie who moved into position took aim and swung the strap at the shame-faced Emily's exposed and unprotected buttocks. Mesmerised by his words, her face bright red with shame, Emily was silent for a split second, until the strap struck home and her attention became much focused.

"Aaaarrrgggghhhh!" she screamed. A pause then, "Nyyaah! Fuck! Fuck! Noooooooooooooo!" and again as the second blow landed. "Yowsee!"

Jamie waited for Emily to fight through the first pain barrier before applying stroke number three to her already inflamed cheeks. Sara moved forward and grasped Emily's face to hold the girl's thrashing head as tears started to stream down her face as she panted noisily, the pain from her bottom registering. Jamie waited until the girl's bottom finished its reaction to the first three strikes and both he and the professor moved closer to study the smarting buttocks reddening almost to a purple hue before their eyes.

"A little pause, as unlike the sharper bite of the cane, the strap is more of a spreading sting. We will allow her to fully appreciate its wondrous effect for a moment. Then we will have these next strokes placed on top of the first three please, Porter."

135

Emily sobbed loudly, tightening her stricken cheeks in anticipation of the pain to come as she saw the strap raised high. The sound of the contact echoed around the room as Emily's body bucked in response before the screams she released filled the room in a cacophony of tortured noise. Jamie laid the fifth stroke right across the middle of her cheeks before taking careful aim with the final stroke, targeting the tight stretched vulnerable skin at the top of her bottom crack. Whop! The sixth stroke landed, causing Emily to jolt so much that the table would have crashed to the ground bar the fixings holding it against the wall.

"Yaaaaaaaaaaaaah! Fuck it! Naaaaarr! Ow, ow, ow, oh my arse, oh, oh, oh."

Celia moved her chair over and sat between Emily's legs looking at the throbbing flaps of her pussy and the rapidly opening and closing arsehole that was twitching in the shock and pain of the extraordinary sensations.

"Of course that should be your thrashing over but as you have seen fit to act in a way that is clearly underhand and treacherous I have no choice but to add a coup de grace to your ordeal. Jamie, please hand me the knotted whip."

The professor took the wicked implement from Jamie and smacked it into his hand. It was a small whip with a thick leather handle with its single lash featured with knots every few centimetres. As Emily gradually recovered from the initial impact of the strap's wicked sting she looked aghast with horror at the professor standing aside her looking down and back at her exposed parts.

"One stroke, Emily, one will be enough I can assure you. I use this extreme punishment rarely due to the fact that it is so very painful but I believe, Emily, that you must receive this so that you understand how seriously you have misbehaved. You do accept that his must be done, I presume?" He dangled the whip so that three of the knots lay on her sex lips while another nestled into the crater of her anus.

"Oh God, I am so sorry sir, oh please, oh no sir, you surely are not going to whip my pussy, sir? Oh sir, it would hurt so much, sir." She looked beseechingly at him forlornly before grimacing and continuing in total submission. "Yes sir, of course, you absolutely must do this sir, I am so sorry that I betrayed you sir, thank you sir. Whip me please."

"Well said, young lady, indeed I will, although I doubt you will be feeling quite so full of bravado in a minute."

He raised the whip just to his shoulder and then, with his eyes fixed intensely and steadfastly on her exposed cracks, he flashed the whip down to land expertly as he had intended. The knotted leather landed full down her vaginal crack with the two knots at the tip flicking around and landing in her bottom crack, one nestling into the crevice presenting her arsehole. Emily's eyes bulged open and then she howled and howled as the pain hit home, her eyes rolling in her head to the point whereby Stones thought that she might possibly faint. He doubted that Emily possible could have imagined the searing sensation of the knotted leather's effect on such vulnerable and sensitive body parts. Her back lifted clear off the table as far as her restraints and fastenings allowed, before crashing down as she twisted and bucked in her abandonment and agony. For two minutes she mewed and thrashed about as much as she was able.

Celia moved forward to place her hands on Emily's parted inner thighs and blew onto the girl's reddening vagina.

"Oh you poor girl, look at your poor fanny, oh I wish I could kiss you better. Your fanny is so lovely, God I so want to kiss you better."

Seemingly transfixed by the vision of the suffering girl's open moist sex lips so close to her face, Celia either didn't hear or chose not to hear the professor's warning voice. "Careful, Senior Tutor, careful now."

Fort a moment time stood still and Stones watched as Celia appeared to win an internal struggle and her face edged slightly away from the swollen and throbbing pussy before her. However Emily's voice then cut into the tension hanging in the room.

"Yes, yes. God please yes, do it. Yes, yes, yes, yes, pleeeassse."

Stones could see Celia's attempt at being surreptitious as she leaned forward, presumably to block his view, as two fingers gently stroked Emily's open vagina. In response to Emily's plea, Celia dipped her head and ran her tongue lightly down the length of the exposed reddened crack before her, licking up and down before continuing to the tight crinkled entrance beneath, wet kissing Emily's arsehole and then working back along her vagina to the hard nub of the clitoris amongst the wet folds. She slipped her tongue into the honeyed interior of the pink lush entrance and lapped at the flowing juices as Emily rotated her hips as best she was able. Blissfully unaware of the movement behind her as Stones ushered Sara and Jamie from the room, Celia was sucking on Emily's pubic hairs, moulding the swollen lips with her tongue and fingering and kneading the furry quim expertly. Settling into a steady movement with her tongue, one hand reached up to tweak and pinch an erect nipple, the other slipped down to her arsehole where she teased the opening to the dark hole, lightly caressing the delicate crinkled flesh that surrounded the entrance.

Emily cried out in ecstasy as she gave into a thundering climax that convulsed through her body.

"Yaaaaaaaah!" as she came for a second time before slumping sated in her bindings.

Stones watched dispassionately as Celia raised her head triumphantly before the reality of what she had just done showed in the look of panic that crossed her features, and she spun round to see him sitting a few feet away watching her intensely.

"W-where are Jamie and Sarah?" she asked, mixed juices dribbling from her mouth, realising that the three of them were now alone.

"Well they didn't say goodbye as you seemed preoccupied but I decided to send them home to save them witnessing your shame beyond what they saw before leaving. Firstly you need to go and wash your face so that Emily's vaginal fluids are not obscenely dribbling down your chin while you talk to me and then we need to decide what to do about your act of the highest level of gross misconduct."

Celia gulped; Stones knew that she would be all too aware that she had got carried away and broken the golden rule concerning sexual and emotional relationships between staff and students. That it was an instant dismissal offence and that Stones had rigidly enforced it in the past was not something that Celia could plead ignorance of, having been present to witness painful interviews in the past. With her lust and passion draining away, Celia visibly shrank seeing the cold fury in Stones' eyes, her anxiety and fear becoming so evident.

"Shit, Edward, sorry, I mean Professor. I got carried away, didn't I? Oh God, I'm so, so sorry."

"I believe I told you to go to the bathroom." His voice was like ice.

As Celia scuttled into the bathroom he glanced over at the exhausted dozing Emily, who seemed totally unaware that the population of the room had diminished and that the atmosphere had changed completely. He gently unbuckled her bindings, laid her legs and arms gently down and turned her over to lie on her front, allowing him to inspect the damage to her buttocks. He collected an ice pack, wrapped it in a towel and eased it between the legs, correctly surmising that the result of knotted whiplash was a very sore vagina still throbbing away.

"Shhh, my dear, you doze for a minute and then we'll have a little chat before you go back to face our friend Zoe."

He was tenderly stroking her hair while he considered his next moves, when a red-faced Celia crept back into the room.

"Professor, I can only apologise," she said quietly, surreptitiously and rather anxiously glancing over at Emily.

"A bit late to be concerned at what Emily is taking in, aren't you?" Stones said scornfully.

"Can we gloss over this? She's not aware that I've committed the big 'no-no' in the college, is she?" The professor's scowling face warned her that this was probably not the best line of defence.

"One, Emily is not in the best state of mind at the moment but she is a bright girl and will probably think it through. Two, students are under our care and protection, therefore any sexual exploitative behaviour is considered tantamount to abuse. You know that we walk a thin line here in that respect. Three, you have a position of authority in this college which you have just abused. Four, if Emily was to go public on this we could be on the end of a public disgrace that even with my power, money, influence and contacts I might struggle to contain. Five, this will go to the Mistress and your fate will be in our hands assuming that I can smooth over any issue with Emily. Six, if we didn't go back years and didn't share the history we do, you would already be out on your scrawny arse. The fate of that scrawny arse is now going to rest with me so if I was you I'd get out and leave it to me to start trying to sort things out."

He paused for a moment. "Why in damnation are you still here, Senior Tutor? Get out, get out, get out!" Celia fled, now in tears.

Stones watched her scurry out of his back door with mixed emotions. He was satisfied that she was fully aware that she had crossed a line and her self-recriminations would be to the fore, but only time would tell if Emily felt in any way that she had been unfairly taken advantage of. He doubted it due to the circumstances. Why would Emily ever want anyone to know about her disgraceful conduct on the night that had brought about her presence in the room? However, he needed to play things cautiously and he had also to consider what he would tell the Mistress. They had an agreement that he would not fail to honour, in that he kept no secrets from her regarding anything at all that could have repercussions for the college. The three of them had been colleagues and friends for many years and the Mistress was well aware of the complex relationship between him and Celia, but the staff-student relationship protocol was set in stone and this was a massive breach. The professor knew that Celia's imprudent behaviour was going to infuriate the Mistress and she would want her pound of flesh but he was also confident that he could convince her to allow him to determine Celia's fate as a disciplinary issue.

First things first though, young Emily had betrayed him, whatever credit her very late confession merited. Still, he very much needed her onside as far as dealing with Celia went, and he wanted to float an idea past her anyway.

"How are your personal bits and pieces now, Emily, still feeling the effects?"

"Oh, yes sir. Wow, I don't suppose you get many repeat offenders after receiving that piece of evil just there? My god, that stung, sir. My bum feels like I got beaten with a hot poker then had it shoved up my arse. Oops, language, Emily, sorry sir."

He laughed at the girl's inability not to resort to crudities. "Don't forget that essay I set you to write, it can easily be tasked at double the wording originally proposed if you wish to continue with your potty-mouth antics."

"No sir, sorry sir, I will try my hardest to limit my profanities in future, sir."

"We will see. Now we need to have a little chat and I think you probably deserve a little treat after such a severe thrashing."

Setting himself beside her prone body, Stones opened up his tub of very expensive and luxurious soothing cream and began to gently rub the contents into Emily's bright red buttocks. He was not at all surprised to find that she immediately raised her flanks and parted her legs to allow him full access. A sigh of pleasure was her only heard response though.

"Well I know that this generation seems to be convinced that swearwords are powerless and not offensive, but I do believe in maintaining certain standards, as you know, and I do think it would be to your benefit if you could curtail this liberal use of foul language. But let's talk about the phone recording for young Zoe and her nasty little friends shall we? So, from what you said earlier, you can expect her and at least some of the others to be waiting for your return. Well I think we need to start looking at how we are going to outflank this little lot. Emily, as you are hardly likely to be a fan or acolyte of these trumped-up little buggers, I think you may be amenable to assist in my plot to help bring them down?" He raised an eyebrow quizzically.

"Oh sir, yes please, sir. Nothing would give me more pleasure. What do you want me to do and when can I start, please?" Emily's turned her neck to face him, a face that had come to life, lit up with enthusiasm, her gleeful expression being the perfect response to his proposal.

"Excellent. To start with, you will return to your room as expected with your mobile. They will soon realise that it is of no use and you need to act well enough to convince them that this is news to you and that you had nothing to do with it. They are not to be aware that we know what their game is and that very much includes your friend with the loose tongue, Miss Fawcett-Jones. Go along with whatever they suggest, the more they think of you as someone to trust the more you can help me." The professor could see by her wide, sparkling eyes and rather triumphant grin that she totally engaged in this opportunity to find favour with him.

"I also think that you may be the person I want to stand in for Sara occasionally, particularly for first-year students, facing disciplinary charges, when we start the New Year. I need someone on hand, a friendly face from their peer group to encourage them to face up to punishments ordained and help them through the process. I think someone who has taken a severe thrashing would be perfect and I do see a lot of promise in you, my dear, that perhaps just needs moulding a little."

He could see that Emily was struggling to contain her excitement. "I suggest you save masturbating until after Zoe and her cohorts have left you and you are alone in your bed, young lady." Emily's face quickly reddened, he always knew what she was thinking! That and the fact that her pussy lips were showing distinct signs of moisture!

"Sorry sir, but sir, is there anything I can do for you, sir?" she spoke in her most coquettish voice.

Stones decided that he needed to remind her of the vulnerability of her position. "Well young lady, you have already given yourself rather shamelessly to the Senior Tutor who is in a lot of trouble as she has breached college rules on fraternization with students. Are you now trying to tempt me to do the same?"

"Sir, no, I don't want to cause any problems. I rather obviously didn't mind what the Senior Tutor did, it was lovely. Please can we just forget that happened, sir?"

"Right, Emily, on your feet and bend over, there's a good girl. There is something I need to do."

Emily took a swallow as she look at the professor but then turned and complied. Without being asked further, she opened her legs wide and grasped her ankles. A long shuddering sigh escaped her lips and her whole body trembled.

"Now, it's not a beating so hands on your bottom and I will need those cheeks wide apart."

An audible gulp came from Emily and, as he had anticipated, Stones guessed that she was under the impression that he was about to enter her anally. Enjoying the moment and never one to miss an opportunity to press home an advantage he deliberately adjusted his clothing quite noisily to enhance her expectation.

"Sir, do you mind if I ask you to use plenty of lubricant, please?" queried Emily, her voice very much a tremor. "You are going to fuck me up the arse now, sir, aren't you?"

"Eyes front! Cheeks wide open now, come on, pull those globes apart," was all the response she received.

Her deep breaths gave away the sense of panic she attempted to quell, he was pleased that he had instilled this sense of obedience and compliance but had no intention of carrying out any sexual act with one of the students himself.

"So you are ready for anal intercourse are you, young lady? Is this something you often partake of, young lady?"

"Oh no, sir, most certainly not, sir, I have never done it there. But I have always assumed that I would one day, sir, so I am happy for you to be the first, sir, if you wish. Will you please be careful, sir?" she added rather shyly but with a little of the earlier confidence coming back into her voice now.

"Oh Emily, I think you may just have let your over-active imagination run havoc, I'm afraid. Stand up and turn around."

Emily's expression as she faced the professor was a definition of astonishment. Her jaw dropped, her eyes widened, her mouth formed a perfect circle until her lips pursed as realisation hit her. Stones smiled knowingly at her. His mastery of the mind games he employed with his malefactors gave him no end of satisfaction and keeping them off-balance was a hobby he thoroughly enjoyed.

He pulled a chair over and sat down before her, tapping his lap. Emily immediately draped herself over his knees and raised her buttocks and spread her leg, toes and fingers against the floor. Stones stroked her still reddened cheeks gently and was not in the least surprised that Emily's response was to open her legs even wider and push her bottom up towards him.

Stones did wonder what her creative mind had come up with for her to have not only just made the assumption that she was now to be spanked but presumably to have justified it for him without any words having indicated any such intention.

"What, pray my charming young cherub, would you like me to do now?" he teased.

"Oh you must spank me, sir, spank this naughty girl hard please, sir." She then added very quietly, "I love you, sir."

The professor smiled; his suspicions had been aroused and he had been expecting and waiting to hear those very words.

"Oh Emily, I really just wanted to see what state your poor vagina and anus were in after the lash, to see if it needed any treatment at all, but everything looks OK. So, no anal intercourse and no spanking, just you proving what a subservient soul you have been turned into. We have made progress, haven't we? You don't love me, you silly girl, you just love being dominated by me. Let's start our little proposed partnership and see how things go, shall we?"

Stones had an ulterior motive, of course. Much as he had faith that Emily would never divulge the details of Celia's inappropriate actions, he wanted to ensure that Emily would never have a reason to want anyone to view the CCTV evidence. He was fairly certain that Emily would not wish anyone to witness her blatant display and invitation regarding her anal area!

Emily would know that yet again she had been truly played but she seemed to revel in anything he delivered. Things had not worked out too bad.

"Right-oh! It is time for you to return to face up to Zoe. Get yourself dressed, get things clear in your mind and see how it goes. Deliver that essay to me on Monday please, when I expect a full report on your follow-up chat this evening. You need to write me a little thank-you note for your correction as well, I imagine that you will find that no problem?"

Emily smiled at him and scurried to dress herself although Stones was well aware of the sense of disappointment that the ordeal was over that emanated from her. He imagined that she may have more concerns and worries about how things would go with Zoe than she was about being thrashed and humiliated once more at his hands. She left the room minutes later, her face a picture that illustrated a mind awhirl with many conflicting thoughts and emotions.

CHAPTER 8

IN WHICH EMILY FACES

THE SEVEN SISTERS

The main thought that was flying around in Emily's head was the memory of holding her bum cheeks apart and inviting a very senior and elderly academic to damn well take her up the arse! Of everything that had occurred over the last two hours that was the only incident that she felt regretful about and sincerely hoped that he wouldn't think anything less of her because she had behaved in such a whorish manner. God, she had told him she loved him and had basically turned into some kind of kinky sex slave. *Seriously Em,* she admonished herself, *what is wrong with you?*

Meanwhile back in her rooms, her flatmate Georgina was not enjoying the best of times. For two hours she had had to endure the company of all of the Seven Sisters; Zoe Taylor, Hilary Brook-Boyde, Charlotte Penfold, Helen Smythe, Saffron Cambridge, Miranda Booth and Chloe Tang. They were not best pleased with the length of time Emily had taken to return so had turned their ire on Georgina. It had been bad enough having to take the girls through her humiliating punishment step-by-step, omitting her act of treachery towards them and hoping upon hope that Emily hadn't found out that she had grassed her up and would be coming back with a thirst for revenge. Georgina was aware of the repercussions if the gang discovered her exposure of their plans to the professor and was now very aware of the position she had put Emily in, albeit her fears were mainly, and unashamedly, self-centred.

Things had moved on out of her control, however, and now she was lying stark naked on the coffee table surrounded by the seven students while they studied her beaten, swollen and marked flanks. They were amusing themselves picking up the differing marks of the crop and the cane as well as a few stray finger prints around the edges of her cheeks and thighs. Continually prodding and poking the blistered buttocks, Georgina was suffering the same mortification as when she had been displayed in the professor's room, although thankfully so far they were not as practised in the art of ignominy as the professor had with his quest for the total humiliation of his victims.

"Well, I don't know about you girls," opined Hilary Brook-Boyde, "but I am rather looking forward to inspecting young Emily's arse when she gets back. This is absolutely fascinating and is it me or is this quite a turn-on, ladies?"

There was a lot of nodding in agreement around the room albeit Miranda Booth didn't look quite as enthusiastic as she ran her fingertips tentatively, and with a fearful expression on her face, along the ridges of Georgina's purple-coloured welts.

As Emily approached her rooms she was still thinking back in amazement at how she had just behaved. She knew that she was now past feeling any sense of shame or embarrassment in front of Professor Stones. She appreciated that she had allowed herself to quite willingly be mastered and the buzz that she was feeling inside was like no other sensation or emotion she had felt before. Her bottom was indeed very sore and was going to bruise badly but she realised that she had never before felt as good as she did now.

"Oh finally, where the fuck have you been? Have you been fucking the old git? We've been waiting ages," fired Hilary at Emily as she entered the room.

"Well excuse me for being beaten for hours and subjected to the most painful and humiliating experience of my life!" snapped back Emily, determined to pull the subterfuge off successfully and deciding to take an aggressively defensive response.

"Here's the fucking phone," she said, handing it over to Chloe, the nearest of the gang to her.

The students immediately lost interest in Emily and Georgina and huddled together around Chloe as she found the recording and pressed play. Georgina took her opportunity to slip off the table and went across to hug Emily.

"Was it truly awful?" Georgina asked in hushed tones.

"Yes Georgie, it was. A frigging awful nightmare actually. It's not just my backside that's burning either." Emily was hoping Georgie wasn't going to blurt out that she had told the professor about the recording plan but wasn't surprised at her reluctance in admitting her part in grassing Emily up.

They were interrupted by some choice expressions as it became apparent to the seven that what had been recorded was the professor's choice of music with just a muffled rumbling in the background.

"It's all going to be like this, isn't it? For fuck's sake." Zoe had taken the mobile and was fast forwarding to try the recording at various points.

"What a fucking waste of time. Shit! Shit! Shit! Wasn't such a bright idea after all, shit! It appears that you failed us, Emily. Well don't think you can slide off and have that wank you're probably desperate for yet. Let's see exactly how much you were punished?"

Emily took a breath. The reality was that things were actually going well; these supercool, kids-in-the-know, no-one puts-one-over-on-us, superior-minded Seven Sisters didn't seem to suspect any complicity from Emily or Georgina so far. She could hardly have qualms about showing her bum to this bunch of girls considering what she had been made to put on display in front of the professor's gathering, on the whole it might give them good for thought to see what a college thrashing resulted in.

"Jesus, I've only just put my bloody clothes back on but if you really want to see what I've had done to me, then who am I to deny you ladies?" *Careful Em,* she thought. *Don't do anything out of character when things are so going in the right direction.*

She sighed melodramatically. "OK, let's get this over with, the sooner you've had a look the sooner I can put some more soothing cream on and go to bed for a rest."

"Oh, I think we can help you with the soothing cream, my dear, although I guess from that remark that dirty old Professor Stones has already been giving you some relief, eh?" interjected Hilary, who was in danger of coming across to the others as being a little bit too keen on getting other females naked. A quick glance between some of the others suggested that the thought was indeed occurring to them.

"Yes, apparently the old boy likes to have his wrinkled creamy hands all over your arse when he's finished torturing you, the bloody pervert!" Emily quickly slipped off her clothing and rather dramatically turned her back away from the girls until she pulled down her knickers and then spun and bent, pointing her rather disfigured, blighted and marred buttocks at the group.

There was a long shocked silence from the group and a desolate sob from Georgina.

Chloe spoke first and directed her remarks to Georgina.

150

"Oi, lightweight, why don't you put your knickers back on and get those other bottles of wine you've got taking space up in your fridge? From now on you are just the help, now fuck off!"

Georgina scuttled off to do her bidding, eager not to rile these fearsome women any further.

"That's desecration to mutilate a bottom as beautiful as yours. The man is an evil monster who needs locking up!" This was Miranda, desperate to re-establish her position in the group, aware that her reluctance to partake in anything that seemed too sexually motivated earlier may have been noted by the others.

"No, not locking up, but taking down. Let's really make taking the old bastard down our target, ladies. This will be to our project for next year, we are going to give this fucking pervert his just desserts!" Zoe thundered.

"Look, let's calm down. I transgressed, I got caught, and then I compounded matters by swearing and insulting him. I got a bloody good thrashing and it bloody hurt like fuck, but it's my bottom, not yours, and it's my fight, not yours. If anyone is taking him down it'll be me, so can you lot just butt right out?" Emily hoped her attempt to gain their respect and admiration by taking them on in this manner would not blow up in her face, but she knew that this confrontational mode was one that suited her personality and therefore should be more believable to the glaring students that she was facing up to.

"Hmmmmm, maybe you can be useful, Emily, we may need a sacrificial lamb but we've got Georgina for that! On the other hand you've got a lot of bottle and that might be what's needed here." Hilary's words were gold dust to Emily although there was a notable sob from Georgina in acknowledgement of possible future woes.

"Lie down on the table, Emily, and let's see if we can soothe some of the nasty pain away while you tell us about the whole experience from start to finish." Hilary was already smearing moisturiser into her hands and was clearly eager to get her hands on Emily's beaten bottom as she faked some reluctance, hesitating and creating the impression that she was a bit unsure. She sighed rather dramatically and laid herself down, leaving herself at their disposal.

Hilary's touch was gentle and sensual as she smoothed the moisturiser into Emily's cheeks and down her upper legs. Emily found her legs parting to allow her fingers to run inside her legs and then subtly sweep up so that her fingertips brushed ever so lightly and supposedly accidentally against her pussy lips before resuming their soothing work on her savaged bottom. The others leant in, gently running their fingers along the length of the most prominent welts, and soon Emily was struggling to concentrate on telling a version of her ordeal that would satisfy her present company as well as keeping them sympathetic rather than suspicious.

"Oh my, I think someone's enjoying our attention ladies, look here, someone is dribbling from their coozie. The cooze does ooze!" Zoe revelled in Emily's discomfort, her fingers now pulling Emily's bottom cheeks apart to expose her wet pussy to all of them.

"Would you like us to toss you off?" Zoe was clearly not going to let Emily off the hook now so she bowed her head submissively to let them continue.

"Georgina, bring us the contents of your sex drawer," Charlotte barked at the completely horrified roommate who was almost frozen to the spot at the turn things had taken.

"What, what? I don't know what you mean," Georgina stammered, red-faced in response.

"Oh, don't you? Well let's both of us go and have a look, shall we?"

Charlotte grabbed Georgina by her hair and dragged her into her room, the crashing and banging sounds rather suggesting that Charlotte wasn't taking too much care in her search.

"Wait, wait, I've got something here," Georgina cracking as Charlotte started to trash her room.

"Oh yes, that'll do nicely. Look girls, our dirty little liar Georgina has got a nice big black cock." Charlotte walked back into the room with a large battery-powered vibrator, very thick and indeed, very black.

"Right," said Zoe, "I think we need to get our little Georgie's pants back down for a spanking to teach her not to lie to us. Who wants to help me while some of you put Emily out of her misery with this nice thick cock? That's, of course, if Hilary doesn't mind and can manage to extract her fingers from Emily's fanny?"

Emily almost screamed out to object as Hilary snatched her fingers away from the gentle strokes that she was applying to her wet slit.

"Oops, sorry, being a bit greedy, aren't I? But as you have all gathered I am finding this young lady a bit of a turn-on. Why don't we move her into the bedroom where we can all be more comfortable?" Hilary decided to come clean on what was already apparent to the others. But several pairs of eyes were betraying their alcohol-fuelled lust by now and Hilary was not alone in being visibly enthusiastic for further sexual activity with the two beautiful blondes.

As Zoe and Charlotte grabbed Georgina, Emily found herself being lifted by five pairs of hands and carried through and placed on her back on her bed.

"This seems an unfair split," pointed out Saffron, another, like Hilary, rather betraying that she was finding the intimacy of the situation was bringing forth feelings that she had never experienced, or allowed herself to be subjected to, before.

Known as an uber-cool inclusive and very politically correct woman, Saffron, who was placing pillows behind Emily's head presumably to prop her up so that she would have a good view of whatever transpired, looked decidedly uncomfortable with the ways things had progressed. Emily espied a look of pure longing being directed back towards Georgina as Charlotte removed her roommate's knickers in the doorway to the dining room. The sight of Emily's naked body may have stirred her further but she was clearly struggling with the realisation of how sexually attracted she was to Georgina and she didn't look at all happy with this division of labour that was denying her an opportunity to get her hands properly on Georgina's body under the cover of the proposed spanking. Suddenly all bets seemed to be off as far as restraint was concerned with all members of the group seeming hell bound on taking this opportunity to gorge their hidden desires on these two supposedly unwilling but so far reasonably compliant victims.

Zoe had manoeuvred Georgina over her lap whilst Charlotte had pulled off a cushion cover and was deftly tying the petite blonde's hands together. Saffron had taken the initiative and moved to face Georgina who was still alternating between whining that this so wasn't fair and begging for her tormentors to please not do this.

"Hush now, baby," cooed Saffron, "it'll only be a little old bottom spanking and then your aunties will kiss and stroke you better."

Georgina, mistakenly thinking she was gaining an ally, turned her attention to Saffron with her pleading.

"Oh Saffron please, I didn't mean to tell lies, I was just embarrassed about the thingy…"

"The thingy is a great big black cock, Georgie sweetheart, a great big black cock that little Georgie likes ramming up her tight little cunt, doesn't she?" Saffron immediately dispelled any hopes

Georgina had that she might be there as an ally.

Georgina blanched at the word used so crudely and openly. However her thoughts were soon distracted as Zoe had now got her arranged to her liking and, with a loud crack, delivered a hard smack to the centre of the girl's exposed buttocks.

"Ow, ow, ow, no, no, no." Georgie's entreaties served no purpose as Charlotte then leaned over to deliver her own blow right on top of Zoe's targeted area.

"Waaaaaaah!" Georgina cried out.

"Now I believe Saffron asked you a question. If you don't answer truthfully when we ask you questions then the spanking is going to last a long time," Zoe practically barked at Georgina whose face showed her real fear.

"Oh dear, oh bugger, what do you want me to say, Zoe?"

Zoe spanked her left cheek hard three more times and Charlotte followed suit on her right.

"No! Fuck! Yaaaaaaar! Oh fuck, it hurts, oh, oh, oh. Black cock. Yes, yes, yes. I love putting the black cock in my little girl."

As the three laughed, Saffron gave her a quick kiss on the mouth.

"Priceless, my little princess, your 'little girl', really? Give her some more, ladies. I am sure Georgina can tell us in a bit more detail why she likes her toy so much."

Zoe and Charlotte slapped her together for several seconds, concentrating on one cheek each, her bottom now returning to the deep red of earlier reducing Georgina to almost a continuous wail of complaint.

"Oh, up my you know, cunt, in my cunt, in and out of my cunt, my cunt, my cunt, my pussy, my fanny, big cock, black cock. Fuck! Fuck! Stop! Stop! Fuck! Oh please no more, no more." Yelling frantically, desperately trying to say the words that would appease her captors, Georgina was writhing and twisting, her discomfort heightened as the blows landed on an already very sore pair of beaten buttocks.

"Good girl, good girl. Your aunties are pleased with you now so maybe some cream on those tender little globes and a nice kiss from Auntie Saffron," Saffron whispered as the other two paused in their administrations to her bottom.

Georgina's resistance broken, Saffron tenderly ran her tongue over Georgina's lips before, meeting no resistance, she slipped it into her open mouth. Charlotte having discovered some expensive moisturiser was massaging Georgina's smarting cheeks while Zoe had slipped one hand under her body to play with a nipple, her other tentatively moving under Georgina's stomach to rest against her mons.

The three now worked in tandem as they seduced the no longer resisting or apparently unwilling Georgina. It would be several minutes before Georgina was to climax with a long drawn-out groan of pure pleasure and abandon as Zoe skilfully used her fingers on the conquered and subdued girl's clitoris, Charlotte used the moisturiser to slip a fingertip into her arsehole while Saffron kissed her deeply and continuously with her fingers squeezing gently on Georgina's taut nipples.

Simultaneously Emily had decided that she was going to put up absolutely no resistance at all. She was spread-eagled on her bed as Hilary stroked her hair, and placed fluttering little kisses all over her face, as she murmured endearments and words of encouragement into her ear. Miranda, by far the slowest on the uptake and easily the least forward and enthusiastic for this particular activity, found herself designated Emily's breasts by default as Helen and Chloe had eagerly, and with a greed in their eyes, bagged Emily's lower regions for their own. One on each side of her lower half, they snuggled up very close and intimate on the spacious bed. Both girls had hooked a leg apiece over their shoulders and Emily could just about make out that there were different sets of fingers stroking and probing at her most intimate parts. Not that she in any sort of state to really think logically, strategically or otherwise as the four banes had now become four very attentive, gentle and decidedly carnal lovers. Her mind was awhirl as all her pleasure points were kissed, sucked, stroked, nipped and licked simultaneously in various ways and to differing degrees. The gentle kisses and wistful flicks of Hilary's tongue as she held her head tenderly and manoeuvred her body to block out a sightline to the others suggested to Emily that she could actually be fantasising that she and Emily were alone. But Hilary's administrations were in reality the least in Emily's thoughts as what the other three were doing to her so sensitive places was sending ripples of ecstatic pleasure throughout her whole being. Miranda's sucking of one of her nipples while lightly rubbing the other one between forefinger and thumb had given her erections of the like that she had never experienced before; no man had ever sucked her breasts so well and with such longing and attentiveness. Slightly reluctant participant she may have been to begin with, but Miranda knew exactly how she liked her own breasts to be treated by a lover and was certainly finding that Emily appreciated the thought and execution. Far be it for Emily to worry herself as to whether or not Miranda was getting as much out of the experience as she was!

Meanwhile Chloe had, after some hesitation, begun flicking her tongue into Emily's arse crack. Emily had no idea as to the sexual history of her subjugators but suspected that the levels of enthusiasm indicated that what was happening was more likely to be an experience that had been a hot topic point rather than as actual reality. As Chloe's tongue again flicked against her arsehole and

Helen's lips finally searched out and found Emily's hardened clitoris, she had to resist screaming at them to encourage slightly firmer treatment. She had had some experience of analingus with a guy, had no reservations about the taboo activity, and quite bluntly wanted Chloe to stop tickling and start rimming her properly! At last a wet fingertip explored her opening and Emily wantonly pushed down, causing the bobbing heads of Chloe and Helen to knock together.

"I think our little plaything is rather eager, don't you Hel?" Chloe's voice broke through Emily's lustful thinking.

"Let's see how many fingers she likes up her pussy, shall we?" With that, Helen quite forcefully thrust three fingers into Emily's sodden vaginal opening.

"A thumb up the bum then," said Chloe, as she quickly put her thumb to her mouth before pushing into Emily's back passage with no finesse or tenderness whatsoever.

Emily realised that the atmosphere had become more charged and certainly more punitive as Miranda now bit down on a nipple and only Hilary maintained the more loving and subtle application. As Emily squirmed under Chloe's violent penetration of her bottom, Hilary hushed her whilst throwing a clearly disapproving look at her three accomplices.

"I wouldn't hurt you like that, my precious." Hilary's whispered words seeped into her consciousness as Emily realised, with a detachment that surprised her, that here was the possible weak link in the group if she was to do the professor's bidding.

"I know you wouldn't, my love," she responded, forcing her tongue deep into Hilary's mouth. It occurred to Emily then that this was just like acting a part in one of the theatrical productions she had excelled at during her time at her sixth-form college. Maybe not a part in a play ever likely to be on stage anywhere soon, she pondered, but nonetheless she had always found acting relatively simple and this was just acting in bed with your clothes off, she thought wickedly. Her amusement became plain to Hilary who mistook it for pleasure and joint admiration.

"Just forget about them," she said quietly, "imagine it's my fingers and mouth all over your body." Hilary locked eyes with Emily, almost causing her to laugh out loud in her face but she managed to restrict herself to a big grin.

In fact there had been little shared sexual activity previously with the seven but only once with a female who had been so terrified of what they were going to do with her, once they had forced her to strip off, that they had had found the experience fairly disappointing and a bit of a damp squib on a sexual level. There had been some fun with a couple of rather timid and meek lads that they had snared, without too much effort or resistance from their victims, for fun and sexual experimentation. But that had generally been one-sided action with passive participants easily led and easily intimated into being sworn to secrecy with the promise of further exploits in the future.

Emily had become used to Chloe's thumb plunging in and out of her arsehole, albeit she wished that she would think to apply a little more lubrication, her anus still being tender from the lash, but knew she would be best advised to stay silent. Miranda's pinching and biting of her breasts was becoming a little more than she would have preferred and betrayed much more of an inclination to hurt rather than arouse. However Helen's expert frigging, Emily could tell that most of her hand was now pumping her pussy vigorously, was proving a good enough distraction and she could feel her forthcoming climax building inside. Suddenly Emily felt a tongue lap at her clitoris and realised that Helen had dipped her head again to allow her mouth to encircle Emily's clitoris and began the nodding movement to facilitate her lips sucking, sliding and stimulating Emily's erect walnut.

Emily's quickening breathing and guttural moans indicated to the four that her orgasm was approaching and as one they all increased the intensity of their activities. Thrusting upwards, Emily was now lost in her moment; she had offered little resistance to the sustained sexual assault but knew that she was undoubtedly being taken to a passionate and erotic heaven by their manipulations. This was no gang bang, this was no rape, she had accepted her fate then gone along with it and now she was getting her reward.

"Yes, yes, yes, yes. Fuck! Uh, uh, uh. Aaaaarggghh!" She climaxed noisily, thrusting herself up into Helen's face and slamming down into Chloe, frantically frigging her arsehole with her thumb, Helen having now replaced her hand with her tongue deep inside of her pussy as the women virtually wrestled to maintain their positions against Emily's writhing body.

"Yes girl, you go. Go on, my baby, let it flow. Oooh yes girl, how does that feel? God I wish I had my tongue up you, darling," Hilary whispered to her and cradled her face as Emily lost herself in the throes of a long breath-taking glorious orgasm.

"I wish it was you too, Hilary. God I wish your naked body was on top of mine now." Quietly responding as she came down from her climax, Emily was no longer sure if she was playing a role but she still had the sense to know that Hilary's feelings expressed were real and could be incredibly useful to her. Emily had no compunction with deceiving any of her tormentors, her resolve to assist the professor in bringing these bullies to account was firm and she was quite prepared to lie and scheme with the best of them.

Emily's words were only heard by Hilary and she beamed in excitement to hear that response. She was so obviously incredibly aroused by the situation but Emily could see in her eyes that she was crazy with envy and resentment that her mates were having what she so wanted just for herself. *She definitely wants me for herself,* thought Emily, *and the stupid girl thinks the feeling is reciprocated.*

"Shhh, darling, me too. But it must be our secret. Don't say anything the others could hear." Emily pulled her into her web just that little step more. "It will be me and you soon, my love."

Result! thought Emily. *Maybe this little task of the professor's is going to be a fair bit of fun.* For a moment she had a fleeting regretful thought over whether or not Hilary might not be deserving of the double-cross that she was planning but those thoughts were soon wiped from her mind as Hilary reverted to type and her allegiance to her gang came to the fore.

"I think she's having far too much fun. Let's shove Georgie's black vibrator up her hole, to see if she is slutty enough to take a nice big thick one. Maybe we should ram it up her bum afterwards, eh girls? What fun!"

Emily took the reminder that Hilary was determined that her weakness of heart towards Emily was not going to be apparent to her buddies at face value. She accepted that Hilary needed to make clear who came first as regards where her loyalties lay but put a wounded look on her face to continue the pretence. Emily hoped that the second part of her proposal was just an idle threat, as within seconds Hilary had got hold of the huge appendage and just shoved it up her pussy. Even with an already well-oiled pussy, it was not the most pleasurable experience and Emily certainly was not keen on having that action repeated up her backside.

Once the vibrator was turned on and the plastic cock started moving and rotating inside of her, Emily could feel new sensations as it touched sensitive internal places that she didn't even know she had.

Hilary's finger sneaked around to rub her clitoris while Miranda had resumed her strange love affair with her breasts.

To her astonishment the situation took a different turn as Chloe lifted her skirt, positioned the writhing Emily flat on her back, pulled her tiny briefs aside and sat astride Emily's face presenting her pussy to Emily's mouth.

"Don't see why you should all the fun, bitch, now lick my fanny." Chloe didn't sound like she was prepared to have a discussion on whether this was optional or not and Emily breathed in her secret scent before deftly running her tongue up and down the freely tendered moist lips above her face. As Chloe tugged her knickers clear of her pussy, Emily was treated to the closest she'd ever been to another female's arsehole and whilst her tongue automatically licked at Chloe's vagina as she slid it over her mouth, Emily found herself fascinated by the fluttering of the opening and closing of the narrow little anal slit above her eyes and nose. She certainly decided that Chloe definitely possessed a more attractive arsehole in comparison to the male versions she had been exposed to, tighter and far more compact with tiny little patches of wrinkled and folded skin encased in dark valley walls leading to the winking hole with its nutty peppery scent merging with the sweeter smell of the girl's pussy juices.

Hilary was now accelerating her thrusting of the vibrator and Emily, although not finding it unpleasant, now that her vagina had stretched to accept its size, was definitely more turned on by what Chloe was doing and the taste and sensation of the girl's pussy. She thought it prudent to fake an orgasm before Hilary's quite forceful actions made her sore and she was conscious from the noises, coming from Chloe above her, indicating the Chinese girl was not far off climaxing on her face.

"Yes! Yes, yes, yes," she gurgled into Chloe's fanny, hoping that, muffled by her nether regions the sound accompanied by the bucking of her hips and helped in her play-acting by Miranda now twisting and pinching her nipples in response to what she thought was Emily's orgasm, would be convincing enough.

The redundant Helen had now decided that Chloe's excitement would be enhanced by having a hairbrush smacked against her bottom as she rode Emily's face to her climax and now the room had a cacophony of wildly dissimilar noises. Chloe was beginning to groan, Hilary was murmuring obscenities to herself as she rammed the vibrator into Emily and Miranda had a hand inside her own knickers and was trying discreetly to masturbate quietly but moaning audibly as she did so with her mouth reattached to one of Emily's nipples. Meanwhile Helen was accompanying each slap of the hairbrush with a loud grunt of effort and self-congratulatory shouts as Chloe reached for her orgasm and came loudly, smearing Emily's face with her juices before snatching the hairbrush from Helen's hand and flinging it across the room.

"Enough!" she said, with clear threat in her tone. "That one's going to be banked firmly in my memory, Helen. I'll expect no resistance when I want to return the favour."

Helen paled at her words and Emily wondered what had seemed to have been unleashed in each of them. With Chloe's juices smeared over her face, Emily wasn't surprised when Hilary snaked up her body, replacing the satisfied Chloe. Hilary's tongue licked the other's juices off and her hand started pumping the vibrator faster inside of her fanny. Once more Emily could feel that she was going to come and began to thrust against Hilary's body.

"Fuck me, Hilary, fuck me," she all but commanded as her hand searched down and slid between Hilary's legs to discover the sodden gusset of her knickers. Her fingers slipped inside and she thrust a finger into her pussy and a knuckle firmly against her mound. The two began to work in tandem oblivious to the gathering crowd around them. Hilary's climax was sudden, violent and loud; its impact on Emily was enough to bring her to yet another orgasm and she bit into Hilary's shoulder as her body shuddered in ecstasy and the two bodies firmly locked together in their mutual exhilaration and pleasure, sweat, saliva and sexual juices merging as the two became one for a sublime moment.

Silence hung over the room for a while before the two parted and cast guilty and suspicious looks at each other before noting the atmosphere and realising that they had a full audience around them. The presence of Saffron, Charlotte and Zoe indicated that their episode with Georgina had also reached a finish. Hilary helped Emily up, albeit with a look that didn't bode well. Emily suspected that she was not too impressed that the others had witnessed her being frigged off, but how Hilary thought that was her fault was really beyond belief! Hilary led her behind the others, with a sharp tug on the arm, out of the room as the entourage moved through to the living room. The scene that greeted them was Georgina's still naked and smarting bottom raised high as she knelt on the table, obediently keeping the position that she had been left in.

"Good girl, Georgina," said Zoe as she moved to stroke Georgina's reddened cheeks. She fluttered her fingers in front of the trembling blonde's face. "My fingers still smell of your fanny juice. Lick them clean, there's a dear."

"Yes, good point Zoe. Mine have been up her arse so they'll need a clean next." Saffron positioned herself alongside Zoe, enjoying the stricken look on Georgina's face as she sucked on Zoe's sweeter-tasting fingers before reluctantly taking Saffron's more pungent digits into her mouth.

"Jolly good, all went very well in the end. A good time was had by all. Don't you agree, Emily?" taunted Chloe.

As Emily hesitated to answer, her pride still refusing to let her buckle down completely to the group's bidding, Hilary grabbed her by the neck and forced her head down towards Georgina's exposed bottom.

"Yes she bloody well did, and now she wants to show us all how much she likes licking pussy, don't you, my little dyke whore." Hilary used both hands to force Emily's face against Georgina's bottom, her friends enjoying the spectacle and recognising Hilary's little display of envy decided to give her a hand. Georgina, who had instinctively started to move away from her roommate's face suddenly found it rammed into her arse crack, her shoulders grasped by Chloe and seeing the raised eyebrows of Charlotte was enough to instil fear of the reprisals that her look was suggesting.

Emily took a smothered breath, stiffened her resolve and hoped that a quick show of acquiescence would be enough to satisfy her audience. She tentatively licked Georgina's slit, nestling her nose into the crack of her friend's bottom, surprised by what at one time would have seemed to her an obscene and disgusting act had suddenly become a repetitive experience. Mechanically lapping away at the folds of Georgina's pussy, Emily listened to the laughter and ribald taunts and comments of the seven and hoped and prayed that she would be around when these bitches met their match and got their comeuppance.

"Shut your eyes, ladies, and pretend that you're enjoying yourselves. Smile, Georgina darling. Remember you're having fun, Emily certainly is, I think that she has developed quite a taste for pussy." Zoe's vindictive tone brooked no argument and got immediate compliance from two young ladies who so did not want their time extended or further, harsher punishment applied.

Neither of them became aware that they had been released and that they were no longer being held in place; it wasn't until the muffled laughter raised suspicion that Georgina snapped open her eyes. To her horror she saw that although Chloe was standing close by, the others had all withdrawn to allow Chloe space to manoeuvre around the table while she had clearly filmed Emily and Georgina's activity on her mobile.

"Oh no, no, no fucking hell!" screamed Georgina, alerting Emily in the process. "She's fucking filmed us, Em, oh no, no, no." Clearly distraught, Georgina started to get up before Zoe firmly held her back in place.

"You're such a piece of work." Emily was thinking fast and trying desperately to quell her raising temper. "Just fucking delete it, please Chloe. I'll suck whatever I have to but please fucking well delete it."

Chloe smiled at them both.

"You will continue your little session please. Georgina, bottom up properly now, show Emily the ingredients of the recipe. Emily please continue with your quim-licking, arsehole-sniffing duties. We will see just how obedient you two can be. This little film will be the price of your silence, that's how it works, you keep absolutely schtum about today and so will we. I'm sure you understand. Basically you're at our beck and call now, sweethearts, so please be good girlies and do as you are told. Call it insurance, my dears, we can't have you telling tales out of school now, can we?"

Emily sighed and resigned herself to the situation immediately; there obviously was no grounds for debate on this one. She just hoped that she could give the professor the dirt that he could use against them so that he somehow find a way of deleting that footage before Chloe shared it or it went public. She nuzzled Georgina's pussy lips and returned her nose, as instructed, to her arse crack. Emily had found herself fascinated by the different taste of Georgina's pussy and in all honesty was perfectly happy to return to her pussy lapping duties that had been so rudely interrupted. She licked and slurped away obediently at the wet engorged lips before her. She breathed in the scent of her friend's arsehole whilst finding herself noting and contemplating the differences in the makeup of the close-up views she had now been subjected to of female arseholes. Her mind also considered how this unexpected sexual activity had allowed both girls to virtually forget their sore and swollen buttocks. *Not thoughts I have ever considered before,* she mused ruefully.

"That's enough, slut." Emily's head was yanked away from Georgina by Hilary who had a fistful of her hair wrapped in her hand. Emily and Georgina rose to their feet, their joint venture sitting slightly uncomfortable across both their faces, blushes of embarrassment colouring their cheeks, their eyes patently avoiding each other's.

"Yes, ladies, time's up. That Josie should be coming back from where we banished her to any moment. I think it's time for us to leave these two to their own devices. They'll probably be fucking one another throughout the night now!" A smiling Zoe rose, signalling to the others that she was calling the evening to a close.

The Seven Sisters got their things together and prepared to leave the flat, Hilary holding back to quickly kiss Emily on the lips while whispering.

"No more pussy for you, Emily, I want to be the one you concentrate those particular skills on in the future."

More loudly she said, "She definitely tastes of pussy. What a tart!" Laughing along with her cohorts in a thinly disguised attempt to hide her lust for Emily, Hilary pinched Emily's bottom harshly, embedding her sharp fingernails in the damaged flesh, as she pulled away.

Emily was amazed at her ability to switch personality and roles but smiled back at her as though she'd be waiting with bated breath for her call. *Bitch,* she thought, *you'll get yours soon.* However, the words that came out of her mouth were decidedly at odds with that sentiment!

"Yes, Hilary, oh yes please. I'll be waiting to hear from you, my love."

As they left, they turned back as one, raised a finger to their lips and then ran it across their throats in a clearly practised manoeuvre to emphasise the danger facing their victims if they did not keep their mouths shut.

When Josie walked back into the room a few minutes later, she was greeted by a dishevelled flat and two naked roommates with clearly marked red bottoms, just cuddling each other on the sofa, recovering from their ordeal, but strangely reluctant to discuss any details.

Later alone in her bed, Emily reviewed her day and her hands began to stray as her thoughts became sexually charged. The discussion, with Professor Stones, after her ordeal had been a total shock but one that she was delighted about. The idea of being present for some punishment sessions excited her far too much, she thought, and the idea of being the professor's helper was making her heart race. *What is wrong with me?* she asked herself, as she remembered her aroused feelings as the professor's hands roamed over her cheeks with the silky lotion. She began to imagine what it would be like to cuddle and stroke a young student while the professor's hand came down again and again on a fresh cute little bottom. Emily thought back to the moments after she had experienced the searing pain of the knotted lash striking her pussy and arsehole, she had thought that she had found a place between heaven and hell.

Her rude memories, still so fresh, were enough for her juices to once more moisten between her thighs as she remembered the moment leading to the glorious touch of the Senior Tutor's fingers. Although she had still been very conscious of the full stinging from the cane and the strap they had dulled somewhat and she now realised that there was a long journey to go before you reached the sort of pain that the knotted lash had unleashed on her most tender areas! But how quickly that pain had been turned into something much more erotic and sexual as Celia had applied her tongue to her stricken parts so delicately. Her fingers had worked wonderfully on her throbbing lips that had quickly moistened and been so receptive to her stimulation. The older woman had licked and sucked her clitoris skilfully and in a way that Emily had not experienced before, seeming to know just when and where to be delicate as well as exactly at what point to apply more pressure. The wondrous sensation as her tongue travelled down to moisten her arsehole before heading back into her longing pussy. Celia's tongue had flicked around and into her wet folds, whist she had her nipple twisted to exert just the right amount of painful pleasure. Her virginal anal chamber had opened automatically to embrace a probing wet fingertip, a fingertip she had felt herself encouraging into her wanton arsehole. A fingertip that belonged to one the most senior and revered members of the austere college's staff, for goodness' sake! Emily's silky blonde triangle had been soaked by a mixture of Celia's saliva and her own flowing juices as the experienced tongue and lips had sucked at the erect little clitoris then slid down into the lower folds; her pussy juices had seemed to become an endless stream oozing out of her saturated vagina. As the liquids merged and dribbled down into her arse crack she had been so aware of Celia's finger scooping it up and into her anal opening, before she had fully embedded the finger deep into her arsehole. Under Celia's expert tuition Emily had built quickly to a state of orgasm and the culmination of a supreme woman-to-woman sexual experience. When Celia had finally fastened her lips around her clitoris and sucked it fervently she had felt as though her head would explode. As her body bucked and tremors ran through it, Celia had tightened the hold on her nipple, twisting and pinching, while the finger in her arsehole had slid to its full extent in that most private of orifices. As she relived those moments her fingers fluttered at great speed as she approached her fourth orgasm of the day and she grasped the pillow and bit down hard. The shuddering sensation of her climax spread through her as she writhed and groaned, her body spasms violent and uncontrolled, her sweat-covered face glistening and she gasped and moaned in pleasure once more.

Exhausted, she had soon drifted off into a deep sleep, her battered body still sore and stinging, but her lust and desire sated and satisfied as never before.

CHAPTER 9

YISHEN IS RE-INTRODUCED

TO THE BAMBOO

As agreed, Jamie arrived at the professor's rooms an hour before Yishen was due, the two men enjoying a cup of coffee each as they sat watching the film of Yishen's last appearance. As per usual, the professor had captured the scene perfectly with his state-of-the-art CCTV equipment, every angle covered and expertly edited as was his wont. Jamie had read the transcript but his wide eyes and open mouth betrayed that he still found the Chinese girl's complete acquiescence, as she recounted her tale of woe, quite shocking to watch.

"I get the impression that there will not be much in the way of resistance from this young lady," he ventured.

"Absolutely, I would be most surprised if this punishment isn't a thing of pure beauty. A delightful and very pleasant girl with an air of innocent sweetness that most lasses totally fail to possess. Charming, absolutely charming, I am very much looking forward to her defrocking and seeing her over my knees, Porter," mulled the professor, smiling, who often used Jamie's nomenclature from BADS, the fetish club that he had actively recruited Jamie to.

"I think that I should begin her punishment to start with, I will spank and paddle her and you should deliver the important second stage. I am leaning towards the cat-of-nine-tails followed by a choice of the bamboo canes I have bought in especially. This is a thrashing that I feel we should very much enjoy and treasure, but let us not count our chickens, Porter, things don't always work out as they appear to promise. We must remember that this is going to be a very difficult ordeal and experience for the poor girl, who, I believe, does have a purity of spirit not possessed by most of the rascals whose bottoms have been seen to in this room over the years."

The professor confirmed that that both the College Senior Tutor, Celia, and the Graduates Administrator, Sara, would be joining the gathering. "Probably going to come as a surprise to young Yishen though, I am pretty sure that she thinks this is going to be a private party for just the two of us." This pronouncement caused him much mirth. "However I am a firm believer that the humiliation of a rogue is as much part of the punishment and the rehabilitation as the physical pain of a good flogging."

The buzzer went and Stones checked his screen and then facilitated the entry of Celia and Sara.

"Celia, Sara, welcome back. All recovered from yesterday's activities, nice to have our little gang back together again so soon." He chuckled and the four of them reminisced about the previous evening for a few minutes, with Celia struggling to stay composed as she waited for the professor to take her to task. She had been fretting all night and had run through many possible scenarios and outcomes that her act of lust and madness had created. She was well aware that she had, in theory at least, committed an act of gross misconduct and as such she could have been dismissed from her position, a position she had worked diligently towards and held for many years and a position that she hoped to hold for a good few more.

"OK people, let's quickly clarify things before the star turn arrives. I will lead, orchestrate and kick things off and then Porter will give the second and more serious part of the thrashing. Sara will give support and guidance to our miscreant and Celia is here to ensure fair play all round. Anyone have any questions?"

No one had, and the conversation moved on to general University chit chat and the four relaxed in a manner quite incongruous with what was about to occur. A few seconds before her allotted time the buzzer sounded and Stones allowed Yishen entry into the room. As expected, she was clearly confused and taken aback to face an audience of four but gathered herself and greeted the professor formally.

"Good evening Professor, Senior Tutor, Lady and Sir. I am here to receive my punishment as agreed, sir. Am I too early? Are you busy, sir? Should I wait outside or come back later, sir?" she proffered, possibly more in hope than expectation.

"No, most certainly not. Good evening to you. Please strip off your dress and shoes and then place your hands on your head, Yishen. The Senior Tutor is here to ensure that the punishment is just and fair, she likes to oversee our most serious cases, so that a true and fair record is acknowledged and seen to be conducted in a just manner for the record."

Yishen's expression became glummer as the glimmer of hope drained from her face. She took a deep breath and began to undress.

"This is Porter, he is here to carry out some of your punishment," continued the professor.

Yishen paused, frozen in the act of placing her folded dress on a chair, her perfectly formed back facing them, framed resplendently by her gleaming white matching underwear. Just a single word escaped from her lips.

"But…"

"Oh yes indeed, Yishen. Due to my ongoing years I find I don't have quite the strength and stamina to do myself justice when giving my wretched delinquents their just desserts so I have enlisted Porter here to assist me. Porter will be able to give you a much harder thrashing and perhaps more likely match your father's strength in punishing you. I do hope that you don't have a problem with my decision?"

"Oh no sir, it will be an honour sir," Yishen rather whimpered, glancing shyly at Jamie, a look of concern crossing her features as she took in his rather impressive physique, which certainly indicated the possibility that he might have a stronger arm than the almost equally as well built, but decidedly older, professor.

Stones smiled in response; this young lady really had the most delightful good manners, he thought. Jamie assessed the beautiful Chinese girl before him trying to maintain some sort of professional detachment but his cock was already starting to strain at his trousers and he was definitely pleased he had gone for a reasonably thick, loose-fitting pair for this. The girl's knicker-clad bottom looked divine, he thought, concerned that he might struggle to concentrate on his main duty to come.

"Right-oh, young lady, let's make a start on giving you this punishment that you have requested due to your disgraceful behaviour the other day. The others have all reviewed the history of why we are here and, in truth, are all rather horrified and disgusted at your performance."

As always the professor had chosen his words to instil maximum shame and humiliation and was pleased to see the deep blush that spread across the errant student's face and the top of her chest.

"I think we need to get started to see if we can get the colour of your bottom cheeks to match that of your face. Take off your brassiere now, there's no reason why a disgrace such as you should be afforded any rights to modesty, is there Yishen?"

"No sir, yes sir, I mean whatever is your command, sir." She removed her bra, releasing beautiful full breasts, showing very distinct and dark nipples, and stood before him in just her panties.

"I'll have the pleasure of removing your knickers once you are in place. So come along now, child, place yourself across my knees and I will warm your bottom up to get us underway."

Again she took a deep breath, before she gracefully draped herself over his knees in the classic spanking position. Stones stroked the bottom before him appreciating the truly fine form with her trim ankles, slender calves and legs, her blemish-free back and an absolutely divine-looking bottom. He hesitated, relishing the moment before sliding the panties down her legs.

There was a silence in the room as the occupants all gazed upon the perfect specimen now fully exposed. Her bottom was perfection, her cheeks like hand-crafted porcelain orbs, split in perfect symmetry by her crack. As she parted her legs obeying Stones' flicking fingers, he was entranced as he exposed her perfectly formed anus, a shimmering star surrounded by small, silky, fine dark hairs. Stones exchanged glances with his companions, all were as spellbound as he with the classic and pure beauty of the naked girl before them. He motioned for Sara to take her allotted place, kneeling before Yishen and taking the girl's head in her hands.

"Perfect, Sara, if you could keep her as calm as required and wipe away any liquid, tears or other unpleasantness from her face whilst I deliver the punishment she has requested." Stones paused, stroking her cheeks slowly, pulling one cheek aside and then the other, knowing that his victim would be aware of the exposure of her arsehole and lower pussy lips, to increase the sense of powerlessness and self-awareness of the position his offenders had found themselves in. Shame and humiliation were his favourite companions to the pain and discomfort that he delivered, he afforded them equal footing and would brook no argument against his stance. He always liked to reiterate that these formal punishment sessions were by the student's request, always ensuring that the point was well made for his recordings and documentation. "Almost seems a pity to put a blot on the landscape of such perfection. Your bottom is divine, young lady, but needs must as the devil drives and as such I need to do this." With those words his hand cracked down hard on her right buttock, immediately followed by a similar crack on her left.

Yishen lay prostrate and uncomplaining as his arm rose and fell again and again, her cheeks turning first pink and then red, and then redder still as the spanks first numbered double figures and then a minute later went past 100. Not a murmur passed her lips as the professor finished the hand spanking a few moment later, gently stroking the glowing flesh and enjoying the feel of her pristine cheeks.

"Well done Yishen, taken like a trooper. Porter, please fetch me the round-ended wooden paddle from my cabinet. Time to inflict some serious harm, I feel. It should help this young lady in her quest for some sense of closure and satisfaction in paying her just dues. Sara, please attend to Yishen, you know the position. Right, now young lady, let's see what you are made of. I will now deliver fifty strokes with the paddle before we move on to the most serious part of your punishment."

From the head bowed motionless close to the carpeted floor came a steady and clear response.

"Yes sir, thank you Professor Stones. It is my honour to be punished thus for my shame."

Stones could only admire the girl's fortitude and courage; she had received one hundred and fifty full-blooded spanks on her bare bottom without making a sound. Normally he liked a challenge but could not really foresee any pleasure in breaking this girl down, however he knew it had to be done and was confident that there would be no other result.

Taking the paddle from Jamie he immediately brought it crashing down on the parted crack of Yishen's globes and then followed it with five more quick strokes on the same spot, with still no reaction from the supplicant below him. He continued to beat the same spot for fifteen further strokes. Changing strategy, he then methodically placed the next thirty alternating from one buttock to the other, hitting the same sore point on each cheek over and over again. His reward was a quiet weeping from his victim and the sight of Sara leaning in to hold her head, which at last was starting to bob up and down as the pain level reached a point where she was now struggling to bear the punishment with the stout-heartedness and resolve she had clearly been determined to do.

Stones was pleased to see Yishen's buttocks now jiggling and clenching as she tried to shake away some of the intense pain caused by the expert and intense application of the paddle. As he put aside the implement on completion of the fifty-stroke ordeal, she let loose a long sob and her whole body shuddered.

"Right, up with you and bend over and touch your toes, legs apart and let us have a look at the results so far," snarled Stones, determined to rattle the stoicism of the courageous student. Much as he admired her resolve and compliance, her dignity was far too intact for the professor to feel that her punishment was being truly effective. Although he had to admit he admired the girl tremendously and did believe that her errant behaviour was a one-off, it was important, in his eyes, that she succumbed utterly and completely to his will and reached the point where her resolve and will were truly defeated. In his eyes there was just not an acceptable outcome other than a crushed dignity, a broken spirit, utter humiliation, accepted shame and plentiful tears.

The Senior Tutor went over to the rudely displayed girl and inspected her buttocks at close quarters. "Good job, Dean, nice red rosy cheeks." She ran her hands over the girl's bottom, feeling the heat radiate from her.

"Some good marks here. Are they sore, girl? Has the professor got through to you yet?"

These were the little moments Stones cherished, adding much to his overall enjoyment. Yishen reacted with a jolt to the unfamiliar touch of another woman's fingers on her nether regions. His joy level was increased moments later as Celia allowed her fingers to flutter between Yishen's cheeks causing a complete stiffening of the supplant.

"Yes miss, truly miss, the professor has paid me the honour of thrashing me well, miss. Oh, Miss. Ooooh."

Yishen's composure finally cracked as Celia ran a finger down the girl's bottom crack to settle on her anus. Stones' smile broadened as the girl's whole body froze and her bottom tightened dramatically as she tried to move away from the unwelcome pressure of her fingertip in this most private of places.

"Naughty, naughty. Stay still, girl! I think we now know what her weak spot is, eh Professor?" smirked the Senior Tutor, applying two sharp smacks to the back of Yishen's legs, as she moved to resume her seat.

"Your turn, I believe, Porter," she continued. "I suspect that the professor would like to see if you can make this little rascal yell!"

With a nod from the professor, Jamie moved to the girl and peered at her bottom. Running his hands over her cheeks, Jamie's admiration of the beautiful bottom plain to see, the glint in his eye showing that he was eager to carry out his part of the task in hand.

"Yes indeed, well delivered and well taken, your conduct has been admirable and a pleasure to see. However I believe that the professor would now like to see whether you can take a flogging with the same resilience, before I deliver the coup de grace that has been kindly arranged for you."

Her buttocks were indeed entrancing, so rounded, so firm and, so smooth. She was like a Michelangelo statue of a Roman Goddess, thought Stones, thinking that although the thrashing was well deserved, justified and appropriate, all he really want to do was to sink to his knees and worship these wonderful orbs.

Sensing Sara move restlessly beside him he brought his mind swiftly back to the matter in hand, not before noticing the glint of what clearly looked like angry envy in her eyes, giving him a degree of satisfaction that his interpretation of her feelings towards Jamie was correct. He smiled disarmingly at her and mischievously decided to add an extra element into the mix.

"Right Sara, I have a crucial role for you now. As this wretch's bottom is quite rosy red already, I think I'll afford her a timely moment of respite in view of what's coming, so if you could please turn around and present your back to our scoundrel I think I'll have her draped over your shoulders if you think that you could cope with that?" Sara nodded and moved into position to stand in front of Yishen as Jamie, with an obvious lingering look at the divine arsehole on show, took hold of her arms and positioned her behind Sara, placing her arms over his colleague's shoulders.

"Link your hands, Yishen and Sara, if you could, now please

enfold her arms, locking her into place with yours and do your upmost to hold her still please." As Yishen was slightly taller than Sara, this position allowed Jamie to force her legs apart, whilst still keeping her head on Sara's shoulder and her back conveniently straight.

Jamie selected the cat-of-nine-tails, a wooden-handled implement covered in leather with nine black, braided suede tails. Jamie had never used this form of punishment flogger before but was well aware that it was the impact of the nine tails that lashed down individually combined with the stings of the raised knot-like braids that caused the intense stabbing pains of the lash.

Aiming high on Yishen's back he swung the cat and lashed it down hard and fast. The crack on her back resounded impressively in the room but Yishen herself remained quiet, although her whitened knuckles gave evidence that there was an increase in pressure applied as Sara found the grip around her shoulders and neck tighten as Yishen absorbed the shock of the spreading pain.

"A tickle to start then, Porter, now stop playing and remember that this is a student who has disgraced herself and this college. Flog her and flog her hard, man, I want to hear this angel scream and those angelic cheeks whipped without mercy!" The professor was clearly determined to hear audible evidence of Yishen's suffering.

Porter smiled; the two shared a glance that suggested that he was just as impressed with Yishen's strength of mind and character as well as her strong-mindedness and pluck as Stones was. Splat, splat, splat, splat, splat. Jamie covered her back in angry thin lines criss-crossing completely over the whole area. But apart from gasps of quickly drawn in or expelled air there were still no cries, squeals, begging for mercy, pleas or words of protest from the thrashed girl.

Stones held up a hand to still Jamie's onslaught and pointed at the tops of Yishen's legs. However impressed he was with her fortitude and bravery, he very much wanted to break her spirit without delay. It was not just a target but a necessity now.

"Harder and faster, Porter. No mercy, thrash her, man, thrash her!" The harsh words resounded around the room and if any of the occupants had ever doubted the hard-heartedness of the professor, those doubts were dispelled in that moment.

Changing aim, Jamie swiped hard at her lower legs, then worked quickly up her body to the high point of her legs just beneath her buttocks. Finally as the lashes cracked against the sensitive skin at the top of her legs, Yishen's body buckled and a cry escaped from her lips.

Jamie paused, his eyes meeting the professor's; the nod he received meant no words needed to be said. The sensitivity of the tops of Yishen's legs had been clearly discovered and now the true test of her spirit would begin. Jamie pulled back his arm and swung hard and true at exactly the same spot.

"Eeeee!" screamed Yishen in response as her forbearance deserted her and she finally gave in to the searing pain. The professor held up five fingers and Jamie swung quickly and as each one landed, Yishen shrieked, twisting her body, and Sara struggled to keep her upright, her weight falling more and more on her upper body as Yishen's legs lost their firm contact with the floor and kicked in protest.

"Let her down to the ground, Sara, well done, well held," said the professor, bringing the session to a halt.

"Excellent delivery, Porter. Yishen, please be so good as to crawl over to Porter's feet and thank him for flogging you so well."

Yishen, who was now in an undignified heap on the floor, sobbing loudly and clutching at the backs of her legs, failed to respond. The professor immediately got to his feet and tugged the girl up by her hair, spun her round sharply and his huge open hand came down on her bottom as he delivered a twelve-slap cascade of mighty blows.

"You naughty child, how dare you ignore me? Take that and that, I won't have disobedience in this room, you rude girl."

Yishen openly sobbing now, tried desperately to pull herself together and regain some control as the blows landed on her sore bottom.

"Sir, Professor sir. Yow, yow, yow. I am so sorry, sir. Yow, yow, sir please sir, may I thank Porter sir, now? Yow, yow please sir. Aaaaiieeoow! Sir, I beg your forgiveness for my offence and disrespect, sir. Yaaaah! Porter, sir, Yishen would like to thank you for such a fine flogging. My skin is truly on fire, I believe that you have truly beaten the badness from me, sir."

Jamie shared a smile with the professor. "Oh, I think we can do better than that, Yishen. Shall I apply the cane now, Professor?"

"Oh yes, let Yishen see what a treat I have in store for her."

Jamie went over to the professor's storeroom-cum-cupboard and walked to the back to pick up the three to four-foot-long, thick bamboo canes that he had sourced especially for Yishen's punishment.

As he brought his wicked handful of canes back into the room, Yishen's eyes widened in terror, filling with tears.

"Oh sir, I beg your forgiveness once more, sir. I feel truly repentant from my beating, sir. Oh sir, I am so ashamed of my fearfulness, sir." Her head dropped and she started to tremble.

"Oh, don't worry about being ashamed, Yishen. Shame is good for you when you have misbehaved, along with disgrace, embarrassment and humiliation. I do try to being them all to the table for my naughty girls that require improvement."

"Yes sir, indeed sir, Yishen is all of these things, sir," she responded as copious tears rolled down her face.

"OK Yishen, you are a very honest young lady, so you can tell me exactly what your father would do now?"

"Oh sir, I am sorry that I am so cowardly, sir. I am sorry sirs, madams, I am so sorry I am so worthless." Yishen was now completely distraught and the professor felt that they needed to calm her down before anything else.

"Yishen, I want you to take a break. There's a small study through there, Sara, take her through and we will let her have a moment to pull herself together." Stones indicated one of the discreet doors that led off from the main room and Sara helped the struggling student through to the small study.

"Fetch her a drink from the kitchen please, Sara, and anything you want yourself."

The professor signalled to Celia and Jamie to sit down and took a moment himself to think things through.

After a few moments he spoke. "I very rarely cull a punishment thrashing but I am reconsidering my original decision to give her twenty strokes of the bamboo. She has behaved so well, taken punishment and stood tall in apologising fully to the offended parties, no small thing to have to stand before our porters and apologise for throwing up and covering their staff area with urine! She's taken a good hiding very well and been honest and polite all through the process. I am finding it difficult to insist that she deserves quite such a severe punishment sentence and would like to hear your thoughts."

Celia took the lead. "Tricky one, Professor, as it was a disgusting exhibition by this girl. However, I agree that this is behaviour outside of what would be expected from this particular young lady, and there are times when mercy should be shown. Mistakes do happen, maybe we should err on the side of compassion and allow that she is seriously contrite and extremely unlikely to do anything like this again."

"Yes, I rather thought that you'd take that line considering your own breach of college rules yesterday." The put-down struck home as Stones stared directly into Celia's eyes. Celia blushed and averted her face away from Jamie. Her horrified look and reddening face reward in itself to Stones, who relished bringing her shame up in front of Jamie.

"Yes Celia, you may well feel embarrassed. Your behaviour yesterday has put the college at risk. Porter here is not stupid, you broke the golden rule and you will pay your dues, he needs to know that there are consequences to straying outside the strict rules we act by and that we are not playing a game for your benefit. Do you understand?"

"Yes Edward, sorry, Professor I mean, I am sorry and apologise to you, to Emily, to Sara, to Porter, to the Mistress, to everyone. I did let myself get carried away and I do accept that I will have to pay penance."

"That is to be decided, but thank you for your apology. You will have the opportunity to apologise to the Mistress, Sara and Emily later, but we need to concentrate on Yishen for the moment, Senior Tutor. Porter, what's your view?"

"I would suggest that she does need to feel the cane, Professor. It may well bring closure to what I see as her dilemma, as she does seem to need to feel that she has been appropriately punished, and in a manner that reassures her that justice has been done. The bamboo cane will hurt dreadfully but as there will be no lasting damage, I feel that a straightforward dozen of the best would be an acceptable compromise."

The professor nodded his thanks, and sat back and deliberated on the issue for a few minutes while Celia and Jamie shared a quite uncomfortable silence. Eventually he rose and went to his study where he found Yishen cuddled up in Sara's arms on a large armchair.

"It is time to come back into the room to see about bringing an end to your unfortunate episode now, Yishen. Sara, escort her through please so that she can present herself to us."

He went back into the room and arranged four chairs in semicircle, inviting his companions to take a seat. Yishen stood naked, still slightly trembling but with regained composure, before them. It was all Stones could do to stop himself applauding her as she raised her hands, clasped them on the top of her head and displayed her exquisite beauty. Her superbly formed breasts, with the deep brown nipples standing proud, were a study of such sublime elegance and grace that not to take a moment to appreciate and drink it in would have been criminal in the professor's eyes. They all took a moment to appreciate her form before the professor nonchalantly used a finger signal to direct her to turn round. The marks of her beatings so far were distinct, from her calves to her shoulders, the individual implements leaving raised marks and lines that betrayed their speciality, with the stunning bottom a carpeted scarlet centrepiece of her previously unblemished skin.

"Bend over and touch your toes. Legs apart, further girl, come on, open that crack up, come on please, you should have learnt that much surely."

Yishen quickly adjusted her erroneously chosen original stance and complied with whispered apologies. She now presented her audience with the glorious view of her rounded, firm, symmetrical buttocks parted to display her dainty little arsehole and the lower lips of her neat and perfectly formed pussy slit.

"Extraordinary how beautiful a lady's rear view can be and she certainly does set a very high standard, doesn't she?"

No one chose to answer although all three of the others sat staring in slight awe of this Asian woman and her beauty so exposed for their eyes to take in.

"Anyway," he continued. "After some thought about whether or not you have been punished enough, I have decided to come back to my earlier question."

Yishen tensed, her bottom muscles tightening rigid, her breathing quickened.

"Oh stand up, child, much as your derrière is a lovely sight, let's see your face when you speak. And you are going to speak now," he ordered.

"Yes sir, sorry sir. I do feel I have been punished sufficiently, sir, and I am truly sorry. I will never drink alcohol again, sir, and I will never shame the college again, sir. I would also like to thank you both for punishing me, sirs, so that I have been fully shown the error of my ways, but..." She stuttered to a halt.

"But..." prompted the professor.

"But sir," she took a deep breath and paused again. "Sir, my father would feel that it was his duty to cane me and it would be my duty to accept this. Please sir, I would ask that you now apply the bamboo to my bottom as agreed, sir. I would like my punishment complete please."

The respect for the student rose even higher as all four nodded in admiration for this principled young woman.

"Bend over the desk, girl," snapped the professor, returning quickly to character. "Celia, Sara please strap her down, you know the drill. Porter, prepare yourself to deliver twelve hard strokes with this cane. Each one will be counted and I expect to hear words of gratitude from you, wretch, to acknowledge our efforts to assist you in correcting your appalling behaviour." He handed the longest of the bamboos to Jamie who swished it experimentally through the air, the length of the cane creating a particular air stirring swooshing noise.

Sara knelt in front of Yishen, holding her face and whispering words of support as Celia moved round to watch.

"Yes Senior Tutor, you watch closely, you get a good view of a bamboo caning from the watcher's perspective. For now!" The professor gave her an evil smile that Celia knew was not an empty threat, she suddenly didn't feel quite so keen on watching what was about to happen.

"Porter, beat this scallywag, please, and beat her hard and true."

Yishen was now strapped securely in place and displayed fully. Her legs wide apart, her bottom raised by the carefully positioned padded mound on the desk. Jamie tapped the beautiful bottom lightly, watching the slit of an anus almost disappear to nothing as the terrified young girl tensed in anticipation of the thrashing to come. There was no hiding the coming of the bamboo as it whistled through the air and the thwack of the impact echoed around the room soon joined by a piercing scream as Yishen found no stoicism level that could hold back her reaction to the fearsome pain.

Jamie waited and watched, fascinated as the line of the strike went white, then red then slowly swelled into a ridge of deep rouge.

Comforted and encouraged by Sara, the stricken student struggled to get out the supplicant words desired. "Oh, oh, oh, one sir. Ooh, oh. Thank you, sir. It is my honour to have received such a painful stroke, sirs and madams."

Jamie took his time and it was almost twenty minutes later before he swung the cane for the twelfth time. Putting all his strength into the final swing, he applied it accurately, landing on the lower cheeks exactly where the sixth stroke had landed. The recipient's screaming, which had become louder and more desperate as the caning had progressed, was broken as the severity of the stroke rendered stunned

Yishen into silence. The ferocity of the impact seemingly freezing her vocal cords numb. Her head slumped down until the pain reached her consciousness, before she then let loose an almighty screech of pain.

Jamie stood back to admire his handiwork, the twelve accurately placed strokes having created six long, furiously purple welts raised like tramlines across her bottom.

Yishen, sobbing noisily blurted out, "Twelve, sir, oh thank you, sirs. Twelve, twelve, oh, oh, yaaa, yaaa, yaaa! Oh please, sir."

Her body racked between shudders and gasping breaths, tears cascading down her face, she struggled to find words that would signal that her torment was over.

"Thank you again, sir, I have so much pain. Please sir, I am so sorry, sir, please sir. I thank you, sirs and madams, I am so thankful you have beaten me hard such as I truly deserved, but please no more, sir." Her burbling became incomprehensible as the weeping and distress overcame her.

The professor nodded to Sara and Celia and they released the broken girl who struggled to stand up.

"There's iced water in the bidet, Sara. Ten minutes will be required to soothe the stinging and swelling, and will bring out the bruising more quickly. Then I think we can apply some cream to her poor bottom, before finally allowing her to write us a nice thank-you letter."

Ten minutes later a much calmer student was face down on the couch while Celia, at the professor's request, was gently applying soothing cream to her blistered cheeks. From the demur and timid look she gave him, Stones was aware that Celia knew that she was being tested and toyed with. He hoped that any enjoyment she would normally have been allowed in such circumstances, as she massaged the beauty's enticing and desirable, if for the moment not quite so perfect, bottom, was being somewhat curtailed.

"A word, Porter," said the professor, moving Jamie across the room and out of earshot of Celia.

"I am going to keep Celia back to deal with her rule breach yesterday, and in the circumstances I will not involve you in what is an internal personnel issue for the college to deal with. She will be subject to appropriately severe punishment but not totally of a corporal nature and this may well be delivered over an undetermined period of time. I may involve other staff members but do not feel that it would be fitting to include someone from outside the college. I hope you understand?"

"Oh absolutely, Professor, in fact I had assumed that exactly this would happen and completely understand."

The professor nodded his approval and went back to the three females. Celia and Sara were just, rather tentatively, helping an unsteady Yishen to her feet.

"Now, my girl, let's have a look and see if we have done a satisfactory job." The professor settled himself in his favourite chair, beckoning the young woman to him.

Yishen moved in front of him, as the other three gathered around his chair, automatically knowing to turn and bend over to present her beaten buttocks.

"Excellent, but legs apart please." The professor leaned in to peer at the fine detail of the angry raised welts, her bottom already turning into a kaleidoscope of colours.

"A really good job, Porter. Oh yes, the welts are well pronounced and should last days to remind young Yishen what happens when you disgrace yourself," Stones announced as he spent several seconds running his hands quite roughly over the beaten girl's exposed flanks, ignoring her intakes of breath as he touched her most intimate of places without qualm or compunction.

"I hope that your father would approve of the beating you have received, Yishen, maybe you should thank Porter properly for his fine effort. You may rise and face us now, girl."

The beaten student was finally able to stand upright and look at her persecutors, her face bright red from the blood rush of hanging her head low as well as the total shame of having the professor explore her bottom in such detail. She was a sexually inexperienced woman and it had patently been a rude awakening to have been subject to this handling from, and under the instructions of, such an eminent and important scholar. Stones knew from experience while his miscreants often became at ease with their nudity before an audience, the personal and intimate touching throughout the ritual generally disturbed them as much as the physical beating they endured. It was his intention that this would insure that the whole experience would remain very much etched in their minds.

"Mr Professor, sir, thank you very much for showing me the correct path to take to achieve my aims and aspirations at college, I will not let you down again. Mr Porter, thank you very much for my flogging, sir. It was truly earned by my disgraceful self and I thank you for beating me so hard to help me on the true path to redemption. I believe my father would be happy with my punishment and hope that I have satisfied you all in receiving it and that I have made you all pleased. It will be my honour to write as you wish, Professor, to thank you all for my just, deserved and merciful punishment."

The virtuous and contrite young woman had them all nodding in agreement and approval as Stones handed her pen and paper and indicated for her to take a seat at a desk to fulfil her final obligation.

"Just get this done quickly, and then you may dress and leave. Jamie and Sara, your work here is done, thank you. Sara, I will see you later as agreed." A wink to Sara out of Celia's sight boded badly as to what that might mean for the slightly apprehensive Senior Tutor, now that the morning's activities has been completed.

Moments later Yishen had dressed and left, bowing politely and still thanking the professor repeatedly. Stones and Celia were alone.

CHAPTER 10

IN WHICH CELIA PAYS HER DUES

Stones was in his element as Celia stood before him, trembling slightly, signs of the utmost apprehension radiating from her whole being, as she waited for the college's feared Dean of Discipline to explain what was to become of her. Long-term lover, friend and confidante he may be, but the college and its rules came first and she had severely transgressed with little justification or excuse that she could offer.

Celia would be aware that he would have had a discussion with the Mistress and any subsequent fall-out and embarrassment of that she had yet to face up to. He fixed her with a stare that relayed a hundred words in the circumstances, deliberately stoking the fires of her apprehension. His intention to convey his displeasure was an undoubted success; Stones recognised that she had been present at punishment sessions and witnessed his methods enough times to know that, in an attempt to truly punish her, he would seek ways to humiliate her that would most likely involve others. He doubted that Celia expected any sense of mercy to be shown and that their long friendship would most likely count against her rather than work in her favour. As she withered before his gaze he wondered if she would belittle herself and argue against the effectiveness of his tactics. Tactics that she had been present to assist in as it had proved time and time again to be the most efficient and emphatically successful lines of punishment that had broken many forceful and arrogant miscreants. The very limited numbers of repeat offenders that Stones had to deal with spoke volumes for the effectiveness of his strategy. Celia had heard his mantra about shame, humiliation, punishment, submission, correction and improvement enough times over the years to have no doubt that she would be shown no deviation or mercy.

"Well, Senior Tutor, a sorry state indeed. We will skip any further apologies, explanations, justification and promises for the future, if you don't mind. I suspect that you realise that there is nothing you could say that would work in your favour. On the contrary, as I would find it insulting and tiresome if you did so, I can assure you that the only amendment that you could influence would involve the punishment becoming more severe. Think on that for a moment before you say anything unwise, because the punishment I have decided upon is already at a level that has not been surpassed in this room."

The professor immediately wrong-footed Celia and caused her to dry up before she'd even begun with her planned entreaties and the like. Of course, he'd yet again outflanked her and she bowed her head in acknowledgment of his superiority and power over her.

"Remove your clothing please."

Celia nodded, it appeared that she did not trust herself to speak, and moved quickly to take her top, skirt and underwear off. She had spent a long time naked in front of and with the professor so had no shame whatsoever in standing unclothed and vulnerable before him. He knew her well enough to know that any fear of the beating to come would be superficial as she could not deny that the delivered thrashings of the past had been anything other than a massive turn-on sexually and that she had a capacity for taking punishment beyond nearly all the students he had ever admonished. His power over her was his ability to produce the unexpected combined with her fear of the unknown; the continual flicking of her eyes to the door betrayed her unease at what he might have planned and who would be a part of it.

"Bend over, hands down to the floor, legs planted far apart. A straightforward walloping with my fiercest paddle with no warm-up spanking should wake you up a bit and get us nicely started."

The professor tried to channel his thoughts towards the lesson that needed to be taught and the punishment that needed to be delivered. Normally he could thrash Celia without compunction and with complete freedom, but at those times the beating would be a part of what was always a lengthy, jointly fulfilling, truly sexual and ultimately a loving experience. This time wasn't to be about enjoyment, and certainly not about her enjoyment although Stones knew he wouldn't relish causing her real anguish but if that is what the situation required then that was what he would intend to deliver.

A paddle beating was generally only slightly more effective and painful on tight, bent-over cheeks than in a prone or standing position with the buttocks at ease and not taut. However the situation was slightly different if the paddle was wooden, thick and heavy. Stones' cricket bat styled long paddle was definitely all three of those, although he rarely applied it to bent-over buttocks as the risk of bruising was so much higher, the exception being to those who were really well-endowed and fleshy in the bottom cheeks department! However he was keen for Celia to see that different rules were in play and she needed this to be a memorable thrashing in more ways than one. Severe, long-lasting bruising would certainly tick that box, he thought. A normal punishment would follow a long-established route of developing the severity gradually as the designated discipline was carried out. The recipient thereby being allowed some grace and mercy in that they would be allowed to grow used to the increase in intensity of the level of pain as the punishment progressed. Stones had decided that Celia did not deserve that luxury and leniency and intended to let her know that he truly meant business.

Before he started he drank in the sight of her, her body had barely seemed to have changed in the time he had known her. Still pretty and attractive, her breasts were firm and pert, her stomach was as flat as it had ever been, her legs sleek and slender, her back was smooth and unblemished, a very sexy back indeed, he had always thought. She had one of those naturally beautifully designed vaginas, the folds blending into each other perfectly and with an almost artistic quality, topped off by a neatly trimmed but quite bushy pubic mound. Her bottom was gorgeous, no blemishes apart from the occasional recovering stripes, bruises, scratches and bite marks delivered by himself, quite full cheeks for a slim woman but not heavy, and perfectly symmetrical with sexy dimples. Her bottom crack was a joy to part, hiding twirling soft brown curls that surrounded a delicate and intricately puckered light brown rosette of an anal hole.

Looking down at her bottom now, he longed to drop to his knees and nestle his nose at that hole's opening and slide his tongue down the length of the beautiful pussy lips below, but he took a breath to harden his resolve and brought the paddle down in a long swing to land in the centre of the proffered cheeks. Apart from a sharp intake of breath and a quick adjustment of her feet to aid her balance, there was no reaction from the college's Senior Tutor; Celia had always been able to absorb the pain of a beating well and he knew it would need a few more strokes to force a response. Concentrating on the lower half of her bottom and the tops of her legs, the professor slammed the paddle down again and again until Celia stumbled before her legs buckled and she fell face forward to the floor.

"Stay there and lay flat, full out," Stones snapped at her.

He dropped to his knees beside her and began to paddle the tops of her cheeks. Celia was fully sobbing now, her body jerking as each stinging blow struck, her bottom glowing bright red. He allowed her no respite, no recovery time and beat her quickly and severely. After thirty full-blooded blows, he rose and returned the paddle to his cabinet. He selected a thin, whippy cane and unbuckled the thick belt from his trousers before he sat down beside her prone body.

"There's a bucket of water in the bathroom, I want you to crawl over to it and to start drinking. You are going to drink it all." He followed behind as Celia painfully crawled over to the bucket and swiped her buttocks with the thin cane. There were straws floating in the water and Celia began to suck while the professor stood watching over her.

From the look of defeat that flashed across her face it was clear to Stones that Celia realised that this would be all part of his plan to humiliate and shame her. Merely being forced to suck water from a bucket through multi-coloured kiddies' party straws was nothing but a minor element in the great scheme of things, displaying a bright red bottom whilst doing so purely an added inconvenience. He guessed that Celia would appreciate that the bigger picture would involve her filling her bladder up and therefore needing to urinate in front of him was likely to be on the agenda as a device to embarrass her. That thought probably wouldn't be bothering her to a great extent, they'd shared so much intimate detail the years, his plan was to be one-step ahead of her attempts to double guess him, however.

"More, woman, I'll tell you when to stop." His harshly spoken words snapped Celia out of any sense of relaxation.

Deciding to up the ante, Stones suddenly grabbed her neck and pushed her face into the bucket which caused her to gasp and splutter.

Stones' belt caught Celia full across her raised cheeks as she went back to sucking on the straws.

"Yaaaahh!" The surprise more than the pain causing her to yell out.

She sucked quickly, taking as much water in as she could as the professor whipped the belt down on her stinging bottom. After a dozen blows, which she stoically took in silence, he stopped as abruptly as he'd begun, leaving Celia's bottom streaked in thick, angry red lines on top of the paddle blows.

"Now dip your arse in the bucket to cool your throbbing bottom cheeks down for a few minutes, but don't let any water spill out. You'll be carrying on drinking soon so I wouldn't pee or fart into it if I was you." The professor went off into peals of laughter at his own wit. Celia raised her eyebrows at him, possibly not amused by the professor's toilet humour at her expense! Perhaps not fully concentrating on the job in hand, Celia failed to get her balance right straight away and some water splashed over the sides.

"Oh dear," was all she would have ominously heard from Stones, signalling that there would be repercussions.

Stones disappeared back into the main room, as Celia was left to enjoy the relief given to her beaten bottom by the cold water.

Stones made as much noise as possible as he got ready for the next stage of her punishment. He wanted her imagination to be concentrating on worrying about what he may have gone in to prepare for her, he was certain that her mind would be awhirl and that she'd hardly be thinking that it would be anything that she could look forward to. He switched the equipment on and off, creating a whirring and a swishing noise from the room which she could hardly have failed to hear.

Stones appeared at the doorway and was glad to see the look of foreboding that she gave him.

"Now get up and be careful not to spill any more precious water. Bend over, legs apart and I'll dry you off." His words sent a series of involuntarily shivers racking through her body and she presented herself once more.

There was not much in the way of a gentle towelling down to follow as he very roughly wiped a towel between her legs, around her bottom and then cruelly rubbed backwards and forwards up and down her bottom crack.

"Now on your knees and start licking up all the split water." The small whippy cane had appeared in his hand once more, and it lashed down across her back as she bent to lick the bathroom. "Obviously the quicker you lick the floor clean the less damage I'll have time to do with this!"

It was difficult for Celia to concentrate on licking the small puddles of water up as the cane flayed her back, her bottom and then the backs of her legs. She jerked and twisted, smearing her face on the floor as she tried to alleviate the stinging and yet still successfully lap much like a cat to get all the water up.

"That'll do, now have another drink," he ordered. "You have probably realised that we need to get your bladder nice and full so that I can cause you some more unpleasantness and grief. Yes, think about that, why don't you? Try and see where this is going to lead. Gives you something to think about, eh?"

Of course, Celia would know that he was deliberately torturing her mentally. That he was well aware that for her to pee in front of him, and that she would fear that it might not only be him, would cause her maximum embarrassment and a large dose of inner turmoil. Celia had watched so many times before, as he tormented offending students in front of her, and had revelled in his ability to find their weak spots, both physical and mental, and then go to town. Exposing a particular body part and then shaming them, or touching them casually somewhere deemed taboo, sometimes just using words and language that would cause them untold shame and disgrace, let alone applying the corporal punishment that they most dreaded. She had partaken and assisted him in his breaking down all resistance in others and both of them were well aware that she had found it arousing and stimulating. Celia had admitted to Stones that she often masturbated in private while reliving their almost sadistic behaviour and this had led to him insisting that she masturbated in front of him whilst he replayed his filmed footage of their latest conquests on a regular basis. He may religiously stick to his discipline of never having sex with a current student but Celia was aware more than anyone else that he might not physically fuck the students but he sure as hell mind-fucked them. He prided himself on his success to prey and play on her dread and fear, as he did with the students, knowing that instilling dread of forthcoming acts was a punishment all of its own.

Grabbing her by the hair, the professor with a look of pure malice on his face, dragged her through to his room and pushed her over his punishment desk, now released from its hidden location set amongst his table and cabinet. Pushed face down over the desk, to enable him to affix the strappings, forced with no option but to look between her legs under the table she would be able to make out the small machine that she had heard earlier.

"Can you see my new toy, Senior Tutor? Lucky you, you will be my guinea pig, my virgin user, my little experimental lamb to the slaughter. Ho, ho!"

Celia would've not needed to study the contraption for long without it being obvious that what she could see was a mobile spanking machine. A long sigh escaped from her mouth and Stones appreciated that she had accepted her fate and would waste no words on entreaties to his better nature or any pleas for leniency or clemency. His aim was to break down any remaining dignity or sense of self-worth. She obediently settled her pussy on the raised mound of the table edge, pushing her legs apart, making her bottom cheeks widen and her bottom crack open up.

"Lovely as ever, I never tire of looking at your lovely pussy slit or your cute little anus, my dear. It is such a pity I am going to have to inflict pain on this delightful bottom rather than seek pleasure in two of my favourite holes, but it has to be done. First I am going to give you the treat of being the first to feel the effects of my new plaything, it's a rather expensive spanking machine, top of the range, of course, and it will be interesting and hopefully fun, for me anyway, to see what it can do."

Strapped down and with hardly any option for movement, Celia took deep breaths; the inference that he might strike her most sensitive and private places was plain to hear and understand. Celia knew more than anyone else the punishment he had imposed on the unfortunate Emily and it was clear that the promise for her to undergo that same discomfort and shame was real. Celia had experienced the luxury of watching when Emily had taken the knotted whip down her pussy and arsehole and Stones had not seen her bat an eyelid when the blow had landed. The challenge here was that Celia would be determined to prove that she could take anything he served up and her pride would drive her to want to take her just dues with dignity and make him proud of her and her commitment, fortitude and acquiescence. The lack of sexual contact so far was intended to disconcert her, he wanted her to forget that they were lovers and start to realise that this was not going to be a thrashing of a sexual nature but a true punishment flogging. He steeled himself as he prepared to commit to giving her a beating unlike any other that he had subjected her to previously. Some of those episodes had been very harsh and, on occasion, he had made her wait so long before he introduced any sexual element into the play. However the difference to the present situation was that she had always known it was coming and that was enough to heighten her arousal until he deemed fit to give her what she wanted. He sensed that, for the first time in a very long time, Celia found herself rather anxious and not a little frightened as to what her fate would be at the hands of her long term lover.

Like many submissives, there was often a point at which the pain became almost overwhelming, all-encompassing and you questioned the reality of what was happening. In the moment you would give anything for the punishment to cease, for respite and release from the blazing stinging but it would be just for then; soon the longing for the impact against your flesh would envelop you again, the desire would return, you would beg for the lash, the whip-crack, the biting cut. Stones hoped that Celia would believe that there was a potential reward for her if she was to take her punishment in an exemplary manner, that he would maybe take pity on her and fuck her afterwards. He really wanted her to have those presumptions and hopes, to have that lust and desire, so that he could have the pleasure of adding that disappointment to her experience at his hands. Stones picked up a remote control panel and the room's silence was broken by the whir of the spanking machine starting, a rapid swish and then the explosive crack against her protruding buttocks.

"Ah ha," exclaimed Stones. "Fair and square, perfect, should be another one coming soon. I've set it on a six-position setting to change every stroke position, ten seconds apart, medium on the scale of severity. Obviously I'll be looking to turn that up as we proceed, more severe, faster and concentrated should be where we end up. Imagine that, Celia, maybe fifty whipping cracks a couple of seconds apart landing unerringly on the same spot, over and over and over again. What a treat to look forward to, lucky you. Think on!"

As the second stroke landed just above the first, Celia looked like she was trying very hard not to think on, in fact. With a human hand controlling the beating there tended to be some temporary respite with inaccuracy, inconsistency and growing weariness or pure exhaustion on the part of the beater offering some reprieve. This machine was not going to offer any escape or let up and the third blow hit hard as the ten seconds passed and the position again altered to strike just above the previous stroke.

"I presume that you are finding this bearable because it's moving, Celia, and it's not going to mistakenly hit the same spot twice. However, you should perhaps be aware that the sequence repeats after every sixth stroke so the seventh will hit exactly the same spot as the first and so on. Until the time comes when I decide to change the sequence or maybe the speed. Then again maybe I'll change the severity level and swing strength. Or all of them even. What japes!" Stones taunted the recipient of strokes five and six and was delighted to see her buttocks tense as the first repetition approached.

To his delight as the stroke landed perfectly on top of the earlier one, Celia let out a slight yelp before dropping her head submissively as the next struck home. Stones lent forward and pulled her head up by her hair, turning her to face him. As each stroke arrived with unerring accuracy Celia's face contorted, her eyes squeezed shut and her mouth began to hang open. Every minute brought six more strokes on top of the previous six and as the time ticked up, Stones suspected that Celia had accepted the fact that without a human being on the end of whatever implement you were being thrashed with, then the sexual and erotic side of the punishment rather wanes and the painful side is totally predominant. By the landing of the nineteenth stroke, being the beginning of the fourth round of the cycle, Celia's resolve to fight was gone and she began to sob in pain, discomfort and self-pity. Any pretence at being able to stifle a response abandoned as her little whimpers of pain became longer and louder.

Stones now placed himself out of her line of vision and watched intently and with complete fascination as his expensive new contraption seemingly passed its trial with flying colours. Celia had a high threshold of pain, as he had learnt over their relationship of many years, but the machine had reduced her to tears much quicker than he himself would have done. He had no sympathy as she had crossed the line and she knew it. There had been times in the past when both of them had come close to taking, or mainly in Celia's case, watching, assisting and participating rather than actually delivering, a punishment to an extreme wherein the beating and shaming had perhaps passed the line where it was possibly no longer appropriate or fitting for the crime that had been committed. He loved her in his own way, he accepted, but he felt no regret, no hesitation and certainly suffered no recriminations when he reduced her to tears, sometimes causing her so much discomfort that he had seen her walking awkwardly in the college grounds many days after a thrashing. He knew that she kept a padded cushion in her desk for when her bottom was so sore that sitting down to work was a challenge. Celia would never bring herself to admit to being a masochist but Stones failed to see how she could really deny it, but he saw any dilemma she went through as of no real concern to him and rarely wasted any time pondering on the subject.

As the device cycle ended after its eighth repetition and stroke number forty-eight seared into the fierce raised welt along the top of her cheeks, Celia's sobs, groans and yelps had by now changed into howls amidst choking gasps of breath. A totally unmoved Stones shifted position to study the marks that were swelling and blistering; he was pretty much an expert at assessing when one of his reprobate's bottoms was approaching the point when the skin could break. He was proud of the fact that he had never broken skin in his years of applying severe floggings and even with the aim of Celia's punishment being as harsh as he could possibly apply, he still had no wish to risk scarring her.

"Last six, my dear, that lovely bottom is going to catch fire soon. Let's enjoy these last ones and then get you back to your bucket."

Celia jumped in surprise as he spoke, jerked out of the reverie she was lost in under the torment of the continual lashing, and then yelled in pain as the cycle restarted.

"Thank you, Dean." Celia forced herself as a matter of pride to respond to his liking. Somehow managing to acknowledge his words as the next stroke landed and tears coursed down her face. Forty seconds later she heard the click and slow whirring finish as the machine was switched off and she found herself sobbing uncontrollably in relief. He unstrapped her and led her to the bathroom and eased her form onto the bucket which was still more than three quarters full as Stones had added ice since she had last used it. The shock of the water was of no real consequence as she sighed with plain joy at the easing of the stinging it induced in her throbbing cheeks.

"Three minutes, no longer, then put the straws back in, have a long drink."

Celia may have thought her wry smile was discreet enough for the professor not to notice, but notice he did and he guessed that she was hoping to be able to claim to need the loo soon so that she could get the planned spectacle of peeing in front of him over and done with before anyone else joined them. Stones kept his face impassive, he had no intention of allowing her to double-guess his designs on her and anyway the next part of his plan took into account his anticipation of her need to pee. The professor had planned visitors, but it was nothing whatsoever to do with making Celia suffer the indignity of relieving herself in front of an audience. Total humiliation was planned but there was a painful path to cross before he intended to break her spirit utterly and completely.

Guessing correctly that the three minutes was about up, Celia took no chances in making a bad choice and decided to ask his permission.

"I am happy to be wiped dry now if you wish, sir. I would like to thank you for my well-deserved punishment so far, sir, and I would be honoured if you wish to continue. I believe that my dreadful behaviour merits further admonishment and I would be privileged to suffer any disciplinary action that would serve to teach me the lesson I so clearly deserve and require to amend my behaviour to match the college's demands, sir."

Stones picked up the towel and gestured for her to rise and bend over, he again gave her bottom and groin areas a perfunctory but rough wipe down. As before he pushed her head down to the bucket and Celia obediently grasped a straw and began to drink deeply. Seconds later she was taken by an ear and dragged back into the main room and over to the door, then led to the lobby, to his concealed garden. Celia winced inwardly as he produced a collar and lead, pushed her down onto all fours and affixed them to her.

"It is time for you to have some fresh air and exercise, bitch."

His reward was Celia's horrified expression and the look of pleading directed towards him. If ever anyone illustrated the expression *with a sinking heart*, this was it, he mused. His garden was not overlooked but she was aware that various college personnel and a handful of his friends, colleagues, certain staff members such as gardeners, housekeeping domestics and his brother, used the garden entrance to access his quarters on an inconsistent but reasonably regular basis. Naked in a collar and on the end of a lead, she was dragged with great reluctance to a post where Stones attached the lead. Celia was limited in movement to about fifteen feet, with very little cover within that distance. Part of the lawn and a small shrub border were the limit to her range and there would be little chance that she would be able to stay out of sight if anyone entered. Added to the fact that she had an obviously thoroughly beaten backside glowing a reddish purple that would stand little interpretation as to how it came to be so!

She kept her mouth shut and her head down; she knew the professor far too well to dare risk antagonising him further. He placed a dog bowl full of water just within reach.

"Keep lapping up the water, I'll be keeping an occasional eye on you, of course. You know that the whole garden is covered by my CCTV system. If you need to go to the loo, bark and scratch at the door until I come. Otherwise take the opportunity to have a little run round and I expect you also to bark to forewarn me if any visitors turn up, please. But no biting of ankles!" The professor meandered back inside, chuckling away at his own wit much to Celia's obvious annoyance, let alone the fear of what the hell she would do if anyone was to come through the back gate.

Inside the professor continued with his preparation of the equipment required for Celia's finale as far as the thrashing was concerned and then made a couple of phone calls to confirm that his denouement would hopefully go to plan and time. The professor was well aware that Celia was attempting to predict his every move but suspected that, with that knowledge, he was always going to have the advantage of being at least one step ahead of her. That and the fact that actually he didn't think that Celia was as hard-hearted and deviously minded as he was and therefore not capable of dreaming up the scenarios that he could when it came to applying punishment.

After cowering in fear of being discovered, Celia's need to empty her bladder had become paramount and Stones watched on his screen as she seemed to argue with herself as to her next move. Stones expected that she would want to get the belittling process over and done with before any visitors appeared. His suspicion was that she would be secretly hoping that the threat and possibility of others joining them was just that and he was happy to allow her to raise her hopes that her indignity would bear no witness. Celia had watched him belittle enough recipients of his own form of punishment to know exactly how effective such mind games and implications were in undermining and shaming arrogant students. Of course, Stones' advantage at the moment was that she had no idea if any others had arrived whilst she was locked outside, so he was content for her to wait outside with her mind playing its own games. As he watched her indecisively move towards the door and then stop in her tracks for the second time, he bided his time. Finally she seemed to make a decision and half-crawled and half-hopped to the door. There was a pause and then Stones heard her begin to scratch and whimper in a passable impression of an unhappy dog to his great amusement. He ignored her for a while and watched her intently on the screen as she squatted expectantly waiting for the door to open. As the time stretched out, he smiled as her look went from irritated at his failure to let her in, to one of trepidation as she perhaps wondered what part of his great plan to humiliate her this was and finally to a dejected and rather ridiculous sulky expression. He saw her then take in a deep calming breath as if to steady herself then once again began to scratch at the door. As Stones finally rose he was surprised and quite impressed to hear Celia begin to do her best impression of a barking dog.

Stones opened the door and snapped at her. "Be quiet, you naughty dog!"

"Oh Professor, I am sorry, sir but I do need to use the facilities please." Celia looked up at him with pure apprehension written all over her face, the tip of her tongue poking between her lips.

As Stones opened the door wider, Celia tried to crawl through the gap, and was taken aback as Stones blocked her off.

"No. No. No. You old silly thing. We don't let the animals pee in the house now, do we? Over here to the border."

He pulled on the lead and to Celia's absolute horror dragged her to the small shrub border.

"Now dig yourself a nice little hole to relieve yourself in. Come on, little doggy, dig."

Celia bowed her head in total defeat, yet again he had played her to perfection, and her despondent look was, for Stones, a joy to behold.

Stones could not fail to admire her spirit as resolute as ever she visibly steeled herself to obey him. The thrashings he knew she could endure but he could see that this level of humiliation was so hard for her. Which, of course, was the point, was exactly why his punishments were so effective and why he didn't get very many repeat offenders. She sighed, took in a ragged breath, a little sob escaping from her mouth before she turned and without looking his way dug a shallow hole in the dirt with her fingers. Celia used her cupped hands to scoop out loose soil and arranged it in small piles around the crater she created, ready to cover her disgrace. She looked up at him modestly and moved with great reluctance to squat over her hole.

"No. No. No. Silly doggy. You lift a leg up against the wall and then pee down. Remember you're a dog."

Celia grimaced and a single tear ran down her bright red face as she cocked her leg, displaying herself so blatantly and squeezed her eyes shut as she willed herself to relax her muscles and allow her bladder to empty.

"Look at me while you pee please, doggy."

A flash of anger crossed her face as she bravely risked a rather rebellious glare but holding his gaze, her protesting bladder got its own way and a stream of urine erupted from between her legs.

"Good dog, make sure your aim is accurate please, don't want to kill the shrubs, do we?" The professor watched her shame with a cold heart. He was pretty sure that his point was being well made and that Celia's transgression would be a one-off but he certainly was not going to curtail what he had planned. Better to over punish than under, was his philosophy.

Her stream ended and the professor held out a dock leaf.

"Wipe the drips off, dear, and then cover your deposit," he ordered, a stony look on his face.

She quickly dabbed herself, dropped the leaf into the wetted earth and scrabbled to scoop the loose dirt over her shame.

"Now I am going to take you for a walk around the garden. There's something I want to show you but first I just wanted to let you know that I did spot the disobedient little glare before you did your business. So bottom up, please."

As Celia dropped her head and raised her flanks, Stones double looped the lead over his hand and whipped down six times, aiming at the sensitive skin at the tops of her legs. Celia had barely time to register the intense singing pain before he tugged sharply on the lead and she had no course other than to crawl snivelling behind him. But then she focused on the direction they were taking and froze, bringing Stones to a halt and almost pulled the lead from his hand.

"Oh no, no Edward, please. Not the nettles, no, oh please no, no, no." Celia looked up at Stones with beseeching eyes, her whole body trembling as she espied a nettles clump and her body trembled with fear.

Stones immediately stopped and once more wrapped the long leash around his hand before he moved behind Celia. She knew only too well what was coming and automatically dropped her head, parted her legs and raised her bottom high, completely exposing herself. He didn't prove her wrong; the leash whipped down hard and fast onto her buttocks, eleven strokes landing horizontally across her already injured cheeks. The final one caught her completely unawares as he lashed down in a vertical strike, the leash landing accurately in the centre of her opened crack, her anus taking the full hit. Celia shrieked in response, the extreme pain centring on her sensitive puckered hole and she rolled away from him in a ball.

"How dare you?" he roared.

Terrified by his clear fury, Celia desperately tried to gather herself, her hand going to her arsehole in a desperate attempt to help absorb the painfulness of the moment.

"Get back into position. I haven't said I am finished with your beating yet," Stones barked.

Celia immediately obeyed, presenting her bottom again as Stones leaned in to stare in fascination as her arsehole twitched open and closed in reaction to the pain. Stones had to steel himself not to move in to kiss and lick the offended opening, now bright red and visibly showing signs of swelling.

"S…s…sorry, sir. So sorry, sir. The nettles, sir, please sir, no." Celia was now sobbing openly and very distressed.

The professor pulled on the lead and led her to the edge of the wild garden area where the nettles dominated, Celia compliant but now a blubbering wreck.

"As it happens, you stupid bitch, I was just going to show you how things could have got much worse for you if you had not been co-operative. This is what you have avoided because you have taken your punishment very well so far. But then you've almost spoilt it by your little show of disobedience and resistance. Now I am not sure whether you need a little taste of nettle to just ensure that you continue to behave."

Celia gulped, her relief palpable but terror still in her eyes.

"Sir, I am sorry but I am so scared, sir. I beg you please do not make me crawl into the nettles, sir. Anything but that, please sir."

Stones fixed her with one of his most fearsome stares and cupping her chin with one huge hand brought her face up to look at him.

"Oh I wasn't going to make you go into them, I was just going to ask you to select one for me. Then I was going to run it down the crack of your bottom and up the valley of your vagina before whipping your breasts with it."

Celia held her breath and her body seemingly frozen in fear as she waited for his next words.

"For now, I am assuming that the threat of the nettles is having the right effect. You are seemingly contrite and very regretful for your inappropriate sexual behaviour so I will impose no further punishment further to what I have previously determined. So inside now, I have plans for you."

He led her inside on the leash and unclipped her once through the outer door.

"Stand up, your stint as an animal is over. Through to the bathroom as we'd better get you cleaned up."

He led her to the shower and gave her instructions. "Wash the dirt off your hands, knees and feet and I'll run you a quick bath so I can properly scrub you up to ensure that you are sweet and clean for your final stage."

It was an ominous promise and Celia shuddered in anticipation of him now upping the game as they headed towards the finish of her punishment. Quickly washing herself down in the shower as he ran the bath, she stepped out and was directed to get straight into the bath.

"Hands on head, legs apart."

Celia tried to stand stock still as he soaked under her arms and her breasts vigorously before sliding down her legs and up between them. Then he turned her around and bent her forward forcing her to place her hands upon the wall, making her bottom push out towards him. Quickly he soaped her back and legs before scrubbing at her buttocks and then roughly delving down her crack, a long soapy finger sliding into her anus. He then pushed her down into the water and knelt beside her with a flannel, washing all the lather off.

"Dry yourself off and come through for the rest of your punishment," Stones snapped, leaving the bathroom.

Minutes later Celia stepped back into the main room to see that he had brought out the contraption that had been the scene of her indiscretion with Emily. There was no surprise apparent as she viewed the bench with its restrictive cuffs and pulley system, nor did she look particularly perturbed, it was clearly what she had expected he might feel was the most appropriate action. Stones hoped that her guard was down as much as it looked, he had noted her glance around the room and the spark come back into her eyes as she had realised that they were still alone.

"Would I be correct in thinking that you appear relieved that no one has been invited to join us for your final humiliating punishment, Celia?"

Completely stymied and aghast that yet again he had got inside her head, Celia was totally lost for a response.

"You know where this is going, so on the table on your back while I strap you in place please. There will be a couple of little additions to add a bit of mystery."

As Celia sat herself into the massage table, Stones produced both headphones and a blindfold to Celia's total consternation. Her eyes betrayed her sense of panic as he approached and suddenly she leaned forward and touched the clear bulge of his erection through his trousers.

"Oh sir, I can see you are troubled. Can I humbly request that you use me to relieve yourself, so that you are not distracted in your commitment to fully punish me for my sinful acts?"

Stones laughed.

"Nice try, Senior Tutor, nice try. Good tactics, well played. However as an obvious tactic to distract me from applying the headset and blindfold, which, with your lack of a poker face means that I can read you like a very simple book, it fails completely. But you have a point, I have always admired your naked body and that bottom is definitely a favourite of mine as well as a joy to thrash. So you are correct that I am struggling to focus completely on ensuring that this is the most painful day of your life and giving you a lesson you'll never forget, so a little relief would be welcome. We have just about got time for a minor distraction."

Celia didn't have long to think about what that last comment implied as Stones took a handful of hair and dragged her into the bathroom.

As Celia sighed in disappointment and resignation; Stones surmised that she had probably worked out that the reason they were now in the bathroom was because it would be off camera, which, of course, confirmed that her humiliation had been and was being recorded. He doubted that she was overly surprised in all honesty as she would have known that her place as his lover would always come second to his role as Dean of Discipline, and whilst he had assured her that their lovemaking sessions were never recorded without her knowledge and were a matter of privacy that they shared, her transgression was a college disciplinary issue and as such was on the record. She may suspect the Mistress would be given access to a live feed but he was damn sure that she hoped and prayed that it wasn't so. Stones was not willing to raise any hopes she had; his quiet fury at her fragrant breach of protocol was long-lasting and only mildly tempered by the discipline he had so far delivered. His arousal and erection, usually most welcome, were a distraction and he certainly did not want his focus to stray from the main theme of the day. His intention was not just to inflict pain and humiliation on the errant Senior Tutor but to instil fear and a guarantee that she would think long and hard before ever attempting to take advantage of their special relationship and situation again.

With his trousers and shorts now round his ankles and his huge protuberance swinging free, Celia further angered him as she inadvertently licked her lips in preparation as he forced her to her knees facing him. Without any pretence at caring if Celia was ready or not, the professor pushed his large stiff cock into her mouth. He felt Celia's tongue swirl rapidly around his cock, working her mouth to produce enough saliva to smooth his passage as he started to thrust in and out. Normally a favourite pastime of Celia's, she had always lingered in this particular activity, she loved having him in her mouth and he acknowledged that she was an expert in the art of fellatio, but this time he was just purely fucking her mouth with no pretence that her comfort or satisfaction was of interest. She may have been glad but not totally surprised when he pulled right out of her mouth and turned her around; he doubted that she was expecting anything other than what he intended to do next. He forced her over the rim of the bathtub so that her bottom was presented to him. As she scrabbled to get her hands down to support herself he forced his knees between her legs and without any hesitation or preparation he positioned his spit-wet cock up against the entrance to her arsehole and brutally forced his way into her. His intimate knowledge of her body meant that he felt the sensations around his cock as she attempted to relax her protesting anal muscles to allow him an open entrance but his aim of causing her discomfort and not pleasure was proved successful as she squealed in pain and protest. The professor ignored her gasping entreaties, grabbed her thighs and slammed himself deep into her rectum again and again. They had both thoroughly enjoyed anal action and full anal intercourse together on many occasions and because he was aware that it wasn't something she especially craved, he had always taken the time to prepare and ensure that he brought her to a level of sexual excitement to help her lose her inhibitions and welcome the variety of sexual acts that he had introduced her to. Lubrication had always been used whether it be gel, her own juices or indeed just a lot of his saliva as he could easily spend thirty minutes or so kissing, licking and probing her arsehole with his tongue. She had once admitted that the thrill of having him tease her open and dribble saliva into her back passage made her feel both disgustingly depraved and wildly excited which, when combined with his fingers or a vibrator sliding in and out of her pussy, would soon ensure that she would lose herself in a pure paradise of debauchery. Stones realised that, like a lot of women, Celia far preferred a finger, thumb, nose or tongue teasing her anally than full-blown intercourse, the size of her lover's cock being a particular issue with Stones as it took practice to accept a man of his girth into an initially tight chamber. They had, to her approval, turned anal into something that was an aspect of their lovemaking rather than an essential and over the years she had thoroughly embraced his adventurous spirit in introducing various sex toys and household articles into their anal play. A vibrating butt plug fully inserted whilst being caned was near top of the list as far as Celia's sexual cravings went and Stones made sure that she needed to feel no shame or guilt concerning any so-called deviant behaviour, the majority of which were practices he had introduced her to. Their sexual activity was of such variety; sometimes ferocious, sometimes pure mind-blowingly climatic, often decidedly crude and downright dirty but always totally consensual and equally satisfying for both of them. Stones and Celia's relationship was of the utmost importance to both of their well-being and happiness although he suspected that ultimately she placed a higher value on their trysts than he did. They had on many occasions discussed her dilemma of holding firm to feminist principles whilst allowing Stones to master and dominant her so completely. She often found it difficult to balance the way she behaved with him and her submissiveness with such a dominant practitioner of the sexual dark arts, but they had both agreed that the reality was that it was a joint enterprise that suited and satisfied them both equally. This, however, was a totally different kettle of fish and Stones wondered briefly if Celia recognised that she was being well and truly buggered, plain and simple. Stones plunged into her darkest recess forcibly, pulling almost all the way out and allowing her ring and muscle to close up around his tip each time, before aggressively slamming into her with his full length to the hilt.

Fortunately it was not to last long as after several deep hard thrusts he pulled out of her and spun her back around and down. Celia had never before taken him into her mouth directly from her arsehole but would know better than to attempt any resistance at this juncture. He noted the brief expression of unease cross her face, signalling reluctance at the idea, but then fade as she quelled her instincts and opened her mouth fully as he pushed down on her head.

"Clean me, my little tart," he snapped.

He would brook no argument as she had many times performed analingus on him and he expected her trust and obedience now. He had always adored her tongue rimming and slipping inside his own arsehole, so would be used to his taste albeit he had never before put her in the position of tasting her own most secret inner place. This was a new act and with entirely a different set of circumstances in play as he ensured that she was left in no doubt whatsoever that she was being used and abused. He wanted her to feel defiled and pushed his cock deep towards the back of her throat, moving her head around so that his cock swirled around in her mouth. What he was not expecting, however, was to sense her enthusiasm in the act! He was astounded as she began to suck methodically and wholeheartedly and within a matter of seconds he found himself approaching a climax. Unable to hold himself back any longer be began to pump her mouth faster and faster and then roared in ecstatic relief as his orgasm came. Celia swallowed rapidly, allowing the warm sperm jets of his come to shoot down her throat, his fingers clenched in her hair, her face rammed into his groin.

"Done," he said, perfunctorily wiping his dribbling cock across her face and pushing her away dismissively.

"Come on, clean and dress me," he said, dragging her across to the sink and she quickly filled the bowl and began to gently soak and wash his cock and balls. She towelled him dry and then pulled up his trousers and pants, before looking up at him expectantly, a trail of his come still running down her cheek.

"Wash your mouth out and clean yourself up, then get out there and get on the massage table. Not that it is going to be a massage you'll be receiving. Much more of a message, in truth. Oh, I am so going to enjoy what is to come." He walked away laughing in that evil villain manner he had that struck fear into most of those who ever had the misfortune to stand before him.

Looking back as Celia speedily washed her face and rinsed her mouth out, he felt rather self-satisfied that he had left her with the knowledge that all she had done was to delay the inevitable by volunteering herself as a vessel for him to relieve himself into. Putting things off for a quarter of an hour in exchange for a sore backside, now internally as well as externally, and a bitter taste in the back of her throat, was maybe not the best plan she had ever had.

As she reluctantly returned to the scene of her forthcoming punishment and laid herself down, Celia looked at him with fear and suspicion in her eyes as she saw that he had picked up the headphones. As she settled obediently onto the cushioned bench he placed the headphones over her ears and put a thick blindfold in place covering her eyes. Her stomach churned loudly and her breathing quickened, as he attached her hands to the restraints above her head before moving down to spread her legs and snap the ankle bracelets into place. Purely for his own amusement, he jangled the hanging chains above her head and was rewarded as she winced dramatically and a tiny whimper escaped from her lips. Whilst Celia would have expected him to recreate the scenario of her transgression with young Emily, he suspected that, now that she was fully attached, the reality of the situation was hitting home. She began to shake uncontrollably and he again jangled the chains to imply that he was ready to begin the process that would winch her legs up over her upper body, raising her buttocks and forcing them apart. If she was terrified now, Stones mused, then his coup de grace, shortly to be applied should be sublime!

That terror appeared to reach a new level seconds later when she was to hear the door buzzer go and Stones savoured the words he had been waiting to torment her with.

"Ah, looks like my next guests are here, very punctual. I think it is time to entertain you with some music to listen to. That should disorientate you a bit and add to our fun, don't you think? A flick of a switch, Celia, and now you can enjoy the sounds of a Bach piano concerto. Please don't allow yourself to be distracted from the wonderful music by allowing your mind to race frantically wondering who has been invited to share your disgrace and denouement. Ha, ha!"

The professor chuckled as he pulled fast the blindfold and, moving a headphone aside shushed Celia as she spluttered in protest.

"Any further unrequested responses or outbursts and I'll have you gagged and the soles of your feet whipped." As tugging and pulling switches he hoisted Celia's legs into the air so that her bottom was suspended clear of the leather mattress and her legs were splayed wide, before being pulled towards her shoulders, her body being displayed and suspended in a most vulnerable and demeaning position.

Stones went across to open the door, welcoming both Emily and Sara in at the specific time as he had requested.

"Oh my god!" was the stunned response as Emily's eyes fell upon the naked exposed body of the college's esteemed Senior Tutor.

Sara was just standing gulping in air at the situation presented before her. They both had been briefed by the professor that he wished them to witness 'the Senior Tutor's disgrace' as he had put it. The reality of what that meant was now becoming very apparent, the angry red marks covering Celia's bottom clearly making evident what had been taking place earlier on in the room. Emily's face coloured whether in embarrassment and sympathy for Celia or both, Stones did not know, but he hoped that she had a vengeful nature of sorts to ensure that her inclusion was a correct decision. He was pretty sure that Emily may have a bit of a dilemma in that the person who had actually made her punishment, on this very table, much less unbearable than it could have been otherwise, was now clearly paying for her actions! Stones had discussed with her in fairly casual terms to explain that, in theory at least, she had been taken advantage of by the Senior Tutor, and regardless of Emily's enjoyment of the cunnilingus received, which Emily had proclaimed to be a wonderful sexual experience that had served as a beautiful interlude and distraction from the severe thrashing she had received, she had still broken college regulations. At that point, of course, Emily had no idea where the conversation, if anywhere, was leading but had no thought that she would herself bear witness to the college's highly respected Senior Tutor's comeuppance. But amidst the shock, confusion and sympathy displayed Stones suspected that he spotted an element of excitement and he was reasonably confident that his assessment of Emily's nature would prove to be accurate. Sara plainly just didn't know where to look, this was her boss on display in the most lewd manner with evidence that she had received a most thorough and severe beating and Stones was concerned that her expression was one of horror, and she was obviously very uncomfortable.

"Now ladies, please relax. She doesn't know that you are here although she does know that someone is. I won't be telling her that you were present so it is very much up to you whether you want to keep it between yourselves or not. I would advise most strongly that it would be best to leave the Senior Tutor none the wiser. You will not discuss this other than in the present company. It is unlikely that your time at the college will last very much longer if you do so. I hope we all understand each other?" Stones raised his eyebrows at them both, receiving a frantic nodding from Emily and a quiet affirmative response from the still shaken Sara.

Sara and Emily exchanged concerned looks; witnessing this shaming of a college senior member of staff was not something that appeared to sit that happily with either of them. Stones imagined that they would be unlikely to want Celia to know that they had been in the room at any point to see her in all her shameless glory.

"Sir, I think that we are both uncomfortable with the situation and would rather that the Senior Tutor were to never know that we were present," Sara spoke tentatively and looked to Emily for support and the student nodded vigorously in agreement.

"Fair enough, my dears. However you do each have a designated role in her punishment which will add to her sense of disgrace and total submission. If you were to decide not to take part in this little scenario then I would have to consider a higher level of actual physical punishment to be dispensed as an alternative. The humiliation and self-awareness that the Senior Tutor will suffer knowing that her disgrace has been viewed at close quarters by persons unknown, will torment her as much as any thrashing. I would also be disappointed in you but accept that you perhaps are not cut out to be part of my little team going forward." The message from the professor was clear to the two women who were visibly thrown by what he had implied.

Sara took the lead in responding.

"Professor, I am happy to follow your instructions and certainly do not wish to be the cause of any additional physical punishment being applied to the Senior Tutor."

Emily was quick to follow her lead.

"Absolutely, sir, what would you like me to do?" offered Emily quietly. There was a breathlessness about her pronouncement which didn't quite disguise the glint of sexual excitement that was now coming to the fore. Any earlier reticence had disappeared.

"Oh Emily, I think you can tell the room exactly what you are thinking, why don't you?" His cheerful demeanour prompted the student to be brazen.

"Yes sir, of course sir," she responded with enthusiasm. "I have to admit that my mind has been in turmoil following my recent, and well deserved, walloping, followed by the Senior Tutor's act of indiscretion, which I believe was kindly meant, and the later scenes with those damn seven bitches, sir. I feel that the Senior Tutor has brought out a very liberal sexual side of me, sir, and I also know that I made a blatant and embarrassing offer to you, sir. I have to say, sir, that the orgasm I experienced when the Senior Tutor worked her magic with her tongue and lips had undoubtedly been the best climax of my life and seeing her displayed so rudely is definitely creating a stirring inside of me, sir."

Red-faced she looked directly at the professor, and he was so aware that she wanted his approval. Ever the game player, he just ignored her and turned to Sara, who he could see was staring intently at Celia's exposed sex.

"Sara, if you could bear to tear your wanton eyes away from the Senior Tutor's groin for a moment. I just want you to stroke her face while she undergoes the final stage of her punishment. As you ladies can see, she has already been given a quite thorough beating, which is commensurate and proportionate with the appalling violation of trust displayed by a senior member of staff who must have known better. It is only correct that Sara, as a member of her team, should evidence with your own eyes that rules are there to be obeyed and there are serious consequences when any breach such as this takes place."

Sara now blushed deeply as the professor's eyes bored into hers; he was certain that she was remembering her own minor indiscretion in front of him and her composure was rocked as her face betrayed a rising panic.

Since her involvement with Jamie, Sara had ceased her occasional visits to an ex-student called Jenny Goldman and had brought the sexual relationship that had developed to an end. A dangerous game had been called off as Sara had breached college rules in a way that was far beyond the actions that Celia was being so taken to task for today. The fact that Sara and Jenny had enjoyed a mutually beneficial relationship of equal standing would hold no sway if their secret was to come out. The liaison would be deemed unacceptable and, as a decision-making member of staff with influence and a certain amount of authority, her action would be seen as unacceptable. Sara now lived in fear that her history would be exposed and dreaded the thought of repercussions that that unveiling could bring. For now her secret was undisclosed but Stones' suspicions were now raised and Sara was living on borrowed time.

"Emily, you have a decision to make. This implement is the

braided, or knotted, whip. As you can see it is the whip that I used to apply to your personal areas. I suspect that you remember it rather well, in fact I can see that all the blood appears to have drained from your face so you obviously do recall it. Which is entirely the point. It is supposed to give the recipient a lasting memory so that they ensure that they never have to endure it a second time. I can see by your reaction that this would appear to be the case proving that it probably works rather well as a deterrent. You may respond, child," he finished in a deliberately patronising tone, worded to remind Emily that she was totally under his control. Her reaction illustrated her compliance as she was once again rendered subservient and meek.

"Yes sir," she stammered in response. "I would certainly not wish to upset or disappoint you to the degree that you felt you needed to use it on me again." Her eyes were downcast as she took on the mannerism and appearance of a whipped dog.

"As the Senior Tutor is supposed to set the standards and lead by example, she has let herself and the college down and her punishment has to reflect this. Therefore before I strap her, and deliver the final instalment of her beating, I intend to lash her with the knotted whip between her legs. The decision I have made it that her poor behaviour and misguided judgment is of such a high level to warrant the maximum penalty of six strokes of the whip in her most intimate places."

Both Emily and Sara gasped in horror. As the former recipient of one mind-numbing, head-blowing, extremely painful stinging stroke, Emily's reaction was most pertinent. She looked aghast at the professor's intention to apply such a severe punishment. Sara may have only watched when Emily had received the stroke but the memory of the event had clearly struck a chord as she swallowed repeatedly, her concerns apparent.

"You are both right to feel the terror you do, six strokes would cause her extreme pain for a long time, however ladies, I am prepared to deliver five of those strokes to her buttocks rather than down her vagina and anal crack. Emily you have the power to decide if that is the route I take."

Emily jumped at the chance offered to save Celia from part of her punishment, it was obvious that she was horrified at the prospect of Celia's most sensitive and private orifices being abused in the way he suggested. Stones was well aware that it would have been the soothing tongue and lips of Celia that had distracted her from the pain of the stroke and that she had shown no real concern that the Senior Tutor had supposedly taken advantage. Emily did not appear to see herself as the poor abused victim of the older predator that the professor presented her role as. Stones surmised that as far as Emily was concerned Celia had been sympathetic, loving and supportive, and he had witnessed her given a fantastic sexual experience and an earth-shattering orgasm.

"I will happily do whatever I need to do, sir. Six strokes would be unbearable. What do you need me to do?"

The professor smiled with a wicked glint in his eyes.

"Oh it would just be applying like-for-like so to speak, or should I say lick-for-lick!" he chuckled to himself as realisation began to dawn on Emily. From the look on Sara's face, Stones could see that the same thoughts had entered her head.

"Yes Emily, I think justice would be served just as well if the Senior Tutor was subjected to a most appropriate but surely far more lenient and enjoyable alternative. To save her from the torturous lashes of my wicked little whip, you can return the treatment that was applied to you without your permission or with my authority. Revenge is a dish best served cold after all! Emily your options are simple; sexual assault or physical assault. You can choose to return the treatment and violation imposed on you, without permission and against college rules by the Senior Tutor, and enjoy yourself in experimenting with the goods displayed or you can watch carefully while I lash her private parts and take her to a hell that will haunt her for years. Up to you, Emily, this is the power I give you. Choose her fate."

Emily looked at her feet; she was both perceptive enough and intelligent enough to realise that he was toying with her for his own amusement and yet she felt complete powerless and helpless to do anything other than his bidding.

"Professor, this is so unfair of you. This puts me in a position of being forced to participate in your belittling and game-playing. Of course I cannot condemn Dr Ford to the six lashes option but I am not happy at being manipulated into having oral sex with her." Emily bravely showed some spirit and resistance to his will, albeit her unhappy features showed she spoke with a heavy heart and dread of his response.

He smiled and fixed her with a steely gaze.

"Firstly young lady, Celia has already accepted her fate and requested that she be thrashed without mercy to pay for her disgraceful conduct. Secondly, you can leave the room now if you wish and obviously strike off any arrangements we had discussed as regards your future at this college. Thirdly, if you ever speak to me like that again you will find that, to continue your stay at this college, you will need to volunteer to be strung up and flayed from head to toe in front of an audience to make amends. Please don't doubt this for one moment. I think we both know that your future at this college relies heavily on my support and I do believe that we can be useful to each other over the coming couple of years and that this will be mutually beneficial. Finally young lady, we both know that you are shortly going to apply that sharp little tongue of yours to the Senior Tutor's labia and that you are aroused at the thought so can we please not pretend otherwise? You may move into position between her legs when you are ready, presuming you have finished your pompous little oration."

He turned away from her dismissively as Emily's face coloured in proof of the truth of his insightful words.

"Let me just adjust her position and bring her down to make her more accessible, we can have her hoisted high again when we continue with her thrashing."

A quick manipulation of the hoisting system brought Celia's bottom down to partly be supported by the table while her legs were still parted wide and her pussy and arsehole openly displayed in front of Emily as she moved the chair in to perch, with her eyes looking through Celia's legs as Sara bent forward to stroke her forehead, murmuring unheard hushing sounds to try and still a trembling Celia, suffering much consternation having now felt and sensed the unknown company by her naked, defenceless body.

Emily leaned in and kissed Celia's stomach, allowing her hands to settle on the inside of Celia's thighs, feeling the older woman tense in anticipation of what might follow. She began kissing slowly and nuzzling and nipping with her teeth, biting gently; she savoured the taste of her skin and very, very slowly began to edge her mouth down towards the glistening wet folds of the woman's open vagina. She ran her tongue around Celia's belly button, impressed with the toning of a woman over twenty-five years her senior. Dropping her hands slightly lower she positioned her thumbs either side of the puckered hole below her pussy. Emily felt her own pussy moisten as she dipped her head to hold her mouth inches away from the beautiful folds of the pussy that perceptively pulsed in front of her. Celia's demeanour had now changed as the older woman realised what was occurring and her body visibly relaxed as though in longing for the touch of the unknown female's tongue. Celia may well have suspected that it was Emily who was about to perform cunnilingus on her but Stones, being so attuned to her sexual needs, knew that the pure excitement of not knowing exactly who was about to delve into her secret sexual places would be tipping her close to the edge with desire. Although Celia and the professor did not have an exclusive arrangement as far as their sexual activities were concerned, she had rarely ventured outside and hadn't, in fact, been in a lovemaking situation with another of the same sex for twenty years, notwithstanding that there had been times when the two of them had been joined by a second female. Now as she jolted her lower regions up towards where she could feel the hot breath of the other woman, she caused Emily to instinctively lick the offered dish, relishing the taste of another woman for the second time in days after Helen, Chloe, Miranda and Hilary of the Seven Sisters group had all taken advantage of her naked body in one way or another before forcing her and Georgina to indulge each other.

Taking a breath, Emily plunged her tongue into Celia's pussy, whose breathing became increasingly enthusiastic, groans of pleasure escaping from her mouth and she writhed in her binding. Emily revelled in the bitter citrus taste of the bound woman, Celia's copious juices flowing from her pussy and being lapped up by a now positively rampant and no longer reluctant student. She barely broke to pause for a moment as she heard the words of the professor as he slipped something into her hand.

"Wet her anus with her juices and your saliva, your tongue if you wish, then I would like you to imbed this monster into her rear end, Emily."

With no hesitation Emily dipped her head again, with one hand lifting up Celia's bottom to force her tongue into the little slit of an entrance winking becomingly below. For the first time in her life Emily had her tongue deep in another's arsehole; Stones had never doubted that she would resist and hoped that she would appreciate the texture and the acrid taste of Celia's dank dark tunnel as much as he did. Celia herself was almost lost in ecstasy, her body straining at every bound point, tossing and twisting on the bed within the tight restraints.

"Pinch her nipples hard, Sara, bite her breasts. I know you want to, I can see it in your eyes." The professor taunted the other woman, bringing her face to flush bright red yet again, but she did as requested and clamped her mouth over an erect nipple and grasped the other breast with a fierce hold.

Emily slipped her tongue out of Celia's arsehole, and slid the large butt plug vibrator Stones had given her into her soaking pussy, covering it with her juices, before she moved it to the entrance of twitching dark hole beneath. Emily may have originally shown apprehension when she had first realised the thickness of the vibrator but now her beaming face was a picture of fascinated incredulity as Celia's anal ring began to stretch as she applied gentle pressure to slowly push the implement against the resisting muscle of her arsehole.

"In and out slowly and lick my cunt, lick my cunt, don't force it, gently does it, in and fucking out. Up my arse, up my arse, lick my cunt, you beauty, oh fuck me fuck me fuck me oh please, for God's sake lick my fucking cunt and ram that fucker up my arsehole!" screamed Celia, rather shocking both Sara and Emily, as unlike the professor they were unused to hearing this senior and rather proper figure use such language. Seeing Professor Stones' nodding approval,

Emily gave Celia's pussy a long lingering French kiss before sucking hard on the erect little tip of her clitoris. Following Celia's wishes she eased the vibrating butt plug backwards and forwards into her arsehole, until the implement seemed to be sucked from her grasp deep inside Celia, causing her to scream out in wild abandon, now completely infiltrated with Emily's thumb also firmly wedged in her pussy.

Celia had clearly moved beyond words, any cares, fears or inhibitions lost as she headed towards a tumultuous orgasm. The sensation of the piercing, twisting grip on one breast with the powerful suction of Sara's lips on the other, the huge device now vibrating and throbbing inside her rectum, with a thumb pumping inside of her pussy while Emily's lips sucked hard on her clit, seemed to have taken Celia to some place beyond where she had ventured before and her climax exploded inside of her, almost tossing Sara off of her as her body bucked violently and her scream filled the room.

Emily didn't want this moment to stop as she swallowed mouthfuls of the bittersweet nectar almost pouring from Celia's soaking fanny. She pulled her as close as she could, her mouth almost welded to the juddering pussy, wanting to just bury her face into the delectable folds and enticing pink inners of Celia. The two thrust together as Celia came again and again, her pleasure-filled yells and screams seemed to bounce and echo off the walls.

Suddenly the giant figure of the professor loomed over the three of them and with a handful of Emily and Sara's hair, he literally yanked their heads from Celia's body, causing a low moaning wail of displeasure and objection from Celia. Releasing the other two, Stones leant over and slapped Celia hard around the face. Celia burst into tears, realising immediately that the fun part of the evening had been brought to a close and the reality of what was likely to follow became a terrifying dread.

"Emily, draw back the chair to allow me to swing the strap, I think that I will leave the whip until last. You seem to have made her vaginal lips quite swollen all on your own so I'll leave them to return to normal before I apply the grand finale."

Emily settled back onto the chair as the professor adjusted the bonds again to raise Celia's bottom back into the air. Emily's eyes fixed to the exposed treasure trove of Celia's pussy and the bulging anal lips with the triangle of pink plastic that made up the vibrator's tip lewdly poking from the filled hole. Stones watched her face as she adjusted to what had just occurred, a picture of perplexity, happiness and eagerness over the act she had just performed. He marvelled at the young woman's high charged sexuality and ability to switch into her appointed roles with relish. There was no part of the act that she hadn't seemed to enjoy and not for the first time he wondered if he had somehow released the hidden lesbian inside of her.

Raising the strap high, Stones watched as Celia tightened her buttocks as she sensed that the final instalment of her beating was about to start. He paused, waiting several seconds until she naturally relaxed and her cheeks unclenched and then brought the thick leather down hard and fast to thwack soundly against the tops of Celia's bottom.

Even caught unawares Celia was able to tighten her lips, grimace in pain, and remain stoically silent. The second stroke landed a fraction lower and Celia took a sharp intake of breath before loudly exhaling as the third stroke landed about an inch lower. The fourth stroke caused her to moan quietly, the fifth to let slip a guttural groan of complaint. As the sixth landed almost at the centre point of her buttocks, Celia allowed a small cry to escape. She would of course be totally aware of his precision with aim and would be expecting that he would work methodically down the complete surface of her behind before, he was sure, she would be anticipating a repeat of the process. Stones had great respect for Celia's ability to take a severe thrashing without too much fuss and had no doubt that she had resolved to try her hardest to retain some dignity now that she knew that she had a participatory audience. His new aim was to belittle those attempts and break her ambition in front of two women.

With her lips squeezed so tightly together she managed the next three strokes with nothing more than discreet grunts but the tenth stroke moved downwards to the lower more sensitive areas of her battered bottom and she let loose a little squeal of pain. The next two breached her resistance as they slammed down at the top of her thighs, Stones methodically increasing the pressure in his quest to break her will. The squeal turned into a yelp and then a scream as he landed several blows in a blink of an eye, taking her unawares. To his delight and surely to her consternation the loss of control caused her to eject the anal vibrator from her arsehole with some force and no small amount of pain as her rectum stretched wide open and then snapped closed.

Emily's hand had strayed between her legs and her eyes locked with Stones, her face betraying both trepidation and longing.

"Oh Emily, you don't know whether you want to be her or beat her, do you? Now keep your fingers away from yourself please, and try not to leave a damp patch on my chair, young lady. I can see you are thirsting for more, you greedy little thing, but you'd also like to take her place, wouldn't you?"

As though completely spellbound, Emily just nodded in agreement and clasped her wayward hands together, whispering just the one, quietly spoken word. "Yes."

The professor continued his vicious beating, working his way back up her stricken buttocks, unrelenting and savage. Each stroke now landing on top of the previous ones as he began the reverse process of working back up her buttocks. Celia now found out expectation was one thing, the reality of the lashing impact of consecutive strokes hitting the same strip of flesh over and over again was something else entirely. Celia shrieked and bucked as each bite of the strap hit home and then that one shriek turned into another and another until the cries merged into one long wailing lament, as Stones was merciless in applying the stinging lashes. Tears poured from under the sodden blindfold as finally, and to the professor's great delight, Celia finally begged to be spared any further punishment.

"No more please, no more, Dean. Please stop, I am so sorry, please... aaaaaaarrgggghh!"

Her words were rudely interrupted as he continued the ferocious beating, his own breath becoming faster and heavier under the effort he was extending in tearing into the exposed cheeks with the heavy leather strap. He had never laid on the strap with such force and for so many times and when the fiftieth stroke landed he took a few deep breaths, threw down the strap and picked up the knotted whip.

"Just the end game to go and then I think that we consider her duly punished," said Stones as he viciously whipped the lash down vertically on her flaming cheeks. Ignoring the heart-rending screams from Celia, he brought the whip down three more times before switching to apply the fifth stroke horizontally. Her bottom was now a mass of purple-red stripes and raised abrasions and with total dedication the professor paused took careful aim and lashed down between her cheeks, the lash landing with total accuracy down her vulva and into the cleft of her bottom. For several seconds Celia was silent before letting loose a banshee of a wail as the pain of the stroke sunk into her consciousness. He picked up his implements and casually walked over to the cabinet humming to return the items to their allotted hooks and slots.

"Sara, your Senior Tutor will need a different type of comforting now so I will need you to please return your attention to soothing her fevered brow," he said nonchalantly, indicating for Sara to retake her abandoned seat at Celia's head.

"Emily, here's some soothing cream which I am sure you would like to massage into her poor little bottom." He smirked at them both, recognising full well that they had enjoyed their roles and the parts that they had just played.

Sara and Emily exchanged sympathetic glances but neither of them could fail to be aware of the sexual and lustful gleam in each other's eyes.

"Take your time, ladies, enjoy your final moments before you take your leave and I let this naughty rascal back into the land of sight and sound. Just remember that she will never hear from me who was in the room and what parts they had played in her chastisement, so I trust that you will not betray any confidences. I doubt that you would want to face me if I ever heard of tittle-tattle concerning anything that occurs in this room."

The implied threat and the steely gaze of the professor had both women nodding acquiescence and almost swearing allegiance to the cause. Quite exhausted from his energetic activities he retired to his couch and watched as the two tendered to the gently weeping and still keening Senior Tutor.

Thirty minutes later Celia was standing in the corner, hands on head, still unclear exactly who had been in the room having played parts in her chastisement, her sexual abandonment and the most welcome soothing treatment afterwards. Stones had released her and rather dismissively sent her to the corner to contemplate her actions that had led to this day. Celia did indeed feel like a very naughty schoolgirl, but accepted that she did in fact find that quite a turn-on and couldn't really argue that she hadn't rather been the cause of her own demise. She was still in a lot of pain and knew that the throbbing from her most private and sensitive areas was something that was going to give her cause for reflection for a few days. The fact that her buttocks were badly bruised, blistered and stinging severely was of no real concern to her. Once the punishment was over she felt strangely complete and fulfilled, similar to the excitement she felt when she knew that a beating was on the agenda. She also revelled in the vulnerability of being naked and exposed to her mentor, and had no objection to his belittling and humiliating her. It was just the actual pain of each individual stroke that she was not so keen on!

"Seems like you have finally managed to pull yourself together at last. You may thank me and get dressed and get out. Oh, you'll find your knickers have gone, one of my guests wanted to keep a souvenir. Perhaps they'll be returned to you one day. Who knows?"

Under his challenging look, Celia knew better than to question him and coloured up once more at the thought of her knickers in someone else's possession.

"Of course," she managed to say. "Thank you, Professor. Thank you for everything. It was a well-deserved thrashing and the memory of this pain will remind me of my dereliction of duty for a long time. I hope that I will never let you down again and apologise profusely once more for my appalling behaviour."

Seeing Stones looking off to his side, she realised that she had been dismissed and very quickly pulled her remaining clothes on and rather scurried from the room.

The professor smiled at a satisfactory job well done and turned to bring his overhead screen down, simultaneously setting his CCTV recorder to replay the eventful couple of hours just passed. As he watched he slipped his trousers down, releasing his throbbing penis and began to stroke it. After a few minutes he felt inside his pocket for Celia's panties and began to pump his fist hard, covering the tip of his pulsating cock with her underwear.

CHAPTER 11

SARA HAS A STORY TO TELL JAMIE

Sara Morgan smiled as she thought back a couple of weeks to when she had blatantly initiated her relationship with Jamie. Sara had never felt as forward as she did on the day that she had emailed Jamie at his work address on some pretext of checking a student's whereabouts and attendance at a function at Parkinson College. She had asked Jamie if he could unofficially check a minor detail and ring her back at some point. Jamie had responded instantly and had been enthusiastic in his response and gone so far as to state how pleased he had been to hear from her. Sara had been thrilled to read that she had not been far from his thoughts since the punishment sessions of Georgina, Emily and Yishen and the connection he felt sure that they had both made with each other. Jamie had asked Sara if they could meet to discuss what they had shared in the Dean of Discipline's rooms, to which Sara had immediately accepted and the two had agreed to meet in a local wine bar and brasserie for the evening. They had enjoyed each other's company until almost midnight before Sara pleaded an early start and a need for some sleep. Jamie drove her home on the outskirts of the city, had pulled up outside a neat little semi-detached house, and Sara had waited to allow him an opportunity to make a move. There had been a long and telling silence as they had both stared anywhere but at each other and Sara had wondered whether the moment was going to be missed. She needn't had worried, as Sara broke the pause and had unbuckled her seat belt their eyes had met and it became the most natural thing in the world to fall into each other's arms, a long and deep kiss had ensued. Hardly a word was spoken in the next few minutes as their lips explored each other's mouths so when Sara left the car, slightly flustered but beaming with joy, they both knew that something special had just started.

A few days later they had been in Jamie's house, he had cooked a nice meal and they had watched a DVD, Sara nestling in the crook of his arm, stealing occasional kisses. As the credits rolled they began to kiss properly and with no words being spoken they began to undress each other, slowly at first then more and more frantically. Jamie had barely time to register that he was unveiling a true beauty before they were on the rug naked, his fingers plunging into her soaking wet pussy, her hands grasping his hard dick and raking his back. As Jamie had dropped down to taste her and his tongue lapped at her sensitive clit, she had opened her legs wide without a thought of reticence, shame or doubt to allow him a first view of her sex and the dark forbidden spider web surrounded hole of her arsehole. Even in these moments of unbridled joy and passion she was able to register that her hand was filled with a much larger penis than she had ever handled and there was just a moment when her mind registered a fear of her ability to encompass such a size inside of her. However it had been a fleeting moment and the fear turned to a thrill of anticipation as fingers and tongue expertly opened up her sexual flower and her juices began to flow in abundance.

Sara had lost any inhibitions she had and had soon found herself grinding her pussy into his face, forcing his nose hard against her clit as she began the quest for her first climax with him. Using the wet slickness of his pussy-juice covered fingers, Jamie lubricated his cock and presented it at the entrance of her garden of paradise. Sara nodded her consent as Jamie's eyes questioned hers and he gently and slowly began to edge his cock inside of her. Too slowly for Sara as in her lust she leaned forward and grabbed Jamie's hips, forcefully pulling him deep into her.

"Yaaaaaaaaaaaaaaaaaaaaaaaaaaaa!" she screamed as his full length invaded the deep, wet, tight tunnel of her sex. She knew that she was heading towards an orgasmic explosion and her body was convulsing in pleasure and sexual abandon. Her nails scratched and dug into his buttocks, pulling him into her deeper and deeper as they bucked together. Her screams of ecstasy pushed Jamie over the edge and grasping her bottom cheeks in his large hands his slammed his cock deep into her again and again until with a final violent jerk of his body he emptied inside of her as she shook and trembled in her own climax beneath him.

"Fuck," said Sara.

"Fuck indeed," smiled back Jamie as they both recognised the joining of both their minds and bodies.

"Next time, and yes, Jamie, I so want there to be a next time. I promise there will be time to take things slower and really get to know each other's bodies, yes?" Sara murmured into his ear as she reluctantly ushered him out of her front door, excited but quite nervous about how quickly her feelings for Jamie had developed. Sara's head wanted her to tread carefully but was fighting her heart's inclination to throw herself at Jamie's feet!

"Indeed, Sara, oh yes, indeed. I can't wait for a chance to worship your body properly, my love, my beautiful lady." Jamie's whispered, parting words sent thrills throughout her body.

They chatted constantly over the phone over the next few days and agreed to meet for drinks to give them an opportunity to get to know each other without the pressure of the possibility of sex intruding, although in truth they both recognised that most lines of conversation had a hidden, often not too well disguised, element of passion brewing away beneath the surface. Jamie was happy to talk about losing his wife with someone for the first time and Sara had found an understanding kindred spirit who seemed to understand her issues, her anxieties and her doubts particularly after a marriage that had promised so much and delivered so little. They swapped childhood backgrounds, school tales, holiday reminiscences and work records. They exchanged so much information about themselves in their quest to know each other that they almost had to force themselves to calm things down and take a step back. Past experience had taught both of them that there could be a danger of doing too much too soon and that they should allow themselves to cherish learning about each other. They had both already considered that maybe they had the rest of their lives to truly discover each other and they both found that thought uplifting as well as a little bit terrifying.

As the relationship intensified in a very short time, they both realised that they were skirting around discussing the elephant in the room and Jamie tentatively asked Sara about her relationship with the Dean of Discipline and how she had come to become involved in his punishment regime. The time now seemed right to discuss the paths they had taken that led to them meeting in the professor's room for the thrashings of the three girls. Trusting that Sara would reciprocate likewise, Jamie had tentatively divulged the story of his original communication that had eventually led to the visit to the Bondage and Domination Society meeting and how he had met the professor. After swearing her to secrecy, as the society had underlined the importance of confidentiality concerning their activities, he spared little and had trusted to his instincts that she would not be too shocked. Sara's mouth did drop open at several points but she was at ease with this man and in truth had realised that his past must contain sexual elements of sadism and masochism of a type for them to have met as they did. Jamie finished his tale and turned to his blushing and quite aroused lover; he waited with concern apparent in his eyes and whispered into her ear the fear that she would be shocked and disgusted, the hope that maybe had a secret of her own to tell. Sara took a moment and then told her story...

Purely by chance one day, returning from an external afternoon meeting, Sara had espied a student that she recognised sitting on a bench in small, wooded park close to the college. Seeing that the young lady, a Jenny Goldman, was clearly distressed and crying, Sara had stopped to speak to her. Dissolving into tears and falling into her arms, Jenny told Sara that she was overdue for a meeting with the college's Dean of Discipline, that she was due to be punished but she couldn't face going to his rooms to take her dues. In her hand she had some rolled up sheets of paper, sensing that this was connected Sara had asked her if she could see. Not long into her position at the college, Sara had been aware of the idiosyncrasies of its strict rules and regulations regarding behaviour and the college's unusual commitment to the upbringing and pastoral care of the students under its control. She was of course aware of the college's reputation and the whispered comments about the unusually old fashioned and more traditional methods of achieving the aims and ambitions of the institution. The college's modus operandi was renowned and its popularity within certain circles, and an awful lot of envy, due mainly to its phenomenal success rate in producing successful movers and shakers in the world outside of academia.

Sara had opened the sheets and her eyes had got wider and wider as she read what was essentially a confession and note of contrition from the poor girl. Apparently after being warned both by the college's housekeeping and portering departments concerning her continual inability to remember to switch off her hairstyling tongs, she had left them on, placed on top of a basket of rack of papers belonging to one of the college's teaching Fellows, a Professor Martin Flanagan. She had returned hours later to find that she had caused a fire in her room, setting off fire alarms throughout her accommodation block, causing an evacuation of that part of the college and a fire engine to attend albeit the college porters had reacted quickly to the alarm and extinguished the fire before any real damage had been done. A shame-faced and horrified Jenny had been taken by her tutor to see both the furious Fellow whose papers she had destroyed and the Mistress of the college to explain herself and apologise for what she had done. After being reduced to floods of tears by the rage of the Fellow, the Mistress had fixed her with an icy glare and told her that this was an offence that she could well be sent down for.

Whilst Professor Flanagan had clearly thought that this would have been an appropriate punishment for the crime of destroying his valuable documents, the Mistress was keener to get Jenny to understand that her actions had been dangerous and indeed could have been life-threatening. She had told Jenny that she would be forwarding one report to the Senior Tutor and Domestic Bursar to recommend that Jenny undergo a course on health and safety in the home and another to the Dean of Discipline wherein she would recommend a severe punishment with the alternative of expulsion in disgrace if she failed to submit herself voluntarily to a fitting chastisement.

Jenny was by now hiding her head in the crook of Sara's arm as she felt Sara's body tense and stiffen as she read on. The interview with the Dean of Discipline had not really gone very well; Jenny had lost any sense of composure and had ended up on her knees begging for mercy. Sara found herself both astonished and fascinated to read the words that Jenny had clearly been advised to write to save her tenure at the college. Jenny had accepted full responsibility for her action, apologised profusely to everyone concerned including an individual personalised communication to every single person who she had inconvenienced because of her lapse and had agreed that the only way forward was for her to submit to corporal punishment to teach her a lesson once and for all.

Sara continued with reading through as Jenny had detailed that she wished – WISHED, thought Sara in amazement – to be thoroughly thrashed on her bare bottom in penance. Not only that, as Sara's mind whirled, she read that Jenny had asked if the thrashing could be of the most severe possible and that she was happy to accept the Dean's view on the most appropriate punishment and would welcome whatever was determined to be suitable. Sara understood the poor student's desire not to be sent down in disgrace, this would clearly be unacceptable in the circles her family moved in, as professional and social judgement and the accompanying shame would surely be forthcoming and would undoubtedly be very hard to withstand. However Sara had to admire her fortitude, up until this point at least, in facing up to the consequences of her foolish action.

Sara took a breath and turned the snivelling girl around to face her. She knew that it was her duty to the college to move this young lady along and, in truth, was quite keen to see inside the most vaunted Dean of Discipline's rooms.

"Come on, let's go and see the Dean. Think of it like having a

243

nasty bit of dentistry work, the sooner it's done the sooner the pain will go and the sooner you can move on and put this behind you," she said, helping the student to her feet and without giving her a chance to say no or resist she slipped her arm through Jenny's and steered her towards the Dean's quarters. She pushed the buzzer at the Dean's front door and looked up into the camera above her. The door opened and Sara helped Jenny into the entrance area as the further door in front of them automatically opened. Sara led Jenny into the room.

"Enter, ladies. So, Jenny Goldman, did you get lost? Presumably so, otherwise I am sure that you wouldn't be so late, eh?" spoke Professor Stones. "Good day to you, Sara, need some help to get here did she?" he queried.

As Jenny appeared to be unable to form any words at that moment, Sara had answered for them both.

"Yes Dean, I found her on the way here but rather distraught and upset. I thought I'd better get her to you, she has shown me this report for you and I have read it, Professor, I hope that's OK?"

The professor took Jenny's report and fixed her with a stern gaze.

"Jenny Goodman will you stand up straight, let go of Sara's arm and put your hands on your head. I will not put up with this snivelling for long before it will land you in even hotter water than you are presently in."

At this Jenny gulped, began to sob and wilted even more, forcing Stones to react.

"UPRIGHT NOW, hands on head, now!" he barked and Jenny immediately responded and arranged herself as instructed albeit with tears running down her face.

"Sorry sir, yes sir," she whimpered.

"Shall I leave her to you now, Professor?" asked Sara, at which point Jenny turned and grabbed her again.

"Please don't go, please can she stay, Professor?" Sara looked at Stones, slightly bewildered at the way this was going as he shrugged and stared at her in a contemplative way.

"She is going to be a pain to punish I suspect, so it might serve me well if you were to stay to assist if you are happy to do so. I can easily arrange the time with your office if you can spare it?"

Jenny looked at Sara with imploring eyes.

"Please Sara, please," begged the recalcitrant student.

The professor stood up and walked around behind Jenny.

"You have read her little essay, Sara, so you do presumably understand full well that this young lady is due to undergo what should be a very unpleasant experience for her?" he asked Sara with eyebrows raised questioningly.

"Yes Professor, if you think it would help I am sure I have the time."

He stood behind Jenny.

"Hmmmm. I need to be assured that Sara's presence here will mean that you will be compliant during your thrashing, Miss Goodman."

Jenny frantically nodded and looked in gratitude at Sara.

"Well let's have a little tester, shall we? You were late after all, which is an offence earning additional punishment. So remain standing as you are, please."

The professor then then bent and lifted Jenny's dress by the hem, exposing bright white little panties housing a fully rounded but quite pert bottom. Tucking the skirt into the waistband, he quickly yanked the knickers down; Jenny gasped and exhaled noisily but just managed to stay in position as the professor swung his arm back then down rapidly to slap hard against her naked cheeks. Holding her firmly around her stomach with one hand his other swung again and again, the slaps resounding around the room, as Sara stood transfixed, her eyes riveted to Jenny's bottom as it swiftly changed colour to a crimson red. Jenny yelped and jolted but otherwise stood firm and after a minute or two it was over.

"Good girl, that is impressive. It appears that you do know how to take a spanking at least," encouraged Stones. "Right, I am happy to deliver you the punishment you have requested so take the rest of your clothes off, fold them neatly and place them on the chair, then stand facing the bookshelves hands on head. Sara if you would be so kind as to make the two of us a cup of coffee please, the kitchen is through that door there, everything is out, milk's in the fridge. No sugar for me."

With that, Sara dutifully went through to the gorgeous and modern kitchen behind the leather door that opened by sensors as she approached; Sara was pleased that it remained fully open so that she was able to stay in sight of the scenario developing. She watched as Stones sat down at his desk after having quickly flicked through the little clutch bag that Jenny had put down with her clothes.

"Good girl, no phone as I ordered, correct display of dress and white underwear, so you can obey instructions when you want to," he smiled as he looked at the girl whose bottom was about to receive a very thorough whopping. It was a smile that Sara thought she wouldn't ever want directed at her, her insides curdled at the look of pure malice from the granite-like face of Professor Stones.

"You will take your hands away from your groin now and put them on your head like I asked please," Stones said, rising and walking around the girl inspecting her body, seeing a well-proportioned figure with generous breasts and dark nipples, lovely unblemished skin and finished off with the fleshy and full set of small nicely shaped buttocks.

"Yes, a good bottom for beating," he said in a disconcerting manner as he nonchalantly prodded both of Jenny's bottom cheeks with his finger before he walked back to his desk to read her report. "Wall, girl, wall. Over there, nose against the bookshelves, I don't want to see your naughty face."

Sara was relieved on Jenny's behalf to see Stones nodding in approval at Jenny's written efforts. As far as Sara was concerned it showed full responsibility accepted, a complete understanding of the danger she had caused, a full and wholesome apology and most importantly a total acceptance that she deserved a severe punishment. As Sara finished making the coffee she realised that the waiting game was part of the experience for Jenny as Stones made idle conversation as they sat and sipped at their beverages. The two members of staff had not spent many moments together but she sensed his approval of her and was delighted when he informed her that he had long formed the opinion that he needed assistance to support and provide a bit of pastoral care and hand-holding to some of his less arrogant miscreants. He told her that he was looking to build a little team to oversee and assist in his disciplinary duties and intimated she seemed an ideal candidate for what he had in mind. Sara guessed that she was on trial and that he was now about to test her to see whether there could be a useful role in the future for her. She reddened in embarrassment when he let on that he had been watching her with his peripheral vision as he had exposed Jenny's buttocks and then proceeded to spank them. Sara had been totally unaware of his observation but could find no words to correct or challenge him when he told her that he had duly noted the sparkle and glint in her eyes as he had done so.

"Right, young lady, let's get started on your involvement in giving this reprobate a damned good hiding, shall we?" the professor concluded, very conversationally, as though they were just running through a tutorial session.

"Get started, sir?" Jenny unwisely queried, her still sore bottom giving lie to any thought that things had yet to begin!

"Oh yes, those little slaps were just a reminder about my views on tardiness and good time-keeping. Think of that little moment as a reminder, an aide memoire so to speak." He grinned at the disconcerted girl who was starting to get a true idea of how awful this whole ordeal was likely to be. He took Jenny by the earlobe and led her over to his chair. Before he sat down he leant behind Jenny and at rapid speed gave the backs of her legs four sharp slaps.

"That's just a gentle reminder that you do not offer an opinion unless invited. We will ensure that by the time you leave this room you will have learnt respect, obedience, and humility and I will strive to help you become a better human being."

Stones smoothed his trousers and patted his lap.

"Over my knee now, legs apart, adopt the standard position please," he ordered Jenny. "Sara, could you kneel at her head and hold her hands nice and tightly for this little spanking please? I think Jenny may appreciate a little bit of assistance in coming to terms with the seriousness of her punishment from now on. Jenny, I will now spank your bottom 100 times and while I do so I want you to think about your actions that have led you to this shameful point and hopefully we can get you started on a true path of improvement and contrition. It will be my honour and duty to assist in your venture."

Sara was entranced, by his words and Jenny's nakedness, as she took the silently weeping Jenny's hands, feeling the suspense build while he talked and disarmingly stroked Jenny's trembling bottom whilst doing so. Sara had no idea how Jenny must be feeling but the professor was certainly playing havoc with her emotions and thought processes. She almost wanted to yell at him to get on with it, finding her anticipation and eagerness to witness the suffering of another quitter disconcerting but undoubtedly exciting. Seconds later the huge hand of the professor slammed down hard on first one buttock then the other and Sara's mind was suddenly concentrated on the job in hand as Jenny jolted in pain and surprise before starting to struggle against her hold. The screaming started in earnest when he changed the sequence to five at a time on one buttock and then five on the other. The backs of Jenny's legs were not to be spared when she lost concentration and closed them in her writhing.

"Open legs, girl, open legs. Let me see the target, your anus is the bullseye, my girl, that's what I centre on my aim on so keep showing me it please. Come on, legs wide apart, cheeks open." Jenny lifted her head and stared at Sara with real horror at this rather descriptive reference to the display of her open bottom as she struggled to retain any composure and dignity; the professor's taunting words, as he had indeed promised, being a further punishment and lesson all by themselves.

Sara was to find out that it hardly takes any time at all to deliver one hundred spanks, plus a few extra punishment ones, but those couple of minutes must have felt like a lifetime to Jenny as the poor recipient; once more tears streamed down her face and she desperately gripped Sara's hands to keep her balance and just a modicum of self-respect. Sara remembered vividly how her bottom had once stung like never before with memories of her mother and her large hairbrush that had served to keep her on a straight path in a few of her formative years. She had in truth only received the sting of the hairbrush on three occasions during her childhood, but the discomfort caused had meant that just the threat of the brush had generally been enough to curb any bad behaviour.

"Up you get now, that was your real warming up," said the professor after his hand had landed for the final time and Jenny's bottom had turned a very deep scarlet.

"Lovely spankable cheeks, my dear, I must say, a pleasure to spank indeed. Enough padding to make it a joy to land a hand on, small enough to be covered quite easily and plump enough to cause a good sting and my, you have turned a gorgeous colour, hasn't she Sara?" His eyes twinkled as he directed his voice towards a rather spellbound Sara.

"Oh, what? Yes, sorry Professor, what were you asking? I'm afraid I was a bit preoccupied," she replied, her face colouring, as she helped Jenny up off the professor's lap.

"I was just saying what a perfect specimen of a bottom we are being treated to. Give the poor girl a nice rub, Sara, I'm sure she'd appreciate a bit of comforting. Bend over the padded chair there Jenny if you would like Sara to help rub some of the stinging away."

Sara and Jenny automatically complied and as Jenny bent over the chair, Sara gently laid soothing hand over the hot cheeks. Sara's head was spinning, she felt drugged with the pure thrill she was feeling as she anticipated the further punishment that was to come on these very cheeks. She was aware that Stones seemed to know exactly the state she was in and realised that he was creating a memorable shared experience for all three of them.

"On the chair, knees on the seat, legs as far apart as you can, please, now bend over the back raising your bottom high and stretch yourself down and hold the chair legs." A whimpering Jenny followed his instructions with Sara aiding her and whispering words of encouragement and calmness.

"Come on sweetheart, it's well underway now so let's just get it over with," she said as she aided a now rather compliant and gently weeping Jenny into position.

Sara and the professor watched as Jenny held herself perfectly before she suddenly worked out that her bottom cheeks were now spread and she was presenting him with a parted crack with her arsehole on show. She threw her hand back covering her open cleft, exclaiming, "Oh no, you can see my whole crinkle."

Both Stones and Sara quietly laughed at her cute, childish expression and pointless action.

"My dear child, I can assure you that I am going to be very familiar with your sweet little crinkle over the next few minutes so please don't be silly," chuckled Stones.

Sara took the girl's hand away and helped her reposition it correctly on the chair leg.

"Crinkle you say, don't suppose you called your vagina your winkle did you?" The professor was obviously amusing himself now. Sara nudged Jenny to prompt a response.

"Er no sir. That was my mother's name for my brother's penis, my um, um, v-v-vagina was called my Winnie, sir." Stones laughed as he parted her cheeks with his fingers he peered at her intently.

"Crinkle, eh, how quaint but actually quite appropriate considering you certainly do have a crinkly little anus. Pretty though, yes, quite lovely. Sara do come and have a look, it's always interesting to compare the wonderful variety of designs of the private places of our miscreants. Stay perfectly still, Jenny, or you will pay the price and relax those cheeks so Sara can have a proper look at your crinkle and your Winnie."

Jenny howled in despair and grabbed the chair legs as Sara released her and rather tentatively joined the professor with her head inches from the bright red buttocks bent so exposed over the chair back. Jenny automatically tightened her cheeks as Sara leant in and as quickly relaxed them at a warning growl from the professor.

"Take a good sniff, Sara. I always like the challenge of seeing if I can spot the scent of the shower gel or body lotion used on the anuses of my naughty young ladies."

Sara found herself even more flustered as she rather cautiously smelt another female's backside for the first time in her life! She obeyed, more for fear of consequences if she refused than desire or curiosity and again Jenny clenched her cheeks at the suggested intrusion.

"No further warnings. Next step will be a rather large implement that will most certainly force those anal lips open!" he barked threateningly.

Sara shushed her urgently to try to stop her reacting and gently stroked down her crack to try and relax her. Sara was certainly getting an understanding of the techniques the professor used to break down the last remaining vestiges of dignity and pride. There could be no place more private and taboo than your arsehole, and this invasion and violation of one's most personal area was truly a masterpiece of torturous humiliation.

"It's OK, Jenny. It's OK. Just take deep breaths and relax. There you go, good girl." And an aside to the professor, "I plump for mango, sir, what did you think?"

Stones moved in again and using two fingers he roughly parted Jenny's cheeks to their fullest extent and virtually plunged his face into her crack causing the already distraught student to shriek at the encroachment as his nose tip actually breached her anal opening.

"Yes maybe you are correct, Sara. I'd thought apricot initially. Well Jenny, do divulge your anal presentation preference. Mango, apricot or some other as rather undetermined fruit scent?"

"It's mango and pineapple moisturiser, sir. Oh my god! I can't believe this, this is appalling, awful, oh my, oh help me someone, help me!" Jenny voice betrayed her brokenness and Sarah's heart felt for her.

Stones just laughed, nodded to himself in a very self-satisfied manner and walked across to his wall cabinet with Sara feeling rather in awe of the way in which he was, piece by piece, breaking Jenny down. As the cabinet door swung wide open, the sight revealed caused Sara to audibly draw her breath in, as her eyes took in the array of punishment items hanging there. Stones withdrew a leather paddle, a thin cane and a narrow leather strap.

"These should do the trick," he said quietly. "I'm going to paddle her now, Sara, fifty wallops hard and fast so back to your station and hold her tight please. Jenny, prepare yourself, the spanking may have warmed you up, but the paddle is going to set you on fire."

Jenny trembled in Sara's arms and Sara tightened her grip in readiness. Splat! Splat! Splat! The paddle landed rapidly across the already swollen buttocks, as true to his word Stones' arm came down in a very fast cavalcade of painful blows. Jenny struggled in vain and yelped as each blow struck home, her bottom flattening and reshaping in time to accept the next stinging swipe. Closing her legs as an automatic response without thinking proved to be a mistake as additional blows struck the backs of her legs.

"Open, open, all the time open, please young lady. Keep that little crinkle winking away at me," was more than enough of a reminder!

The pummelling from the paddle continued until, excluding the additional ones on her legs, the paddle had landed fifty times and Jenny was sobbing uncontrollably and in total distress.

"You're halfway through your thrashing now, young Jenny, so let's try and keep some decorum. Sadly for you the more painful half is about to begin, but maybe you are learning important lessons about health and safety in the home, so it's not all bad, eh?" Stones offered, not so helpfully.

"Soothe her, Sara please, blow her nose and wipe her tears and then we will move onto the more serious improvers… that is the cane and the strap to you, my young novice," he imparted to Sara, causing her heart to flip and her stomach to gurgle.

Sara was bewildered to feel so exhilarated to be referred to as such. Her mind was still whirling with the whole occasion, but she recognised that she was seriously enjoying herself in this surreal moment in the presence of this man of such great magnitude and prominence in the revered world of academia. Sara, having wiped Jenny's face, picked up on Stones' intimation that he should escort Jenny over to the sofa across the room and she did so, sensing correctly that she should lay her face down, bottom up. Sara began to stroke Jenny's poor battered arse cheeks, leaning forward to whisper in her ear.

"Good girl, good girl. It's all OK, soon to be over, my sweet," she whispered as she kissed the girl's tear-stained cheeks whilst her fingers fluttered lightly over her bottom, round and round, feeling the intense heat generated by the fierce beating.

"Harder please, can you rub a bit harder? It really helps then," simpered Jenny and Sara increased the pressure, squeezing and kneading the swollen cheeks. Sara couldn't help but watch, rather enthralled, as the kneading of Jenny's cheeks opened up both her pussy lips and the arsehole above.

The professor watched the interaction closely; he was impressed by Sara's commitment to the process and was aware that he had created a scenario that was awakening desires within her.

"Time to proceed to the next stage, Sara, off to the end of the sofa and hold her legs out straight and tight please, I will put leg straighteners on her I think, I very much doubt that she will have the resilience to remain in position without them once I lay the strap on."

Jenny sobbed and went to twist over onto her back but Sara held her down with plenty of force, keeping the girl's body firmly across the end of the furniture.

"No, Jenny, do as the professor says now. This is all part of you learning obedience as well as acknowledging and accepting that irresponsible and uncaring behaviour results in repercussions and accountability. You do the crime, you do the time."

Sara wasn't exactly sure where all that came from but was pleased to see the approving nods from Stones. He fixed the restraints into placing, adjusting them to stretch her legs wide and rudely apart, presenting her buttocks taut and firm, the crack stretched open. Stones forced a couple of cushions under her, raising her bottom up and exposing her pussy lips beneath her now very prominent arsehole. "Lovely display, Jenny, perfectly presented. I am looking forward to helping to improve you, it's going to be an absolute pleasure strapping these beauties. Oh and look at that lovely crinkle now, you see you are starting to show it off most proudly." As he said the taunting words he ran his hand lazily over her bottom, the combination of his words and his fingers causing her to desperately clench her bottom trying to hide her arsehole from his view and touch. Sara moved into position at the student's head and placed her hands firmly on Jenny's shoulders.

"Yes, quite a lovely picture. Don't clench so much, my dear, it's far better to take a walloping on relaxed cheeks."

Stones winked at Sara and she realised that this was all part of the upping of the game, this gentle and consistent humiliation and degrading of his culprit's nature and psyche. She certainly now understood that it wasn't only about physical chastisement and retribution, it was about character building and mettle development. It was about humiliation, breaking down of the spirit and shaming. As the professor had often stated, this was about improvement.

Sara watched in total fascination as he picked up the strap, her eyes wide and fixed on the leather implement.

"You've behaved quite well so far, Jenny, so it's the light strap and twenty lashes for you now." He let the strap dangle in her arse crack and peering over the top of Jenny's head, Sara saw the terrified girl's bottom start to tremble as she anticipated the first blow. The professor lifted the strap and paused, waiting for the moment Jenny naturally allowed her bottom muscles to relax and the tension to leave her cheeks, he then brought the leather down with speed, force and expertise, producing a resounding crack.

"Yaaaaahhhhhhh!" was Jenny's response as a furious red mark developed across the centre of her buttocks, followed by an equally inarticulate, "Guuuuurrrrr," before the next blow struck home higher on her cheeks which produced a more primal scream from its victim. Again he cracked her with the strap and again she screamed. Holding her firmly, Sara found herself alive with excitement as she waited for the strap to fall once more. She suddenly didn't care that this was a clearly deviant side of herself materialising, she just wanted to watch this girl's bottom writhing under the onslaught. She squeezed her legs tightly together as she realised, with some shock, that she could feel her pussy becoming moist. Jenny yelped and hollered as every stroke landed; the professor had readjusted his aim now that her whole bottom had been covered with angry red weals and had begun to strike her with diagonal lashes. Finally the strap dropped from his hand and Sara pulled the weeping young woman's face into her arms. She kissed her tears away and stroked her hair, whispering soothing words of comfort until Stones' voice broke into their private moment.

"Use this oil on her bottom, Sara, if you can tear yourself away for a moment, massage away some of the pain. She's doing rather well, in fact, you are both doing very well. I am very pleased so far with the way things have gone. Well done, ladies, good job."

Sara, intrigued again to recognise the thrill she received from being included in the professor's words of praise, took the oil from him with a beaming smile and moved behind Jenny's bent over body, putting her hand over her mouth as she now saw the full extent of the damage wrought by the strap. Jenny's whole bottom was a fiery deep red colour and Sara almost dared not touch it. She leaned forward, closing her eyes and gently kissed each bottom cheek then gasped in horror to look up and see the professor's smiling and knowing face watching her. Sara started to massage the oil into the red cheeks, fully aware that her own face probably matched Jenny's colour. Sara was shocked to realise that she was staring lustily at the pink moist pussy lips inches from her fingers and that Jenny was quietly mewing as her fingers brushed over her swollen bottom. Her fingers lingered as she reached down to Jenny's lower bottom cheeks, parting them gently and exposing more of the girl's sex beneath. Sara felt mesmerised and confused, it's just the circumstances she thought brushing off the desire to dip her head to kiss and lick the girl's entrancing folds.

"Enough, ladies, take Jenny over to the desk now please, Sara." Stones again broke into the erotic fantasy world Sara's mind was drifting into.

Sara shook her head again to try and clear the worrying feelings that were invading her head, shocked to think that some kind of anomalous, for her anyway, force had been let loose from deep inside of her. She had never before in her life considered the options that had been flashing through her head as she approached Jenny's pussy; she knew it had been lust and probably a little bit of love produced surely just by the peculiar situation and the sight of Jenny being laid so open and fragile before her. Tenderly Sara helped Jenny to get to her feet and walked over to the desk that had been pulled out, noting the ankle and wrist cuffs on each leg and wondering about the odd-looking leather mount similar to a bicycle seat fixed to the top front edge.

"Feet to the restraints, strap her to the legs, Sara, please."

A shaking and shaken Jenny still seemed in a daze as Sara quickly positioned her legs apart and fixed the cuffs to her ankles.

"Bend over the desk, arms down the sides, hands reaching firm to the legs at the back. Position yourself centrally onto the support mound there please," said Stones, snapping her hands in the wrist cuffs as Jenny compliantly prostrated herself.

Feeling the leather support between her legs Jenny found her upper legs forced apart and the realisation had clearly dawned that the desk was lower at the front which had forced her bottom to be raised into the air by both her positioning and the leather support.

"There now, you should be able to feel a nice sensation of air between your bottom cheeks to freshen you up a bit now we have got you fully stretched open. Nice to see that beautiful crinkle on display again, isn't it Sara?" Stones said provocatively. "Lovely display of her vagina too in this pose, don't you think? Right, round the front you go, leave me with the business end to deal with," he continued, absentmindedly letting his fingers run along the inside of Jenny's bottom crack. Jenny froze as she suddenly seemed to snap aware of what was happening.

"Oh my god, please stop, I don't want this, stop now please sir."

The professor smiled as, removing his fingers from the valley between her bottom cheeks, he went across to select a thin, whippy cane from his cabinet.

"Too late for a change of mind now, young lady, don't spoil things now by misbehaving. Or misbehaving any further, I should say. Remember that you wrote to me and specifically asked if you could have this form of punishment. I am just following up on your request and delivering what you ordered! You've just got your caning to go and then hopefully you will have learnt a lesson that you'll remember for a long time. Good girls need a little lesson every now and then too, and I suspect that you are mostly a good girl who just does the occasional naughty thing. Which, for the moment anyway, makes you a naughty girl, but don't worry, Jenny, I don't think you are beyond repair and restitution, sometimes a good thrashing is all that is required to get a miscreant back on the road to righteousness. It is our pleasure to administer this and help guide you to an improved state. Now I will need these counting and you will thank me clearly, and with real meaning and sincerity, for each stroke."

"You are sodding joking. I will not, now let me go!" cried out Jenny. Barely able to move, she seemed unaware that she was in no position to be making such an unwise choice of words. Sara's efforts to smother her face and muffle her provocative words were to no avail.

"Oh dear, oh dear, oh dear. Not clever at all. How very disappointing and more worryingly, quite unintelligent and stupid. Firstly, that will be two extra strokes for disobedience and rudeness. Secondly, any further repetition of such behaviour will earn you six extra strokes which will be applied to the backs of your legs, and thirdly, you will now apologise and confirm that you understood and accept my earlier request in regard to the counting of the strokes."

Sara looked at the set jaw of the harnessed girl and knew that she needed to pull herself together before landing herself in even deeper trouble. Sara slapped her face and grasped the shocked girl's jaw in one hand.

"Jenny, listen to me. Do exactly what the professor has asked. Quickly!"

It was enough to bring Jenny to her senses. "Oh God, I am so sorry, sir. I didn't mean it, sir. I am just so scared, sir. Yes sir, I will count the strokes, sir, and thank you for each one, sir, I am so sorry," Jenny gabbled.

The professor began to hum and started to swish the cane close to Jenny's face.

"Would you like your caning now, Jenny?" he asked. Jenny made a small, strangled sound but as Sara cupped her chin once more in encouragement.

She blurted out, "Please sir, I would like my caning now pleeeeeeeeaaassse. Ooooooowwwwwyeeee!" The cane lashed down against her raised cheeks with force, cutting off Jenny's words.

"One, sir, thank you sir," whispered Sara in her ear.

"One. One. One. Oh, sir one, sir, thank you sir, oh my," Jenny responded.

Each stroke of the cane felt like a red-hot poker and been applied to her bottom and Jenny's screams filled the room before, with Sara's encouragement, she gainfully managed to force out the requested words. Sara gripped the girl's face between her hands and after the twelfth stroke was surprised and delighted when Jenny pushed her face forward and kissed her on the lips.

"Thank you. I love you, Sara," she whispered.

Shocked but suddenly aflame with desire, Sara kissed her back. "I love you too, my darling," before their little distraction was cruelly interrupted as stroke number thirteen bit into Jenny's lower cheeks.

"Aeeeeoooooowwww! Oooh, sir, oh, oh, oh, thirteen sir, thank you sir," she yelled.

"Now I'd like you to add a request for your next stroke after you've counted the stroke and thanked me for my delivery."

"What, sir? Sorry sir, w-w-what do you mean?" stammered Jenny.

"Oh dear, Sara, hopefully you can tear yourself away from your little seduction routine to translate my request into words of one syllable so that this seemingly stupid girl can understand and obey. Meanwhile here's a little something to remind her to listen and answer quickly and intelligently when I ask her a question." With that, the professor tucked the cane under his arm and proceeded to begin slapping Jenny's bottom with his hand.

"Quickly Jenny, just tell him that you are ready for the next stroke and ask him to cane you." Sara, although flustered herself at realising that her little moment with Jenny had been witnessed, murmured into Jenny's ear, desperate to appease the angry academic.

"Just do whatever he tells you to, sweetheart, the sooner you do the sooner this will all be over." Jenny took a second to contemplate Sara's words of wisdom, and tear her concentration away from the constant stinging of her battered bottom, before the penny finally dropped.

"Ouch, ouch, oh Professor, sir. I am sorry sir, please sir, I am ready sir, ouch, ouch, ouch. Oh, yes sir, cane me again please, sir. Can I have my next stroke, sir, please sir?"

Stones knew that she was close to the moment of full submission and that he had succeeded in taking her to the point he reached with almost every single miscreant he had thrashed in the past. He lifted the cane again and brought it swiftly down very high on her cheeks where there was less fatty flesh in protection. Her reaction was exactly why he saved this spot for specific moments during a caning. Jenny let loose an incredibly long and high-pitched scream as the cane-virgin flesh sung fearsomely and she once again burst into floods of tears.

"Come on, darling, talk to us, say the words," Sara urged Jenny, who was struggling to control the absolute despair she had been reduced to.

After a few seconds' pause Jenny managed to blurt out the required words rather laboriously. "Fourteen, sir, thank you so much, sir. Please sir." Stopping to sob and sniff loudly she then continued, "I am ready for my next stroke, sir."

"Certainly, my dear girl, happy to do so," teased the professor in the manner he employed aimed at increasing the whole sense of degradation and humiliation for his victim, as he swung the cane in its unforgiving arc again to land squarely across the centre of her bottom. There was little reaction from Jenny other than a slumping of her body, a relaxing of the tension.

"Fifteen sir, thank you sir. Please sir, I am ready for my next stroke, thank you, sir," she whimpered quietly.

He smiled. The submission stage had been reached, there would be no further resistance.

The next few strokes were far less harsh from Stones as was his inclination once his sufferer had been bested, although he laid on the final strike with full force just to ensure that the memory of the beating was lasting and memorable.

"Yaaaaaaaaaaaaaaaaaah! Oh twenty-two sir, thank you sir, sorry sir… ow, ow, ow. I am ready for my next stroke now, sir," Jenny half shouted out in the pain of the stroke and being so conditioned now to obedience that she had truly forgotten that she had just received what was scheduled to be her last stroke.

"No!" Sara knew that she had to curtail the girl's automatic response. "Just thank him properly for punishing you and apologise for being so naughty," she desperately prompted, but the professor was having none of it.

"Oh, you want more, fair enough," as he brought the cane down harshly for the twenty-third time on the bright red bottom, raising yet another welt across her flanks.

"Yo! Yaaah! Yo!" was the incoherent response before Jenny gathered herself. "Twenty-three, thank you sir. Sir, I am so sorry for my disgraceful behaviour, sir, and I would like to thank you for punishing me so well, sir."

Stones bent down to inspect her thoroughly beaten buttocks, gesturing Sara to join him. "A fine job, if I say so myself, oh yes, there are some beautiful lines here, can you see my dear?"

Sara leant in next to the professor as she peered totally fascinated at the angry red lines criss-crossing over Jenny's bottom but was a bit shocked when he once more rather cruelly yanked her swollen cheeks further apart.

"One last look at that lovely little crinkle. Any further issues with fire regulations and I'll be aiming the cane just there," he said, tapping his finger emphatically against Jenny's arsehole, causing Jenny to desperately squeeze the open cavern as tight as she could, undoubtedly while trying not to imagine the damage that a cane would do to such a tender spot.

Stones laughed. "The humiliation is a good half of the punishment, you get that, don't you, Sara?" he whispered conspiratorially. Sara nodded, yes, she did indeed, she had really gotten an insight and an appreciation into the way the professor worked. She was also well aware that she had exposed herself to him in a way that she hadn't possibly imagined doing, letting loose feelings that she had not dreamed she possessed. Had she handed him power over her? Had her lapse exposed her to a tricky disciplinary situation? Surely he would forgive her a moment caught off guard, she thought to herself apprehensively...

The professor opened a drawer and handed Sara a different tub of cream, then unhooked Jenny from the restraints, allowing her to get up and stretch, her hands then automatically going to her damaged rear quarters. Her eyes widening as she felt the raised welts and twisted trying to see the results of what she could feel.

"Take her into the bathroom, Sara. There's a full-length mirror in there, Jenny dear, since you seem to have a desire to see what damage your behaviour has caused to your buttocks. Then, Sara, please help her to sit on the bidet, it's been full of iced water for a while so should be perfect now to take the sting out of her poor cheeks. Give her five minutes or so ice water treatment, then towel her down and apply a good thick layer of this cream. The bruises will come through soon then in a few days, Jenny, probably about a week or so later your bottom should be restored to its original unblemished beauty."

A few minutes later Sara had finished the intimate towelling down of a truly subdued and chastened Jenny. Having been originally apprehensive about touching the girl's most private areas, Sara had then realised that Jenny had totally succumbed to the idea of Sara as her protector and guardian angel. With Jenny now face down reposing, legs apart on the professor's chaise longue, Sara was rubbing the thick cream into her glowing cheeks and enjoying every moment of the experience. At first, Sara thought that she was imagining the subtle movements of Jenny's posterior as she worked the cream in, but then she heard the younger girl's change of breath and gentle sighs, she knew that the recipient was getting as much out of this as the giver!

"Right ladies, let's remember that this is a punishment session please." The professor's voice intruded into the separate world that the two females were drifting into. Sara froze, she had to get a grip, that was the second time she had let her emotions take control, or was it passion or lust, she thought, a little bit disturbed at how things had developed.

"Jenny, against the wall, please, hands on head. Time for you to have some moments of reflection on what has occurred today. Sara, you may leave now but I'd very much like to have a chat with you tomorrow lunchtime if you find the time please. Thank you very much for your assistance today though, it was truly invaluable and mainly professional." The professor said, raising an eyebrow at her, immediately causing her cheeks to redden yet again.

"I'd also propose that Jenny, and please don't think about speaking, girl, you are reflecting, remember?" he sharply reminded the girl. "As I was saying I'd also propose that Jenny and you get together shortly so you can check on her recovery and Jenny can have the opportunity to thank you properly for all the help you have given her. Off you pop now, Sara. Goodbye."

Sara learnt later that after about an hour, which seemed more like half a lifetime to Jenny, the professor finally barked out an instruction ordering her to dress and with a warning about any recurrence of issues with her, had given her a final slap on her still-throbbing bare backside one more time to hasten her on her way and had dismissed her with that air of indifference he had perfected. Jenny had dressed as fast as she could and made her way out, beaten and defeated.

Whilst Sara was happy to honestly recount the session's details to Jamie, she refrained from adding the specifics of what happened afterwards. She didn't realise that he was later going to find out.

She did tell him about the rather cringing chat she'd had to undergo with the professor the next day when she had stood red-faced in front of this quite imposing man. The professor had reminded her quite formally about the college rules concerning fraternizing in any way with students under the care of the staff and teaching body. For a while Sara was concerned that she had put her position at the college in danger and then had been hit by the fleeting thought that perhaps she could find herself being subject to the professor's preferred form of discipline. However Stones had seemed content to stick to a verbal dressing down on this occasion, although he made it quite clear to Sara that there was a line not to be crossed with the students and she had stepped close. Certain words in that excruciating conversation were etched in her memory and would come back to haunt her later.

"It is Gross Misconduct if you cross the line, Sara, do please remember that. Whilst the college would be reluctant to dismiss staff members for this sort of violation, it does happen, albeit in certain cases in can be an option for the culprit to choose an alternate form of severe punishment. I think you know what I am referring to, Sara, but this is at the discretion of the Mistress and me. Acts that are deemed to be of Gross Misconduct can clearly risk the college's reputation so by necessity any punishment must be harsh." The professor leaned back in his chair and peered at her in silence for a while.

Sara broke the silence. "Professor, I am so sorry, I don't really know what came over me. I think I was just caught up in the moment and acted quite out of character. I do apologise and of course accept any stricture you feel appropriate." Sara was gambling very much in hitting the right tone and choosing the right words, hoping desperately that they wouldn't be interpreted as a request to undergo corporal punishment of any sort.

She was relieved when he suddenly changed tone.

"You are forgiven, Sara. You were generally exceptional with your assistance and I would very much like to set things in action to make you available to assist me in future, um, let's call them, projects. I hope that you would consider helping me out again on a regular basis?" He beamed at her.

Sara didn't hesitate. "Of course, sir, it would be my pleasure and an honour to get to work with you again, sir. Thank you, sir."

Thus setting in place an arrangement that had led to some interesting times for Sara over the last couple of years, as well as a nice increase in her salary, as she became his go-to assistant when dealing with and supporting students of a certain manner and type in disciplinary situations.

CHAPTER 12

WHEN JAMIE AND SARA GOT

VERY INTIMATE

Sara was very still as she realised that Jamie's face could only be inches away from her open bottom crack. *Yes,* she prayed. *Oh, please yes.*

"God, your bottom is so beautiful," he whispered. "Your cheeks are so soft and pure; your crack is such a tease with its soft little brown hairs twirling around that absolutely divine-looking arsehole. I feel so lucky to have this chance to worship such perfection, it looks wonderful, it smells so enticing, rich musky and oh so sexy. I have to taste it and yet I don't want to hurry as this moment is just awesomeness in itself and I could look at these divine cracks of beauty and just be content to worship them for ever."

Sara felt herself relax as any tension and anxiety over being so exposed was just melting away with his seductive, rather poetic and calming words. She could feel her pussy responding to his hypnotic tone and longed for him to make contact but knew, like Jamie, that this was a moment in time to treasure. This wondrous feeling of opening herself so totally and absolutely to this man, a moment of trust and devotion to be savoured, she could feel herself almost crying in joy at this sensual and erotic sensation. She was totally his now, in this moment, she knew that there would be no resistance from her, she was giving herself to a man in a manner that she had never come close to before. Jamie inched even closer to this centre of her being; she waited in awe as she felt her puckered rosebud relax, as she let the tension go, and knew her arsehole was welcoming him. Sara could smell her own sexual aroma and knew full well that the evidence of her excitement and anticipation as her pussy visibly became more moist and ready for attention would be so obvious to her lover. Jamie's hands reached around her body and gently grasped her hanging breasts and she could feel the racing and thumping of her heart as she started to pant short breaths in her passion, losing herself to sexual arousal and desire.

He paused, with her nipples taut beneath his pinching fingers, and she nearly screamed in frustration as she felt his mouth within licking distance of the wetness of her pussy lips. Jamie reached back beneath her with one hand, sliding it under her deliberately just barely brushing her pussy. She tensed again, an almost complaining murmur escaping from her lips as he stilled his hand and let his inner wrist rest against her wetness whilst he gently placed two fingers either side of her arsehole. She trembled as ever so slowly; he moved the fingertips nearer and nearer to the dark centre. Jamie squeezed harder with his left hand, the nipple like a hard nub between his fingers. She grimaced in pain but not a word of complaint passed her lips.

Slowly he ran a single fingertip around the external ring of her arsehole; Sara convulsed and bucked.

"Shhh," he entreated. "Shhh, my darling, shush now."

Sara willed herself to stay still but felt her emotions twirl, she wanted him so much to do whatever he wished but she also wanted this feeling to last forever and didn't want to make any moves that would hasten him and fast forward this perfect moment in her sexual education. She knew her arsehole was opening and closing as she became more and more worked up and briefly wondered at the picture she was presenting at close quarters. Sara hoped that he truly appreciated that she was allowing him freedom and access in a way she had never done before to an erstwhile lover. She had never exposed her herself so wantonly before, and doubted Jamie would be aware that he was so privileged to be allowed this access to Sara's most private and most secretive entrance. She reached down as Jamie moved round so that she had access to the hardness in his shorts that strained to be released, her fingers encircling the rigid length and longed to accommodate it inside her wet love hole. Sara groaned, in both excitement and frustration, as she started to truly long for more contact from her oh so patient lover. She deftly unzipped his shorts and freed the large erect penis inside, her eyes widening as she took in the length of his manhood.

Jamie groaned in response to the contact; he moved his fingers from her bottom and stroked her pussy lips, causing Sara to buck in sexual pleasure and increased anticipation as his fingers slid along the wet vagina to her hard clit. Her bottom jerked back and her arsehole met his perfectly positioned mouth.

Sara shrieked in uncontrolled pleasure and lust as a finger breached her slit and his wet lips met her anal lips, forming a perfect sealed circle. Her body immediately jolted in mind-exploding sexual passion and in massive relief and her body racked with shudders as the build-up of sexual tension was partially released. Jamie sucked lustily at her anus, his tongue flicked at the very centre of her being, his fingers continued to probe her pussy, flick at her clitoris and twist her nipples in turn bringing her quickly to the climax that had been building. Sara squealed in ecstasy, her closed fist now pumping his cock, her body in turmoil as wave after wave of climax shook her body from head to toe. Taking a breath, Jamie leaned back and then plunged his tongue deep inside the open dark hole of her arse. Sara could hardly contain herself at the feelings she experienced as he fully probed her anal chamber, and began to dip his tongue in and out with speed as she opened up. Sara's head shot backwards as she finally enjoyed the joint sweet pleasures of a lover's rasping tongue deep in her previously forbidden and virginal arsehole, while so in tune with the fluttering fingers simultaneously tweaking and invading her pussy. Releasing her breast, Jamie suddenly brought his other hand back and round her. Plunging another finger deep in her sex and twisting it around to cover it with her sticky juices, he then slid it expertly and without resistance into her wet and welcoming arsehole lubricated fully by his tongue. Deep into her arsehole and pussy he probed, forcing her wider open before Jamie then slid a second finger into each entrance. Sara felt her rectal muscles protest at the much tighter fit and larger intrusion and she squeezed his fingers as the invasion stretched her like never before. Jamie's tongue moved to lap at the wet folds and dribbling love juices underneath as his other hand frigged her pussy rapidly.

Inexperienced at anal, she may be, but Sara found that she was learning fast as she relaxed her muscles to allow his fingers to fully penetrate her arsehole as Jamie forced them up to the knuckle, ramming her hard. Sara's eyes and mouth were now wide open as she recovered from the initial discomfort and shock of a second digit invading her inner sanctum so forcibly but as Jamie went to work with his mouth in her pussy she found the sensation of the total submission in accepting the anal invasion the most incredible turn-on. She was his totally and completely she realised, he had mastered her and was quite shocked at her total capitulation and happiness at being conquered thus.

"Jamie, my love, my hero, my master," sighed Sara. "Please may I have permission to suck your lovely cock?"

This was as forward as Sara had ever been during her limited, in quality if not in quantity, sexual life. A handful of teenage gropes and sexual adventures had preceded an ill-fated and fairly loveless marriage that had left her unfulfilled sexually; at no time during her previous lovemaking sessions had she ever ventured such words! Empowered by giving herself so completely to a lover, she felt that the beast inside of her had finally been let off the leash. She wanted more of this and she wanted it now.

As Jamie eased his fingers out of her tight rear portal she imagined him watching as she felt her muscles pause, leaving him the opportunity to see inside her wide open arsehole momentarily, before the natural contraction occurred and her ring tightened and her anus closed up. Sara yelped at the movement and the sudden void inside of her as both his fingers and tongue left her most private openings. Jamie shifted position to fully lie alongside her, head to toe and Sara did not need any encouragement to lift her legs over his face and bend down to completely free the giant protuberance gripped in her fingers. He lifted his bottom to allow her to slide off his remaining garments, his erection throbbing wildly as she released it. Jamie lay perfectly still and she could sense his anticipation as she guided the swollen member to her salivating mouth. With one hand wrapped gently around his cock Sara softly teased the helmet of his erection with a sensitive touch. Jamie cried out in ecstasy as she moved her hand lightly up and down his stem, hovering around the tip, enjoying the moment and the control she felt.

Completely relaxed now, even knowing that her pussy and arsehole had been penetrated, were wide open to his view and surely tempting him again as she slowly dipped her head to breathe on his tip. She felt Jamie tense and suspected that the tension was almost unbearable as he waited for her to ease his hardness into her waiting wet mouth. Suddenly he forced his face in between the cheeks of her bottom, his nose nestling against her arsehole, the tip sliding into the dark, dampened hole, his lips tantalisingly close to her dripping pussy. The touch of his nose there almost sent Sara into another climax as she struggled to believe the obscene thoughts that were running through her head; she was trying to cope with the astonishing fact that she was on the verge of begging him to fill both of her entrances, and she didn't care what with.

Sara took his large penis deep into her mouth; she was now used to the fact that Jamie was of above average length and thickness and had realised that there was probably no down side to taking this giant inside of her. Her mouth melded around the huge length, delighting her as she enjoyed the sensation of his sliding foreskin. His penetration of her body with his fingers had been wonderful and she was eager to take this colossus into her pussy once more. The thought of accommodating such a monster into her arsehole, however, caused her to shiver inwardly, but she brushed that thought away, still amazed at her sudden ability to have such crude and wanton thoughts. Her dalliances with the student, Jenny, she had filed as understandable aberrations and a thirst for adventure and new experiences. Although, in reality, she was aware that locked away, unfulfilled sexual desire had been released by Jenny and the reality now was that she was eager to make up for lost time. Having almost reached her fortieth year before feeling a pair of male lips sucking and licking between her cheeks she still struggled not to think at herself as filthy, sluttish and dirty for even daring to consider something she had previously viewed as gross behaviour, such was her previous mind-set from a marriage to a puritanical man with low sexual desire and needs. Now as she began to bob her head up and down this thick rampant cock, her saliva coating and dripping down the full length, she found herself pushing her bottom back into Jamie's face to force his nose further into her dark hole while her pussy was frantically sliding over his open mouth, her rock-hard nub searching for the tip of his tongue and her mound pressing on his chin as she once more built towards a climax. Again one of his hands grasped and squeezed her nipples in turn and she revelled in the painful jolts as he pinched and twisted, seemingly knowing that she had a penchant for a certain amount of rough behaviour; his other hand moved against her pussy as his tongue flicked around it. A thumb suddenly dipped deep inside of her as he began a fucking movement, pulling it almost out and plunging it fiercely back again deep inside of her wet gash. Matching his own body movements, Sara sensed Jamie being close to his own orgasm as his tongue replaced his thumb, ploughing deep inside of her pussy. He pulled his face back from her bottom and expertly slid his thumb into the dark recess of her open anus stretched by his nose to readily accommodate the thicker, larger digit. Sara was pushed over the edge and her body began to spasm in another glorious mind-blowing climax. Resisting the urge to release his cock from her mouth so that she could let loose the scream of abandon that was building within her, she sucked hard and deep and licking her fingers, reached under him, two fingers parting his bottom cheeks whilst she pushed a saliva-covered middle finger tentatively into his arsehole, a virgin act for her she was hesitant until she heard his groan of undoubted appreciation and pushed in to the full length of her digit.

Jamie let out a blood-curdling strangled scream as his cock flooded her mouth with his come as they both now bucked and shook, rocking and hanging on to each other as waves of ecstasy hit them both like jolts of electricity. Sara came again, rediscovering the meaning of the term multiple orgasm, as she swallowed Jamie's offering greedily and drained the last thick droplets of spunk from his softening cock with unbridled enthusiasm. She slipped from him and they lay side by side, exhausted, until she crawled into his arms and entwined they laid silently, their passion subsiding as their bodies gradually recovered from their exertions.

A few days later as Sara lay supine relishing the feel of Jamie's hands all over her body as he finished massaging her with oils, following a luxurious bath, she felt ready and turned her head to stare into her lover's eyes and although no words were spoken, Sara sensed that they were as one. Had the time finally come, thought Sara, for her to lose her anal virginity as Jamie lay down behind her and she raised her bottom invitingly in the air. "My heart is yours, my pussy is yours, and now my love, my arsehole is yours. Take what you want, my love, I want to give myself to you completely." Her voice trembled slightly as she contemplated the invasion that she was inviting; this surely was the ultimate prize and honour a woman could give her lover. She relaxed her cheeks and took a deep breath as she widened her legs to expose herself fully. She could feel Jamie's eyes feasting on the shimmering starfish of her arsehole as she twitched the opening before him. There was a lovely sensation as Jamie blew softly into the crevice. Sara's arsehole immediately began to spasm, taunting him as the tight, dark hole beckoned him on. Jamie moved in and kissed her rim, his tongue tip teasing her. Sara shuddered and a moan escaped her lips. She could feel her pussy twitching brazenly; she sighed with anticipation as she heard the giveaway buzz of a vibrator and sensed the touch just seconds before Jamie ran it down her wet folds and then up to her throbbing hard clit. He continued to lap at her arsehole, running his tongue round and round, dipping in and out as he prepared her for a moment she believed would put the seal on their developing love.

Jamie turned on his back, pulled her on top of him and slid between her open legs to plant a kiss on her pussy. She straddled his face as he began to suck on her swollen clit, switched the vibrator to her rear opening and just held it lightly to the centre of her rear entrance. Sara was now completely lost in the moment as she approached orgasm, her clitoris reacting to his fierce suction, and started to mew and moan as her body surrendered to her lust and desire. Her body shook and rocked as the climax took hold of her. Jamie held her tightly before he planted a final kiss on her pussy and slid from beneath her, reaching for the lubricant on the bedside table. Carefully he turned her over and laid her on her back and presented his erect penis to her mouth and Sara quickly seized the throbbing dick and closed her lips around it. Climbing onto her, his legs either side of her head, his muscular buttocks above her face, Jamie squeezed the lubricant onto his fingers and reached down to work it into her puckered arsehole; she clenched tightly around the invading fingers as her sensitive membranes reacted to the different texture of the lotion.

Sara groaned fervidly as his lubricated fingers rotated in her passage as he prepared the way for his penis, stretching her gradually, accepting Jamie's thumb as it smoothly replaced the smaller fingers, her anus opening to accommodate his larger digit. Returning the vibrator to her twitching arsehole, Jamie inserted the tip and held it there for a few seconds before gradually sliding it in to fully penetrate her arse. Sara sucked hard on his cock as she prepared herself for the penetration that she knew was seconds away, her fingers grazing his bottom cheeks as she dragged her nails along the tempting buttocks over her face. Taking his cock from her mouth he coated it with lubricant and moved around and positioned himself between her welcoming legs, lifting them and forcing her knees towards her breasts with his shoulders beneath supporting her and holding her ready and steady.

Her legs were now forced far apart and her arsehole was stretched wide open as Jamie presented his cock at the entrance of her dark, deep hole. One hand reached around and under her to help guide his cock into the entrance, his other hand flicked at the top of her pussy lips to distract her from the unnatural feel of his thick shaft probing her bottom. Sara almost screamed half in anticipation, half in fear, as the helmet of his cock slipped inside of her pulsating anus. *How could this be a shameful act,* she thought, *when I am virtually bursting with pleasure and longing?* She wanted to scream "ram it in" at him as he oh so slowly edged his cock through the tight neck of her delicate arsehole. Then suddenly the resistance gave, the muscle relaxed and he filled her anal canal entirely; both of them exhaled noisily and smiled as they gazed into each other's eyes.

"You have me now completely," she whispered. "I love you."

Jamie kissed her. "I love you too, my sweet, and now I am going to fuck you and come into your gorgeous arse."

He started to thrust, his mouth going to her breast to suck on a nipple. His thrusts began to accelerate and as his orgasm approached he lifted his head to gaze into her eyes. With a deep slow groan he exploded into her rectum, flooding her chamber with his warm spunk. They both knew in their moments of passion of such depth, that they were sealing the importance and closeness of their relationship. Sara sighed deeply as she finally discovered the intimacy and affection of giving her most secret and forbidden opening to a lover who clearly cherished and appreciated her.

Slipping out of her warm pleasure hole, Jamie bent down to her cheeks and taking a tissue gently wiped away the small flow of mixed come and lubricant dribbling out of her arse.

Feeling her tense, he said, "It would be an honour for me to suck out the rest of my come, would you allow me the honour of doing so, please, my sweet?"

Sara felt her face on fire; in a short space of time with this man, she had received his fingers, his tongue, a vibrator and then his penis inside of her most secret chamber. He had deflowered her virgin rear hole and spurted his come inside of her. Could she really feel shame if he now licked his own juices from her bottom? So disgusting, so dirty, so decadent, so filthy, thought Sara in both wonder and horror at exposing herself and behaving like this.

"Oh God, yes please, yes, yes, yes, do it, Jamie, do it please," she huskily breathed.

She wasn't sure if she would be able to meet his gaze if he came to her now. *Oh God, he's actually sucking my spunk-filled arsehole, can this really be happening to me?* Her stunned mind was whirling. Feeling disgusted with herself, her wanton and slutty self, as well as trying to understand the sense of wonder and elation that filled her, she held still as his tongue now probed as deep inside of her arsehole as he could force it. She felt it swirl round inside of her as he wholeheartedly licked the dark tunnel out. Sara's mind was in a whirl, how could something so disgusting feel so wonderful, so intimate and so loving? Jamie's fingers then began to stroke her pussy lips again and she felt her body respond instantly as another climax gripped her body. Sara convulsed in sexual ecstasy once more as the combination of sensations drove her over the brink. *You're not fooling anyone,* thought Sara wryly, as she trembled in exhaustion and fulfilled desire. *You are loving this — debasing and demeaning yourself is clearly what ticks your boxes.* Her head sank down submissively as, to her final consternation and dismay, her bottom noisily spat forth a last globule of Jamie's sperm. Jamie chuckled and planted a last slow, wet kiss on her still-twitching arsehole. Lapping up the creamy blob into his mouth, he turned his pink-faced blushing lover around opened his mouth and leaned towards her. Sara closed her eyes, not able to look directly at him and to her further surprise he covered her mouth with his and smeared her with the spunky solution, using his tongue to transfer it into her mouth. Sara automatically swallowed and felt the sour stinging sensation at the back of her throat.

"My god," she whispered. "What have you unleashed in me? I can't believe what you are doing to me."

Jamie just smiled and kissed her deeply. They cuddled, and entwined in each other's arms fell asleep, sated, exhausted, contented, and totally at ease with all in the world.

CHAPTER 13

JULIE AND SONYA HAVE THEIR

FATES DECIDED

Sonya's return to the Dean of Discipline's office was something that she had postponed and put off as many times as possible before a telephone call from the Mistress had spelt out the dangers of prevaricating any longer. Leaving the college on her own terms but with bad grace and without the support of the powerful governing body was not an option. It had been made quite clear to her how far the tentacles of the college's powerful figureheads stretched and her career in academia would surely come to a dramatic halt if she left in anger.

As she stood in front of the Dean of Discipline, she felt reduced in stature, age and size. This man exuded power and authority and the trembling of her body was surely visible to him as he fixed her with his foreboding stare.

"Well, I've read your effort at negotiating a way out of the punishment that you clearly admit that you deserve but desperately seek to avoid. My opinion of it is thus." At which the professor slowly tore up the proffered document and dropped the remnants onto the floor. He stood up and walked slowly around the trembling Pastoral Care Tutor. His hand reached to the back of her neck and stroked her hair.

"You appear to have wet hair, Sonya. Is this because you have come straight from the shower?"

"Er, yes, Professor Stones," she answered hesitantly. "Yes, yes I did."

Stones just smiled at her for several seconds and let the pause develop. Sonya became more and more uncomfortable and eventually, as the professor knew she would, she broke the silence.

"It doesn't mean anything, Professor Stones. I don't understand why you are making something out of the fact that I've just happened to shower before leaving my room to come here."

Stones smiled again.

"Oh Sonya, we both know exactly why you have felt the need to clean your body before attending my office to discuss your serious disciplinary breach. Please face up to the fact that you have put your career at risk and have clearly realised that you need to accept your one route to redemption and reparation. I suggest that you begin this process by removing your clothes and we will take it from there."

Sonya blanched and gulped for air. "Oh no, please sir. I can't take my clothes off in front of you, sir. I am so scared of being punished. Oh please sir, can I just have another punishment, sir? Anything sir, please."

The smile dropped from the professor's face.

"Enough!" he barked. "No more, either take your clothes off in preparation for a thorough thrashing or get out and go and pack up your belongings. I am not prepared to discuss this further."

A tear ran down Sonya's face but with trembling hands she began to unbutton her top. Stones picked up a pad and pen and turned his back on the distressed woman. She slowly slipped her skirt down and stepped out of her shoes before hesitating.

"Sir, please may I keep my underwear on?" she pleaded.

Stones glanced around at her and to Sonya's amazement answered in the affirmative.

"Yes that's fine, just leave your other clothes neatly on the chair there and go and stand against the wall, hands on your head whilst you think about what you are shortly going to write. I assume that you are now prepared to request a thorough thrashing to help make amends for your disgraceful conduct?"

Sonya murmured her assent and took the position indicated against the book-lined shelves, obediently placing her hands on her head.

Stones left her a couple of minutes before walking over to give her the pad and pen.

"No prevarication, no ambiguity, no waffling. Just a straightforward plea to be severely punished using whatever implements thought necessary to punish you for your shameful behaviour. Please confirm how you transgressed and how you wish to make amends clearly and unequivocally. You have five minutes, so get on with it."

Sonya took the pad and taking a deep breath began writing straight away as she tried to find the resolve that she knew she'd need to get through the trauma that she had reluctantly accepted was her fate. Within the designated five minutes she was handing the paper back to the professor before resuming her former position.

"It will just about do, Sonya. Barely acceptable but I will take it as a genuine script of contrition if you will just state clearly for me what you wish to happen now."

Sonya gulped; she clearly knew that she was playing with fire as she had struggled to put down on paper the punishment that she knew was forthcoming, but Stones was confident that she was on the verge of reluctant submission.

"Oh sir, please. Do I really have to say it?" She turned with pleading eyes to meet the steely gaze of a man who was just now starting to show signs of tiring of her reticence. He didn't speak and, as he had expected, once again the nervous Pastoral Care Tutor broke the silence.

"Oh sir. I am sorry sir about my behaviour and how I have let you, myself and the college down. Sir, I believe that I deserve to be punished severely for this, sir, and, and, and…" She began to stumble but the fierce look from her persecutor encouraged her to force the words out.

"Sir, I would like you to thrash my bottom, sir, please. I know that I deserve it and wish for you to carry out my punishment please."

Stones nodded and flicking his fingers to signal that she was to resume facing the wall, he went over to his cabinet and Sonya watched out of the corner of her eye, a look of sheer terror crossing her face as he selected a flat wooden paddle, a swishy cane and the thick black leather strap before returning to his desk. Sonya began to tremble as the reality of what would soon be happening hit home.

Seconds later a buzzer sounded in the room and Sonya spun around as the professor flicked a switch and the door gradually opened. In a flash he crossed the room, grabbing her by the hair and dragging her over to the chair positioned in the centre. Sonya barely had time to register that Julie had entered the room before she found herself face down across the professor's knees with his hand slamming down on her knicker-clad behind.

"Have you learnt nothing at all? How dare you move without permission? Take that and that," he thundered as his large hand struck her again and again. Sonya screeched as the shock and pain registered and tears soon flowed from her eyes as she kicked her legs feebly, locked in his unbreakable grasp. Twenty strokes later, he paused and turned his attention to Julie.

"Julie, thank you for attending for your punishment, as you can see I am busy but you can assist in the Pastoral Care Tutor's road to redemption. Please remove her brassiere, she is very much under some illusion that she gets to decide what she wears during punishment so let's disabuse her, shall we?"

A flummoxed and clearly surprised Julie quickly assessed the situation and moved straight away to follow the barked instructions and unfastened the struggling woman's bra, allowing her breasts to swing free as Sonya continued to struggle pointlessly on the lap of the man who had just delivered a fearsome stinging sensation to her buttocks, the likes of which she had never before experienced. Seconds later Sonya's screams of pain returned to the air as Stones' hand continued the torturous onslaught for several minutes further. Eventually he paused but as Sonya took a breath in the expectation that this part of her punishment was over she was horrified to feel fingers inside her panties and, in a thrice, they were unceremoniously pulled from her legs and she was fully exposed.

"Noooooooooooooooo! No, no, no, no, no. Not my knickers. No! No!" Sonya yelled as she tried desperately to cover her bottom crack with her hands.

"Stop it now, you ridiculous woman. How dare you presume that you would be allowed to keep your dignity in this room?"

The professor shoved her from his lap to the floor and once more grabbed her by the hair and flung her face down over a nearby table.

Sonya was again caught unprepared at the speed of her tormentor as without much time to process any thoughts of resistance her hands were cuffed as she sprawled face down. Unable to move her arms she had little ability to resist as Stones kicked her legs apart and buckled her ankles against the desk legs. As the reality of the situation dawned upon her she was horrified to feel the professor's hands between her legs as he manoeuvred the rubber protrusion at the table edge underneath her pubic mound, which forced her bottom higher whilst spreading her legs further apart.

Stones was delighted to see from her facial expressions that Julie's mind was reeling as she watched the much maligned but oh-so-proper Pastoral Care Tutor displayed before her. She was looking wide-eyed at the raised and opened buttocks rudely on show and unable to help a smile playing cross her lips at the belittling of this haughty member of staff.

"Stop looking so self-satisfied Julie. You'll be joining Miss Coombs shortly, now sign the voluntary punishment form that is on my desk then get your own clothes off and add them to this reprobate's apparel over there." The professor broke into her reverie and Julie's mind suddenly became a bit more focused on why she was there!

"This is outrageous, Professor Stones, you said I could keep my underwear on... oh, ouch! Ow! Ow! Ow! Ow! Yeooow!" Sonya's unwise words were interrupted as she received a further short, sharp spanking in response. Unwisely she waited for him to stop before continuing her ill-thought-out resistance.

"This is ridiculous. I am a respected member of staff and a grown independent woman. I will not be treated like this."

Stones let her words hang in the air, suspecting that this newly injected confidence and arrogance would prove to be a false dawn.

"Miss Coombs if you speak again out of turn, I will double your punishment and you will be lucky if you are able to walk out of this room unaided. You have still the opportunity to leave virtually unpunished. You will, of course, have avoided a painful hour or so and a few days of recovering from your ordeal. You will have to find another position, which I suspect, you may find challenging given the reason for your situation here today. But you do have the right to leave this institution immediately. You may rise, get dressed and then I will escort out through my garden into the street to begin your new life. Otherwise you will damn well do as you are told, and as you have requested in writing, take your agreed discipline so that we can file this matter away for good. Your call, Miss Coombs. Do you understand?" Stones placed a large hand across the crack of Sonya's bottom and squeezed hard to prompt her.

"Oh lord, this is so humiliating, please Professor, I just don't want this." Sonya paused as a silence fell in the room, her mind in a whirl as she considered the words she had just uttered and the repercussion if she were allowed to follow her wishes through.

"I will ignore that last comment and refer you back to my question concerning your understanding of how this process will work. You can have two minutes to reflect whilst I place Julie in her punishment position and you might like to take note of how she sets the example of how to behave in my office. Julie, come here and bend over, legs apart, spread your arms out to the cuffs."

Stones had moved to unfasten attachments under the table that released a section of the table enabling him to double its length. Julie, who had clearly made the call that she was not going to earn herself anything further than already ordained, now came obediently to the opposite end to where Sonya's upper torso was lain prone and spread-eagled and allowed Stones to place her over the table so that her hands just touched Sonya's and the two came face to face in their undignified positions. As Julie looked into the tearful, terrified eyes of the pastoral care tutor she instinctively moved her fingers to entwine with the stricken woman's. Stones was not at all surprised when the two locked eyes and all previous animosity between the women seemingly drained away as they contemplated their fates and grew some solace and strength from their mutual suffering and fear. Fastened down securely, Julie took a deep breath in as she felt the hands of the professor as he delved between her legs to position the mounded leather support to force her thighs apart. As his knuckle rubbed against her sex lips she moaned in pleasure and automatically pushed her groin against the hardness.

"Oh you really are a brazen hussy. Do control yourself, young lady. I know that the idea of a blazing bottom turns you on but you really are insatiable aren't you? You're absolutely dripping wet!" He pulled her legs and cheeks wider apart and stared at her hairless vagina and anus. "Such a pretty display though, lovely to see this bald anus again. A delightful sight, my dear, very pretty indeed. Now please try and curb your lustful thoughts, you are soon going to be howling in agony so think on that." He slapped her bottom and finished fastening her ankles securely.

"Oh sir, thank you sir."

"I can't believe that you are looking forward to this," whispered Sonya, aghast at the young student's forward behaviour in such a vulnerable state.

"Silence!" barked the professor. "The only words I want to hear from you are an apology for your outburst and a request to be properly and deservingly thrashed."

As he completed Julie's restraint, the professor leaned in behind, grasped her buttocks pulling them apart and took a deep breath in.

"Very strong scent of lemons from your sweet cheeks today I believe, young lady?" he queried.

Sonya gasped as Julie laughed, saying, "Citrus Blush, sir, actually. From my mother's favourite department store as usual. Although I doubt she expected me to be discussing it in these circumstances!"

The professor smiled, admiring the young woman's pluck and fortitude.

"Not so amusing as far as you are concerned, I suspect, my straight-laced pastoral care tutor?" Stones moved around behind Sonya and, knowing the ignominy that would be caused, he grasped her buttocks pulled them wide apart and leaning close in to her anal opening sniffed noisily.

"What have we here, let me think… wet soil, a grassy field after rain maybe, quite earthy definitely. Not a great believer in artificial or perfumed scenting in your nether regions then?"

Sonya's anus tightened involuntarily, bringing a beaming smile to Stones' face, as he breathed noisily close to her very centre.

"Fascinating this jungle of little black hairs filling your anal cleft and so much pubic hair spouting from between your legs… such a delightful contrast with our shaven friend across the table." The professor continued, casually running his fingers down her bottom crack as he spoke, knowing the discomfort he was causing Sonya. "I think I am ready to hear your decision on whether or not you wish to take your punishment now, young lady. It's time to start so I need you to confirm that you wish to remain in your position, in more than one way, or not."

"Please Professor, can you not touch me in my personal places? I do not give you permission to touch me there!"

Professor Stones very gently stroked around the rim of her tightly clenched anus before twiddling his fingers in the dark hairs surrounding her reluctant orifice. He spoke quietly but menacingly.

"Miss Coombs, you are fully aware that you have transgressed very severely but seem sadly reluctant to accept the agreed punishment. Do not interrupt me, keep your mouth firmly closed and listen. You are stretching my patience and I am starting to doubt whether or not you are worth the effort. If you wish I will release you and you may dress, clear your desk and leave the college. If you decide to stay, you will be thoroughly and soundly thrashed, you will be humiliated, belittled and your body will be at my mercy. At the end of this session, you will hopefully leave here a sore but chastened woman, having learnt a valuable life lesson. You will still be in a very good job with a prestigious institution earning well above the market rate. You will have learnt never to breach fundamental college rules and you will have cleansed this misdemeanour from your conscience. I will now expect to hear you state that you understand this and wish to be appropriately punished at my discretion for as long and in whichever way I see fit. Now take a breath and think very carefully before you next speak."

"I am sorry, sir. I am just not used to being dealt with like this. I do want to stay and keep my job but this is difficult for me to take. I am just not used to it, sir. I accept the punishment, Professor, but I forbid you to touch me intimately."

"This is just waffle and nonsense, you need to cut to the chase, young lady," Stones interrupted her. "Might I remind you about your home situation? I believe that the college is kindly allowing you and your partner to reside in college property at rather favourable rates and assisting you in securing a home of your own through our property team? You presumably realise the consequences on your living arrangements if you were to have to leave the college? Now, have you been sensible and discussed this with your husband? I hope you understand that that it is going to be clearly apparent, from the state your backside will be in, that you have been soundly beaten."

Sonya seemed to shrivel as she processed the professor's words. There was no doubt that her whole life would change if she lost her position in the college and Stones waited for her to think things through and come to her own conclusion that she needed to accept the fate that her own stupid actions had created. He had studied her file and noted that she had taken care to keep her private life and work life apart, keeping her maiden name for work and barely referring to the fact that she was married to colleagues.

Finally she took a long shuddering breath and clearly collecting herself, pronounced.

"Yes sir, again I apologise, and yes I have told my husband about today and the circumstances that led to me being here. He wasn't overly sympathetic. I suppose that's my own fault, I do give him a hard time quite often and I know that he wished that he had the gumption to put me over his knee himself! I think he will be secretly pleased when I come home with a sore behind, sir. So, yes sir, I am ready to accept my punishment now and apologise again, both to you and Julie for my intolerable behaviour the other day and for my childishness and poor attitude so far today."

"Well hurrah for that! At last, sense prevails and the light dawns." As he spoke, the professor ran his hands over Sonya's rounded buttocks, deliberately allowing his fingers to trail into her cleft and touching first her anus and then slipping lower to brush very lightly against her vaginal lips. Sonya jolted but Stones could feel her concentrating on not reacting, perhaps finally becoming aware of the rules of this ritual that he practiced so thoroughly.

"Of course, young Julie is setting a fine example to you in how to behave whilst awaiting punishment. However," he said, moving round to behind the young prostrate student, "I am not overly impressed, as I am fully aware that the gentle rocking motion is not caused by fear or trepidation of what is to come." As he spoke he slipped his fingers between Julie's legs and brought them out, and waved them in Sonya's face. "As you can see, or indeed smell, our young friend is looking forward to her thrashing with a fair degree of self-gratification." Stones walked into the bathroom and came out with a towel that he roughly pushed between Julie's legs.

"I'd rather my table wasn't stained by your sexual juices, you insatiable harlot. Now stop your masturbatory antics please and if you are a good girl I may help you pleasure yourself once I've caned you."

Stones' words brought a beam of absolute pleasure to Julie's features as she responded, "Oh sir, thank you sir. Whatever you wish, sir."

"Now be quiet, child, and lay still. One further thing, Miss Coombs, is that your thrashing will be carried out by my assistant for the evening and to preserve his anonymity, you will be wearing this." Suddenly he slipped a breathing hood over Sonya's head, blocking her vision completely.

"It is completely safe and will provide ample ventilation for breathing whilst sufficiently constructed to allow you to cry buckets without affecting your air intake if we discover that you're a big blubber."

Sonya started to object but a tap on her right buttock from the professor reminded her of the futility of any objection. Her intensified breathing betrayed her disturbance at this latest psychological twist and he suspected that she would assume that the visitor about to join them would be Jamie, his new sidekick.

"Yes, a younger man, with perhaps more stamina and a stronger right arm than me possibly. I do so believe in sharing, ladies, and it will be a treat for my visitor to see you presented like this on his arrival. Think on, ladies, think on. Although in your case, Julie, I suppose that this just adds to your sexual thrill. Sonya, however, I know will now be feeling the pain of her impending humiliation to a much higher degree." Stones moved around behind Sonya, chuckling away to himself.

"Oh, please sir," she ventured with trepidation. "This is not fair on my husband, exposing his wife to others like this, he will be very upset."

"Really Sonya, I wonder if this is true. Perhaps the poor unfortunate man will be delighted to know that you have been given a damn good thrashing for your disgraceful performance. Maybe he will think you have finally got what you deserved."

The lack of a response suggested that Stones had achieved his aim of giving given Sonya food for thought; her hooded head dropped to the table top, giving the appearance of an abject surrender.

The door buzzer sounded and the professor turn up the music playing in the background to signal that the time had come to move things on. Stones moved to greet his guest and conducted a short, whispered conversation out of the hearing of the prostrate females.

Julie's face showed her intrigue and Stones could see that she had quickly worked out that this was not likely to be the porter that she had undoubtedly heard mentioned. The professor had one eye on Julie as he escorted Sonya's husband Ian into the room and immediately suspected that she was working things out.

"Julie I suggest that you stop before you start, young lady. Additional punishment strokes are freely available and can be applied in the most painful places, I remind you."

Julie's mouth snapped closed, earning her a knowing nod of approval from Stones.

"So here she is, as discussed, my friend, ready and prepared for her just desserts! As you can see Sonya is a hirsute female, lovely bushy hair decorating her fine crack and luscious-looking vagina and anus... Oh look, a nice tight squeeze of embarrassment. I am afraid Sonya is not really used to displaying her intimate areas to an audience yet. Not to worry, we'll soon have her forgetting her modesty and offering herself up without any sense of shame and dignity."

Sonya response was a low groan and Stones thought that she was probably thankful that her face was covered as he could imagine her cheeks burning red with embarrassment. He continued with his belittling.

"Have a closer look and smell in her scent, let me open her cheeks up so you can see properly." Sonya yelped as his fingers dug into her bottom cheeks, prising them even further apart and lifting her to display her pussy fully. With Stones' encouragement her husband moved in and blew lightly into her crevice before taking an audible long sniff. Sonya trembled as her husband's breath disturbed the hairs surrounding her arsehole before the two conniving men shared extremely self-satisfied grins with each other.

"A lovely sight and a nice earthy scent from one who seems somewhat disturbed by having an unknown man taking in the delights of her anus. Now come and have a look at a total opposite. This is Julie and she is as relaxed with displaying herself as Sonya is uptight, she is also a total opposite in hair covering, see?"

The two men moved around to Julie's posterior, Stones placing his large hands either side of the buttocks.

"As you can see we have a younger, slimmer model on display here. Cheeks nowhere near so rounded, much perter, more delicate which isn't such good news in a way for our culprit as she has little padding to protect her from the bite of a hard caning and the severe lash of a good strapping. However the coup de grace is her absolute lack of any bodily hair on her private parts. Have a close look, see."

The professor lifted and separated her buttocks and thighs to their limits whilst exposing her clean-shaven zones.

"See, as bald as a newly born baby's. Admittedly sodden with her sexual juices as she is such a wanton vamp desperate for the pain that will give her the satisfaction she craves for. But not to worry, I have a plan to ensure that this isn't too enjoyable for her!" he said as he pinched Julie's bottom cheeks hard between his fingers causing her to buck and squeal.

"Right, let us make a start. As we talked about earlier, I will give Sonya her first stroke as a tester or a taster and then you try your swing on young Julie's backside, then we'll swap over for their thrashings with me going first on Julie and you following on Sonya. So no messing, twenty-four of the cane each, hard and true, let's make these scoundrels and their bottoms sing, shall we?"

The contrast between the two females couldn't have been more different at this point. Julie sighing and relaxing, offering up her bare fully opened bottom, her excitement levels at fever pitch, obviously yearning for the beating to start. Sonya, however, had begun trembling and shaking with her bottom clenched tight, almost trying to force her body into the tabletop in a pointless attempt to try and alleviate the impact that was coming.

"Right-oh, my friend, please observe and then nip around to Julie and follow suit." The professor raised a thick cane above his shoulder, swung in lightly to tap Sonya's bottom twice and then drew back a third time and brought his arm down in a blur to slam across the centre of the woman's bare buttocks. The resulting scream from Sonya certainly gave authority to the accuracy and intent of the stroke as her bottom bucked furiously and the first angry red stripe appeared as Sonya tasted the bite of the cane for the very first time in her life.

"Now remember our earlier chats," said the professor, alluding to the long conversations that the two had shared in preparation for this. "It does hurt, it will be damn sore but no lasting effect other than a young lady who might remember what happens if she's naughty and breaks the rules."

The plan was for Ian to stay anonymous to his wife until Julie had left the room and then move things to another level in teaching the pastoral care tutor a life and relationship lesson on top of saving her position at the college. Stones had been stunned to hear how Sonya had dominated Ian for most of their time together and had had no hesitation in joining forces with the vengeful husband. Soon they had planned their subterfuge to teach Sonya a lesson that Ian hoped would add a power balance shift as well as an extra element of excitement to their partnership. There was a gamble involved that Ian was fully prepared to take, the downside seemed minimal, and he had told Stones that he was confident his wife truly loved him and that their relationship could survive the turmoil that any backfire in his assessment of how she would take this might cause. The upside was that he was going to make the absolute most of the situation that she had created and intended in the short term to avail himself of this opportunity in every way he could. He also fervently hoped that this session could be a lightbulb moment for Sonya and that the direction of their future sex life could be determined by the way that things went over the next hour or so. Meanwhile he was lost in a world dominated by the gorgeous display of nakedness of the clearly aroused pretty young student bound and bent over before him. Copying the professor as best he could he swung the cane down on a naked female bottom for the first time ever. The crack of the impact on Julie's small, hard, round buttocks was far louder than the impact that Stones had produced on his wife's cheeks and Stones could sense his fascination and arousal as the red line appeared and the student gasped and squeezed her bottom tight, Ian able to view the crack closing fast for a few seconds before relaxing and re-presenting that spellbinding view of her open cracks and most private orifices.

"Excellent," said the professor as he came round to admire Ian's handiwork. "Lovely first stroke, as you can see it's nice and straight and central with a lovely red glow to the stripe. Take one more shot at this little rascal and then we will swap over and you can apply those fine arm muscles to giving Sonya her painful lesson. Try for the same spot and see if you can get a reaction other than exciting this rather lustful female any further." At this Stones used his fingers to fully expose her vaginal folds which showed clearly the glistening lips and the obvious signs of sexual readiness that Julie was in.

"Minx is like a tap, certainly needs a severe thrashing to get through to her that this isn't meant to be fun or foreplay!" He nodded at Ian who swung the cane with a lot of force, producing a resounding crack and a strangled half-scream from the recipient.

"Good, good," muttered Stones. "I'll do my best to get close to matching that severity. Come and prepare yourself to take over with Sonya, let's get her splendid bottom singing shall we?"

Stones lashed his cane down hard again and Sonya predictably replicated her earlier howl of anguish, before Stones moved aside and moved back around behind Julie. With the two men now positioned behind their designated targets, Stones raised his cane and swung it down to the more fleshy lower cheeks of Julie's bottom. A stifled scream was his reward and with a nod to Ian to proceed, he stood back to wait for him to finally take the opportunity to apply the cane to his wife's bottom. After a slight hesitation Ian took a deep breath in before he swung the cane down onto Sonya's fleshy and rounded buttocks.

"Naaaaaaaeggghhhhhhhhhh!!!" The reaction from Sonya had none of the restraint or control that Julie was able to bring to the occasion.

The hooded head shook and rolled as the yell of agony was quickly followed by heart-rending sobs. The professor swung down on Julie again to deliver another blow, this time hitting the tighter skin stretched across the top of Julie's bottom crack. As she writhed and began to whimper, Ian applied his second stroke to Sonya, her scream again filling the room. The two kept the thrashing up in perfect tandem, Julie now letting loose discreet yips and grunts of pain which filled the slight gaps between Sonya's full-throttled screams as she paused only to take noisy spluttering breaths in. Eventually, as Stones signalled to Ian to apply the final strokes together, the two men took almighty swings and laid the canes ferociously across the centre of the two female's bucking bottoms.

As his arm dropped for the last time Ian was joined by Stones and he handed the cane back to his companion. Stones could see that Ian was transfixed by his wife's glorious bottom, her dark brown arsehole framed by the swarm of deep black curly hairs, her crack squeezing tight then springing open as Sonya tried to absorb the fierce burning of the cane strokes. He looked at the glowing red haphazard lines showing evidence that Ian lacked the skill it took to lay the strokes on in a consistent pattern. Ian's trousers were not hiding a throbbing erection clearly showing evidence of the excitement that the flogging of his wife had caused. A slight doubt and sense of guilt crossed his face as he watched his wife still struggling and mewing pitifully, bound and hooded.

"Well done, my friend, a necessary duty excellently executed. Not at all bad for a novice, I do have to say." The two men leaned in to peer shamelessly at Sonya's twitching cheeks before Stones then ran his hands over the swollen cane marks of Sonya's sore bottom.

"With practice those lines will get straighter but the application was certainly successful by the looks of these raised welts. A good hard six with the strap shortly will definitely set those off perfectly. A very good and solid foundation laid, I look forward to hearing her sing when she feels the force of the thick strap considering the ridiculous fuss she's been making from a caning." Words which set off a fresh litany of sobbing from Sonya as her head sank down once more and she unwisely vocalised her distress.

"Oh please Professor, no more, no more. It hurts so much. Please can that be the end? Yaaaarrrrhhhh!" Her words were strangled off as Stones pinched and twisted a group of her anal hairs.

"I hope you haven't got anything else to say, young lady. Unless of course you'd like your strapping to be doubled to twelve lashes."

Sonya's only answer was a wretched snivel as she belatedly seemed to accept her fate.

"Just try and remember that your quick temper and disgraceful hot-headed attitude landed you in this predicament and part of the lesson today is about you learning compliance and control. Do you understand that, young lady?"

Sonya was quick to answer. "Oh sir, yes sir, sorry sir. Thank you, Professor, thank you."

This earned her sore buttocks a gentle caress of approval as Stones rather cooed at her, fluttering his fingers over her throbbing cheeks.

"Good girl, good girl," winking at Ian as he did so.

"Now then Julie, I can see that you are trying at least to be a bit discreet but I am aware of your movement and that you are basically making love to the raised mound of rubber between your legs."

The two men now moved behind Julie with the professor indicating to Ian to join him in studying his work.

"As you can see this young minx is rather damp down here and well on her way to the little treat she thinks she deserves. I suspect she'd very much like some assistance but unfortunately for her the rule is that we don't take advantage of the students regardless of their thoughts on the subject. But I am happy to allow her this brief interlude and distraction as she has taken her caning very well. On the downside is the fact that I now intend to give her twelve, rather than six, serious swipes with my thick leather strap. Much as Julie thinks the thought of a thorough beating is sexually exciting I suspect that she will find a severe strapping a different matter entirely. My aim will certainly be to ensure that the strapping will not form part of any sexual fantasies that she'll be masturbating over in the future. She's been enjoying herself rather too much but let's allow her to relieve herself and then see if we can deliver something that will bring her no sexual satisfaction whatsoever." He reached around and unbuckled Julie's right hand and with a triumphant cry she plunged her hand under her body and her fingers delved straight into her soaking wet vagina.

Both men watched in silence as the rampant student thrust her fingers unashamedly and without finesse or dignity into her gaping pussy.

"Fuck, yes, yes, oh fuck yes. Spank me now! Spank my naughty arse, pleeeeaase," she wailed as her hind quarters bucked in her bindings as she rammed herself against the hard rubber mound that separated her legs.

"Hmmmmm. Seems only fair to help her out. I'll hold her shoulders down firmly while you give her as many slaps as it takes to get her to her desired pleasure point."

The professor pushed down hard on Julie's upper body making her buttocks even more prominent as her sodden fingers worked frantically on her pussy. Ian did not need asking twice and began to spank the writhing cheeks of the already quite marked bottom in front of him.

"Gurrrrrrrrrrrrrrrrrrrr! Ooooooooo! Ah yes I'm come, come, coming. Oh fuck yes, yes, yes, fuck, fuuuucccckkk! Fuck, oh yes here we go. Guuuuuuurrrrrrrrrr!!!!" There was no restraint from the young student as she embraced the sensations exploding within her.

Stones noticed Sonya wincing as her hand was squeezed so tightly as the student writhed in her climax, he could only imagine what she was thinking with her vision denied and the sounds of spanking and sexual ecstasy filling the air. Gradually he could see the grip relax and eventually her hand was released as Julie's breathing slowly returned to normal. The professor moved away but quickly reappeared beside Julie with a warm and damp flannel and after gently removing Julie's hand from between her legs, he proceeded to rather tenderly wipe the young woman's love juices from her fingers before refastening her into the buckle.

The two men stood back as the young body finally ceased to buck and shudder before them, Stones moving across to pick up the thick heavy strap laying it across Julie's back.

"Just allow her a moment more for this little episode she's having to subside completely and then I anticipate that I will be able to introduce you to a young lady with a rather different demeanour in a few moments time," he said mysteriously, before continuing. "Listen up, Sonya, this will give you food for thought. Young Julie will be receiving twice the six you're going to get but this will give you a clue to the flaying that you will shortly be experiencing."

With that Stones drew back his arm and, after pausing for dramatic effect, he whipped down fast and slammed the thick leather hard against the taut buttocks facing him. There was a short pause before Julie's scream tore through the room. Stones allowed her no recovery time and laid on the next five strokes of the strap rapidly, covering the complete surface of her bottom in seconds. Julie's yells and sobs were now constant, her distress total, as the ferocious pain drove any thought of sexual pleasure from her.

"No more, no more please Professor. No, please, it hurts so much. Oh God, please no more." Julie's plaintive cries landed on deaf ears as the strap was raised high again before swinging down to land perfectly across the top of her bottom.

Once more ear-splitting screams echoed around the room joined by before interruptions of the crack of the strap hitting home again. As the young student hollered in agony, Sonya began to cry again herself, squeezing Julie's hands tightly, partly in sympathy towards Julie but no doubt partly in sheer terror of what she was due to receive. Again the strap slammed down as the professor put all his strength into the ninth blow, watching with satisfaction as it landed just below the previous two, the top half of the ravaged bottom before him turning bright scarlet as the savagery of the beating took full effect.

"Now my friend, you've seen how it's done. Why don't you finish off the final three strokes here before we move on to the equally naughty Sonya's more ample cheeks?" he said, passing the strap to Ian.

Julie gulped in air as her body was wracked with sobs while Sonya began to visibly tremble once more as she anticipated the fate shortly to befall her.

Ian took the strap and positioned himself, they had agreed this in advance, so that the professor could monitor and tutor him to ensure he delivered the beating his errant wife deserved. His erection strained against his trousers as he again drank in the sight of the open legs displaying Julie's hairless crotch and tight, bald splayed buttocks before him. He had discussed with the professor his concerns about his ability to dish out a severe punishment to his beloved partner whilst maintaining the silent treatment that the professor had deemed essential to the fulfilment of his planned discipline. Stones could see that on reflection he need not have worried, Ian had kept his concentration well. It looked as though he had found that the sexual high he was receiving from this experience was of such a level that keeping his mouth shut to extend the session was little price to pay for the reward that the thrashing of the two women was providing.

Julie's discomfit proved no barrier to his willingness to be the provider of further pain and he laid the strap across the centre of the youngster's bottom with relish. The scream in response just spurred him on. He waited a moment to allow Julie to settle then slammed the strap down hard across the top of her buttocks. Spotting Stones' signal to end the punishment with a forceful stroke on the suffering student's lower cheeks, he applied an extra hard stroke that almost caused Julie to lift the table off the floor.

The resulting final scream from Julie was just reward for his efforts as he stood back to join the professor in admiring the results of their joint work. Her scarlet buttocks were still moving as she sought relief in squeezing her suffering cheeks tightly and then releasing, the white strip of her open crack suddenly appearing starkly against the redness of the enflamed cheeks. She sobbed and groaned in agony and Stones was confident that she had found little sexual pleasure in so severe a thrashing.

"A damn good job all round, I'd say," said the professor approvingly, as Julie's distress was clear evidence of a severe punishment duly applied successfully.

"So let's pause for breath and contemplate the fine buttocks of our errant pastoral care tutor before we apply the final instalment of today's thrashings."

Sonya groaned and a violent tremor worked its way through her body. Stones' experience and expertise meant that he had become a good judge of the variance of pain levels they were capable of withstanding and their recovery rate response. In his view the pain of Sonya's caning would, by now, be reduced to no more than a mild throbbing and the sensation of a sore but dulling discomfort. However having just heard the far more resilient student be reduced to a writhing screeching banshee by the lick of the strap he could understand why Sonya would be absolutely terrified of the six lashes that were going to be delivered shortly. Hearing the two men behind her and studying her fully displayed open legs and buttocks no longer seemed to cause her any consternation, she had adapted to the humiliation aspect remarkably quickly. In that sense Stones felt that being hooded had spared her some shame in having to meet the eyes of this mysterious man assisting the professor but the initial shock and horror of her not knowing who was present had undoubtedly added to the punishment in his view. Stones had deliberately not allowed her the time to ponder on the clear and deliberate effort taken to ensure that she did not see him and that he did not speak. The thought that it was one of her colleagues, the Head Porter or one of his team maybe, would, he hoped, have caused her much despair. He again deliberately distracted her by suddenly running his hands over her bruised buttocks, leaving his fingers dangling between her cleft; he decided now was the time to bring her fears of the strapping to the fore.

"I think our Sonya is close to having her fitting punishment complete, her cheeks look nice and sore, we've got some good raised welts here that should give her a few days of contemplation. Let us now proceed with the strapping, good and hard please, my friend. Give her something to truly remember this day by."

Sonya's body tensed and she held her breath as the men

positioned themselves and she kept herself very still as she waited for the dreaded rush of air that would signal the strap approaching. There was a blur through the air and then a moment of total silence that followed the resounding crack as her husband slammed the thick leather downward across the middle of her waiting bottom. Then the shock of the impact registered.

"Yaaaaaaaaaaaaaaaaaaaaaarrrrrrrrrrrrrrrr!" hollered Sonya and Stones was confident that this was pain unlike she had ever received or felt before in her life, pain that she had no previous experience of, pain that she certainly would not want to repeat.

He watched contentedly as Julie grasped Sonya's hands tightly and begun to whisper words of support and encouragement to the stricken woman. Unfortunately though, for Julie, loud enough for Stones to catch an ill-judged remark referring to himself in four-letter terms. Quickly going to his cabinet and selecting a 30-inch-long leather-covered crop made from fibreglass, he marched around behind Julie. As Ian brought the strap down hard across Sonya's bottom for the second time, Stones whipped the crop down diagonally across the already severely blemished and throbbing cheeks of the foolhardy Julie.

The two females screamed in tandem and the table bucked and quaked as they both convulsed in agony.

"You will learn to keep your foul-mouthed thoughts to yourself, young lady," growled the professor as he repeated the stroke immediately indicating for Ian to follow suit.

"Make sure that you strap the tender top of buttocks and the lower cheeks, my friend. I don't think Sonya will want me to feel the need to double her punishment due to you holding back. Is that right, Sonya?"

Not that Sonya was in a position to hold a conversation at that point as the strap indeed landed across the tighter skin top of her bottom crack and she howled in distress.

However Stones knew to wait whilst she processed both the pain from her beleaguered bottom and the threatening words just left hanging in the air. The professor loudly cleared his throat which was enough of a prompt for Sonya to blubber just about coherently.

"Oh no, oh please, I mean yes, please beat me properly, oh my word, it hurts so much, oh no, oh, oh, oooh! Please just do it, just damn well do it."

Again the two men raised their implements and lashed them down together and yet again watched enthralled as the beaten prostrate bodies beneath them were wracked with pain and fire.

"Let's do them both justice with these final two, one after the other on the same spot on their lower cheeks. Let's ensure that they will both think twice about behaving in a manner that requires them to attend this office for discipline ever again."

As both women began to babble their compliance they received almighty cracks across the fleshy cheeks where their buttocks joined their thighs which brought an end to their pointless entreaties. Not allowing them time to recover, the final strokes were laid on top of the ravished strips of flesh and their protagonists were rewarded with ear-piercing shrieks from both.

"An excellent job if I say so myself," said the professor as he peered intently at Julie's writhing buttocks.

"Such a lovely sight. Your hairless orifices have add an extra element of delight to today's task I must say." Stones ran his hands over the thoroughly thrashed cheeks before moving round to inspect the work of his partner in this joint endeavour.

"Such a lovely contrast," he sighed approvingly as he placed both hands on Sonya's twitching bottom pulling her cheeks apart to the widest extreme and breathing in the aroma of her forested arse crack.

Both women were beyond further humiliation and Stones knew that yet again he had conquered and totally defeated the miscreants before him.

Bringing over ice packs, he indicated for Ian to hold them against the raw redness of his wife's throbbing, naked cheeks whilst he went over and unbuckled the sobbing Julie from her bindings.

"Iced water in the bidet for you, young lady, go and sit through there for a few minutes to take some of the sting out and get the bruising process underway. You are your own worst enemy, my dear, and you are going to be suffering for some days yet. Pull yourself together now and let's have a bit of decorum." He gave Julie tissues and a towel and helped settle her onto the bidet, holding her down as she struggled against the shock of the cold water.

"Take a deep breath, and relax yourself, this is for your own good. You will stay there until I say otherwise."

Julie continued to weep as he wrapped the towel around her shoulders, her body trembling as it suffered the joint impact of the freezing water around her nether regions combined with the searing throbbing caused by her almighty thrashing. Stones had been determined that everything would turn out to have been so much worse than she had expected and he felt that he may just have instilled a real sense of shame in the errant young woman, as she thought back on her overtly sexual behaviour in front of the two men. His wish was that anything she had gained from her sexual gratification had been completely overshadowed by the following strapping, and the wicked cut of the crop for the first time. Stones was interested in whether or not he may actually have broken the link between the thrill and pain of a beating and her sexual desires. If so, he mused, maybe that would be a good thing and maybe a more straightforward sexual life could now be ahead of her. If not, then he suspected that he would enjoy the sight of her shaven slits again!

He turned his thoughts back to Sonya. It appeared as though she was recovering her wits fast and with the ordeal seemingly over his assessment would be that she just wanted to do whatever would get her the quickest route out of this room. The ice packs that Ian held against her stinging cheeks would do a fair job of masking the pain from her beleaguered buttocks and his experience told him that she might now feel a strange euphoria knowing that the punishment had come to an end and that she had survived this traumatic day.

"I'll take over here, my friend, you can put your feet up and enjoy the glass of Malbec I've poured." Sonya felt the ice packs lift from her bottom, before being immediately replaced as Professor Stones took over the task of applying fresh packs.

"Yes, a jolly good job all round, albeit you have got off lightly considering your appalling aptitude previously. I am not totally convinced that you have had a fitting punishment yet, my dear. I'll muse on that for a few moments."

Sonya stiffened in horror at these words, and yet again fell victim to the professor's cleverly targeted teasing.

"Professor I can assure you that I am truly sorry and surely the punishment has been severe enough to have satisfied you that I have suffered enough. Thrashed and flogged like a naughty schoolgirl, hooded like a villain, pawed over and exposed to all and sundry like some cheap whore just for your bloody entertainment. For pity's sake Professor, surely that is enough pain and humiliation to inflict on one person! I think it's about time I was allowed to take this ridiculous hood off and be unbuckled." Sonya's voice was rising as she concluded and the tone had gone from suppliant to a rather unwise challenging note as her sense of injustice was starting to develop.

Bullseye, thought Stones. There was a long pause before the professor spoke in a chilling and threatening voice.

"Well thank you for your input, Miss Coombs. I think we will leave your buttocks to air for a while but you can certainly stay exactly where you are for a little while longer. You clearly seem not to have taken on board some of the lessons I was hoping you would have learnt today."

Sonya by now was clearly regretting her words of pique. "Oh God, I am so sorry, Professor. I didn't mean it. Please forgive me. I just forgot myself for a moment."

Sonya was yet again subjected to one of his hands fluttering across her bottom, his fingers blatantly lingering in her hirsute crack.

"Futile words, young lady, you have made your true thoughts perfectly clear and now I must decide what action to take."

Sonya sobbed, her forehead dropping to the table yet again, as she was left to contemplate the thought that she may have inadvertently set herself up for another dose of the professor's rather particular form of disciplinary action. Satisfied that he had taken Sonya's newly found confidence and bravery right away, Stones went back to a sniffling Julie.

"Right Julie, let's get that bottom dried and creamed and then I think you might take your leave from us. I presume you are happy that you have received the appropriate punishment you deserved?" Stones adopted his usual end-game persona, clearly encouraging his victim to accept ownership of her ordeal.

"Oh yes sir, very much so, sir. I am truly sorry I misbehaved, sir, and I would like to thank you for punishing me so harshly, sir." Julie, having heard his conversation with Sonya, was a quick enough learner to know the tone to take and the words required to ensure that her ordeal was not extended. A brief look at the red welts on Sonya's crudely displayed open buttocks looked to be enough to caution her not to speak out of turn. Julie was totally compliant as the professor positioned her leaning forward against his desk and spread her legs apart. She dipped her back at his touch to allow him to wipe the luxurious towel between her legs. She barely moved as the towel was replaced by the feel of luxurious cream-covered fingers stroking her tender globes, working the thick soothing lotion into her inflamed skin. A very quiet moan escaped from her lips as this man who had minutes earlier delivered the most savage and severe beating now so tenderly worked sensual magic with nimble fingers. As a finger strayed down her open bottom crack and over her arsehole before stopping tantalisingly close to her pussy. Julie pushed her bottom up invitingly but her reverie was broken by his voice in her ear.

"Tut-tut, dear. That's enough of that, I can smell your arousal, you little hussy. Maybe you need a cold shower before you take your leave?"

Red-faced, Julie stuttered out an apology. "Oh sir, no sir, I am so sorry."

Stones spun her round and took one last look at her flushing naked body. Her nipples were ramrod erect, pointing almost lewdly directly at him, her breathing fast, her cheeks flushed.

"Very well, Julie. You may get dressed, sign your form to confirm you have received the punishment as we agreed and state your appreciation for the trouble we have taken to give you correction, and then you may leave. I have business to take care of that means I am just about willing to overlook your wanton display now and put it down to a confused mind. However it has crossed my mind that you may well benefit from a quick few strokes of a whippy cane down your vaginal crack to help you understand the difference between punishment and foreplay!"

Julie's eyes widened and her legs automatically clamped together at his words. He sensed that she was reluctant to leave the room in which she had suffered pain and total humiliation beyond her wildest dreams, and he watched her as she dressed slowly while the two men seated themselves and sipped glasses of wine. Sonya was silent apart from an occasional quiet sob and Stones could see Julie keeping an eye on her as though torn between feeling sorry for her and wishing that she could stay and watch whatever additional fate she was about to endure. Spotting the disproving gaze of the professor settling on her, she pulled on her top and moved to the desk to sign off the punishment form, making sure that she emphasised her consent and approval of her ordeal and thanking the professor for his trouble in arranging the punishment. He appeared beside her, nodded his approval of her written words and before she knew it Julie was ushered from the building.

"Right, Sonya, time for you to receive the final part of your punishment. My friend will take his leave now as what I have planned requires no assistance or audience. Thank you, my good fellow, take a last look at the rather delicious display and the results of the excellent job we have carried out. Your work is done." With the background noise of the classical music and the disorientation of the hood, Sonya was completely fooled by this prepared charade between the two men and took it as said that the opening and closing of the door signalled that she was now alone with the Dean of Discipline. Stones approached her, his mouth by her right ear.

"Now my dear, much as the beauty of your split buttocks tempts my thoughts to stray into areas of carnal desire, that is not really the point of you being here is it?"

Stones let the words hang in the air as he moved across to his cabinet to select a fierce-looking knotted whip and a thick cane. He swished them both through the air before lashing them down on the space recently vacated by Julie. Sonya yelped involuntarily as the table shuddered with the force of the blows, her bottom twitching automatically at the thought of her extremely sore cheeks receiving further punishment. Ian stood motionless and silent behind her drinking in the sight of the thrashed buttocks and upper thighs and the sweat-drenched hair down his wife's crack and surrounding her arsehole. As the professor moved around beside Ian he nudged him forward and indicated that he should fondle the trembling cheeks.

"Much as I'd rather kiss them than give them a good licking so to speak," he guffawed at his own humour, "I suppose you'd rather I just got on and apply this final thrashing with my trusty scream-makers, as I like to call them for obvious reasons."

As expected Sonya saw the thread of a life belt and grabbed with both hands.

"Oh sir, I wouldn't mind if you really wanted to kiss me there instead," she stuttered as she offered up her final remaining grain of dignity. Stones and Ian exchanged smiles; the professor had predicted that this stage would be reached as Sonya accepted that there was no shame left to lose and was ready to offer anything this man wanted to avoid further beating, not realising that she was being completely played and manipulated to plan.

"Well, this is not a path I would take with a student obviously but we are consenting adults alone so maybe just this once I would be open to suggestion. However I would like you to make it very clear as to what exactly you are offering to trade to avoid this final part of your well-deserved castigation by thrashing. Then I will consider your offer and see if I feel that it would be a fair exchange."

Sonya's long sigh in resignation as his words struck home and the acknowledgement that she was going to be required to virtually beg him to use her sexually in whatever way he wished. Stones waited patiently for her to think things through, he felt that, by now, she should fully understand that this was the way he worked and there was little point in trying to save any last tiny shred of pride by being coy or ambiguous. He had promised Ian that he would reduce her to a broken and submissive woman by the time he had finished and the signs were that he was almost there.

"Oh sir, you can use me in whatever way you wish. Please Professor Stones, my body is yours and I would be honoured if you were to enjoy yourself by allowing me to please you sexually in any way you wish. Just please do not beat me anymore, sir, I beg you."

At a nod from Stones, Sonya's husband, now naked as they'd agreed, moved in to run his fingers over her pussy, a pussy that was showing signs of moistness already, causing her to groan in pleasure. Stones could see from his expression that Ian, rather than be concerned over his wife's lack of loyalty to him sexually, was rather obviously aroused and excited at his partner's blatant submission, unfaithfulness and display of sexual desire.

"Let's be clear here, Miss Coombs, please specify exactly what you are offering. I don't want any misunderstandings of what you are asking for. Clarity, please my dear, clarity," Stones continued, his body close enough to Ian's that Sonya had no chance to become aware of their duplicity.

Sonya gulped as the fingers expertly stroked her slippery vaginal lips. Unaware that it was her husband's fingers, who knew exactly her personal triggers, she very rapidly became lubricated and ready for penetration, her swollen labia and seeping juices providing clear evidence before both men. Stones very much doubted that Sonya had ever before been subject to the description of wanton, sexually rampant, desirous and lustful that she was now acting out. He had unleashed a side of her that he suspected her husband had never been privy to before. However it didn't look as though this was a negative to Ian, whose face betrayed pure sexual greed and unadulterated excitement at his wife's behaviour, his cock twitching wildly in its fully erect state.

"Oh sir, oh yes, just there, oh fuck, everything is yours, sir, oh yes, that's good, oh my, oh yes. Please just fucking well shag me!"

With a signal from Stones, Ian dropped his head and kissed the anal rosebud openly displayed before him, rimming her with his tongue, before pulling back to allow the professor to speak to continue the deception and subterfuge. Sonya had automatically tightened her arsehole at the touch of his lips and was quick to respond.

"Oh sir, please sir, er that was quite nice but I'd rather you didn't penetrate me there though sir. Please sir."

The professor smiled and indicated to Ian to finger her anal opening with his fingertip.

"Oh but Miss Coombs, I do so like anal. Not necessary with my penis, my dear, but surely you are used to having tongue and fingers up this lovely little dark tunnel?"

Sonya response was music to Ian's ears.

"Oh God, sir, it's complicated. I had an old boyfriend who was a bit obsessed with anal sex and while I didn't mind it occasionally when maybe I was a bit drunk and feeling slutty, it was never my number one choice. With him it became his preferred way of making love and eventually led to us parting but not until experiencing some rather brutal sessions which caused me quite a lot of pain and discomfort, sir. So when my relationship with my husband began, I told him that I'd never had anal and was very much against it. So Ian thinks I am a nice, well brought-up young lady, who would never partake in such dirty and deviant sexual behaviour. I know he'd like to go there, sir, as he clearly loves my bottom but I daren't run the risk of him ending up like my ex and becoming obsessed with my arsehole. Excuse my language, sir."

Stones looked at Ian, his face a picture at his wife's confession and enlightening announcement, and Stones could see his mind whirling as he replayed private and intense conversations in the past.

"Your secret is safe with me, my dear, but let's have a moment or two paying homage to such a tasty and attractive anus." Saying this, he nodded to Ian who automatically dipped his head and began to lick at his wife's dark hole, finally tasting the subject of so many of his fantasies. His lust overcoming his anger and hurt at his wife's deceit, he feasted on her open hole, delving deep with his tongue, ecstatic in this pleasure denied to him for so long. He wrapped his arm around her and eased his finger into her pussy, massaging her clitoris in a motion that matched the swirling on his tongue in her rear. Ian was in heaven as he delighted in savouring the dark musky taste of his lover's most secret of orifices, his cock now ramrod erect and leaking pre-come from the top. Gradually she began to rotate her hips to replicate his motions and her breaths became louder within the constraints of the hood. Ian felt her buttocks push back against his face, allowing him to ease his tongue further into the aromatic bitterness of her arsehole which wilfully opened wider to accommodate the intrusion.

"Oh. Oh. Ooooh." Sonya became lost in her own lustful heaven as all resistance ceased and her body lost all of its previous tension.

Ian enthusiastically continued his penetration of her bottom whilst his fingers worked expertly in her pussy as Sonya began to writhe rhythmically before him. She seemed to have recovered from her throbbing and sore posterior, had put aside the humiliating ritual she had endured and succumbed to what she could only be aware of as acts of betrayal and subterfuge that she would be hiding from her husband. Her panting became louder as she thrust her body back and forth in her bindings as she embraced her building excitement and coming orgasm.

"Going to come, Professor, going to fucking well come soon," Sonya squealed as her orgasm approached.

Stones signalled to Ian to get ready to mount his wife, and moved to Sonya's head and with one hand holding her neck down he ripped the hood from her head. Unable to move her head, it took a moment for Sonya to realise that the man beside her, as her eyes adapted to the sudden light, couldn't possibly be the same man whose cock was just sliding into her sodden pussy.

"Oh, now you can come whenever you want as my friend here is clearly ready to unload the contents of his swollen testes into your rather brazen vagina, my dear. Enjoy!" He released her and moved aside as Sonya strove towards the unstoppable force that was her approaching climax. Leaving her surely still trying to process the fact that the man currently slamming his cock into her, the man who had just been feasting out of her anus, the man, she presumed, who had thrashed her and seen her beaten, humiliated and demeaned beyond belief was possibly a member of staff that she worked daily alongside. Any horror turned to joy and relief as she twisted her head round to see her husband and erstwhile lover's scrunched up face as he accelerated his own pummelling of her pussy and headed towards his own orgasm. Screaming in joy, Sonya climaxed.

"Oh thank heavens, oh Ian, oh my love, thank Christ, it's you it's you it's you my love. Yaaaaaaaaasarrrgggghhhhhhhh. Yaaar. Oh fuck oh fuck, my love. Fuck. Fuck. Yaaar. Yaaar. Yaaar Oh. Oh. Ooh!"

With a massive groan building to a shouted low, drawn-out grunt, her husband unloaded his spunk into his wife's dripping fanny, ramming a finger deep and hard into her arsehole as he spurted.

Stones watched in a detached manner as the couple exhausted themselves with their climaxes, Sonya clearly coming multiple times, her body writhing and shuddering within the confines of her restraints.

"Sonya will now suck and lick you clean, Ian, if you could present to her mouth please. Make sure she cleans your penis up properly then give her the fingers that enjoyed her anus to suck clean. It's important that she now understands that she has some serious making up to do, and a good start would be a little reminder of where your fingers have been and the new experiences that she has now opened up to you."

Sonya acquiesced without delay or sign of argument. Minutes later as her husband's fingers slid from her mouth, she began to throw herself on his mercy.

"My love, my darling, I am so very sorry, I don't know what to say but you know everything now, my love. You have seen me laid bare, completely exposed, and I know I have deserved everything that has been done to me. I am so sorry, please forgive me my darling."

The professor moved across to her, saying, "Save it until you are alone, my work here is complete. Your punishment is over, let's get you out of these bindings and dressed and gone. You can continue conversations about your marital arrangements in privacy. I have no interest in you any further, Miss Coombs, other than I might suggest that your husband should consider sending you to me in the future if you step out of line. I do have more severe punishments that can be delivered to especially naughty young ladies and I would expect you to present yourself to me if your husband ever so wishes."

Sonya gulped but Stones could see that she would agree to

anything that would preserve her attachment to the man that she perhaps now finally accepted was the ingredient that made her complete. She, however, looked just as shocked as her rather triumphant-looking husband when Stones continued.

"Of course, that applies to you too, my newest dear friend," as he grabbed and squeezed Ian's left buttock hard. "I am quite partial to thrashing a nice pair of manly cheeks too if the situation deserves it, so please feel free to drag him along here if these gorgeous, sweet dimples of his ever need to taste the cane, my dear."

Sonya's face turned ecstatically happy as she watched the shock and dread spread over the face of her truly astonished husband who wriggled to escape the firm grip of Stones' huge hand and received a well-aimed slap across his flanks for his efforts.

"Oh really, Professor Stones. I don't think so, no. No, not at all," Ian blustered rather unconvincingly as he struggled to assert himself as he stood naked, his spent cock wilting, in front of the rather overawing figure.

"Stand still, young man. Put your hands on your head. Do not dare to answer me back or by God, man, I'll have you bound and bent over now!"

Seeing the look of pure glee spreading over Sonya's face as she revelled in her husband's discomfort, Stones turned his attention back towards her.

"Oh the thought of that gives you pleasure, does it, you wicked little minx? Well let's show you what you will be introduced to if I have to have you back in here for any further punishment."

With that, Stones moved over to the panelled door that housed the most prized possession of his punishment collection. He rolled down the enclosed massage table out with its attached buckles, chains and restraints, into the room he pulled Sonya over beside him.

"Imagine, if you please, bring laid on your back, your legs and arms buckled and spread wide, your derrière raised off the mattress and your knees winched towards your shoulders. Think of the site of your splayed thighs showing the glory of your totally unprotected open vagina and anus and ponder on what it would feel like to have this lash swinging through the air on its way to whipping you down your labia and down into your split cheeks." Whilst talking the professor had walked over to this cabinet and unhooked one of his braided cat-of-nine-tails whips and placed it into Sonya's hands.

"Yes young lady, think on. These tight leather knots landing on your most sensitive parts at pace, eh? Can you imagine the pain, Miss Coombs?"

Sonya froze in horror as she stared at the contraption.

"Nothing to say, young lady. I presume that you are not volunteering to have a little taste of what could befall you if you ever step out of line again. Hmmmm. I thought not. Now both of you go and shower yourselves and then we just have the little task of you writing a thank-you note for the service given today and then you can be out of here."

Grabbing her husband's hand, Sonya scurried off towards the bathroom, now keen to get away from the scene of her total humiliation and brutal comeuppance.

Stones prepared the desk ready for Sonya's last act and packed away the instruments used, glancing through the half-open door, watching as the showers occupants quickly washed each other down. He noted Ian's erection was back and suspected that the two would have a further coupling not much later that evening. He thought it was quite likely that he would have the two of them back in his parlour at some point in the future and his own erection hardened as he watched Sonya as she soaped her husband's decidedly firm and peachy buttocks.

Minutes later he was nodding in approval as he read the pastoral care tutor's carefully worded piece, clearly and openly expressing her admission of guilt, her contrition, her desire to undertake corporal punishment and her heart-felt gratitude to the professor for carrying out her sanctioning in the form of a thorough and deserved thrashing. At Stones' suggestion she also raised no argument against adding a sentence volunteering that her future behaviour be monitored and that she would present herself, without objection, for further castigation if called upon to do so. The approving nod of the head from her husband, his poise now recovered, and the meekness with which Sonya deferred to him, suggested to Stones that their relationship may have undergone some enlightenment in the confines of his room.

He thanked them for their time and waved them out. Another job well done, at least for the time being, he speculated thoughtfully.

Coming early in 2021, the further adventures at St. James' college.

CHAPTER 1

WHEN JAMIE MET THE PROFESSOR

Jamie and Professor Stones had met in unusual circumstances even when you considered their joint interest in spanking; Jamie had been bent over a very robust and rather intimidating woman's knees whilst completely naked at the time!

Jamie's interest and yearning for some wholehearted spanking action had finally led him, via internet searching, to a national group of likeminded gatherings spread throughout the country but linked by a national site that allowed communication by web-based chats that ensured a certain level of privacy. He had come across BADS, Bondage and Disciplinary Society, and after a bit of thought, Jamie had made contact and exchanged views and been politely questioned online as to his intentions in contacting the group. After a few weeks Jamie was invited to choose from three meetings in adjoining counties – apparently only the most confident and nonchalant members participated in gatherings close to home – and had plumped for a one-hour drive to a location just across the county border. Jamie received clear instructions concerning attending his first meeting, known as a Munch, in a pub, and was also informed that to ensure the protection of members' identities and privacy, he should only refer to himself by his BADS name, which he selected as

Porter for ease, and was required to pledge to respect everyone else's wishes regarding anonymity.

It was with a fair degree of trepidation that Jamie accepted his invitation to attend a first meeting, particularly as Cain, who had introduced himself online as the Regional Facilitator, had stressed that Jamie would have to undergo further assessment as to his suitability for group membership before he would be introduced fully to other group members. His final words had almost put Jamie off of his chosen course of action.

"Just come prepared for anything! Normally first nights are just a chance for us to feel each other out, so to speak, but sometimes if things look like that they are going smoothly it can progress quite quickly."

It had been delivered as what seemed like a friendly enough piece of advice but had still sent a shiver of wariness and apprehension through Jamie, although he had to admit a certain thrill as well. So freshly showered, shaved and dressed carefully to try and hit the smart, but casual and confident mark, Jamie had followed instructions and driven to the designated public house in the market town, just across the county border. Less than an hour later and arriving just before the agreed time, he had taken a deep breath and pushed through the doors at the rear entrance to the pub that, as promised, was clearly marked as 'PRIVATE PARKING – INVITATION ONLY'. A chap about Jamie's age, and to Jamie's relief dressed in similar garb to his own choice, was sitting on a stool in the small foyer sipping a class of red wine.

"Evening, are you here for the BADS meeting?" he queried politely as Jamie approached.

"Yes," said Jamie. "The name is Porter," he related as per Cain's online instructions.

"Ah, thought so, you're a new prospective member aren't you? One of two being given the once-over tonight, so you're not on your own, as the young lady is already here and is with our President and Chairman just having a private chat, so to speak. It's just committee and long-term members tonight as we are finalising our first social of the year which is in a fortnight's time. Let me introduce you to a couple of the committee and they'll get you a drink and settle you in until our Pres is ready for you. Name's Joseph, by the way, as in the cloak of many colours. Pleased to meet you."

So far so good, thought Jamie, *he seems friendly enough,* as he followed Joseph into the bar, where there were just eight other people divided into two tables poring over drawings, plans and lists.

"Heads up, gang," called Joseph. "Here's our other guest tonight... Gang, this is Porter, Porter this is the gang, names as we go along, we won't overload you yet."

Which Jamie surmised was the polite and diplomatic way of getting round not letting Jamie know too much information before he had passed muster.

"Thanks Joseph," said a tall, rather striking man in his fifties. "Hi Porter, I'm Tom, as in the Piper's son who stole a pig and away he ran," he chuckled. "Come and sit with me at the bar for a while, I'll get you a drink and you can relax with me until Her Highness, El Presidente, is ready to see you! What's your poison?"

Jamie opted for a small draft cider due to his driving situation and his host slipped round the other side of the bar and skilfully poured, so Jamie surmised was likely to be either very well connected to the Landlord or indeed was the Landlord himself. The following conversation was both quite bizarre and yet strangely normal and everyday as the subjects meandered through the weather, sport, parking and then seamlessly onto the reason why

Jamie was actually there.

"So I am a submissive, as are most of us here. We have a shortage of dominants so your contact was quite timely and to be honest quite a relief for a few of the subs. El Presidente, or more formerly and to her face The President, but she'll ask you to call her Pres, is, as you have now surmised a woman, and, as I am sure you will find out, quite a formidable woman. She is also a Dom, which is just as well for all of us subs who like being mastered by the fairer sex. However we have three other females at this little meeting tonight, Jezebel, Isobel and Sloth. Wave, ladies, although as you'll probably find out, 'ladies' isn't really an appropriate term!"

The three woman seated all smiled and waved. "All three of them are subs and frankly we are all rather hoping that you cut the mustard, old chap, as they have all become a little bored of the few Doms we have and having to wait in turn to be serviced, especially as their appetites are quite veracious and hard to satisfy. A certain amount of variety being the spice of life, of course, no disrespect to established Doms intended. Furthermore they are all ready to move onto a higher level of submission and disciplinary measures and we really need new blood and an experienced hand to carry that through. What's your speciality?"

Jamie had prepared himself well for this question.

"Role-play, discipline-based of course, is my area of expertise, generally working on scenarios such as teacher-pupil, doctor-nurse, manager-employee, master-servant and countless other varieties along those lines. I am happy with bondage, chains, bandages, rope, and have a selection of my own correctors to punish appropriately for crimes and rule-breaking. I generally only apply punishment to bare bottoms and I expect and demand obedience, acceptance and appreciation from any rascal I have to deal with," he stated firmly and confidently.

Joseph reappeared at that moment. "President will see you now, Jamie," he said.

Escorted up a flight of stairs off the main room, Jamie was shown into a fairly bare, poorly lit room in which a large, formidable-looking woman sat at a table in the centre, although Jamie sensed a further presence in a dark alcove at the far end of the floor. Joseph left them alone as the woman beckoned him to her.

"Welcome to our little group," she announced. "As you have been told," and she motioned towards a device on the table indicating that she had listened to his earlier conversations below, "I am the President of our little society and you should refer to me by that name or the accepted shortening of 'Pres', nothing else. You are Porter and that is the only name you can henceforth be referred to if you are invited to participate in our gatherings. I see from the record of your online conversations that you have stated that you have read and understood our rules and that you are willing to undertake any little initiation rites proposed to fully reassure us of your purpose for being here. My friend over there in the dark shadows has done due diligence on your application and has given me his nod of approval and now I just have to amuse myself at your expense to fully satisfy us." She stated this with a look that contained a fair degree of menace to Jamie.

"Yes indeed, President," he replied as a sharp slapping sound was heard from across the room followed swiftly by a snapped command.

"Get your tongue right up between the toes, you snivelling wretch!" A deep and severe voice barked before the servile response came.

"So sorry, Master. I will, I will."

As his eyes adjusted to the dim lighting, Jamie could now make out the form of a seated and substantial-looking man. He guessed him to be about sixty, with a young lady naked at his feet, crouched down, in collar and chain, clearly sucking his uncovered toes.

"Ignore the Professor," President said. "He's just putting our other new member through her paces. She's a submissive and a potential new slave if she behaves herself. It's always good to have a new piece of meat for the members to enjoy. Anyway, you can get your rags off and let me have a look at what you've got to offer. Come on now, look lively. You'll soon find that I am completely intolerant of slovenly behaviour and slackers!"

Gulping and feeling very apprehensive and fighting an impulse to flee, Jamie took a deep breath and stripped quickly to his briefs before hesitating.

"For heaven's sake, don't stop there, this is the interesting bit. Off with the knickers now, get a move on."

Red-faced and feeling totally self-conscious, Jamie now stood totally naked before her.

"Hands on your head, now come along. Oh dear, this is neither complimentary nor promising, is it Professor?" She smirked and bent to lift his flaccid penis with the tip of a finger. The older man had appeared beside her.

"Give him a chance, Pres. There are signs that he may have something worth seeing purely judging by the limp version."

Pres strolled around Jamie, admiring his physique. "Certainly not bad shape for a man who's seen his thirties off," she opined. "Oh, and hold the front page," were her next words in exclamation. "An arse to die for, I do believe! Well this has just improved my day considerably. Yummy!"

She stroked his buttocks lightly, nonchalantly running a finger up the crack of his bottom and Jamie felt the first signs of interest stirring.

"Lean forward, hands on the table, stick your cute little butt right out, spread your legs," she instructed in a barking tone. Jamie immediately complied.

"I noted that you put in your earlier commentary that you liked the occasional 'switch' so now we shall put that little claim to the test."

Pres was referring to the admission of Jamie's when completing the online questionnaire that every now and then he and Angie had changed roles and he had been on the recipient's end of a harsh thrashing or two and had played the submissive role in being well abused by Angie wearing a strap-on cock to ream and peg his arse. Pres bent down and settled on her haunches behind him. Jamie could feel her breath on his cheeks that were now rather quivering in anticipation. One hand was reaching round to firmly grasp his building erection.

"Hello!" she cooed approvingly. "Definite competition here, Professor. He feels as long and as thick as you, and he's clearly got a yearning to have his bottom in play as his cock is now really throbbing in excitement," she continued as she slapped his bottom playfully.

"Get Wretch over here to suck your cock, Professor, and we can have a little comparison. But first of all I think I'll have a little taster of the new meat." Jamie had succumbed to the expert hand rolling his foreskin and tweaking his sensitive penis tip. *She can do what she wants,* he thought, as she parted his bottom cheeks and took a deep sniff between them.

"Ah good, a lovely a nice rustic scent, good and manly."

These were the last words he heard from her before her tongue and lips sealed around his anus as she began to suck and lick alternatively on his opening. Soon his hole was relaxed enough to allow her long full tongue to inch its way up his rear tunnel, before it was suddenly replaced by a probing finger. Jamie's legs started to buckle as his whole body trembled with sexual ecstasy and he knew that she was taking him towards a climax. Suddenly her finger was pulled out unceremoniously and the large woman shuffled around in front of him, pushing him upright and dipped her head to engulf his total length into her mouth and after taking one long, lingering suck she allowed his cock to spring out. Using him to support her substantial weight she pulled herself up in front of him.

"Enjoyable though this all is, I have the order of the day to be getting on with," she said and handed him a blindfold. "Put that on and hands back to your head. It's time this naughty little boy had his bottom thrashed." The last thing Jamie saw as he covered his eyes was the Professor with his trousers and underwear around his ankles as Wretch, Jamie presumed that this was her Society given name, knelt naked before him with his huge cock sliding in and out of her mouth. As the darkness took over and his sight went, Jamie conceded in his mind that not only had the Professor probably got at least a similar length, if not fractionally longer, cock to his, but he had to concede that it might well be thicker!

Jamie stood for a moment and heard the scrape of a moving chair before he was snapped out of his contemplation as Pres pulled him by the arms and he found himself head down, arse up across her lap.

"A spanking to warm us both up for a few minutes and then I am going to let you have the honour of feeling my favourite switch. Now is the moment you say. 'Yes please. Pres, thank you.' There was no hesitation from Jamie as he meekly repeated her words and tensed for the first slap. The switch he was less sure about; while he had seen that it did not look as substantial as a cane he had also seen that it looked quite whippy and was double pronged to increase the effect.

Jamie's muscles tightened automatically as he imagined the feel of it cracking against his backside.

"Excuse me, Mister. Unclench, legs wider apart, relax those gorgeous cheeks and let me see you pointing your jam roll at me."

Jamie knew enough cockney rhyming slang to know what rhymed with jam roll and quickly opened his body up, unclenched his cheeks and raised himself to expose his arsehole completely.

"That's better," said Pres, clamping his cock between her huge thighs, "and now it begins."

The first blow was a real shock; Pres' huge hand was hard and her arm powerful and within seconds his arse cheeks were burning. *Wow,* thought Jamie, *she can certainly spank.* He was struggling not to cry out as her large hand continued to fall punishingly on his rear cheeks. Much as he enjoyed a spanking and in particular the after-glow sensation, he was verging on begging for mercy as his eyes filled with tears. Previous spankings he had received, had been delivered by his late wife Angie and an earlier girlfriend, but neither women had possessed the power, intent and stamina of the assault his poor scarlet bottom was currently undergoing. They had also been delivered by a loving partner with an element of fun involved and no malice or real intent to hurt. This was most definitely not the case here. The blows were delivered in a methodical, consistent manner, the constant slaps often hitting the same spot over and over again. He gritted his teeth and tried to concentrate his mind on counting but painfully aware that his erection was subsiding and that the sexually exciting element of this and somewhat gone astray!

"That's two hundred, my poor love. Well done, Porter, most crack and start their pathetic pleas and whimpers for mercy before the end," Pres commented to Jamie's relief. "Now up you pop and we'll move things up a notch to finish this part off," she continued ominously, pulling his blindfold off.

Up stood Jamie, trying not to look too ungainly and self-conscious as his half-erection swung free and his eyes blinked rapidly as he adjusted to the light. He tried to avoid staring as he saw Wretch still slurping rather noisily and with pure pleasure on the other man's cock. Grabbing her hair, the Professor, as Jamie assumed his moniker here was, detached the young girl nonchalantly and virtually shoved her to the floor.

"Eyes down and follow me on all fours, be close by me on my right-hand side. Otherwise I'll be fetching a whip to your skinny little baby backside," he threatened.

Jamie was snapped back to full attention by his own assailant.

"Don't relax too much, Porter, I'm quite loving your ass, get over here and present in the correct manner over the table. Grip the edges, legs wide apart pointing that jam roll up at me."

Jamie prostrated himself over the table and raised his buttocks, relaxing his arse cheeks to show his arsehole (jam roll), inviting her approval.

"Good boy," she said and moved forward and tickled the welcoming dark hole. Jamie sighed, he had little resistance to anal massage of any sort and his body immediately betrayed this as his arsehole opened beckoning her finger on and in.

"Oh you do like a bit of anal don't you, new boy?" Jamie relaxed as he wallowed in the expert fingering so it was a bit of a shock when the switch she had picked up without him noticing swung wickedly through the air before smacking across his raised bottom cheeks as her finger was snatched away.

"Aaaaarhghhh!" he let loose inadvertently, caught unaware, as the shocking pain spread across his unready arse. Pres showed little interest in his discomfort as she wielded the switch with great accuracy, a fearful force and no sympathy. WHOP! WHOP! WHOP! The switch cracked down hard as Jamie tried desperately to retain some sense of composure and dignity. Red weals were rising on his thrashed cheeks and the punishment continued without relent as Jamie slumped over the table feeling defeated and truly mastered by this awesome woman, clearly illustrating why she was such an in-demand dominatrix. At last she threw the switch down and to Jamie's delight she dropped to her knees behind him and began to stroke, lick and kiss his beaten bottom.

"Yes. Make it nice and wet, my dear, and then I think I'll have a little bit of fun to finish him off." The Professor's voice sent a tremble through his body but Jamie held it together as Pres treated him to a long, lingering anal kiss before moving aside. Jamie heard the swish of the switch a heartbeat before it landed. Gritting his teeth, Jamie was determined not to let this old man best him, no way was he going to cry out. Twelve times the switch slashed down on his unprotected buttocks, Jamie's eyes were closed shut as he focused on absorbing the pain and trying desperately to think of what this sacrifice could lead to. Then it was over and again he felt the hands and lips of Pres on his poor throbbing bottom. His erection which had subsided considerably as the thrashing intensified now twitched back to full length. Pres reached round and began to toss him, causing Jamie to immediately react, forcing his bottom back into Pres' face, his arsehole clearly welcoming her probing tongue which she dutifully forced deeper into him in response.

"That's enough," barked the Professor, who clearly had the authority to call the shots. "It's your turn now to show us what you can do, Porter. Get those clothes off, Pres. Jamie you may put your clothes back on."

Jamie was happy to comply and watched in awe as this formidable woman submissively obeyed the instruction and quickly unshipped her clothing to stand naked before them.

"Right Porter, she's all yours. Forget her standing, for now she is a naughty girl that needs a bloody good sorting out. Don't hold back, let's see how you deal with this miserable piece of utter disrepute. Sort her out, man, sort her out and make this reprobate sorry."

Jamie barely hesitated as his eyes soaked up the magnificent creature so exposed before him. Huge breasts with the longest and largest nipples and areolae that he had ever seen let alone the veritable forest of pubic hair that presumably covered her pussy. Her body scent was pure sex; Jamie could honesty say they he had never smelt such a strong and erotic sexual aroma. *She oozes sex,* he thought.

"Hands on head, eyes to the floor, you disgusting piece of filth," Jamie ordered, he was not going to take this challenge lightly. "Turn around, let me see the target, bitch."

Pres turned as instructed, giving Jamie his first sight of her enormous bottom. Fantastically formed, far firmer than Jamie had expected and indeed was nicely in proportion to the rest of her, Jamie couldn't help but lick his lips. He could see that this was a challenge and his mind whirled with what move to take next.

ABOUT THE AUTHOR

Dee Vee Curzon was born in May 1976 and is a widow and the mother of two grown up young ladies. Working in academia for many years, she has an insight into the machinations, idiosyncrasies and vagaries of day-to-day University life but has never, ever delivered a spanking to a student!

Printed in Great Britain
by Amazon